nancy moser
& vonette bright

'round the corner

the Sister Circle series book 2

TYNDALE HOUSE PUBLISHERS, INC.

Carol Stream, Illinois

Visit Tyndale's exciting Web site at www.tyndale.com

'Round the Corner

Designed by Jennifer Ghionzoli

Edited by Kathryn S. Olson

The Library of Congress has cataloged the original edition as follows:

Bright, Vonette
  'Round the corner / Vonette Bright & Nancy Moser.
    p. cm. — (The sister circle ; #2)
  ISBN 0-8423-7190-7
    1. Female friendship—Fiction. 2. Boardinghouses—Fiction. 3. Widows—Fiction. I. Title: 'Round the corner.
II. Moser, Nancy. III. Title.
PS3602.R53 17R68 2003
813'.6—dc21   2003008301

ISBN-13: 978-1-4143-1674-1
ISBN-10: 1-4143-1674-7

Printed in the United States of America

14   13   12   11   10   09   08
  7   6   5   4   3   2   1

Nancy Moser dedicates this book to
Emily, our firstborn,
who searches for what life has to offer 'round the corner
with an open heart and an ever-willing hand.

The Lord is wonderfully good to those
who wait for Him and seek Him.
LAMENTATIONS 3:25

•   •   •

Vonette Bright dedicates this book to
my two beloved granddaughters:
Rebecca Dawn,
with her depth of character and sensitivity of spirit
with biblical understanding,
and
Noel Victoria,
with her vivacious, enthusiastic imagination
and inquiring spirit.
Both of you have a heart for God
and give me confidence that something very special
awaits you 'round the corner.

Commit everything you do to the Lord.
Trust Him, and He will help you.
He will make your innocence as clear as the dawn,
and the justice of your cause
will shine like the noonday sun.
PSALM 37:5-6

*E*velyn stood in the kitchen of her boardinghouse, Peerbaugh Place. The room was lit only by the light from the fridge. Gone were Mae's zucchini and bean sprouts, gone were Tessa's labeled Tupperware containing dabs of this and that, gone were Audra's Diet Coke and Summer's yogurt with sprinkles.

Her appetite left her. Who would have thought the food in a refrigerator could tell such a story?

Or rather, the lack of food in a refrigerator.

She shut the door, throwing the room into darkness. It was depressing. After vibrating with life for nine months, Peerbaugh Place was empty once more—and had been for two weeks now.

Evelyn let her eyes adjust to the dark before she snaked her way past the kitchen table to the light switch. With the lights blazing, with the clutter of coupons and recipes on the counter and the yellow curtains at the window, it looked like a cozy, lived-in place. The scent of last night's split pea soup lingered.

But without the sounds of her dear friends—her sisters—it was a hollow coziness and a phantom family. There one minute, gone the next.

At least that's what it felt like.

In truth, the emptying of Peerbaugh Place had been gradual—and joyful. In the ten months since the death of her husband, in the nine months since she'd opened her Victorian home to boarders, Evelyn had been witness to some wonderful milestones in the lives of her friends.

Tessa Klein had won a national contest and was off on a three-month world cruise. Just last week, Evelyn had received a postcard from Naples picturing a mosaic wall from Pompeii. History and Tessa Klein were the perfect match—if Tessa didn't make a pest of herself correcting the tour guides. But a cruise? Evelyn had trouble imagining Tessa lounging in a deck chair, sipping a drink with an umbrella in it. But maybe her good fortune had loosened Tessa up. Or not.

And Mae Fitzpatrick was—as of a month ago—Mae Ames, the boisterous and loving wife of their neighbor Collier. As expected, she'd defected to Collier's house across the street, so Evelyn still got to see her, but somehow having Mae visit was not the same as having Mae in-house, akin to ordering a bowl of apple brown Betty but having someone pull it away after only taking a nibble. She felt unsatisfied and a bit cheated.

Evelyn was drawn toward a picture that hung in the place of honor above the phone and straightened it. The artist was five-year-old Summer. The biggest blessing amidst the wistfulness was that Summer was officially hers now. With Audra's marriage to Evelyn's son, Russell, nearly two weeks ago on the Saturday after Christmas, Evelyn had become an instant grandma. And once the three of them got back from the honeymoon, Evelyn would resume her child-care duties with Summer on weekdays before and after school. That was a continued blessing she needed to count. But until then . . .

The clock in the entry chimed the hour: six o'clock. She'd been wandering through the house for over an hour. The world was waking. She might as well get something done besides wallowing, wandering, and worrying.

She was unsuccessful. During the next hour, Evelyn's entire achievement—other than making herself a cup of coffee and getting dressed—was to worry and wander some more.

She'd grabbed up her cat, Peppers, and together they had visited each empty room, trying to see things as a prospective boarder might see them. Though she'd been running an ad in the *Carson Creek Chronicle* for over a month now—with first Mae's room up for grabs, then Tessa's, and now Audra and Summer's—she'd had lookers but no takers. The reasons cited had been varied: too small, not enough sun, too much sun, too many antiques, no modem hookup. Evelyn hadn't dared ask what a modem was.

She strolled through Mae's room, ran a hand along the walnut dresser that had belonged to Grandma Peerbaugh, and straightened the seascape painting that now hung over the bed, since Mae had taken her awful Picasso. From the very beginning Evelyn had removed most of the family knickknacks, providing space for each boarder to add her own pretties, but now she wondered if the rooms looked too bare. Too sanitized. Maybe if she put the fancies back people would sign a lease?

She moved to Tessa's room. It was painted a pale pink. Was pink in style anymore? Maybe she should paint the walls a neutral beige. And the quilt on the bed in the room that Audra and Summer had shared . . . it had been in the Peerbaugh family for generations, but boarders wouldn't care about such things. They would see only the faded colors and the slight fraying at the corners. Maybe she should call her friend Piper over to redecorate all the rental rooms. Piper had been such a help giving the master bedroom a redo, helping to turn it from Aaron's and Evelyn's room into Evelyn's.

Evelyn let her doubts push her onto the bed. Why was this happening? When she'd first made the decision to open her home to

3

boarders, the rooms had virtually rented themselves. Within twenty-four hours of calling out to God in desperation after her husband's death and learning of the unexpected financial crisis, after getting the idea to hang the old *Peerbaugh Place, Rooms 4 Rent* sign she'd found in the attic, the rooms were rented. It had happened in a blink, as if the thought and reality were one and the same.

Evelyn never regretted the decision. With the full house and new friends, she'd found the strength to carry on after Aaron's death.

"But now they've all deserted me." Evelyn hadn't meant to say the words aloud, and upon hearing her voice, realized how angry she sounded. Did she really begrudge Mae her new husband, Audra and Summer her son, or Tessa her cruise? Was she really that selfish?

She nodded, propelling herself off the bed. Enough of this pouting. She had work to do. She'd call Piper and have her stop over after work and take a look at the rooms. Piper was great at decorating on a shoestring, which was good, because that's all Evelyn had.

She went downstairs to call, but detoured onto the front porch, wrapping her sweater around her torso. A scattering of leaves skittered over the snow and up the steps to meet her. The *Peerbaugh Place, Rooms 4 Rent* sign swayed in the breeze, and Evelyn found herself wondering if a coat of fresh paint would help draw attention to it. Maybe if she used some neon color?

A garish sign on her lovely Victorian home? That would never do. Besides, such a move would shout desperation.

She watched her breath vaporize in the cold yet didn't want to go in quite yet. The cold woke her up and helped her think. She hoped she was a smarter landlord this time around. Where she'd filled Peerbaugh Place with Mae, Tessa, Audra and Summer without so much as a renter's application, this time she was prepared. It's not that she'd had a bad experience. Just the opposite. It had been a God thing.

No, that wasn't exactly true. Evelyn knew God was behind
the filling of Peerbaugh Place the first time. But this time, she felt
it was her responsibility to be wiser and show God she'd matured
as a businesswoman. She was prepared to have applicants fill out
the paperwork; then she'd check references . . . the whole schmear.

She heard the screen door slam across the street.

"Well, top o' the morning to you, Evie." Mae zipped up a ski
coat and headed toward her, diverting through a pile of snow
Evelyn had watched Collier shovel the day before.

Once again, Evelyn was amazed at Mae's gumption.
"Collier's not going to appreciate you messing up his hard work."

"Oh, pooh," Mae said, coming up the walk. "What good are
piles and puddles if you can't walk through them?"

Evelyn thought of her own late husband. How would Aaron
have reacted if Evelyn had walked through a pile of just-shoveled
snow? The question was moot. Evelyn would never consider
walking through snow, and that knowledge made her kind of sad.
Sometimes she felt like an extremely elderly fifty-seven-year-old,
while Mae made over-fifty look positively youthful.

Mae took the porch steps two at a time and snapped her on
the shoulder. "How's the landlord business? How many you got
filled?"

"None."

"None?"

Evelyn shook her head.

"What's up with this town? They don't know what they're
missing. I loved my months at Peerbaugh Place."

"Care to move back in?"

Mae leaned close. "You'll find people, Evie."

Evelyn turned her ring—the silver friendship ring Mae had
made for each of them. "But it's taking so long. I'm beginning to
wonder if the whole thing was a mistake. Maybe I should close
her down."

"Gracious geckos, Evie, Peerbaugh Place is a wonderful home." She stilled Evelyn's hand and held up her own to show her matching ring. "It was the birthplace of our sister circle. And it will be again, to another set of ladies."

"It won't be the same. They won't be sisters."

"We weren't sisters either. Not at first."

"But why is it taking so long?"

Mae stepped back. "I don't know."

Evelyn was surprised—and *not* comforted. Mae always had an opinion. About everything. "I was thinking I should redecorate the rooms," she said. "Take out some of the antiques and replace them with some modern furniture."

"Don't you dare. Who wants to live in a Victorian house decorated with Danish modern?"

"Then what's the answer?"

"Stop thinking so much."

"Huh?"

Mae knocked some snow off the railing. "You're analyzing this thing to death. You've done everything *you* can do to get the place rented, right?"

"Right."

"Then quit dissecting the problem and let the big Landlord of landlords rent it for you."

"God?"

"He did it the first time, didn't He? We've all admitted that."

Evelyn put a hand over her eyes. "Oh dear . . . I'm so ashamed. I didn't pray; I haven't asked—"

"Hey, better late than never."

Evelyn looked over the yard and watched some leftover leaves relinquish their hold and fall into the graceful care of the breeze. Where would they land? There was no way to tell. And maybe it didn't matter. Why not enjoy the journey?

Relinquish your hold, Evelyn. I've got you.

Evelyn turned back to Mae, taking her hand. "Will you pray with me?"

"You betcha."

They bowed their heads. As they said "Amen," they saw Collier come out of the house across the street. He eyed the scattered snow pile. He looked up and saw them. "Mae!"

She sprang from the porch. "Coming, Mr. Husband."

*   *   *

Evelyn answered the phone.

A woman's voice. "I'm calling about the room for rent?"

Lord, could this be a yes?

Evelyn told the woman about the rooms available. "Would you like to come see them?"

"If it's not too much trouble I'll be right over."

Amen.

*   *   *

Heddy Wainsworth walked through the three bedrooms a second time. Evelyn stood aside in the hallway, trying to pray, but not quite knowing what to pray for. Heddy was a prospective tenant. Evelyn needed a tenant. But was Heddy the kind of person she could live with? All external clues said yes, and yet . . .

Heddy was the essence of polite, calling Evelyn "Mrs. Peerbaugh" and saying "yes, ma'am" and "no, ma'am." Her nose kept her from crossing the line from pretty to beautiful, and her long wavy hair and pale skin joined with her delicate frame to give her an ethereal quality. She wore a voile skirt that undulated around her legs, along with a classic cardigan set in the palest sea-foam green. Both reinforced her femininity yet were a bit disconcerting, being out of season.

As for her age? It was hard to say. Definitely over thirty, but beyond that, Evelyn wasn't sure. Whatever her age, her lissome daintiness made Evelyn a bit pouty about the fifteen extra pounds that had settled around her middle since her fortieth birthday. While Evelyn walked through a room, Heddy seemed to float. Her movements reminded Evelyn of Isadora Duncan, that dancer at the turn of the century who used all the flowing scarves. The woman gave the notion that she was there but not there, that any moment a breeze would pass through the room and take her away, leaving an observer wondering if anyone had ever been there at all.

Heddy made a third trip back to Mae's old room. "I like this one best. I adore the balcony. If it's all right with you, Mrs. Peerbaugh, I'll take it."

Evelyn blinked twice, shocked to actually hear the words she'd been waiting—and praying—to hear. "That's wonderful."

"I have good references," Heddy said.

Evelyn had nearly forgotten her landlord duties. "I'm sure you do. Let's go downstairs. I have an application for you to fill out."

They descended into the dining room, and Heddy meticulously filled out the form and handed it to Evelyn. "When will I know if I can have the room? I'm very eager to move in."

Evelyn looked over the form, so neatly filled out with a cursive that would make a calligrapher envious. Heddy had last lived in nearby Jackson. Five years in the same apartment. Surely that indicated stability. Did Evelyn really have to call her references? Couldn't she just tell Heddy yes right now?

Heddy had gotten up from the table and was taking in the room. "This furniture is lovely. They don't make pieces like this anymore. Solid. Graceful detail. I don't abide by modern-looking pieces with straight lines and no adornment."

She likes antiques. "They're family heirlooms."

Heddy ran a finger along the walnut hutch. "Hmm . . . family . . ."

"Do you have family?"

Heddy opened her mouth to answer, then closed it. "Some." She moved to the silver tea service that sat on a cart by the window. "Ooh, do you use this often?"

"Not really. But I remember my mother-in-law using it when we used to come to Sunday supper."

"So you didn't grow up here?"

"It's my husband's family home. But he and I moved in nearly thirty years ago. We raised our son here."

"A child. How wonderful."

Evelyn noticed a pensive look to her eyes. She glanced at Heddy's ring finger. It was bare. "Have you ever been married?"

Heddy suddenly looked at her watch. "I'm sorry. I have to get to work. It's a new job. They want to show me around."

"Where are you working?"

"I just got a job as the hostess at Ruby's Diner. I hope I do a good job for them." She headed toward the door. Evelyn was impressed with her sincerity. She glanced at the application form, then at Heddy, whose hand was on the doorknob. "I think we can dispense with the formalities. You want the room, it's yours."

Heddy smiled wide, revealing a perfect set of teeth. "That would be grand. When can I move in?"

"Anytime."

"This afternoon? I'll be off work at two."

Evelyn was a bit taken aback, but said, "Certainly."

They shook hands, but as soon as Heddy left, Evelyn felt a stitch in her stomach. *Now that's an odd reaction.*

She pushed the feeling away.

One room down. Two to go.

•   •   •

The doorbell rang. A knock followed. Before Evelyn could get to the landing, another knock.

"Coming!" Evelyn saw the shadow of a woman through the leaded glass. The bell rang again just as she opened the door. Evelyn had rarely seen such a large woman. She was dressed stylishly, but two Evelyns could have fit into her clothes.

"You have a room for rent?" She waved a hand at the Peerbaugh Place sign swinging in the breeze.

Evelyn caught her mouth before it gaped. The idea of this woman sleeping in one of her delicate antique beds . . . the woman was waiting. "I . . . yes. I have two rooms for rent."

"Then show me. My name is Anabelle Griese." She stuck out a hand.

They shook hands across the doorway. "Evelyn Peerbaugh."

There was a moment of awkward silence. "Well?"

The hint of impatience added to the first impression made Evelyn want to say no. But in an instant, she realized propriety demanded that she show the room. She let Anabelle in and racked her brain for points that would make this woman *not* want to live here. She showed her the parlor. "The tenants have their own bedroom and access to the rest of the public areas here on the first floor. There is a sunroom out back, the dining room, the kitchen with an eating area, and—"

"Is that the only TV?" Anabelle pointed to the small set in the corner of the parlor.

Evelyn jumped on her interest. Maybe she preferred one of those monster TVs. "Yes, I'm afraid that's it. Actually, we don't do a lot of TV watching. We like Peerbaugh Place to be a quiet—"

"Good. I hate TV. Our lives would be better without it."

Okay, forget that tack.

"The rooms to rent are upstairs, aren't they?"

Evelyn started up the steps. "There are four bedrooms on the upper level, including mine."

"How many bathrooms?"

Evelyn felt a slice of hope. "Only two. The rooms have to share, though there is a small shower in the powder room off the kitchen. I've just recently opened, but Peerbaugh Place was a boardinghouse back in the fifties. At that time my father-in-law had an extra shower installed down there for the boarders." She hesitated. "But it's a very small shower. Tiny really."

"So I'd have to share a bathroom?"

"Yes."

"I figured as much."

Evelyn showed Anabelle the two rooms left to rent. Going up the stairs caused her to breathe heavily, so much so that Evelyn feared for her health. Anabelle didn't say much but seemed to take in everything. Her eyes slid over the details of each room, her jaw set in a look of disapproval. When they returned downstairs to the parlor, Evelyn expected her to offer a brusque regret and leave.

"I have a few questions before we wrap this thing up," Anabelle said. When she headed to an old walnut rocker, Evelyn instinctively took two steps forward, her hand outstretched. "No! Not—"

Anabelle turned, and her eyes zeroed in on Evelyn's hand. Evelyn lowered it and felt herself blush. "Why don't we sit over here?"

Evelyn sat at one end of the couch and Anabelle, the other. Anabelle squirmed to get comfortable in the deep cushions. Evelyn thought about saying something about the chair incident, but couldn't find any words that wouldn't make it worse.

Anabelle broke the silence. "How are meals handled?"

Evelyn immediately found herself wondering how much food a woman of Anabelle's size consumed. The usual four-way split of the grocery bill might not be appropriate. A lie surfaced. "We buy our own, but we do take turns cooking. That is, unless someone has very specialized needs or . . . ah, wants . . . then we would have to adjust the system." Lame. Very lame.

A crease appeared between Anabelle's eyes. "Adjust the system to compensate for a fat pig like me?"

The words were a slap. "Oh no, I didn't—"

"You did. You were thinking those very words, weren't you?"

"No. We just want the expense to be fair to everyone." Oh dear. Evelyn looked away. She wished she could replay the last fifteen minutes. She wouldn't even open the door.

Anabelle pulled her purse to her lap and retrieved a folded sheet of paper. "Here are my references. I'd like a room here, Mrs. Peerbaugh. I'm a good tenant and would be an asset to this establishment. All I'd like from you is your fair, unprejudiced consideration."

The way Anabelle stressed the words caused mental warning bells. But before Evelyn could think further, Anabelle pushed herself to standing. She shook Evelyn's hand, meeting her eyes. "Thank you for your time. I'll be waiting for your call."

Oh dear, indeed.

●   ●   ●

Evelyn sipped a cup of chamomile tea. Her stomach was still unsettled. Between the menacing mood Anabelle had left behind and the not-quite-right sensation Heddy had produced, Evelyn considered pulling the Peerbaugh Place sign from its hangers and locking the door. She wasn't cut out to be a landlord. The first round of tenants had been a fluke. The people who had answered the ad this time gave her all the wrong feelings. Where was the sense of family? the feeling they'd known each other forever, even though they'd just met? Where was the potential for sisterhood?

Anabelle's aggressive nature made Evelyn want to crawl into a corner. She couldn't have Anabelle as a tenant. She just couldn't. She didn't even plan to call any of her references. And yet she had an awful feeling that if she didn't . . . Evelyn couldn't imagine Anabelle Griese taking no for an answer without a fight.

And then there was Heddy. With Heddy it was a done deal. Any minute now, she would appear on the doorstep with boxes of belongings, descending upon Peerbaugh Place like a fog, someone who could be seen and felt but not defined.

Evelyn shivered and with a start realized she was working herself into quite a mood. She'd prayed for tenants and she'd gotten one. But just one. Heddy was moving in, and no one was forcing her to accept Anabelle. She had every right to turn down a tenant's application. So there.

Her strong-woman number lasted ten seconds—until the doorbell rang again, signaling round two of her bout with doubt.

Heddy was at the door with two suitcases. She was still dressed in her flowing skirt. "Here I am, Mrs. Peerbaugh."

Evelyn opened the front door wide, looking past her to the car. "Please call me Evelyn. I'll go help with your other things."

"There are no other things. This is it."

Evelyn did a double take at the suitcases. "That's all?"

"It's a furnished room, isn't it?"

"Yes, yes, but usually—"

Heddy put a hand on Evelyn's arm. "Thank you, Evelyn, but I'll be fine. I don't want to trouble you one little bit." She headed up the stairs. "I'll let you know if I need anything."

How was it possible to gain a tenant yet feel more alone than before?

• • •

Evelyn pinched a dead bloom off the African violets in the sun-room. She looked up when she heard footsteps in the kitchen.

"Here you are," Piper said.

Evelyn dropped the flower debris in a trash can. "Are you done with work already?" Piper was a counselor at the high school, and even though school wasn't resuming its second semester until next week, she'd had to report in.

"Just. Hey, don't let me stop your work."

"Nonsense. I need an excuse. I'm afraid these violets can't take much more attention. I'm pinching them to death."

"Aha. A frustrated gardener waiting for spring?"

"A frustrated landlord who's finding release wherever she can."

Piper sat on the morris chair, putting her feet on the ottoman. "I met your new tenant. I heard rumblings upstairs and thought she was you. Her door was ajar and I went in. She's pretty in a camellia, Southern belle sort of way." She stretched. "The point is, you finally rented a room. So why are you frustrated?"

Confronted with putting her frustration into words, Evelyn found there weren't any. "You notice anything unusual about her?"

"She only wears pastels."

"Really?"

Piper nodded. "Her closet door was open. All her clothes were pastels. But maybe I only noticed because I like deep tones and it's winter. Your new tenant appears to clothe herself in shades of eternal springtime."

"Maybe that's it. The springtime. It goes beyond the clothes. She's so . . . polite."

"Is that a bad thing?"

"Of course not." Evelyn sank into the rocker, glancing toward the kitchen. She kept her voice low. "Maybe it's just me, but I can't

14

shake the feeling that something isn't quite right about her. That the manners—the correctness—are forced. A front."

"Ah yes, that happens all the time. I can see the headline now: 'Crazed Psychotic Criminal Uses Good Manners to Lull Victim into Submission.'"

Evelyn looked at the windowsill packed with violets. She'd missed a yellowed leaf. "I'm sure it's nothing."

"Actually . . . " Piper leaned close. "You might be onto something. When I went in her room, she was sitting on her little porch. In the cold. I think she'd been crying."

"Oh dear. Then there *is* something."

"Maybe. But a few tears doesn't mean it's anything to be worried about. Lots of women cry. Especially during times of change."

Evelyn fingered her lower lip. "And Heddy is going through change. She used to live in Jackson and she just got a new job at Ruby's."

"New town, new home, new job. There you have it."

Evelyn wanted her wariness to dissipate, but it didn't.

"You're not convinced," Piper said.

"There are a few other things. More things left unsaid than things said."

"Like what?"

"She seemed to clam up when family was mentioned. I mentioned bringing up Russell here and she got wistful-looking. And when I asked if she'd been married, she suddenly had to go to work."

"Sounds like the woman has a secret."

"You think so?"

Piper pinched a piece of lint off her sleeve. "Perhaps something happened to her. Something she doesn't want to talk about."

Evelyn let her mind replay the moments spent with Heddy. "And something else. When she came to move in she only had two suitcases. Isn't that strange? Everyone comes with much more than that."

"What did her references say about her?"

Evelyn studied her flower-stained fingers. "I didn't check them."

She didn't like the look of disapproval on Piper's face. But it was no worse than the look Russell would give her when he found out. "She *does* like antiques."

"Well then."

"It does earn her brownie points."

"The main thing I want to know is why she's moving into a boardinghouse in the first place." Piper said.

"She didn't say."

"Why did she leave her last home?"

"She didn't say."

"Was she in a boardinghouse before?"

Evelyn was relieved to know the answer to that one. "She lived in that big apartment complex on the east side of Jackson. She lived there five years. That's why I didn't ask any more questions. Five years is a long time for an apartment dweller. That should prove she's stable."

"But where are all her possessions from the apartment?"

Evelyn was feeling more and more foolish. "I don't know."

"And why would she give all that up? Downsize like that? There's a story here. Something happened to her to bring her from point A to point B—or should I say, point PP for Peerbaugh Place."

Evelyn's lungs deflated. "There's a story I should have discovered before I let her move in. There's a story that's causing her to cry."

A moment of silence was Piper's answer.

"Oh dear. I thought I was getting over acting impulsively. I thought I was getting good at being a landlord."

"You'll be fine. She'll be fine. Everything will—"

Piper's voice broke, and for the first time Evelyn noticed a worry line etched between her eyes. It made her look older than her thirty-four years. "What's going on, Piper?"

She looked up, then down. "My mom and dad called. They're coming home."

"So soon? Why?" In October Wanda and Wayne Wellington had sold their house and taken off for a retirement life of traveling in their new RV.

"Dad wouldn't say. But I'm worried."

"Maybe they miss you."

"It's only been a few months."

"Maybe they're close and they're just swinging by."

"They were calling from South Carolina. Hardly within swinging-by distance."

Evelyn hesitated. "I'm sure it's nothing."

"I'm sure it's something. Dad's voice . . . it didn't sound right."

Suddenly Evelyn's concerns about Heddy and Anabelle seemed inconsequential. "When will they be here?"

"Saturday."

"But they don't have a house anymore. Do they need a place to stay? They can stay here."

"Thanks, but they can stay in my apartment. I'll sleep on the foldout, or they can always sleep in the RV. We'll be fine." She stood and headed to leave. "I'd better go. Thanks for listening."

"But I didn't—"

Piper turned, her eyes misty. "Say a prayer, Evelyn. I'd appreciate it."

Evelyn saw Piper to the front door. Piper, the person who'd led Evelyn to Christ, was asking *her* to pray. Evelyn had a bad feeling about this. But she did what Piper asked and added a prayer about Heddy Wainsworth, just in case.

•   •   •

Evelyn stood in the upstairs hall and stared at Mae's—now Heddy's—closed door. Piper had found it ajar. She'd gone in and seen Heddy sitting on the porch. In the cold. Crying. Now the door was closed. It made a mute statement: Do not enter. Leave me alone.

"I'll let you know if I need anything, Evelyn." Not exactly an invitation for chitchat. But it had been hours now. And it was nearing dinnertime.

Evelyn tiptoed over to the door, held her breath, put her ear close, and listened. She heard the rustle of movement and soft humming. As the humming grew closer, Evelyn instinctively stepped back. The door opened.

Heddy put a hand to her chest. "You frightened me."

"Sorry." Evelyn took another step back. "I was coming to ask if six o'clock was all right for dinner."

"Oh, I'm sorry, Evelyn. I should have told you. I'm going out for dinner with—I won't be joining you this evening. In fact, I'll be working through most meals, so . . ."

"Oh."

"Forgive my negligence in not telling you sooner. I wasn't thinking."

"It's okay," Evelyn said. But it wasn't. It really wasn't.

Heddy came into the hall, closed the door, and checked to see if it was locked.

Evelyn found the action disconcerting. Though all the bedrooms had keyed locks, no one ever used them. In fact, Mae, Audra, and Tessa had usually left their doors wide open.

They stood in the hall, two strangers standing too close.

Heddy looked at her watch. "I really have to—"

Evelyn stepped aside. "Of course. Have a nice evening."

"I will." Heddy descended the stairs and was gone.

Evelyn let the silence fill the gap caused by Heddy's departure. She sensed the invitation for a pity party being written in her mind. "This is ridiculous. I don't have to be alone." She had plenty of friends.

She phoned Mae and Collier, but they were going to choir practice. Russell and Audra were still out of town. Piper was getting ready for her parents' return. One by one she mentally scanned her friendship list but found it lacking. Since Aaron's death she'd let her entire life get wrapped up in Peerbaugh Place and its tenants. Now that they weren't so readily available, she felt like a wallflower at a dance with the music of life playing around her.

Evelyn headed to the kitchen, ready to let the pity party begin full force. There was some Rocky Road ice cream in the freezer. That would make a good first course.

*   *   *

The phone rang just as Evelyn finished her second helping of ice cream—probably preventing a third.

"Russell!"

"Hey, Mom. How are things?"

"Never mind me; how are you and the girls?"

"Fine, fine. But you first."

She did a quick mental scan and decided to let the healing work of the Rocky Road be sufficient and not burden her son. "Everything's fine here, honey. I rented one of the rooms."

A pause. "I don't hear an exclamation point at the end of that statement."

"You can't *hear* an exclamation point."

"Exactly. I didn't *hear* an exclamation point. So what's wrong?"

Evelyn had to laugh. "If *you* can hear or not hear an exclamation point, then I can *see* Audra's good influence on you."

"How so?"

"Some of her woman's intuition is rubbing off on you."

"Sounds messy."

"Oh, you . . ."

"So what *aren't* you telling me, Mom?"

Evelyn wrapped the phone cord around her finger, trying to decide what her newly sensitive son would comprehend. "Let's just say my new tenant is unusual. She's a bit . . . ethereal."

"Are you being 'touched by an angel'?"

"No, no, not that kind of ethereal. Hard-to-pin-down ethereal. Elusive."

"Mysterious?"

"Kind of. She has a secret."

"Ah. Curiouser and curiouser."

"It's probably nothing," she said. "I'm just used to the openness of Audra and Summer."

"And Mae and Tessa. Four heart-on-their-sleeve kind of women."

"Sisters." For the second time that day, Evelyn looked down at the silver friendship ring Mae had made for each of them—including little Summer. She never took it off.

Russell seemed momentarily distracted. "I have two of your sisters pestering me right here. Audra and Summer say hi."

In the background she heard Summer's voice: "See you Sunday night, Aunt Evelyn!"

"I know. Can't wait, sweetie," Evelyn called into the phone.

"We've had a good time," Russell said, "but she's anxious to get home to see you and to start her second semester of kinder-garten Monday. Be prepared for constant talking when you take her before and after school."

"I'll look forward to it. But remind her that I'm her grandma now. No more 'Aunt' Evelyn."

"I know. Bizarre, isn't it? Aunt Evelyn is now Grandma Evelyn, and your 'sister' Audra is now your daughter-in-law."

"But you're still my baby boy."

"Mom . . ."

"Thirty-one or eighty-one, that won't change. Bye, honey. See you Sunday."

Four more days. Just four more days.

2

My problems go from bad to worse.
Oh, save me from them all!
Feel my pain and see my trouble.
Forgive all my sins.

PSALM 25:17-18

*E*velyn let the keys jingle as she climbed the front stairs. But as she reached the landing she palmed them as if their chatter would give her away.

That was ridiculous. The house was empty. Which was exactly the reason Evelyn was choosing this moment to sneak into Heddy's room. Three days of having a tenant who slipped in and out, barely exchanging a word, was too much. Evelyn and Heddy were like two ships passing in the night—one with its lights blazing and the other with its lights off, secretive, coming and going with barely a sound. A smuggler, drug runner, slave ship . . . Evelyn stood before Heddy's door, the master key poised at the lock.

She stopped.

She pulled her hand to her chest and let the crazed thoughts dissipate. Heddy hadn't done a thing to make Evelyn think she was into anything illegal or sordid. Her only crime had been keeping her own counsel. Yet the fact that she hadn't opened up was a direct affront to Evelyn's heart-on-her-sleeve philosophy. She didn't begrudge Heddy a secret or two. But she did need *some*

23

information about her tenant. Small talk might satisfy the males of the species, but for women it was not enough.

Or maybe . . . was it the locked door that had impelled her to this point?

No matter which motivation was driving her, as soon as Heddy slipped out this morning to work the breakfast shift at Ruby's, Evelyn ascended the stairs with the intent of going into her room to snoop.

It's wrong.

She let out the breath she'd been saving and answered the inner voice out loud, "I know."

If only God would use His celestial hand to grab the scruff of her neck and pull her back. She knew it was up to her to decide yay or nay, yet free will could be exhausting. There was no one in the house. She could open the door and look around and no one would ever know.

I'll know.

And God would know.

That was the clincher.

Evelyn backed away from the door. She fled downstairs before she changed her mind. She had to admit she felt a hint of disappointment. It *would* have been interesting to see inside Heddy's room. But she also felt a surge of satisfaction.

She'd done the right thing.

This time.

•   •   •

The phone rang. As soon as Evelyn answered, she wished she could hang up. It was Anabelle Griese.

"I'm calling about the room. When can I move in?"

Evelyn sank into a kitchen chair for support. "I . . . I haven't decided yet, Ms. Griese."

"But I'm sure my references are glowing." A pause. "Weren't they?"

Evelyn hadn't called the references. She wasn't planning to call the references.

Anabelle gave a sigh full of exasperation and impatience. "You didn't call them, did you?"

"I've been very busy."

"Are you singling me out, Mrs. Peerbaugh? Are you discriminating against me because of my size?"

"No, no, I just—"

"Contact my references. I'll call you later to see when I can move in." She hung up.

Evelyn lowered the receiver to her lap, its weight too heavy for her arm to move it to its proper place. How could this one woman make her feel like a squished bug? She shouldn't *have* to take any tenant, should she? She was the landlord. It was her house. Logically, she should have the last say.

But the world wasn't logical anymore. Everyone was defensive. Many were ready to sue at the slightest offense. And being right didn't mean winning such a suit. Not anymore.

Evelyn realized the phone was still in her lap. She hung it up with extra emphasis. She noticed Anabelle's references on the counter and got an idea. If she called them and got bad feedback, she'd have a valid reason for telling Anabelle no beyond the fact that she didn't like her.

Evelyn dialed the first number and asked for the contact person. "I was calling for a reference on Anabelle Griese, who lived in your complex from—"

"Lived in our complex too long, if you want my honest opinion."

Evelyn was taken aback. "Can you explain?"

"Oh, she's a good tenant in the paying-the-bills and keeping-up-the-place ways, but she's a pain in the . . . how do I put this delicately? Anabelle Griese has a chip on her shoulder the size of a laminated beam."

So I've seen. Evelyn remembered the question her son had told her to ask: "So you wouldn't let her rent from you again?"

"Only if I was desperate. But please don't tell her I said all this."

"Why not?"

"I don't want to get on her bad side."

Evelyn changed the phone to the other ear. "Are you implying she's violent?"

"No, nothing like that. But you've met her. She definitely has a presence about her."

"Indeed she does."

"Just be wary, that's all."

Evelyn said her thanks. She didn't need to call anyone else. She'd done her duty. And desperate or no, she'd made her decision.

And yet, the tone of the landlord's warning hung in her memory.

* * *

Piper sprang off the couch in her apartment and paced. Twice. Up and back. Then she sat down again. She looked at her watch. Her dad had said they'd be there at ten. It was five after. Were they all right? Had they had an accident in the RV?

She jumped at the knock on her door. She ran to it, ready to whip it open, only to hesitate at the last moment in order to send up a quick prayer, *Lord, be with us. Please.*

She forced a fresh breath then opened the door. Her father stood behind her mom, his hands on her shoulders. "Hi, Piper-girl."

She searched their faces. They were both a little pale. And was there a slight pull in their smiles?

Her mother drew her into a hug. "It's so good to be here." Then her dad took a turn, his aftershave a woodsy contrast to her mother's floral cologne.

Piper realized they were still in the hall. "Come in, come in."

She took their coats and turned on the small talk. *Maybe if I keep it up they won't be able to tell me the real reason they've come home.* "Would you like something to drink? Some tea? Coffee?"

Her father helped her mother onto a stool by the breakfast bar. Only after she was settled did he answer his daughter. "If you have some chamomile tea, your mother finds that settling."

Her mother raised a hand. "But don't go to any trouble on my account."

Since when was heating up some water trouble? "No trouble. Dad? What about you?"

"Tea's fine here too."

Since when? But come to think of it, Piper could use some stomach-calming chamomile herself. She filled the teapot.

The silence fell like a theatre curtain.

"Is that a new sweater, honey?" her mother finally asked.

Piper looked down. "You gave this to me last Christmas."

"Oh, that's right, that's right."

Her father put a hand on his wife's arm and let it linger. That one gesture of solicitous comfort caused shivers to run a race through Piper's body. She couldn't take it anymore. She had to know. "Why are you back? What's wrong?"

She was expecting—she was praying—the next words would be "Why, nothing's wrong, honey."

But those words weren't hers to hear. Not today. Not again. Not ever?

Wayne Wellington's hand moved from his wife's arm to her hand and squeezed it. They exchanged a wistful smile, and Piper saw the space between their eyes crumple, then flatten, as they each took a breath that seemed to fuel their control.

She wanted to run to her room, slam the door, and curl around a pillow. Let them bang on the door, let them break the door down, she was not going to hear what they had to say. She couldn't hear it. And they shouldn't say it! They had no right to come into her home and blow her world—

Her mother spoke. "I had some chest pains while we were gone. I had some tests. I'm going to need heart surgery."

Piper would forever remember this moment, standing in her small kitchen, the water churning as it began to heat in the teakettle behind her. The clatter of the refrigerator releasing its offering of ice, followed by the whirr of water as it refilled the trays to make more. The counter that separated her parents from herself holding a cute chicken note holder emblazoned with the words *Chicky Notes*, a telephone, and a Christmas poinsettia that needed to have its dead leaves pinched.

Dead.

Pinch *me*. Wake me up!

Her father moved around the counter to be with her. But she was frozen. She couldn't turn toward him to accept his hug, so he awkwardly put an arm around her shoulders and pulled her close. "It'll be all right, Piper-girl. We'll get through this."

Her mom nodded, and Piper suddenly hated herself for taking the focus off her mother, exposing her own pathetic need, when her mom needed *her*.

She forced her body to shake her selfishness away and sucked in a breath so deep, it revealed the fact she'd been holding it since she'd heard the news.

"No." It was all she could say.

Her father let go and took a step back, then returned to his wife's side, finding *her* shoulders to hug, and *her* hand to hold.

"That's what I said too," her mom said. She looked up into her husband's face. "That's what we both said."

"But no amount of no's will change it. It's a fact," said her father. "When Wanda started feeling bad in South Carolina, we took her to a doctor. Or should I say, we *finally* took her to a doctor." He gave his wife a chastising look. "I've since found out she's been having chest pains for some time but didn't bother to tell me."

"I didn't think they were serious," Wanda said. "We've all heard about the symptoms of a heart attack: aching left arm, crushing feeling, shortness of breath. I didn't have those symptoms."

"Women often don't," her father said. "We learned that later. And so she didn't think it was anything major. But it was."

"What kind of surgery are you talking about?" Piper asked.

"I have some blockage. They'll try an angioplasty first."

"When?"

"Monday."

"So soon?"

"The sooner the better." Her mother avoided Piper's eyes. "It's been going on a long time."

"How long?"

"A few months. And so . . . there's some damage."

"What kind of damage?"

Wanda only shrugged.

Piper pointed a finger at her. "That shrug is totally unacceptable. I'm your daughter. I deserve to know the truth! I can't believe you didn't tell me about the pains when they first started. I thought we were close." She put a hand to her mouth, not believing the zeal behind her words. She was shaking. It was disconcerting to have her body act on its own accord. She covered her face and let the tears take over.

"We are close. That's why we're here, honey." Her mother held out her arms and comforted her. Comforted *her.*

Some daughter she was.

• • •

" . . . and then the ostrich says, 'Not with my neck you don't.'"

Piper's father laughed and slapped his thigh. Her mother giggled. Piper couldn't even smile. How could he tell stupid ostrich jokes when her mother needed heart surgery?

Plus, they'd spent the entire lunch telling RV stories, taking over each other's sentences, correcting each other's details, and egging each other on. Piper wanted to scream at them, but she knew another hissy fit would not sit well and might cause her mom to have to comfort her again. She vowed not to be needy.

But she was needy. She needed some answers. If only she knew the questions.

Piper suddenly noticed that her parents weren't talking anymore. They were looking at her.

She smudged a brownie crumb with the end of her finger and licked it away. "What?"

"You're not laughing," Wayne said. "That was a very good joke."

Piper's mother nodded.

Piper found safety in a shrug.

Wanda reached across the table. "I'm not dead, Piper."

Piper pulled back, appalled.

"That *is* how you're acting," her father said. He pushed his brownie plate away. "'Can all your worries add a single moment to your life? Of course not!'"

Her mother raised a finger and added her own verse. "I prefer Matthew: 'So don't worry about tomorrow, for tomorrow will bring its own worries. Today's trouble is enough for today.'"

Piper should have known her parents had this situation covered in the Word. "It's hard not to worry."

"Of course."

"But shouldn't it be easy?"

Her father tilted his head. "No. But it *is* something we're told to do. Did you know that the Bible tells us twenty-eight times not to worry? Jesus Himself says it ten times, the apostle Paul, three. And then there's King David, Samuel, Peter, Luke . . ."

Her mother pegged the table with each repetition. "Don't worry, don't worry, don't worry."

"So we've got to give it our best shot. We've got to. And so do you, Piper-girl. So do you."

"I'll try."

"Thata girl." He slapped the table. "You still have that Parcheesi board? I've been aching to beat you."

"*Au contraire*, Father dear. You haven't beaten me since I was twelve."

"Your memory is failing, child." He turned to his wife. "You in, Wanda?"

"Someone has to keep you two honest."

•   •   •

Piper's parents left to get the RV settled into a campground near town. Piper took advantage of the time to go visit Evelyn. She had a very important question to ask her.

She found her in the kitchen, a stack of cookbooks covering the table. "Hey, Evelyn. Planning a feast?"

Evelyn turned to a page featuring a photograph of a meringue-topped pie. "Maybe. Heddy hasn't had dinner here since she moved in, and I figured if I made a real fancy one, maybe she'd eat in more often."

"You want her to eat in?"

Evelyn shrugged. "Once in a while. How else can I get to know her? She's gone so much." Evelyn pointed to the coffeepot. "Help yourself."

Piper poured herself a mug and freshened Evelyn's before sitting at the table.

"I thought your parents were coming home today."

"They were. They did. They're at the campground getting hooked up."

Evelyn nodded. "And . . . ?"

Piper wanted to ease into it. "I come here with an ulterior motive. I want something from you."

"You got it."

Piper took a fresh breath. "Will you rent me a room?"

Evelyn nearly dropped her coffee. "You? Move in here?"

"For a while."

"But why?"

Piper fingered the corner of a cookbook. There was no easy way to put this. "Mom is having heart problems. She had heart pains while they were gone. She's going in for surgery Monday. They told me they could stay in the RV, but as nice as that is, it's ridiculous for them to be cramped when I have an apartment that would be more comfortable for her. For them."

Evelyn put a hand on hers. "What kind of surgery?"

"An angioplasty."

"That balloon thing?"

Piper nodded. "So can I move in? I'd really like to let them have my apartment all to themselves while they're here."

"Of course." Evelyn leaned over and gave her a hug. "Welcome to Peerbaugh Place, Piper."

•   •   •

After Piper left, Evelyn pumped an arm in the air, but immediately felt guilty for feeling so happy. It had nothing to do with the money part of getting another renter. She didn't plan on charging Piper a thing. She was just thrilled to have a friendly face close. If nothing else, she'd be a buffer between Evelyn and Heddy.

But the circumstances that had brought about her happiness . . . poor Wanda. Evelyn had gotten to know her and Wayne when they'd taken cooking classes together. She'd been excited for them when they'd sold their house and headed off RVing. Now to have their plans cut short . . .

Evelyn felt the need to pray. She bowed her head, asked God's forgiveness for her elation, and asked Him to look after the Wellingtons. She wished there was more she could do.

Pursue faith and love and peace,
and enjoy the companionship of those
who call on the Lord with pure hearts.

2 TIMOTHY 2:22

*E*velyn hung up the suit she'd worn to church, her mind absently pondering whether she should have grilled cheese or a tuna sandwich for lunch.

The doorbell rang.

She pulled on a pair of jeans and whipped a bulky sweater over her head as she called, "Coming!" She took the stairs in a quick *clop-clop, clop-clop* cadence.

A woman with very short hair and wearing a rust wool blazer with jeans, stood at the door, a newspaper in her hand. "Do you have a room for rent?"

She nodded. Wow. Wouldn't it be wonderful if she got the last room rented? "I'm Evelyn Peerbaugh, and you are . . . ?"

The woman's handshake was strong. "Gail Saunders." Gail flicked a finger at her own earlobe but stared at Evelyn's.

Evelyn put a hand to her ears and realized she was still wearing her dangly Austrian crystal earrings. "Oops. Leftovers from church. I suppose they look a little odd with jeans."

"May I come in?"

"Of course." Evelyn pocketed the earrings and stepped aside.

Gail's eyes scanned the foyer. "This is quite a showplace."

Evelyn detoured Peppers with a foot and closed the door behind them. "Thank you. It's been in the Peerbaugh family for generations."

Gail stroked the baluster, letting her hand follow its final curve. "Nice lines. Nice details."

"My father-in-law had that railing carved and—"

Gail faced her. "May I see the room?"

So much for small talk. "Right this way." As Evelyn ascended the stairs she realized Piper had not specified which room she wanted. Which one was available to show? Tessa's or Audra's? She decided to show both. She was sure Piper would be happy with either room.

At the top of the stairs she turned right into Audra and Summer's old room. It had a nice view of the backyard and a window seat. "This room shares a bathroom with the front bedroom."

Gail strode through the bedroom and bath, her hands behind her back like a sergeant making an inspection. Evelyn heard the medicine cabinet open and close.

"Who's in the room up front?"

"Heddy Wainsworth. She's a hostess at Ruby's Diner."

"Hmm. Is there another option?"

"Right this way." Tessa's room also looked out over the back garden. It was slightly smaller and had no window seat. "This room shares a bathroom with me."

Gail opened the walk-in. "This closet is smaller."

"A bit."

She stepped to the window, parted the blinds, and looked outside. "Nice yard."

"Thank you."

She turned and gave Evelyn her complete attention. At that moment, Evelyn realized what was unique about Gail. She seemed to move in blocks of action, as though looking at the closet was one goal, and then looking out the window was a separate goal. Once each was attained, there was a sharp distinction in her body language that signaled she had shifted her attention to the next objective. She moved in abrupt vignettes—a stark contrast to Heddy's continuous flow.

"I'll take a room. I prefer the first one with the window seat." Gail opened a leather shoulder bag that looked more briefcase than purse and handed over a crisp lineny paper. "Here are my references." She reached over and removed a check from the attached paper clip. "And I'd like to leave a deposit as a gesture of my intent."

Evelyn took note of the neatly organized page. "Wouldn't you like to see the rest of the house?"

"I've seen enough. And since the room is ready, I'd like to move in as soon as possible."

Evelyn skimmed over the references. Gail's latest place of residence was a nice set of town houses in Jackson. "The Dunmoor. I've been by those. They're beautiful. Why are you moving?" Before she let Gail answer, she noticed the dates of occupancy. "Oh. But wait. You moved out of those ten years ago. You don't say where you've lived since then."

Gail shrugged and headed to the stairs. "I'd prefer not to get into it, if you don't mind. You'll have to trust that my request for privacy has nothing to do with my qualifications as a tenant or my ability to pay the rent."

"But—"

"I'm looking for a change, that's all. A new, fun experience."

Though Evelyn had only known Gail a few minutes, she couldn't imagine her embracing anything new for fun. Because it fit into her finely delineated plan, because it served a purpose, certainly. But not because it was fun.

Gail headed downstairs.

Evelyn tried to read her personal information while taking the stairs. "Where do you work?"

Gail reached the foyer and did another one of her about-faces. "I am a merchandising consultant to the president at Lanigan Marketing. It's a wonderful job."

"I'm sure it is."

Gail opened the door, extending a hand. "I look forward to hearing from you, Mrs. Peerbaugh. Let me assure you, I will make a competent tenant."

Evelyn had never heard the word *competent* used in a tenant context.

Interesting.

* * * *

Evelyn hung up the phone. Not surprisingly, none of the people who currently worked at Dunmoor Town Homes knew Gail Saunders personally. They had to go back into their records to find any mention of her. She'd paid the rent on time and there were no complaints. That's it.

The reference listed as Gail's residence prior to Dunmoor was in another state, so Evelyn decided not to call. And it was Sunday so she couldn't call Gail's work. She'd never heard of Lanigan Marketing, but that wasn't surprising. It's not like she'd ever needed their services.

It all came down to instinct. Would Gail be an asset to Peerbaugh Place? Was she the right fit? There was Heddy, who was polite but wispy as the wind; Piper, who was a people person, but someone who might be facing hard times with her mom; and Gail?

In ten words or less, how could she define Gail? Evelyn looked down at the sheet of references. Professionally done. Actually, those two words applied to Gail herself. She was profes-

sionally done. Strong, confident, independent, successful. And
to use her word: *competent*. She could take care of herself. Which,
considering the uncertainty of Heddy—and her secret—and
Piper's upcoming need for stability . . .

Evelyn picked up the phone.

Peerbaugh Place was full up. Back in business.

• • •

"Mom! We're back!"

At the sound of Russell's voice, Evelyn nearly dropped the
cake she was putting in the oven. Before she could even shut
the oven door Summer burst into the kitchen and into her arms.
Evelyn lifted the five-year-old off the floor, giving and getting
a kiss.

"Missed you, Grandma!" Summer said. Audra and Russell
came in and there were more hugs.

"How was the honeymoon?" she asked.

Summer answered for all of them. "Mommy says I'm the only
five-year-old in the world who got to go on a honeymoon."

"You're probably right."

"She certainly got plenty of attention because of it," Audra
said.

"How about you two? Did you have a good time?"

"A cruise was definitely the way to go. Plenty of activities for
all of us."

Summer tugged on Evelyn's sleeve. "We got to go on our very
own island that had hammocks and sand toys and stuff."

Russell smoothed her hair. "It wasn't really our own, but it
was the cruise line's special island, visited by a few hundred people at a time. And it was very nice."

Audra put a hand to her stomach. "But too much food. I don't
want to eat for a week."

Evelyn glanced at the oven. She'd made Russell's favorite: fruit cocktail cake. She'd hoped to have it ready to serve before they showed up.

Evelyn heard the front door open, then Mae's voice, "All right, where are the newlyweds?"

"In here," Audra called out.

Mae pushed through the swinging door to the kitchen. She gave all three of them hugs, then put her hands on her hips. "Do I detect a decided glow on three sets of cheeks?"

Audra blushed. "It was hard to come back."

"But reality calls," Russell said.

Summer got out a coloring book and was setting up shop on the kitchen table.

"No, no, baby," Audra said. "We can't stay. Russell and I have to go to work tomorrow morning. We need to get home, unpack, and do laundry."

Evelyn looked wistfully at the oven. So much for the cake.

Summer put the crayons away, then got down and took Mae's hands, swinging them back and forth. "Aunt Mae, guess what?"

"What?"

"I go back to kindergarten tomorrow!"

"I know," Mae said. "Are you excited?"

She nodded vigorously and turned to Evelyn. "Can we have peanut butter and honey tomorrow for lunch?"

"You got it."

Russell looked around. "Where's your new tenant?"

"Working. She works a lot."

"I guess that could be a blessing," he said.

"But is it?" Audra asked.

"I haven't spent enough time with her to know one way or the other."

"I don't think she actually exists," Mae said. "I've yet to catch her coming or going."

"But you know who she is," Evelyn said. "She's the new hostess at Ruby's. You eat there every weekday."

Mae's eyes widened. "That filmy little thing that looks like she could blow away with a good sneeze?"

"That's her."

Mae tapped her mouth with a finger. "My, my. That's the woman who's taken my place?"

"No one could take your place."

The finger stopped tapping. "I stand corrected."

"Her name's Heddy Wainsworth."

Mae made a face. "Sounds like the spoiled heroine in a Southern novel."

Russell peeked in the oven. "I thought I smelled my cake."

Evelyn beamed. "If you can hang around a bit longer . . ."

Russell looked at Audra with his little-boy eyes. "Pretty please?"

Audra looked at her watch. "I suppose. If you don't mind wearing dirty clothes tomorrow."

"Don't mind a bit." Russell took a seat at the table and patted the place beside him. His new wife sat down, and his new daughter climbed into his lap. It was a wonderful scene, and Evelyn suddenly wished Aaron were here to see it.

Mae and Evelyn took the remaining two chairs. "So how many rooms do you have left to rent?" Mae asked.

Evelyn grinned. "None."

"Since when?" Russell asked.

"I just rented the last room an hour ago. To a career woman, Gail Saunders. She's moving in tomorrow."

Audra counted on her fingers. "Heddy is number one of three renters. Gail is number three. Who's number two?"

Evelyn suddenly realized they didn't know about Piper's mother. Audra and Piper were best friends. Should Evelyn tell her the details or let Piper do it? She straightened the salt and pepper shakers while she tried to decide. "Piper's parents are back and need her apartment. Piper's going to be staying here for a while."

"No fair! Talk about bad timing," Audra said. "I move out and Piper moves in? The two of us would have taken Peerbaugh Place by storm."

"No," Mae said. "I was the storm; you two would have been a tiny blip on the radar screen."

"Actually, Tessa was the storm."

They laughed. Tessa had stirred things up like a storm cloud on a sunny day.

Evelyn waited to see if they would ask for any details. If they didn't, she wouldn't say anything. But if they did . . .

Surprisingly, Russell was the one to read between the lines. "You didn't say why her parents needed to stay at her place."

Evelyn took a breath. "Wanda had chest pains while they were gone. She has some blocked arteries. They're operating tomorrow. She wanted to be home for the surgery."

Audra pushed her chair back. "Where's Piper now? I have to talk to her."

"She's probably at her apartment. She won't move in here for a few days. As long as her mom is in the hospital she'll stay at her place with her dad."

Audra looked to Russell. "I have to call her."

He nodded and set Summer to the floor. "We have to go."

"But the cake—" As soon as she said it, Evelyn realized how lame it sounded. It was unimportant amid the reality of chest pains and the need of sister for sister. "The cake can wait. How about coming to dinner tomorrow night? You too, Mae. You and Collier are welcome."

Russell kissed her cheek. "That would be great, Mom. See you then."

As they left, Mae hung back at the door. "Is there anything we can do?" she asked Evelyn.

"Pray?"

"Consider it done. See you tomorrow night. I'll bring a salad."

It was a good idea. Food and prayer. Two staples of life.

●   ●   ●

Evelyn had trouble getting to sleep. It was incredibly strange to have Mae and Audra leave at the end of the day. She felt like a left-behind child who wanted to plead, "Can I go too?"

But she couldn't go. This was her home, and Heddy and Gail would become her new sisters. Maybe. Hopefully.

Thank God for Piper.

Evelyn started to turn over, then stopped as she heard the front door open. The sound of hushed voices. And was that giggling?

She looked at the clock: 10:30. It was the normal time Heddy got home, but who was with her?

Evelyn slipped into the hall in time to hear the kitchen door swing shut. She heard a man's laughter and her breathing stopped. When her heart started to gallop, she put a hand to her chest, reminding herself that the tenants had free use of Peerbaugh Place. If Heddy wanted to bring a boyfriend home after work to chat over a cup of coffee, that was totally acceptable.

As long as a coffee chat was all that transpired.

Evelyn regretted her ignorance of Heddy's social life. Did she have a steady boyfriend? If so, shouldn't Evelyn meet him?

No time like the present.

She backtracked to put on a robe and slippers. She'd say she couldn't sleep and was getting a glass of milk. *Oh, Heddy . . . excuse me. I didn't know you had company.*

Evelyn headed downstairs, tiptoeing like a parent zeroing in on a child who was up to no good. When she got to the kitchen door, she listened. There were no sounds. That was odd. She pushed the door open.

A man had Heddy pressed against the counter—and against each other—kissing. Hard.

Evelyn hadn't meant to gasp, but she must have because Heddy's eyes shot open and looked at her over the man's shoulder. She pushed the man away. "Oh."

The man turned around. "Oh, hello."

"Hello," Evelyn said.

Heddy brushed a hand over her mouth, then let it run through her hair. "Did we wake you?"

"I couldn't sleep. I came down for a glass of milk."

Heddy stepped away from the man. "We were just—" she scanned the counter—"going to have some cake. Would that be all right? I see you've baked. We could smell it when we came in. What kind—?"

Nice try. "Are you going to introduce us?" Evelyn asked.

"Of course. Evelyn this is Bill—"

"Bob," the man said, extending his hand. "Bob Olson."

A sickly puce color swept over Heddy's skin. "Bob, this is Evelyn Peerbaugh, the proprietress of this establishment."

Evelyn shook his hand, wanting him gone—wanting to be gone herself. She was embarrassed for Heddy yet incensed that she'd been drawn in to witness such a thing. To kiss a man and not know his name? What kind of woman was Heddy?

Heddy took Bob's hand and pulled him toward the door. "I think we'd better call it a night."

"Sure, sure. Night, Evelyn."

They left Evelyn alone in the kitchen. She wished there was a back stairway she could take to her room. If only she hadn't heard the giggling, hadn't been curious. Now what was she supposed to do? She didn't want to put herself in the position of being house-mother to her tenants and yet—

Heddy returned but only took a single step into the room. "I wish you hadn't seen that."

"Me too."

"I really did know his name."

"Not well enough."

Heddy got herself a glass of water. "He's been in Ruby's a few times. We've talked. He's a nice man. He sells insurance."

"You don't have to justify yourself to me, Heddy." *But actually* . . .

"I know." She drank the water and set the glass down. "But I don't want you to think I'm the kind of woman who sleeps around. Oh, I've had my share of boyfriends, but—"

Evelyn took a step toward the door. "You don't have to tell me this."

Heddy huffed a breath, as if she'd wanted to tell more, was used to telling more. But Evelyn didn't want to hear it. Ignorance was bliss.

"Maybe you should fill me in on the house rules."

Not this again. Evelyn remembered the stress of making house rules back when her first tenants had moved in. Actually, the only one they'd agreed to was a blanket "Be nice." Couldn't that still be enough?

Heddy turned to lean against the counter, her voile skirt doing a sashay. "For instance," she said, "is it acceptable to have a gentleman up to my room?"

Evelyn felt her right eyebrow raise and thought of the phrase *then he's no gentleman*. She cleared her throat. "I . . . I don't think that would be appropriate. When the other tenants move in this week, they'll want—"

"You've rented the other rooms?"

"Yes."

"To whom?"

They were getting off track. "To two nice ladies. Which brings me back to my point. Since we're all women, I think it's best to keep the second floor female. For the sake of any of us who may want to move around in our robes."

Heddy nodded once. "But on the first floor? Can I bring my beaus here?"

Beaus? Did Heddy consider Bob a beau? Or was any man who paid attention to her a beau in Heddy's eyes? "I suppose that's fine. Though be aware there is no real privacy here. It is a shared house; therefore the public areas are for anyone—at any time." *Which means I can burst in anytime I want. So there.*

"Understood." Heddy put the glass in the dishwasher and headed out. "I think I'll turn in. Sorry to wake you, Evelyn."

Great. Tenant issues. Now Evelyn *really* couldn't sleep.

● ● ●

Heddy closed her bedroom door. And locked it. And leaned her head against it.

That was not good.

It's not that she was ashamed of doing anything so wrong. What was a little kissing among friends? Even if they were new friends? But the fact that Evelyn had caught them . . . Heddy felt dirty.

She moved to the bathroom and flipped on the light. Soon the bathroom wouldn't be just hers. It would be shared with a stranger. She'd known that, of course, but she'd enjoyed her privacy while it had lasted. Living in one room was a big enough change, much less sharing a bath.

But it couldn't be helped. Everything was different now. All that she had was gone. All that she'd planned was over. All that she was . . . ?

What she was, was a fool.

She looked in the mirror above the sink, studying her face.

She pulled at the corner of her eyes, eliminating the crow's-feet that were starting there. She was a pretty woman. She'd bought every cream on the market trying to find one that would keep the wrinkles away. While other women lauded their tans, Heddy took pride in her porcelain skin. She'd like to see them at age fifty and compare skin then. She stroked her cheek as if the hand were not her own. . . .

Her friends had warned her about Carlos. But she'd been so smitten, so sure it was true love. And yes, she'd been flattered that a younger man, ten years her junior, had shown interest in her, a thirty-five-year-old spinster.

She went back to her bedroom and began to undress. She knew *spinster* was an outdated word. The world was not as harsh now as it once had been on women who weren't married by age twenty-five. Nowadays, women often held off until their thirties to marry, and it wasn't a completely bad decision. Maturity had its merits. But if she was supposed to be mature at her age, then why had she let herself be finagled and finessed by Carlos, a handsome man who'd had nothing to offer her except an adorable smile and adoring looks?

She hung up her skirt, holding the hanger a moment, making it sway, enjoying the movement of the fabric. If only life could move along as easily as its movement, as smoothly, as gracefully. But life was full of sharp corners and abrupt turns.

Desperation was the culprit. Forget that society allowed women to delay marriage. The truth was, Heddy didn't want it delayed. Ever since she'd been old enough to play house, she'd dreamt of a home of her own, complete with an organdy apron, matching his-and-her chairs in the bay of a living room window, and even a string of June Cleaver pearls. And children. One boy and one girl. Lovely children with red cheeks just meant for kissing, and soft arms that would wrap around her neck for unlimited hugs.

She held her sweater under her chin and closed her eyes. Oh, to receive such unconditional love . . .

She opened her eyes with a huff. Forget it. She couldn't imagine such a love. And that made her incredibly sad.

Heddy pulled her nightgown over her head and got in bed. She hugged a pillow, knowing that a warm shoulder would provide better comfort. There had been many warm shoulders in her past. But none had stayed long—a hard fact Heddy could not understand.

What was wrong with her?

Be strong and take courage,
all you who put your hope in the Lord!

PSALM 31:24

$\mathcal{H}$eddy didn't need to get up early, but considering what had happened last night with the Bill-Bob-kissing fiasco, she thought it might be a good idea to make an effort. For Evelyn's sake. The poor woman wanted friendship. Perhaps Heddy had been too adamant about keeping her own counsel.

She was whipping up a batch of applesauce pancakes when Evelyn came into the kitchen, tying the belt of her robe.

"Heddy, I . . . why are you up so early?"

"I thought I'd make us some pancakes. You like pancakes, don't you?"

"Of course."

Heddy nodded toward the counter. "Coffee's ready."

Evelyn poured herself a cup, then stood in the middle of the kitchen. "Need some help?"

Heddy ladled two pancakes onto the griddle. "You could get the syrup out and set the table."

Evelyn hesitated the slightest moment before moving to the cupboard.

Perhaps more explanation was needed? After all, Heddy had lived at Peerbaugh Place five days and—until last night—had

49

barely said a dozen words to her landlord. Where were her manners?

Evelyn set the plates.

"I want to apologize again for last night," Heddy said. "For waking you."

"You didn't wake me."

"Then for causing you concern. I don't want you to get the wrong impression."

Evelyn stopped with a fork in her hand. "I want to have the right impression, but I know so little about you."

Heddy turned back to the stove. "I realize I may have been negligent in the social amenities. I'm not usually like this."

"Then why—?"

"I blame my situation."

"Which is?"

It had to come out sometime. But that didn't mean Heddy had to offer up unnecessary details. "I've recently broken up with someone. It still hurts."

"So Bob was a rebound?"

"No!" Heddy was shocked by the power behind her own voice. "I mean, not really." She flipped the pancakes. "I'm just a woman who needs to have a man around. I like men. I like the way they make me feel."

Evelyn poured orange juice. "But if you barely knew him . . ."

"I know. Bringing Bob here, kissing him like that . . . it was a mistake. Give me some kind attention and a few compliments, and I forget myself." She caught Evelyn's raised eyebrow and prepared a lie. "Not like that. Not that way. But if they want a few hugs and kisses?" She shrugged.

"But . . . what if they want more?" Evelyn asked.

Heddy felt heat on her face, and it wasn't rising from the griddle. "I'm careful."

"I hope so. Men don't liked to be teased, led on."

Heddy smiled. "You know this from experience?"

It was Evelyn's turn to blush. "Oh, no, no. I was married to Aaron for thirty-one years. And I only had one other boyfriend before him."

"How long have you been widowed?"

"It will be eleven months on the twenty-seventh."

"Are you dating anyone?"

Evelyn snickered.

"I take that as a no?"

"A definite no."

"Is that for lack of interest or lack of proper suitors?"

"I'd say it's a lack of interest from proper suitors."

"So you're willing?"

Evelyn held the syrup bottle to her chest. "I think so."

"Then what are you doing to get yourself out there?"

"Out there . . . you make it sound like a meat market. Like I have to put myself on display for the picking."

"Unfortunately, that's not far off. But perhaps it *is* a little harsh. Yet if we're truthful about it, aren't we putting ourselves on display anytime we go out in public? We're dressing a certain way, saying and doing certain things in order to elicit a certain response."

"Take me, I'm yours?"

"Not quite," Heddy said. She took up the first two pancakes. "Here you go. Enjoy."

"You have one too."

"No, you go ahead. I'll put more on."

Evelyn sat at the table and poured syrup on top. Heddy waited for her response. "Umm. These are good."

"It's the applesauce and cinnamon."

"I approve. Keep 'em coming."

Heddy adjusted the burner. "Back to men."

"Or our lack thereof."

"Exactly."

Evelyn took another bite. "Why did you and your boyfriend break up?"

I can't go there. She'll think I'm a fool. "Let's just say I discovered some things that made me question his character."

Evelyn didn't say anything, but her face implied she wanted more details. Best to nip that in the bud immediately. Heddy couldn't go into it. At least not yet. "I don't want to say more than to state . . . he wasn't what he seemed."

"Are they ever?"

"I think the better question is are we ever?"

Evelyn hesitated a moment, then nodded. "I like this, Heddy. I like getting to know you better. And I love these pancakes."

There. That wasn't so hard.

•　•　•

"Well." Wanda Wellington sighed deeply.

Yup. That about said it.

Piper squeezed her mom's hand, while her dad stood on the opposite side of the hospital bed and squeezed her other hand. The nurse had come in and inserted an IV. In just a matter of minutes her mother would be wheeled away to surgery.

Wanda looked at Piper, then at her husband. "Come on, you two. This is a good thing. A positive step. Angioplasty is done all the time. It will take care of the blockage."

But what if it comes back?

"So," her mother said, squeezing both their hands. "What kind of pie are you going to have?"

"Pie?"

"While I'm in surgery, I expect you'll saunter down to the cafeteria and have yourself a piece of pie. Wayne, I know you'll take any meringue, but Piper . . . will you go for the cherry or apple?"

This discussion seemed ludicrous, yet Piper went along. If her mother wanted to talk about pie . . . "Cherry, I think."

"With ice cream?"

"If they have it."

Her mother nodded, then turned to Wayne. "But don't drink too much coffee. You know that makes your stomach act up."

He smiled. "Whatever you say, dear."

"You'd better believe it." Her brow dipped for a split second, and in that one slice of time, Piper witnessed the worry she was trying so hard to hide. Yet, in a strange way, it made her feel better. Her mother was so strong and so positive that it gave the whole situation an otherworldly feel. Piper couldn't relate to that. But fear and worry? They were old friends.

The orderly came in. "Ready to go, Mrs. Wellington?"

Her mom nodded.

Piper kissed her cheek. "We'll be waiting for you."

"Praying for me."

"That too."

Her dad leaned close, encasing her head with his arm, rubbing a thumb across her forehead. "I adore you, you know."

She nodded and accepted his kiss.

And she was gone.

Without the bed between Piper and her dad, there was an empty space. An awful void. The symbolism enveloped her. Piper rushed toward her father, eager to make it go away.

He wrapped an arm around her. "Let's go get some of that pie."

•   •   •

Piper wished she was the type of person who couldn't eat in times of crisis. But she had no trouble snarfing up the cherry pie à la mode and even took two bites of her dad's lemon meringue.

He sat next to her, his hands cradling the mug of coffee, the steam rising to fog his glasses. If only she had words.

She touched his hand. "She'll be all right, Dad."

He nodded. "She's my life, Piper-girl. She—and you."

Piper appreciated the addition of her name to his list, but it wasn't necessary. She was a loved child. She knew that and daily thanked God for placing her with such awesome adoptive parents.

He looked up, and Piper once again marveled at the blueness of his eyes. "Why did this happen to her? Why not me?"

How about neither of you? "I don't know, Dad. At least we've done what she asked. We had our pie."

He nodded once. "Now we need to pray."

"I feel like I've been praying constantly for days," Piper said. "A lot of it's been in such short snippets that I barely know when a regular thought appears and a prayer begins."

"Me too." He took her hand. "Shall—?"

Piper saw Evelyn in the doorway of the cafeteria. She waved and called her name.

Evelyn joined them. "I went to the waiting room but they said you were down here."

"Want some pie?" her father asked.

It was a question her mother-the-hostess would normally ask, and Piper was a bit thrown off upon hearing it.

"No, I'm fine," Evelyn said.

Her father pushed his chair back. "Let me get you some coffee."

She didn't object.

He returned with a steaming mug and settled back in. "We were just about to pray," he said. "Care to join us?"

"Oh, absolutely."

He held out his hands to the women on either side of him, and fingers intertwined with fingers. Then they began.

• • •

After their prayers—or as their silent prayers continued—Evelyn, Piper, and Wayne retired to the waiting room. They leafed through old magazines and endured the TV in the corner, which someone had tuned to a shopping channel. An oval, multicolor, ammolite ring was being hawked at the bargain price of $179.98.

Piper's mind absently asked two questions: What was ammolite? And how could anyone ever need it? She needed her mother to have a healthy heart. She needed her dad to smile again. She needed to have her parents around for the rest of her life. She didn't need a ring. Any ring. At any price.

The surgeon, Dr. Baladino, came in, his eyes searching for them. Piper raised a finger. As he came over, she studied his face for clues. He smiled, but it was only a smile of the lips, not the cheeks. Not the eyes. Not the heart.

She gripped the armrest of the chair and found her father's hand there first. Evelyn covered her other hand with her own.

The doctor stopped before them. "We did an angioplasty in the three blockages and put in stents."

"Stents?" Evelyn asked.

"A tiny metal structure that holds the artery open." He looked back to Piper's father. "It went well."

"Well" but not great.

"We're a little concerned with her high blood pressure, but with careful monitoring . . ." His eyes swept over all three of them. "Any questions?"

Her father's head was making an odd figure eight like a doggy head in the back of a car window. Suddenly it stopped. "Can we see her?"

"She's in recovery now. A nurse will come down when it's okay to go in." The doctor put a hand on Wayne's shoulder. "If you have any questions, let me know."

Questions? He wanted questions? Piper had a few. "Why did my mom have chest pains?" Or "Why can't you tell us everything will be wonderful again?"

"She got through," her father said. "That's the first step."

Maybe so, but Piper had the feeling the upcoming journey was going to be very long—and the steps steep.

●　　●　　●

Evelyn didn't know why she lingered in the hospital past the time when she could have left. Most people hated hospitals. Shouldn't she? After all, Aaron had died in a hospital. The memories were still fairly fresh.

And yet . . . as she strolled down the halls, she found a kind of excitement growing inside. Life and death was held captive here, vying for supremacy, trying to prove which one was stronger.

She was too squeamish to be a doctor or even a nurse, but there was something about this place that made her want to stick around and help. Somehow. Some way. People were needy here. She could feel the need emanating from every room.

There was a crash. Up ahead a woman pushing a flower cart had toppled one of the arrangements. The vase lay broken on the floor, water and flowers scattered. Evelyn hurried to help.

"Oh dear, oh dear," the woman said. She wrung her hands and looked around for someone to save her.

But before Evelyn could get to her, a nurse arrived and put a hand to her shoulder. "Don't worry about it, Mabel. There's a broom and dustpan in that storeroom right over there. And towels." She looked down the hall. "I'm sorry I can't help, but Mr. Johnson . . ."

Mabel had collected her wits. "No, no. I can handle it, Nurse Hudson. Thank you."

After the nurse left, Evelyn stepped forward. Mabel was picking up pieces of glass and placing them in the palm of her hand. "Can I help?"

"I've got it, thanks."

Evelyn nodded toward the lone vase still standing on the cart. "It's a good thing this last arrangement didn't topple too."

Mabel nodded, then eyed Evelyn a moment. "You really want to help? Why don't you take those into room 636 over there so I don't have to feel any more guilty."

Evelyn didn't hesitate. "No problem." She picked up the vase of mums and ferns and headed for 636. Not until she knocked on the opened door did she question what she was doing. But then it was too late.

"Yes?" The voice was feeble and sounded old.

Evelyn walked in, holding the flowers as if they were her entry pass. "These are for you," she said.

The old woman's skin was nearly translucent. When she tried to sit up, Evelyn set the flowers down and helped her push the button on the bed so it would do the work for her. She fluffed her pillows and helped her get comfortable. "That better?"

"Much. Thanks."

Evelyn remembered the flowers. She placed them front and center on the tray table. "Aren't these beautiful? Someone must think you're very special."

The woman touched the petals. "Can't imagine who."

The words were full of sorrow and regret. Evelyn plucked the card from the stems and handed it to her. "Then let's see who."

With difficulty, the woman opened the tiny envelope. Her knuckles were swollen and knobby. She pulled out the card, and her face lit up before tears came. She put a hand to her lips. "My son! These are from my son!"

Evelyn felt her own tears threaten. "How wonderful."

"He lives in Cincinnati. I hadn't heard from him. I didn't think he . . ." She looked at Evelyn, beaming. "He sent me flowers!" She held the card so Evelyn could see. "He says he loves me."

"Of course he does. You're his mother."

She shrugged. "Yes, well . . ."

Evelyn hurried past the unspoken back story that was obviously painful. "Would you like to call him?"

"Call?"

Evelyn moved the phone close. The woman shook her head. "It's long distance. It costs money."

Evelyn opened her purse, ruffled through it, and handed the woman a card. "Here. Here's my calling card. Go ahead and call him."

The woman held the card in both hands and looked at it as if it were a winning lottery ticket. Then she looked at Evelyn. "You'd do this for me?"

Evelyn was embarrassed at the gratitude over such a little thing. She handed the woman the receiver.

"I don't know how—"

Evelyn took the card back, dialed the string of numbers, then asked, "What's his number?"

Moments later, "Eugene? It's Mom."

Evelyn saw the woman relax against the pillows. She headed for the door, waving good-bye. Her insides threatened to burst. Mabel and the spilt flowers were gone, as if they were never there. Yet if it weren't for those spilt flowers . . .

Evelyn stopped at the nurses' station. "Excuse me?"

Nurse Hudson came over. "May I help you?"

"What's the name of the woman in 636?"

The nurse smiled. "Oh, that's Accosta Rand. She's such a sweet thing."

"When is she being released?"

Nurse Hudson didn't have to even check a chart. "Tomorrow."

"Do you know if she has anyone coming to get her?"

"I don't know. She hasn't had many visitors." She gave Evelyn a serious look. "Are you volunteering?"

"Maybe."

The nurse winked. "We can always use more volunteers." She wrote down a room number and a name. "Go to the Volunteer Office, talk to Joann, and sign up."

From a good deed to an official volunteer. It was happening so fast. "But—"

The nurse smiled. "I'm sure Accosta would love having a friendly face pick her up tomorrow. Talk to Joann. Then I'll call you. All right?"

"All right."

Evelyn left her name and number. Nurse Hudson took a look at the note, then slipped it into her pocket. "We could use more volunteers like you. God bless you, Evelyn Peerbaugh."

He already had.

●   ●   ●

Evelyn arrived home, still high on her Accosta Rand experience. She found herself thanking God for spilt flowers. And yet there was more to do today, someone else to help, someone at the other end of life's timeline.

She zipped up her coat and sat on the porch swing to wait for Summer. School had let out ten minutes ago. Any moment now the little girl would run up the front walk, all excited about her day.

The swing relaxed Evelyn, as it always did. The simple movement made her think of all the times she'd escaped to the porch when she and Aaron had argued. Or rather, when Aaron had argued. Evelyn didn't argue. She avoided confrontation like a dog avoided an invisible fence. It hadn't taken her long to learn the boundaries of their marriage, to learn where the shocks would come, and to stay back. Or run away. Whatever was appropriate to the moment.

Although being an arguer wasn't good, being an escapist wasn't good either. And one of her biggest regrets was that she hadn't stood to fight—or at least discuss—the issues of their marriage. Would it have been a better marriage if she'd been a different kind of woman? A strong woman? One who had enough self-esteem to at least give an opinion?

She'd never know. But one of the good things that had happened since Aaron's death was that Evelyn had developed a backbone. It wasn't straight and strong yet, but it was getting there. And when she had occasion to stand up tall and take a stand, it felt good. She'd always imagined that at age fifty-seven her character and personality would be a done deal—not much change going on, good or bad. So when she'd discovered this new part of herself and found herself growing in character, it had been a wonderful surprise. Like finding a Christmas gift hidden in a back closet, unexpected yet packaged in a special wrapping of appreciation—with a pretty bow on top.

She heard humming to her left. Summer was skipping down the sidewalk, her eyes down. *Don't step on a crack, or you'll break your mother's back.* Evelyn took a deep breath at the sight of her. The crisp air filled her lungs, sparking to life all that was good and hopeful in the world. She moved to the top of the porch steps, ready to greet her new granddaughter.

Life was good. It was.

• • •

"Where's this little fork go?" Summer asked. "Inside or outside?"

Evelyn turned to see Summer holding up a salad fork.

"Outside, sweetie. You set them so people use the outside ones first, then work in."

Summer nodded and skipped off to the dining room as if learning such intricacies of etiquette were normal for a five-year-old. Only this five-year-old.

Evelyn had never known a child like her. Summer was bright, at ease talking to adults, and was happiest when she was helping. Quite the little gem. And it wasn't Evelyn's grandma status talking. She'd thought that since the first day Audra and Summer had moved into Peerbaugh Place. Funny how one day could change so many lives.

The doorbell rang. Evelyn glanced at the clock. Dinner guests weren't due for ninety minutes.

"I'll get it!" Summer yelled.

Evelyn sighed. "No, sweetie. Remember, only I answer the—"

Too late. Summer had opened the door.

Gail's gaze bypassed the little girl and sought out Evelyn. "Hello, Evelyn. I've got my things. I'm moving in."

For a moment Evelyn's mind was blank. What day was it?

Monday. Gail-moving-in day.

How could she forget?

Gail was standing on the porch, where Evelyn could see a stack of boxes and suitcases. "Do you have something to use to prop the door open?" Gail asked.

"I'll hold it!" Summer said.

Gail seemed to see her for the first time. "Thanks, kid."

Evelyn took a reluctant step forward. "Need some help?"

"Sure." Gail handed a box through the door.

Evelyn took it upstairs, her mind going over the to-do's in the kitchen. She didn't have time for this and yet this was part of her duties. With every step, Evelyn tried to grab on to some feeling of hospitality and gratitude. But all she could think about was the bread that needed to be kneaded.

The need to be needed. Ha.

To be fair, Gail did most of the work. Evelyn only had to take two more boxes upstairs before they were done.

She pushed her hair behind her ears, feeling too warm. "Well then, I'll leave you to get settled." Summer stood in the doorway, hugging the jamb, her cheek pressed to the trim. "Come on, sweetie, leave Gail alone so she can get moved in."

"In a minute, Grandma."

Evelyn sure liked that title and wondered if she'd continue to glow every time she heard it.

She hoped so.

•   •   •

Gail wanted to close the door, but she couldn't because the kid was in the way. The girl kept staring at her. It was annoying.

Gail arranged a suitcase on the bed and opened it. The kid still stayed. Finally, she gave her a direct look. "You can go now. Thanks for the help."

The child didn't budge, but kept hugging the door. And she kept staring at the room. Surely she'd seen it before.

Gail dragged out an armload of blouses and moved into the closet. When she came out the girl still had not moved. Gail put her hands on her hips. "Don't you have something to do?"

The kid shrugged, then pulled in a breath. "This was my room. And my mom's."

Ah, so that's it. Gail's opinion softened. "Where do you live now?"

"We got married."

Gail had to smile. "When did this happen?"

"Two weeks and two days ago. We just got back from the honeymoon last night."

"You went on the honeymoon?"

She nodded. "We went on a cruise. They had an ice sculpture in the shape of a dolphin, and we saw some real dolphins too."

"Cool."

"I started back at kindergarten today."

If the girl was going to keep talking, Gail decided to at least keep working. She opened a box of shoes and took two pairs to the closet.

The little girl let go of the door. "Let me pair them up. I'm good at that."

Gail relinquished the box. "Knock yourself out, kid."

She disappeared into the closet, but kept talking. "What's your name?"

Gail felt like a fool. She was the adult. She should have asked first. "I'm Gail Saunders. And you are?"

"Summer Taylor, but my Mommy just got married so her last name's different than mine."

"What's her name?"

"Peerbaugh. Like Grandma's name."

Gail was starting to get the picture. Mother and child move into boardinghouse, then marry son of landlord. She felt a slight stirring in her stomach. Maybe something good would happen to *her* while she was here. She could use a little good fortune.

The previous month had been the hardest in her life. Nothing was going as she'd planned. She'd never felt so powerless or out of control. It was an unacceptable condition. Moving into Peerbaugh Place had been a last resort, yet a necessity. Gail only hoped she'd hit bottom. She looked around her bedroom. The one-and-only room she could call her own.

How pitiful could you get?

●   ●   ●

Gail stacked the last empty box in the hall outside her door. The sounds of laughter and conversation floated up from the dining room at the foot of the stairs, and Gail regretted turning down

Evelyn's invitation to join them. Why had she done that? With her image as a professional woman, wasn't she supposed to be good at meeting new people, holding her own in lively conversation, participating in the social graces?

She *was* good at those things. Then why had she chosen to remain by herself?

Because you don't want to field their questions. You don't want to lie.

Gail closed her door against the laughter . . . and the truth.

·   ·   ·

Evelyn brought out a box wrapped with silver paper and a slightly squished bow. She put it on the cleared table in front of Audra. "For you and Russell."

"Another wedding present?" Audra asked.

"It arrived last week from Tessa. It was shipped from Venice."

Summer sat on her knees to get a better view. "They have boats and guys with poles in Venice. It's in Italy."

"Where did you learn all that?" her mother asked.

"Aunt Tessa left me a book with lots of pictures about where she'd be going on her trip."

Mae laughed. "Sounds like Tessie. Always trying to teach the rest of us." She put a hand to her chest. "Not that I need to learn a thing."

Collier leaned close, bumping arm to arm. "Yes, dear. We all know how perfect you are."

She kissed her finger and touched it to the tip of his nose. "I just wish you wouldn't make me keep reminding you."

Evelyn moved to the coffee carafe on the buffet. "Anyone for refills?"

Russell raised his cup to his mother, then turned to his wife. "Are you going to open it or not?"

Audra stroked the paper. "It's so pretty."

Russell rolled his eyes. "My wife has all the wedding wrapping paper rolled onto tubes in our hall closet. As if we'll ever use it."

"We will," she said. "I will. I promise."

"We can afford new wrapping paper, luv."

Luv. Evelyn poured the coffee and had to smile. It was so odd to hear her staid son use a term of endearment. Odd, but wonderful.

He turned to his mother. "By the way, I need your help. I'm trying to convince Audra that we need to start looking at houses. My apartment is fine, but now that we're a family . . ."

"I think that sounds wonderful," Evelyn said, returning to her seat. "Audra, why are you hesitating?"

She continued to painstakingly remove the paper. "Summer and I aren't used to big spaces. And haven't we been through enough changes? I'd like to settle into being married before I have to tackle a house."

"Oh, take the house, girlie-girl," Mae said. "Don't look a gift husband in the mouth."

"I'll think about it."

Evelyn was glad Audra wasn't quick to spend Russell's money but hoped she'd change her mind. Summer would flourish in a house with a yard.

The front door opened and all heads turned. It was Heddy. Evelyn stood, feeling awful for never once thinking about Heddy coming home for dinner.

"Heddy. Come meet my family and the neighbors."

Heddy pointed upstairs. "I really need—"

"Ah, come in, Heddy," Mae said. "It's me, Mae. I see you enough at Ruby's. Might as well come meet the rest of the gang."

Heddy took a single step into the room and nodded politely while Evelyn made introductions. "There's more lasagna in the kitchen," Evelyn said. "And cheesecake. If you'd let me know you were going to be here—"

Heddy stepped back into the foyer. "I'll be fine. Nice to meet all of you."

No one said anything until they heard the hinges of the kitchen door squeak. Then Mae leaned forward. "A bit reluctant, is she?"

"She's just shy," Evelyn said.

Mae shook her head. "No, she's not. You should see her flirting with the men who come into Ruby's. Why, she can bat her lashes with the best of us."

"You bat your lashes often?" Collier asked.

She patted his hand. "Not anymore, Mr. Husband. Not anymore."

●　　　●　　　●

Heddy stood in front of the refrigerator. Nothing looked good. Of course, after being around food all day at the diner, that wasn't surprising. Sometimes she thought if she smelled the aroma of a deep-fat fryer one more time her stomach would do something nasty.

She grabbed an apple and closed the fridge just as the back door opened. A woman came in like she owned the place.

"Excuse me," Heddy said. "Don't you think you should knock?"

"Not if I live here."

"You live here?"

"I most certainly do. I just took the last of my boxes outside. You live here too, I take it?"

Heddy didn't like feeling so flustered. She nodded and sat at the kitchen table. She took a bite of her apple.

The woman scanned the kitchen, then made a beeline for the oven. She opened it, revealing the leftover lasagna. "I thought I smelled Italian."

Heddy pointed toward the dining room. "Evelyn's having a fancy dinner for her family and the neighbors."

"I know."

"Why aren't you eating with them?"

"No reason." The woman smudged a finger against the cake plate then licked it. "I should have said yes. Good cooking here."

"You don't cook?"

"Since you make it sound like a character flaw, I assume you love to cook, right?"

She hadn't meant it that way. *Had she?* "I do like to cook. And bake. It calms me."

The woman turned a chair around and straddled it. "So you need calming?"

"No! I mean, I'm fine. Everything's fine."

The woman laughed. "Methinks the lady protests too much."

How had they gotten on this track? Heddy took another bite, buying time. Then she got back to the conversation two newly met tenants should be having. "I'm Heddy Wainsworth. And you are?"

"Gail Saunders." She reached over the table and they shook hands. "Back to your need to be calmed down."

"That's not what I said. I never said that."

"You said cooking calms you."

"A generic comment. It doesn't imply that I'm agitated."

Gail's smile was smug. "You're agitated now."

"Only because you're goading me."

Gail put a hand to her chest. "Me? Goading? How dare I do such a thing?"

Why did everything Gail say come out as a challenge, like a fencer taking a stance and saying "En garde!"? She would not be drawn to this woman's level. Why, Gail didn't even know how to wear makeup. And her ridiculous boy-length hair . . .

Gail gripped the back of the chair and rested her chin on her hands, peering at Heddy too intently. "You're making a judgment against me. I can tell."

Flustered and now disconcerted, Heddy wondered what would be next. "I am doing no such thing."

Gail sat up. "Sure you are. I saw your eyes taking me in, and your mouth—" she made a curlicue with her finger—"it went down at the corners, as if what you saw was distasteful. Sorry I don't meet your standards."

Heddy moved to the sink and got herself a glass of water. She didn't like being face-to-face with Gail, but also didn't like the feeling of having her back exposed.

"You're ignoring me," Gail said.

Heddy realized she was still holding the half-eaten apple. It was the apple's fault. If only she'd gone upstairs as soon as she'd said her greetings to the group in the dining room . . . she tossed the fruit in the trash.

She heard Gail stand. "Well then. I see how it's going to be around here. I'll just go up—"

Reluctantly, Heddy turned around. "Wait, Gail. I think we've started out on the wrong foot. Since we're going to be neighbors—even sharing a bathroom—it's important we be on good terms."

Gail made a dramatic gesture of shock. "You mean—gasp—be friends?"

Heddy couldn't imagine being friends with Gail. "Of course."

"I'm game if you are."

Heddy shrugged.

Gail laughed. "Your lack of enthusiasm is telling. But I'll let that go for now. Perhaps I did come on too strong, delving into your personal life with all guns blazing. You're allowed your secrets."

"And you're allowed yours?"

For the first time, Heddy saw Gail's strong demeanor crack. "And I'm allowed mine." Gail turned to leave.

"Where do you work?" Heddy asked.

There was a moment's hesitation. "I'm a merchandising consultant to the president at Lanigan Marketing. It's a wonderful job."

There was something about the way she said it that made Heddy believe it was anything but wonderful.

"And you?" Gail asked.

"I'm a hostess at Ruby's."

"That diner on the square?"

"I resent the contempt I hear in your voice."

Gail raised a hand. "Hey, don't get me wrong. I like chicken-fried everything as well as the next person, but Ruby's . . ." She shook her head, giving Heddy the once-over. "You don't seem to fit there. You're too . . . too . . ."

Heddy crossed her arms and waited. This, she had to hear. "Yes?"

"Too frilly. Ruby's is a denim-and-T-shirt place. I would think you'd be better suited to some linen-and-maître d' eatery."

"I think I'll take that as a compliment."

Gail flipped a hand. "Hey, it's all yours. Now, I really have to get upstairs. Moving in wiped me out." She paused at the kitchen door. "When do you take a bath?"

"Excuse me?"

"Morning or evening? We're sharing a bathroom. What's your preference?"

"Evening."

"Super. Talk at you later."

Only if absolutely necessary.

With the Lord's authority let me say this:
Live no longer as the ungodly do,
for they are hopelessly confused.

EPHESIANS 4:17

$\mathcal{H}$eddy stood on the stairs, listening to Evelyn getting breakfast in the kitchen. Some early morning talk show was on.

Heddy was hungry, yet she didn't dare go into the kitchen because Evelyn would offer to make her breakfast, and if Heddy ate breakfast—or any meal at Peerbaugh Place—she would be obliged to pay in some money for meals. And after going through her budget last night, she'd realized that wasn't possible.

There was no money. Not anymore.

She'd heard people say she didn't "fit" as the hostess at Ruby's. That was completely true. Heddy hated her job—the slightly coarse atmosphere and the incessant need for chitchat. But the fact that Ruby's allowed her to eat her meals free . . . that was a perk that overruled any fitting or not fitting. If she had her dream job it would involve using her artistic abilities, not showing hungry people to their tables and handing them sticky, laminated menus.

She heard Evelyn's humming rise as if she was coming out to the foyer. Heddy scrambled back upstairs to hide out until it was time to go in to work to cover the lunch crowd.

She closed the door to her room and locked it. The four walls immediately pressed in on her. She felt a bit like a prisoner. Thank goodness for the balcony. Unfortunately, this morning it was too cold to use it. She grabbed a notebook and a pen and settled onto a walnut rocker near the window. She bypassed the many used pages and opened a fresh one. There was something exciting about a fresh piece of paper. Moving into Peerbaugh Place was a fresh start and deserved a fresh plan. A new plan. A revised plan—since her old one had obviously come up short.

Now that was an understatement.

With a careful cursive, Heddy wrote a heading across the top: *My Life*. She underlined it, then created a subheading: *What I Want*.

As she began to make her list, she was a bit disappointed that it hadn't changed from her previous life plans. Considering all that had happened, shouldn't her wants and desires change?

She let the question hang a moment, but decided the answer was no. The desires she kept listing were deep-seated. A part of her. And despite what had happened, she truly didn't believe they were wrong. The wrong came from her choice of how to fulfill those desires.

She tilted the page just so, adjusting the *H* in *husband* to be prettier:

Husband
Two children
Home

She was sure Gail would laugh at her simplistic list. Most people would laugh. While others might list a desire to be president of some company, travel to exotic places, or ease world hunger, Heddy was content with her list. Simple wasn't bad. Simple was stable, secure, comfortable. Not everybody could conquer the world. Heddy was out-of-date and old-fashioned. And proud of it.

But if her desires were so simple, then why were they repeatedly held out of her grasp? Women far less attractive than Heddy had husbands, and women far less maternal than Heddy had children. And to make matters worse, a lot of women who were married with children acted like they didn't want to be. Heddy couldn't imagine.

She thought back to the other night when she'd brought Bob home. A mistake. Just because she'd been feeling a hint of desperation and depression that night didn't mean she should throw away her requirements for a mate.

She turned to that particular page in her book and read the Mate Requirement list:

Nice looking but not necessarily handsome. Nice smile and eyes.
Makes me laugh but can also discuss serious things.
Honest. Has good character.

Heddy stopped reading. She was tempted to make an arrow from the "Honest" entry, moving it to the top of the list, but she couldn't get herself to do it and mess up the neat composition of the page. But mentally . . . mentally, honesty was number one. Thanks to Carlos.

She looked out over the yard of Peerbaugh Place. The pin oaks that canopied the house stubbornly hung on to their leaves. Yet periodically a leaf surrendered its hold and let itself fly free.

Oh yes, she was free now. Completely free of beautiful Carlos with the brown eyes and the delicious smell. Of course all her money was also gone . . .

With a fresh breath she shoved such memories away. Everyone made mistakes—but most people didn't make mistakes that cost them their entire life savings. She'd heard it said that a wise man can see more from the bottom of a well than a fool can see from a mountaintop. She hoped so, because she was certainly at the bottom of a very deep well.

She returned to her list of qualifications:

Attentive. Remembers special occasions.
Polite. Opens doors, holds my chair: a gentleman.
Likes children. Likes spending time as a family.
A good provider. Loves his job (but me more).
Adores me.

It was that last one that ignited the romantic in Heddy. In her past excursions into love, that element had been missing. Heddy had discounted the need for adoration as something above and beyond the capabilities of a true-life, flesh-and-blood male. It was a trait only found in romance-novel characters.

And yet . . . a part of her wouldn't let it go. She knew *she* had the capacity to adore. The trick was finding the right person to adore her back.

Maybe she should move to a big city where the dating pool for thirtysomethings was larger and put her ad in some singles' paper. She shook her head. No way. Though she wasn't a religious person, she liked the idea that God had created one special person for everyone, and certainly His methods would be more creative than using singles' ads. And then there was the fact that people could mess up His plan and choose wrong. Free will and all that.

She'd certainly proved that point with Carlos. And Harry. And Dennis.

She closed the book, hugged it to her chest, then closed her eyes and found herself praying. *God . . . is he out there? Show him to me.*

She opened her eyes, a bit shocked that she'd prayed. But what could it hurt? She could use all the help she could get.

* * *

Evelyn heard the front door close. She looked at the kitchen table, so nicely set for three. So much for sharing breakfast with her tenants. So far, she'd only seen Gail drink coffee, and Heddy's foray into a friendly breakfast was obviously a one-time engagement. At least they'd save money on food. In fact, the question of food money had not come up. With the previous tenants, she and the other women had put fifty dollars a week into a pot and had taken turns buying groceries—and cooking.

Fat chance. Would she have to get used to cooking for one?

The phone rang. It was Nurse Hudson. Accosta Rand was being released at eleven.

Evelyn would be there. At least someone needed her.

* * *

"Thank you, Mr. Burroughs. Have a nice day."

After dealing with a long line of bank customers, Audra could finally take a complete breath. She spotted Russell walking through the lobby on the way to his office. He kissed his fingers and waved.

Susan, in the teller cage next to her, leaned over the partition. "A kissy wave. A nice perk for being married to a vice president."

Yes, it was.

Susan continued. "Having the wife title and the income to go with it must be great."

Audra did a double take. What an odd comment.

"But how do you like having the Peerbaugh name?" Susan made a face. "Quite a change from Taylor."

Yes, it was.

To be truthful, Audra was not thrilled about her new last name. Before meeting Evelyn and Russell, she'd never heard the name *Peerbaugh*. Not once. At least her first name wasn't Polly or Perry. That would have been too much. Audra Peerbaugh. She'd have to get used to it. Get used to a lot of things.

"I suppose you'll be getting a promotion soon."

Ah, so that was it. Audra had to nip this in the bud. "Just because Russell is my husband doesn't mean—"

Susan raised her hands. "Hey, take what you can get; that's what I always say."

I bet you do—say that and do that.

"I didn't have a chance to ask you yesterday . . . how was the honeymoon?" Susan's grin and the suggestive curve of her eyebrows made Audra once again wish that her old friend Gillie had stuck around. She and Gillie had shared some good cage-to-cage discussions. But Gillie had moved to another state and was working with some charity foundation. As far as Audra was concerned, Susan was completely unlikable. Although she applied a professional front for customers one-on-one, with her teller hat off, Susan tended to be rude, lewd, and crude.

"The honeymoon was lovely," Audra said.

"Lovely. Never heard it called that before. By the way, what did you do with the kid?"

"She came with us."

Susan snickered. "I bet that was fun."

"Yes, it was."

New customers came into the lobby. "I guess your idea of fun is different than mine."

"I guess so."

The customers were a blessing.

*   *   *

Evelyn took a side trip before she went to the hospital. She usually used the drive-through, but today she decided to go into the main lobby of the bank. It would be a nice chance to say hi to her new daughter-in-law at work, and if Russell was available, even stick her head into his office.

The tellers were busy, but when Audra looked up and spotted Evelyn, she smiled. Such a nice girl.

Evelyn took her place in line and within a few minutes had Audra's attention. "How are you doing today, Mrs. Peerbaugh?" she asked.

Audra beamed. "Fine. And you, Mrs. Peerbaugh?"

"Peachy keen." She pushed the rental checks forward. "Deposit these, please."

"Certainly." Audra completed the transaction. "Thanks again for dinner last night. You went all out. That cheesecake was delish."

"Thank the cooking classes. Aaron wouldn't touch cheese-cake. He couldn't get past the idea that a cake had cheese in it."

"Cream cheese. That's different."

Evelyn shrugged. "Try telling him that." She saw Audra's eyes flit over her shoulder and glanced behind. There was a line. "I'll see you after work."

"Give Summer a kiss for me."

"Will do."

As Evelyn left the line and placed the deposit receipt in her purse, she was stopped by a hand to her arm. She looked up and saw Anabelle Griese in line.

"Mrs. Peerbaugh."

"Uh . . . hello, Anabelle."

"I haven't heard back from you. When can I move in?"

Evelyn scanned the faces of those in line. They averted their eyes, but she knew their ears were tuned in. She was acquainted with two of the customers. Carson Creek wasn't that big.

"Well?" Anabelle asked.

"I . . . I'm afraid the rooms are rented."

"Since when?"

Evelyn tried to remember which day Anabelle had shown up so she could tweak the answer to her advantage, but her mind was a jumble. "This weekend."

"But I looked at the place on Wednesday. I was there first."

Evelyn edged toward the door. Unfortunately, Anabelle stepped out of line and followed her.

"Did you even call my references?"

"Yes. Yes, I did." An honest answer, but she dreaded the next question.

"What did they say?"

Wording, Lord . . . give me the right wording. "They said there were some problems."

Anabelle dug her fists into her ample hips. "They what?"

All eyes turned. "Can we go outside to discuss this?" Evelyn asked.

Anabelle shoved her way past, clanging the push bar of the door with the force of her motion. Evelyn looked desperately toward Russell's office, then at Audra. Audra nodded and picked up the phone. Help was on its way.

Anabelle backtracked into the foyer, sticking her head in the door. "You coming?"

Audra was speaking into the phone. Maybe if Evelyn stalled . . .

"I don't have all day," Anabelle said.

Evelyn saw Russell come out of his office. As a child, he'd run to her for help. Now the tables were turned.

He hurried to her side. "Mom? What's going on?"

Anabelle stood in the opened door. "She rooked me out of a room at her boardinghouse—that's what's going on."

"We were going outside," Evelyn said.

"Perhaps that's best." Russell extended an arm of invitation. The three of them went outside. Russell led them to a planter area. "Hello. I'm Russell Peerbaugh."

"You're her son?"

"Yes."

"Uh-uh. No fair."

"I assure you, I'll be extremely fair. I'm sure we can work this—"

Anabelle's hair gyrated as she shook her head. "The only way we can work this out is if your mother rents me a room."

Russell looked in his mother's direction. "But I believe her rooms are already rented."

Evelyn nodded, thinking how wonderful it would be if she didn't need to say a word.

"But I was there first. She's discriminating against me because I'm fat."

Evelyn saw Russell's eyebrows rise and knew they were mimicking her own.

Anabelle waved an accusatory finger at them. "Don't give me that shocked look. It's the truth. You should have seen her have a conniption when she thought I'd break one of the antique chairs in her parlor."

Russell looked at his mother, but Evelyn looked down.

"See?" Anabelle said. "She admits it."

So much for staying quiet. "I don't let Russell sit in that chair."

Russell took a step between them. "My mother—any landlord—has the right to rent to whomever they please."

The hair whipped again. "No, they don't. There's the Fair Housing Act that says they can't discriminate."

"Can't discriminate against anyone for race, creed, color, age . . ."

"Exactly."

"Weight is not listed." Russell quickly added, "Not that my mother declined your application for that reason."

"Then what was the reason?"

They both looked to Evelyn. She'd never been good at making

up lies. It was easier to tell the truth. "Your last reference said they wouldn't rent to you again."

Anabelle's eyes widened, and Evelyn was reminded of a cartoon character whose face reddened to the point of explosion. "They what?"

"So then," Russell said, "that's the end of that. My mother can only go by the references you gave her."

"But they're wrong."

Russell shrugged. Evelyn was impressed with his cool demeanor under fire. "Now, if you'll excuse us, my mother and I have some business to attend to."

He herded her into his office, where she hid until Anabelle Griese drove away. Saved by the son.

This time.

●   ●   ●

Evelyn knocked on the door to Accosta's hospital room.

"Come in."

"Morning, Mrs. Rand." Accosta was sitting in the visitor's chair, dressed in a skirt and a heavy, cabled cardigan that couldn't hide her frail frame.

But her smile was anything but frail. "So it's you! Nurse Hudson told me not to call a cab, that someone special was picking me up and taking me home, but she wouldn't tell me who it was."

"Even if she'd said my name you wouldn't have recognized it." Evelyn held out her hand to shake. "We were never properly introduced. Evelyn Peerbaugh."

"Accosta Rand."

"That's an unusual name."

"My parents wanted all us children to have one-of-a-kind names. Peerbaugh's a bit unusual too."

"Unfortunately, I have no story to explain it away."

Accosta attempted to stand and Evelyn helped. "Ring that button there. The nurses said to ring when I was ready to go."

•　　•　　•

Accosta's home was marginal and sat in a neighborhood that had once been filled with families, but now were rental properties. The homes were bisected into apartments that rarely held anyone who was married, much less over the age of thirty. The sound of a stereo vibrated from the house next door.

Accosta caught Evelyn's look in its direction. "Good thing I have a hearing aid I can turn on and off at will. Now, if they'd play some Glenn Miller, I'd be dancing on the porch."

"'Little Brown Jug' is my favorite."

"I like 'Pennsylvania 6-5000.'"

Evelyn liked that one too. The inside of Accosta's house looked as if it hadn't changed for decades, yet the original details of the house were rarely duplicated today except in the most expensive homes: Mission-style oak balusters and railings, with brass rods holding down the flowered stair runner. Columns separated the parlor from a dining room that held a brass light fixture with prisms catching the sun. Wood floors were dotted with Oriental rugs. And there were family photos everywhere, covering every surface. Black-and-white photos of women with bobbed hair, wearing tea dresses, and some with exaggerated leg-o'-mutton sleeves.

"Would you like the suitcase taken upstairs?" Evelyn asked.

"That would be nice."

The upstairs mirrored the first floor, with dated but classic furnishings. It was fairly clean, but could use a good going-over, something Accosta probably wasn't capable of doing. Maybe on another day . . .

When Evelyn returned downstairs, she found Accosta making tea. "You don't have to do that. You're supposed to rest."

"Oh fiddle-dee, I've got all day to rest. Now I have company." She opened a cupboard. "I think I have a tin of butter cookies around here somewhere."

The cupboards were nearly bare. Evelyn made an excuse of finding some milk for tea and opened the refrigerator. It was the same. Forget helping Accosta clean. She had more immediate needs. Like a good meal.

Evelyn allowed Accosta to serve the tea, but was eager to be gone. She had groceries to buy.

• • •

Just once, Piper wished she could find a decent parking place at the hospital. Yes, the exercise was good for her. Yes, there were other visitors who needed to be closer to the building. But still . . . having to walk down a row of twenty-five cars that were there first irked her. Didn't they realize she had to get to her mother's side ASAP? Didn't they understand she'd had an awful day at work, with two problem students needing more counseling than she could ever provide? Didn't they know she hadn't had time to eat lunch because of a fight between two other problem boys? Couldn't they tell she had a hole in her nylons that now encased her big toe and was driving her crazy?

Once in the lobby, Piper saw that all the elevators were on upper floors. Typical. She punched the Call button a half-dozen times and considered taking the stairs. But after her parking-lot trek she decided against it. Besides, it was the principle of the thing—though at the moment she couldn't pinpoint just what that principle might be.

She sensed a white coat move beside her and smelled a musky scent she'd smelled before. She turned to look. It was Dr. Baladino.

He glanced up from a chart. "Oh, Ms. Wellington. How are you?"

She let out an explosion of air coupled with a laugh. "You don't want to know."

"Oh, really."

"Really."

"Your mother's doing fine . . ."

Suddenly, Piper felt like a selfish fool. She covered her face with a hand.

"Ah. I get it."

She peeked through her fingers. "Get what?"

"Your mood has nothing to do with her, does it?"

Piper took a step back. "Stay away from me, Doctor. You are way too right to be safe."

He laughed, then looked at his watch. "Got time for a cup of coffee? or a piece of pie? I missed lunch."

"You buying?"

"Absolutely."

"Then lead on."

Things were definitely looking up.

•   •   •

Why had she never noticed Dr. Baladino's eyes before now? or his long fingers? or the way his left cheek dimpled when he smiled?

As soon as the observations hit her consciousness, Piper tried—*tried*—to shove them away. It was ridiculous. She was acting like a high school girl in the fervor of her first crush. She was thirty-four years old. Sure, she was single. Sure, Dr. Baladino reminded her of Andrea Bocelli (she wondered if he could sing), but that didn't mean she had to obsess about him. Especially when he was merely being nice, rescuing her because she'd made a fool of herself because she'd been having a bad day.

At the moment, her day was drastically improving.

Without meaning to, she glanced at his ring finger. It was devoid of a ring.

"No, I'm not married."

Piper sucked in an extravagant breath and slapped a hand to her chest. "Don't do that!"

"Do what?"

"Catch me doing something I shouldn't. Don't read my mind."

"You're not that hard to read."

"Thanks a lot."

He pushed his empty plate away and sat back, stretching. "And you have it wrong. Having a transparent nature is an attribute. It saves time."

She cocked her head. "I may be transparent, but you are a piece of work, Doctor. Just when I think I know where you're heading with a comment, you add another one that sends me ricocheting off in some other direction."

"I don't mean to."

"As you said to me, it's an attribute. I think. At any rate, it sure keeps my attention. I don't dare slack off or I'll get whiplash."

"I can treat that, you know."

"I'm sure you can."

He looked at his watch again and slid his chair back. "I have to go."

She looked at her own watch. Piper couldn't believe she'd taken forty minutes of his time pouring out the annoyances of her day. "Me too. My mom awaits. And I'm sure Dad needs a break."

Dr. Baladino took their dishes to a cart. "They're very close, aren't they?"

"They're meant for each other. 'What God has joined together . . .'"

His face changed. "Hmm."

"What brought that rain cloud across your face?"

He held the door for her. "Obviously I have my own transparency to deal with."

"Which doesn't answer my question."

They headed back to the elevators. "You mentioned God. I don't believe in God."

Piper was taken aback. "But how can you not? Especially when you see miracles every day."

"I see death just as often. Where is God in that?" His pager beeped. He glanced at it. "Gotta go. I'll check on your mother later."

Piper returned to the elevators. One opened just as she got close.

Why did she want another dose of pie?

•   •   •

Evelyn had never had so much fun buying groceries. She'd wanted it to be a surprise, but had realized that Accosta might have some food restrictions after her surgery—and Evelyn didn't even know what surgery she'd had. So she'd been forced to reveal her intentions and ask a few personal questions about why Accosta had been in the hospital in the first place. She'd had her gallbladder removed, but instead of the way Aaron's had been done ten years ago, they'd used a laser that was less invasive. Amazing.

When Evelyn came back to Accosta's, she went right inside, having left Accosta resting on the couch. When the woman started to get up, she shooed her back down. "No, no. You stay put. I can handle it."

A half hour later, Evelyn brought Accosta a bowl of chicken noodle soup, a turkey sandwich, and a glass of milk.

Accosta's eyes widened. "My, my, this is wonderful. No one's ever treated me like this before."

"Then it's about time."

About time for Accosta to get a little pampering. About time for Evelyn to feel like she made a difference. It was the perfect trade-off.

Your refuge looks strong,
but since it is made of lies,
a hailstorm will knock it down.
Since it is made of deception,
the enemy will come like a flood to sweep it away.

ISAIAH 28:17

*E*velyn ran the dust cloth over the intricate feet of the dresser. The good thing about antiques was their lovely detail; the bad thing was dusting that lovely detail.

She groaned as she stood up, the bending and squatting that came with the job of cleaning Piper's room making her feel old—especially at five thirty in the morning. But it was worth it. After more than a week of living with Gail and nearly two weeks with Heddy, it was clear that her tenants were independent souls. Evelyn looked forward to having a good friend around. She hadn't realized how much she was looking forward to it until she'd awakened early and decided to get going with the work.

There was another positive aspect to Piper's moving in today. It meant her mother was finally coming home from the hospital. There'd been some complications that had kept Wanda hospitalized a few extra days, but everyone was eager to have her settled in a home setting.

Evelyn heard Gail's door open. Why was she up so early?

She stepped into the hall and found Gail tiptoeing down the front stairs.

Gail looked up and froze.

Evelyn moved to the railing and whispered, "What are you doing up?"

Gail's eyes flitted away, then back to Evelyn. "We have a big project due. I want to get a head start."

There was something else odd about this scene besides the time of day. Evelyn pegged it. "Why are you wearing jeans? You always wear such nice suits."

"Uh . . . it's casual day." She moved a black tote bag behind her back. Evelyn had seen her carry that bag to work every day. She'd thought it odd before—most corporate types had briefcases, not soft-sided zipper bags—but now Evelyn sensed that Gail was trying to hide it.

Gail didn't give her time to ask more. "I have to go. I'll be late."

She slipped down the stairs and out the door. *Whoosh.* She was gone.

Something wasn't right.

•   •   •

Gail pulled away from Peerbaugh Place, muttering to herself. How could she have been so dumb? Yes, it was a pain keeping up the pretense of going to work at a corporate office day after day. Yes, it was extra work getting dressed in a suit and hose to leave the house, and again, to return.

But that was no excuse for slacking off by wearing jeans.

Because of the early hour, Gail had thought she would be safe to venture out without the suit. Evelyn didn't usually get up at 5:30. Why today, on the one day Gail had to go to work early because they'd assigned her the dreaded breakfast shift?

As a newbie, it couldn't be helped. She'd only worked at Burger Madness for three weeks and had zero seniority. High school kids were above her. If that wasn't humbling . . .

The black bag containing her uniform slipped off the car seat. She pulled it back. Who would have ever thought that she, Gail Saunders, with a master's degree in business, would be forced to work in a drive-through burger joint and wear an awful red, white, and blue polyester uniform, including a visor? It was the epitome of disgrace.

Wasn't it humiliating enough that she could only afford to live in a boardinghouse? Sure, Peerbaugh Place was clean. Sure, it was nice. But it was a step below an apartment. It was cheap. And inhabited by losers like Heddy or desperate people like Evelyn's friend Piper, who needed a short-term place to stay. Peerbaugh Place was not a residence for anyone who was successful or ambitious. It was *not* a place she was proud of. She had not told anyone.

She turned onto the highway that led to Jackson. The commute was a killer, but necessary. There was safety in distance, a buffer against those who could witness her failure.

Success was important to Gail. She'd grown up being told that success in business was the essence of achievement and the measure of a person's worth. That's why she'd given up her social life in college in order to pull all A's and graduate with "high distinction." She'd been a somebody then.

It wasn't fair that the job offers hadn't come rolling in. Gail had to concede that personality and giving a good interview should have some weight in the hiring process, but the fact that no big corporations had hired her proved they held too much weight.

Lanigan Marketing was the exception. The reality that the position they hired her for was a glorified gofer was another humiliation she'd had to bear. And so what if she exaggerated her job title and duties to friends and family? She *would* be an executive at Lanigan Marketing one day.

Or she would have been if she hadn't been fired.

It was all their fault. Any supervisor who couldn't take constructive criticism was weak. It was hard to believe that no one else had ever told the company where they were going wrong in the way they handled their project placement and administration.

In retrospect, yes, Gail probably could have been a bit more tactful. But to be fired for telling the truth?

Good riddance. She'd find a better job. A great job. Soon. Hopefully.

Gail turned the radio on. Loud. After all, didn't she have to be wide awake to say, "Welcome to Burger Madness. May I help you?"

Pitiful.

* * *

Mae wasn't paying attention to the lunchtime conversation of her friends. She was too busy watching Heddy. Studying Heddy.

Mae considered herself good at analyzing people, pegging them. But Heddy Wainsworth was one tough study. On the surface she was a butterfly, flitting from one point to another. When she sat still and let herself be observed for the beautiful creature she was, Mae felt as if she should be quiet so as not to scare her away. And when Mae watched her interact with the customers that came into Ruby's, it was as if the butterfly that was Heddy was being forced into deep winter where there were no flowers upon which to land. No sustenance. No joy. Only an edge of panic as if she wanted to be anywhere but where she was.

It wasn't that Heddy presented herself as being better than the others who inhabited Ruby's, but she clearly wasn't one of them. Mae's mental image of Heddy placed her on a porch swing with a child on either side, reading a picture book. It was spring and a basket of pink geraniums hung nearby, swaying in the wind. Home and hearth. That was Heddy Wainsworth.

If Mae's assessment was right-on, then a question arose: What was Heddy doing here?

Her friend Doris poked her in the arm with a fork. "Mae! You haven't heard a word I've said."

It was true she hadn't been listening to words, but Mae *had* been listening. The vibes Heddy was sending from across the room were trumpeting full blast. And they were far more intriguing than any story Doris had to tell.

• • •

Audra took a bite of her chimichanga. "Mmm. This is wonderful." She pointed to Russell's plate, which remained untouched. "You haven't tried your enchiladas yet."

He picked up a fork and poked at them.

Uh-oh. Something was wrong. She should have known. Russell never had time to take her to lunch, so when he'd offered today . . .

She set her fork down. "What's wrong?"

He glanced up, said nothing, but offered a deep sigh.

The sigh that spoke a thousand words.

She reached across the table and took his hand. "Russell . . ."

He quit playing with his food. "There's been a little flak about the two of us working for the bank."

She withdrew her hand. "From whom?"

"I won't say, don't even know names, but apparently some employees have complained, insinuating you get special treatment because you are my wife."

"Such as?"

"You just got a raise."

"It was a merit raise." She lifted an eyebrow. "At least that's what I was told. Did you do something to get it for me?"

His hesitation answered for him.

She tossed her napkin on the table. "Russell, I do not want to be treated any differently because we're married. I told you that beforehand."

"I know, and be assured that the raise was coming anyway. But I do think your connection to me had something to do with you getting it now as opposed to later."

"That's not my fault."

He picked up his fork again and cut into the food. "No, it's mine. I wanted you to make more—for your pride's sake—not because we need the money."

There was so much being said behind the words. "Are you implying you're *not* proud of me? That having your wife be a teller is beneath your position?"

"No." His voice had softened but was also tinged with doubt. "No."

They each took a bite, chewing over their thoughts along with their food. "Do you want me to quit?" Audra asked.

"I . . . I don't know." His face brightened. "Would you consider quitting?"

She'd never thought of it. "I don't know."

"Because if you would quit . . . I was thinking that maybe it would be nice for you to remain at home with Summer. Be a stay-at-home mom. It's not like we need the money you make."

"My pittance compared to your windfall."

"I never said—"

"You didn't have to. I know I don't make much, but again, that's not my fault. Maybe you should pay your tellers more."

"I—"

She stopped his words with a hand. "I know. That's not the issue. The bottom line is that you want me to stay home. You don't want me to work."

"Being a homemaker and a mother is plenty of work. And we

were going to buy a house . . . there will be tons of work involved in that." He adjusted his napkin in his lap.

"And?"

He looked up and his eyes betrayed a pleading softness. "The truth is, I'd like us to be more than a couple. I'd like us to be partners. If you were home maybe we could entertain clients, and I could show you off at business lunches and—"

She put her fork down. "Be a trophy wife? You want me to smile pretty and laugh at the clients' jokes?"

He blushed. "No, no. I'm saying it all wrong." He took a few breaths in and out. "My dad never involved my mom. Ever. Except for living in the same house and having me they led completely separate lives. I want our marriage to be more than coexistence; I want *us* to be more, as individuals and as a team. I want *us* to make decisions. I want to tap into your woman's intuition and have you tap into . . . into whatever I have to offer." He smiled. "Assuming you think I have something to offer."

She let her anger subside, squeezed his hand, and gave him the reinforcement he was begging for. "I can think of one or two things." She was amazed at the relief on his face.

He kissed the back of her hand. "I don't want to be just an ordinary small-town banker, Audra. I want to do good things. Make a difference. I can't do that without you."

"You have me, Russell. You know that."

"But if you were home, if we were truly working as a team, focused on the same things . . ."

"Can't we be a team with me working at the bank?"

His eyes flitted away, then back. "Summer needs you too, you know."

"She's doing just fine."

"But she'd do better with you there. And she'd be able to take piano lessons—or dance. Experience new things with your help. You know I'm right."

He was right on all accounts, but a part of Audra rebelled at the idea of *just* being a wife, *just* being a mother and homemaker. Weren't women supposed to do all that *and* have an outside job to prove they could do it all? Wasn't that the measure of success?

"Just think about it," Russell said. He turned to the waiter and ordered another bowl of chips.

• • •

Piper ran ahead of her parents to unlock the door to her apartment. Her mother did not take the steps well because of the incision in her groin that had become infected. Her face was pale and periodically flashed with pain. If only Piper could take the pain away.

Her parents finally reached the door and Piper led the way to the bedroom. She pulled back the bedcovers. "I have it all fixed up for you. I bought one of those cushioned bed chairs, here, and the phone is close, and tissues, and the remote—"

"It's fine, honey. Don't make a fuss over me."

It was the least she could do.

Her father removed her mother's shoes, and helped her swing her legs onto the bed. He tucked her in, then kissed her forehead. "Anything I can get you?"

She shook her head. "I'm worn out. I just want to sleep."

"Whatever you say."

Piper and her dad moved into the living room, leaving the door slightly ajar. When Piper started to say something, he put a finger to his lips and pointed to the kitchen, which would give them more privacy.

Finally, facing each other within the U of the counters, Piper had a chance to notice that her father looked like a whipped puppy. He looked *old*.

And then without warning, the tears came. Her father's tears. "I'm so scared, Piper-girl. I'm so scared."

All she could do was hug him and tell him everything would be all right.

But would it?

•   •   •

Piper cleared away the lunch dishes. Her mother didn't want to eat, but Piper brought her some chicken broth in a thermal mug with a lid so she could eat when she felt like it.

Piper had taken half a day off to get her mom home and move into Evelyn's. But she needed to get the moving done so she could be back at work tomorrow.

She grabbed her suitcases. Her father eyed them as if they were full of radioactive material. "I feel bad."

"Don't. This is best. You and mom need a quiet place for her recuperation. I have the place. And Evelyn has a place for me. It's perfect."

He shook his head. "If things were perfect, we never would have sold our house to go RVing. Your mother wanted to keep it to have a home base, but I insisted. I was obsessed with this travel thing and didn't see any reason to hold on to our past lives with any house."

"You had no way of knowing this would happen."

"Maybe. But I should have listened to her. She had reservations. She kept telling me . . ." His eyes were sad. "Maybe she knew. Maybe she sensed something with that woman's intuition of hers. I wish I'd listened."

"You can't go back, Dad. And now everyone's doing all we can to make it through this. You'll be back RVing before you know it."

"No."

"Don't say no. You love it. You both do."

He didn't say any more, but took one of the suitcases to her car.

•   •   •

Evelyn answered the door to Piper.

"I'm here."

"You're here."

They paused a moment, as if letting the unspoken *reason* for her presence have its say.

"Come in," Evelyn said. She pointed to Tessa's old room at the top of the stairs. "The door just at the top—"

"I know."

She felt herself redden. "Of course you do." Why was she acting so oddly? She'd gotten up at five thirty this morning because she was excited that Piper—her dear friend—was coming, but now she was acting as if Piper were a stranger.

Evelyn took one of the suitcases and headed toward the stairs, but was stopped when Piper put a hand on her arm. "Mom will be fine, Evelyn. I know it."

Evelyn let the relief show. "I'm so glad."

Piper headed up the stairs. "Come help me get settled in."

At that moment, Summer came running out of the kitchen. "Piper!"

The suitcases were set aside to make room for hugs. "How you doing, pip-squeak?"

"I'm fine. We made lemon crisp cookies. I ran the mixer all by myself."

"My, my. Then come help me unpack so we can eat."

•   •   •

Evelyn and Piper sat on Piper's bed chatting about nothing in particular. It was wonderful and brought back memories of the time when Peerbaugh Place was full with Mae, Audra, Summer, and Tessa. Lest Evelyn make those past times too idyllic, she reminded herself that there had been tough times too. Not everything had been happy chatter and laughter. But there had been *sister* times. That's what Evelyn longed for again. More sisters to add to her life. She was willing if only Gail and Heddy—

When the doorbell rang, Summer yelled from the living room, "I'll get it!"

Evelyn got off the bed. How many times had Evelyn told that girl she was not to answer the—

From the stairs, Evelyn spied the postman at the door. He looked from Summer up to her. "Certified letter, Evelyn. You have to sign for it."

Her stomach clenched. *Certified* was another word for important and serious. The last time she'd received anything certified was in regard to the paperwork after Aaron died. She signed the green card and took the envelope. The return address was a lawyer's office in Jackson: Griese Law Practice, Attorney-at-Law. Her mind did a bizarre twist and allowed itself to ponder the absurdity of the title Attorney-at-Law. What else would they be attorneys of? Calypso dancing? Horseback riding?

She was pulled back to reality by Summer's tug on her arm. "What is it, Grandma?"

Piper stood on the bottom step. "Yes, what is it, Grandma?"

Although Evelyn longed to retreat upstairs and get back to their discussion of cute shoes, favorite movies, and good restaurants, she knew she had to open the letter. And maybe it was something good. Maybe she'd won the Publishers Clearing House Sweepstakes or something.

But if so, where were the balloons?

She ripped open the envelope and took out a letter on embossed legal stationery. Evelyn scanned the words, then reread them. As her eyes scanned the letterhead and skipped to the signature at the end, it became clear. So clear that it was terrifying. No way. This wasn't real.

"What's wrong?" Piper asked.

Summer's eyes moved from her grandma to Piper and back again. "Grandma . . ."

Evelyn thrust the letter toward Piper. "I'm being sued."

"By whom?"

"By Anabelle Griese. She looked at the rooms and wanted one. I wouldn't rent to her."

"Why not?"

Evelyn's mind skipped over a possible answer and gave the probable answer. "She didn't get a good recommendation from her last landlord. He said she was a pain."

"Then what's the problem?"

Evelyn pointed at the letter. "She says I didn't rent to her because she's fat."

"Is she?"

"Very. But that wasn't the reason. The lady had an attitude." An attitude that made Gail and Heddy seem like bosom buddies. She pointed to the letterhead. "And to make matters worse, she's a lawyer. She has her own firm."

"That's not good."

"An understatement."

Piper glanced over the letter again. "I've heard of discrimination suits, but never one for obesity. I'm no lawyer, but how is she ever going to prove damages?"

"I don't know . . . because she didn't move in? That's damaging?"

"To her ego. Just because you apply to an apartment complex doesn't mean they'll rent to you. Everybody knows that."

"Anabelle must have been absent the day life taught that lesson."

"What are you going to do?"

Evelyn took the letter and carefully slipped it back into the envelope. "What can I do? There are no more rooms to rent. Peerbaugh Place is full."

"I could leave."

"You will *not* leave. What Anabelle's doing is wrong. Absurd. She can't force her way into this house. I won't let her."

Piper smiled. "My, my. Where did this fire come from?"

Evelyn put a hand to her chest and found her heart doing double time. "I don't know. I don't usually act this way."

"But sometimes you should, Evelyn. Sometimes everyone should. Even Jesus got angry when He witnessed a wrong being done."

"So you agree Anabelle is wrong?"

"Of course she's wrong."

Summer nodded furiously.

Evelyn realized what a joy it was to have the support of people who loved her. She set the letter on the foyer table and extended both hands. "Lawsuits make me hungry. Who's game for some cookies and milk?"

The comfort food did its job. For the time being.

●　　●　　●

Since she'd worked the breakfast shift through lunch, Gail was off work by early afternoon. But she couldn't go home. She'd aroused Evelyn's suspicions by her early exit and couldn't risk more scrutiny by showing up much before five. She'd killed some time hanging around the library, but when she found herself dozing in her carrel, she decided to head home, scrutiny or no scrutiny.

To pad her entrance, she stopped by the grocery store and bought the fixings for alfredo with peas and ham. No, it wasn't made from scratch—the noodles and sauce coming from an envelope—but Evelyn would have to deal with Gail's meager cooking expertise or go hungry. She'd never had an inclination to learn how to cook. Yet after working at Burger Madness, she *was* developing a yearning for food from a kitchen rather than a sack.

She found Evelyn in the kitchen, staring into a cupboard. When she turned around her face was drawn. "Gail. What are you doing home so early?"

Kick in excuse number 283: "Since I went in early, they let me go home early."

"Did you get your big project completed?"

"Yes."

Evelyn turned back to the canned goods. "I'm glad for that and for the fact you're home for dinner. Piper's moved in and I was just getting ready to make—"

"I got groceries," Gail said. "I'll cook for us tonight."

The shock on Evelyn's face was pitiful. Yet there was another emotion present. Relief? She fumbled a can as she put it back in the cupboard. "That would be wonderful."

"It's no big deal." She set the sacks on the counter.

"Do you need help?"

Gail did *not* want an audience. "I can do it. Just tell me how many are going to eat."

"Audra should be here anytime to pick up Summer so there's just me and Piper. I haven't seen Heddy today."

"Does anyone ever see Heddy?"

Evelyn didn't respond and Gail felt a moment of regret for the comment. And guilt. Who was she to talk? "There'll be enough for Heddy if she does show up."

"That's great." Evelyn's sigh was deep and loud. "Truth is, I don't feel like cooking tonight. I don't know how long I'd been standing in front of the cupboard, just staring into it, when you came in."

"Is something wrong?"

Evelyn told her about the lawsuit. Anabelle Griese. What a name. And what an absurd suit. It would be impossible to prove intent on Evelyn's part. Unless she'd said something derogatory about the woman's size . . .

"*Did* you turn her down because—"

"No! Absolutely not."

Gail shrugged. "Doesn't matter to me. I was just curious." She heard Summer's laughter coming from upstairs. "Summer's not in my room, is she?"

"No, no," Evelyn said, heading for the foyer. "She's been helping Piper move in. She's quite the helper, you know."

Whatever.

•   •   •

A green salad from a plastic bag, a bowl of canned peaches, a noodle dish made from an envelope packet (Piper had seen the packet in the trash), and a frozen lemon cream pie coming up for dessert. Interesting . . .

They were just sitting down when Piper heard the front door open. They stopped all movement, listening.

"It must be Heddy," Gail said.

Piper pushed her chair back. "I'll go get her."

"But . . ." Evelyn's voice was oddly hesitant.

"Shouldn't I go get her?" Piper asked. "Shouldn't she eat with us? I haven't even met her yet."

"Sure," Gail said, waving toward the kitchen door. "Give it a shot. Invite her in. I doubt she'll come."

Why wouldn't she?

But they were right. When Piper entered the foyer, she found Heddy going upstairs, clearly couching her steps so as not to make any noise. "Heddy?"

The woman froze. "Yes?"

Piper reached a hand over the railing. "Hi. I'm Piper Wellington. I'm the new tenant." Heddy's handshake was weak. "I'm staying in the room at the top of the stairs while my mother is recuperating from surgery in my apartment."

"That's nice of you."

Piper shrugged. "Your timing's perfect. We're just sitting down to dinner."

Heddy took a step up. "I'm not hungry."

"Then come sit and talk with us. This is my first night here. I'd like to get to know you."

Heddy's panicked look said she found the idea unappealing. But Piper would not take no for an answer. Evelyn had complained about her new tenants and their lack of camaraderie. Maybe Piper could help turn that around. If she acted ignorant about the tension, maybe everyone would ease out of it.

"Come on. Join us."

Heddy glanced toward her room as if it were a sanctuary and she longed to escape into its comforting embrace.

Piper stood there, her arm extended, waiting. *Come on, sister. We won't bite.* She was actually surprised when Heddy turned and descended the stairs. *Thank You, Jesus!*

She took Heddy's arm, patted her hand, and led her into the kitchen. "Look who we have here," Piper said.

"Oh, my." Evelyn stood to get another place setting. "Sit, Heddy, sit."

"I don't want to intrude."

"Oh, please," Gail said. "Don't act like you're a guest. It's your house too. At least in theory."

There was an awkward moment of silence. Piper didn't like Gail very much. She was way too blunt. Honesty was one thing, but rudeness . . .

Heddy sat in the remaining chair while Evelyn set a place before her.

"There," Gail said. "All better. Now pass the pasta; it's getting cold."

"I'd like to offer grace first," Piper said. "If you don't mind?"

Evelyn bowed her head immediately, Heddy nodded, and Gail rolled her eyes. "If you must."

"I must."

From habit she extended her hands, palm up, to link with the others around the table. Evelyn took her hand. Heddy looked a bit nervous, but hooked up with Evelyn. Gail balked, leaving Heddy's and Piper's hands empty.

"Pray if you want, but I don't need the touchy-feely stuff."

"What *do* you need?" As soon as she asked the question, Piper wished she could take it back. So much for camaraderie.

"That was rude," Gail said.

Piper withdrew her hand from Evelyn's and covered her face. "Yes, it was. I'm sorry."

"You're used to being in charge, aren't you, Piper?" Gail asked. "Conquering the room for God."

"All she wanted to do was say grace," Heddy said. "There's nothing aggressive about that."

Evelyn let her hand find its mate in her lap. "Oh dear."

If only Piper could rewind the last minute. How could something as innocent and positive as saying grace turn into an argument full of dissension? "Again, Gail . . . I'm sorry. Old habits die hard."

"So you make it a habit to insult people you've just met?"

Piper pursed her lips together, holding in the words that longed to burst out. *Lord, please help me.* She took a deep breath. "My habit is to say grace. My habit is to hold hands while doing so. My habit is not to make it a point of contention. It's meant to be a time of bonding and gratitude."

"Gail made the dinner," Evelyn offered weakly.

"Which is getting cold," Gail said.

"Then let's eat," Piper said. "Can we try this again, minus the hand-holding?"

"Whatever," Gail said. "Knock yourself out. But make it quick."

Piper bowed her head and said a quick prayer of thanks for the food and the fellowship. "Amen," she ended.

"Amen," Evelyn said.

"Amen," Heddy said.

"Pass the pasta," Gail said.

Hoo-boy.

•   •   •

Heddy found it ironic that she hadn't partaken of the food at Peerbaugh Place because she didn't have the money to contribute for groceries, yet the meager meal Gail had offered probably cost less than five or six dollars. Total. Why couldn't her first meal have been one of Evelyn's feasts of home cooking?

The company was a mixed bag, both in their personalities and in Heddy's opinion of them. Evelyn was a sweet woman who seemed intent on keeping the peace at all costs. Piper was deep. She seemed to have an insight into things that Heddy had never even considered.

That left Gail.

If Heddy proclaimed the sky blue, Gail would argue with her. She might not have the audacity to say it *wasn't* blue, but she would belabor the exact shade of blue. Was it azure, delft, powder, or baby?

Talking with Gail was exhausting, and during dessert—which was a piece of waxy-tasting frozen pie—Heddy counted down the minutes before she could escape to her room.

Piper put her fork down and took a sip of coffee. "Thank you for the meal, Gail."

"You're welcome."

"Yes," Heddy said. "It was nice, but I really need to get going." She pushed her chair back and took her dishes to the dishwasher.

"You have a hot date?" Gail said.

Heddy glanced at Evelyn. "No, no. I just have a few things to work on up in my room."

Gail laughed. "You're kidding, right?" She turned to Evelyn. "No offense, but there's hardly room to sleep in our rooms much less do anything."

"You are free to use the rest of the house," Evelyn said.

"Yeah, yeah, we know that," Gail said. "But let's face it—none of us leads an exciting life." She chuckled. "I mean, look at us."

"Piper's here temporarily," Heddy said. "And even I'm only here as an interim measure. My main goal is to be married and have children."

Gail's jaw dropped. "That's your main goal?"

"It's a good goal," Evelyn said.

"It's my goal too," Piper said. "Though I'm presently coming to terms with the fact that it may never happen."

Heddy shook her head. "I'll never give up."

Gail pushed her chair back, nearly toppling it. She cleared her dishes. "Hey, ladies, let me tell you, it isn't all it's cracked up to be."

Heddy glanced at Evelyn and Piper. They looked as oblivious as she was. "You've been married?" Heddy asked.

Gail rinsed off her plate, but held it a moment longer than necessary under the water. "Sure. Have a kid too."

"Where is she?"

"He," Gail said. "Jacob. He's nine."

"Where is he?"

"With his father."

"His father has custody?" Heddy asked.

Gail pointed a finger at her. "No you don't. I don't need any of your judging tone. You don't know the circumstances. You don't know."

"But the mother usually gets custody," Piper said.

"Stay out of it."

"How often do you see him?" Evelyn asked.

Heddy despised the offhandedness in Gail's shrug. "When I want."

"How often is that?" Heddy asked.

"Not enough for you, I'm sure."

Heddy put a hand to her chest. "Hey, I'm not the one who lost custody of my child."

"Mind your own business."

Heddy shook her head. "If he were my child—"

"But he isn't your child. You don't have children. You don't even have a husband, so I'd thank you to keep your opinions to yourself." Gail waved a hand over the mess she'd made cooking. "I cooked; you clean." She stormed out of the kitchen.

"I had no idea," Evelyn said.

"How could you?" Piper said. "I don't think she meant to tell us now; it just slipped out."

"But isn't Jacob ever coming to visit?" Evelyn asked.

Heddy watched the kitchen door end its swing. "How can she *not* see him? How can any mother not see her own child? She must be an awful mother to act that way—and to lose custody in the first place."

"Whoa there, Heddy," Piper said. "We have to be careful not to jump to conclusions. It sounds as if Gail's been a bit wounded and could use our prayers more than our condemnation."

Heddy wasn't too sure about Piper bringing prayer into the picture all the time, but that was another issue. "Then tell me this," she said. "What maternal qualities have you seen in Gail?"

Evelyn and Piper were silent.

"I rest my case."

•   •   •

While she was getting dressed for bed, there was a gentle tap on her door. Evelyn wanted to pretend she was already asleep. She'd had enough confrontation for one night.

The tap repeated. She had no choice. "Come in."

She was relieved it was Piper. "Can we talk?"

Evelyn removed her khakis from the chair so Piper could sit. Then she hung up her blouse.

"Are you okay, Evelyn?"

She wanted to say, "Sure" but couldn't. Not to Piper. She exited the closet and sat on the bed. "I don't like this."

Piper nodded. "Heddy and Gail are definitely two opposites."

"Who collided. And who will continue to collide." Evelyn pinched the hem of her nightgown. "That's what I'm afraid of. I'm not sure I can handle this kind of arguing all the time. Especially with this Anabelle problem. My nerves are on high alert already."

"Maybe we need to instigate some peace talks."

Evelyn snickered. "The world scene has nothing on Peerbaugh Place."

"They both need us," Piper said. "You do realize that, don't you?"

Evelyn cocked her head. "I don't see what we can do for either one of them. Stubborn and stubborner."

Piper leaned forward, resting her arms on her thighs. "They need our faith, or rather they need to find their own faith."

Evelyn shook her head. "You're good at talking about God and spiritual stuff. I'm not."

"St. Augustine said, 'Preach the gospel. If necessary, use words.'"

Evelyn felt the idea connect. "I like that."

"Me too. Smart man, St. Augustine."

"So I don't have to say anything?"

"If the time is right and you feel led to do so, let it out. But maybe I can do the talking, and we both can do the living. We can show them the comfort of our faith through our actions, through our peace."

"Peace. Ha."

"Don't discount it," Piper said. "You are a lot more peaceful since you put Jesus first. You're stronger too."

"I am?"

Piper reached across the space between them and Evelyn took her hand. "You are. I can see Him in you."

It was a wonderful thought, one that brought about its own peace.

•　　•　　•

Gail lay on her bed and heard the bathwater run in the bathroom she shared with Heddy. Why couldn't she share with Piper or Evelyn? Why did she have to share with the one woman who was the antithesis of everything Gail stood for? Froufrou clothes and dreams to be a stay-at-home mom. Give-me-a-man-to-love Heddy.

Heddy. What kind of dopey name was that anyway?

And what kind of dope are you for letting it slip about Jacob?

Speaking of . . . Gail slipped out of bed and rummaged through a file box of papers. She found what she was looking for: a snapshot of herself holding a four-year-old Jacob on her lap, with Christmas stockings hanging in the background. She touched his face and a longing returned like an abyss opening up in her heart. She sucked in a breath and willed the pain away. Then she removed her fingers from the photo and propped it against the bedside lamp.

There. That was better. Look but don't touch. It was safer that way. And better for everyone.

The Lord will work out His plans for my life—
for Your faithful love, O Lord, endures forever.
Don't abandon me, for You made me.

PSALM 138:8

*A*udra didn't mean to eavesdrop. She was in the storeroom that was attached to the employee eating area, getting some more coffee sweetener, when she heard others come into the kitchen. She was about to join them when she heard her name and took a step back, holding her ground. Audra recognized the voices of two of the tellers: Susan and Kendra.

"Audra pretends it's no big deal, but it is," Susan said.

"I think you're being too hard on her," Kendra said. "Sure, he comes up to talk to her more than us. Sure, she gets taken to lunch—"

"For ninety-minute lunch breaks. Do you and I get that?"

"No, but . . ."

"But it all adds up."

The sound of coffee being poured. Audra nearly panicked when she thought of the missing sweetener. She tried to remember if they took their coffee black. She hoped so.

"Great. We're out of sweetener," Susan said.

Audra stiffened. There was only one way in and out of the storeroom. And there was no place to hide.

"Here's sugar," Kendra said. "Use this."

A moment later Audra heard the sound of a spoon tinkling against a coffee mug. Then chair legs skittered against the tile floor as they sat down. "You're much too suspicious," Kendra said. "I've heard of lots of husband-wife teams working in the same company."

"In different departments maybe. Or in equal positions. But not with one spouse reporting to the other."

"Mmm. You have a point."

"Of course I do."

And Audra was stunned to realize Susan *did* have a point. Up until her lunch with Russell last week, Audra had never imagined there was anything wrong with their job arrangement.

"I assume you heard about her raise?"

"What about it?"

"She wasn't due for another two months, but dear old hubby pushed it through."

Audra inwardly groaned. If she'd known what Russell was up to, she never would have agreed to it. It was all his—

"She got a two-buck-an-hour raise."

"No way," Kendra said.

No way! Audra's raise had been an additional fifty cents an hour, not two dollars.

"It's true," Susan said.

"How do you know?"

"Office grapevine."

Kendra snickered. "I think you'd better take into consideration this is the same office grapevine that said Matthew Dawkins was engaged."

"I still think he was. I think he just chickened out."

"I don't know . . ."

"Wouldn't you if you were engaged to snooty-tooty Ann Lewis?"

They both laughed.

Audra endured ten more minutes of their chitchat, knowing she should be back at her station. Their sniping about other employees ate at her like acid on her skin. After what she'd heard, how could she ever endure working side by side with either of them?

Finally, they got up to leave. "We'd better get going or we'll be late," Kendra said.

"We'd better watch it or they'll dock our pay. Notice how Audra disappears for a half hour at a time and doesn't get into any trouble."

"Maybe she's doing an errand or something."

Susan laughed. "Or something. Come on. Back to the cages. If we're lucky, management will throw us a bone for lunch. But watch, Audra will probably get taken out."

"Maybe she'll bring us back a doggie bag?"

"Scraps for the peons!" Susan said.

If Audra was upset before, their final remarks pushed her over the edge. This is what her colleagues thought of her? How could she work knowing they hated her, or at the very least, resented her?

She made a decision. She left the sweetener behind and left the storeroom.

• • •

Audra tapped on the doorjamb to Russell's office. He turned his chair around. "Hey, luv, what's up?"

She went in and closed the door.

Russell looked nervously out the glass window toward the lobby. "My, my. Why the need for privacy?"

She moved to the edge of his desk. "I quit."

"What?"

She unpinned her name tag and tossed it on his desk. "You

were right. The other employees think I'm getting special treatment—and I *am* getting special treatment." She hated the pitch
of her voice but couldn't seem to change it. "You should never
have pushed my raise ahead of schedule. They all know about it.
They're exaggerating how much it was, but the point is, I *did* get
preferential treatment, and I shouldn't get preferential treatment."

"I didn't mean to upset—"

"No, I'm sure you didn't." She thought of Susan's analogy.
"You threw me a bone and I grabbed on to it greedily. But now
I'm throwing the bone back. I don't want to work here anymore,
Russell. And more on point, I don't want to work with you."

"Audra!"

She knew she should apologize for the cut. She hadn't meant
for it to come out sounding as bad as it had, but she couldn't find
the strength to take it back.

She turned on her heel. "I'll see you at home. Tonight."

"But—"

She flashed him one last look. "You got what you wanted,
Russell, so I don't want to hear another word."

She walked out.

•　　　•　　　•

It didn't hit her until she was nearly home. She'd quit her job.
She'd insulted her new husband. *Welcome to my day.*

Audra considered turning around, driving back to the bank,
marching into Russell's office to apologize and beg forgiveness.
But the thought of suffering through the looks of the other employees . . . she did not want to feed the bank's infamous grapevine.

But she didn't want to go home either. Summer was at school.
All she'd do was brood. She needed to talk to someone. Someone
who would understand. Piper was at work. So that left . . .

She turned toward Peerbaugh Place.

•　　•　　•

Evelyn was sweeping a dusting of snow off the front walk when she saw Audra pull up. She looked at her watch. It was nearly time for Summer to show up from school, not Audra. What was going on?

The sight of Audra's face compounded her feeling of unease. Evelyn leaned on the broom. "Well, hello. What are you—?"

"I quit."

Forget sweeping. Evelyn slipped a hand through Audra's arm and led her inside to the parlor. Once they were settled on the couch she asked, "What happened?"

Audra told her about Russell's comments at lunch a few days previous, plus the overheard conversation between Susan and Kendra. "That's when I decided I'd had enough. I marched into Russell's office and quit."

"Wasn't that a little . . . drastic?"

Audra's face drew tight with panic. "Was it?"

Oh dear. Evelyn hadn't meant to make Audra doubt her actions. And yet it did seem out of character for the usually careful and controlled Audra. "What did Russell say?"

"Unfortunately, I didn't let him say much. In fact, I blamed him."

"How is it his fault?"

"He pushed my raise through and people heard about it. So it's not just rumor that I'm given preferential treatment; it's a fact."

"I'm sure he didn't do it to hurt you."

Her hands found company in each other. "No, he didn't. But I stormed out of his office." Her eyes were plaintive. "It's our first real argument."

Evelyn patted her knee. "Sometimes it's good to argue. I wish I'd argued more."

"What?"

Evelyn hadn't meant to draw the attention to herself. "I gave in a lot—*most* of the time. Evelyn the Peacemaker."

"Peace is good."

"Not at the expense of truth."

"You lied?"

Evelyn shrugged. "In a way. Withholding my true feelings, keeping quiet for the sake of peace alone, was wrong. And dishonest. I think our marriage would have been better with a bit more yelling and fewer 'Yes, dears' on my part."

"You were the polite, complacent wife?"

"I was the weak, insignificant wife."

"Insignificant? That's a little harsh."

"No, it's not. Sometimes I wonder what I added to the marriage besides a clean house and hot meals."

"You belittle yourself."

"I'm honest with myself. Being a person who seeks peace is not the same as being a doormat. Peace is an active thing, not passive."

Audra smiled. "My, my . . . what would Aaron say if he could hear you now?"

"He'd probably be so shocked *he'd* be the one to run out to the porch to hide from this crazy woman who used to be his wife."

"Hiding on the porch . . . I remember you saying that."

Evelyn nodded toward the front of the house. "That swing and I are buddies from way back."

They listened to the clock *ticktock . . . ticktock.* Finally Audra asked, "Did I do the right thing?"

"How do you feel about it?"

"Confused."

"Understandable."

"But kind of relieved too," Audra admitted.

"So it *was* awkward having a husband for your boss?"

"It was hard to know how to act in his presence."

"I can understand that."

Audra moved to the window and looked out over Evelyn's frosted front yard. She hugged herself. "But what do I do now, Evelyn? I worked so hard to get my degree. Summer and I lived with my parents so I'd be able to get it. Now, to stay at home and not use it . . . that seems like such a waste."

Stay at home. Suddenly, those words had a far-reaching connotation. "If you're at home . . . then you won't need me to keep Summer anymore."

Audra swung around. "Oh, Evelyn, I hadn't thought that far."

Evelyn's throat tightened. She slipped her hands under her thighs and looked at the Oriental rug. "I love having her here."

"And she loves being here—with her new grandma." A car drove up. "Great," Audra said. "It's Heddy."

"Don't worry," Evelyn said. "She never sticks around. We can continue talking in a minute."

They were silent while Heddy came inside. "What's going on?" she asked.

"Nothing," Evelyn said.

Heddy shifted her weight to her other foot and looked at Audra. "You're not usually here this early, are you?"

Audra took a huge breath. "If you must know, I quit my job. I'm here to get advice from Evelyn about what to do with the rest of my—"

The familiar sound of Summer's singsong came close. Within moments, they heard her feet on the porch. Coming home to Grandma Evelyn's. For the last time?

As soon as she opened the door, Summer saw her mom. Her backpack slid off her shoulder. "Mommy?"

"Hey, baby."

She closed the door. "What are you doing here?"

Oh dear. Now talking to Evelyn would be next to impossible. But then Heddy stepped forward. "Hi, there, Summer. Your mommy and grandma need to talk over something for a few minutes. What if you and I go get a snack? Then I've got something really special to show you."

Summer stood in the foyer and eyed them all, then looked back to Heddy. "What is it?"

"Surprises can't be told; they have to be shown." She held out her hand. Summer looked wary but took it. They went into the kitchen, leaving Evelyn and Audra alone.

"Speaking of surprises . . ." Evelyn said.

"That was nice of her," Audra said.

Evelyn shook her head, still not over the shock. "Heddy's seen Summer many times, but has never shown much interest. Until now."

"Summer's okay with her, isn't she?"

"Sure," Evelyn said. "Heddy's made it known that one of her life goals is to be married and have a family. That must mean she loves children."

"I will say her offer was well timed." Audra got comfortable on the couch again. "Now, where were we?"

"Figuring out your life."

"I hope Heddy has *lots* of surprises hidden away."

•   •   •

Summer was a jewel and Heddy was immediately charmed—and jealous of Audra. Summer was everything Heddy dreamed about in a little girl: feminine and feisty, smart and sweet. After having an apple and milk together, Heddy led her up to her room.

"Is this where the surprise is?" Summer asked.

Heddy unlocked the door. "Uh-huh." They went inside, and Heddy got down on her hands and knees to retrieve a box from under her bed. "This was mine when I was your age. My grandmother gave her to me and I've kept her ever since."

"Her? Is it a doll?"

"You'll see." She put the box on the bed. "Open it."

Summer carefully took off the lid. She moved the original pink tissue paper aside. "Ooooh. She's beautiful."

Heddy lifted out the bride doll, letting the feel of her curves and the silk of her dress bring back dozens of memories. "Her name is Catherine. She used to sit on my bed. I can't tell you how many weddings I planned for her. I used to design dresses for her bridesmaids and even sewed some of them up. Do you want to see them?"

Summer stroked the lace of the wedding dress. "Oh yes, please."

Heddy got out another box that was full of doll-size bridesmaid creations. "This red velveteen is for a winter wedding and has this white fur muff, and this yellow one is for a spring. . . ."

It was wonderful having someone to share with.

•　•　•

Audra and Evelyn talked for nearly an hour. Nothing was resolved, but Audra *did* feel better about her decision to quit her job at the bank. Her life now contained a certain air of expectancy that had been lacking before. She had a new husband, a new apartment . . . why not a new direction for her work? They'd ended their discussion by praying for *God's* direction. After all, He had it all worked out. The trick was being open enough for Him to share His plan.

They stood in the foyer. Audra called out, "Summer?"

"Up here, Mommy! Come see!"

Audra and Evelyn exchanged a look and headed upstairs. They found Summer and Heddy sitting on Heddy's bed, a dozen doll outfits spread across the coverlet.

"Looky, Mommy. Heddy made these! Aren't they beautiful?"

Audra picked one up. It was an organza gown in sea-foam green with little rosettes at the intersection between straps and bodice.

"There's a shawl that goes with that one," Heddy said, handing it over.

"These are bridesmaid dresses," Summer said. "She planned lots and lots of weddings for her bride doll."

"You made these outfits?" Evelyn examined a coral satin number with slim lines and a self-train.

Heddy shrugged. "I love to sew and design outfits—fancy outfits. Even my baby dolls used to have wedding dresses and ball gowns. They'd own a ball gown before they'd own a nightgown."

"Mommy sews too," Summer said.

"Not like this." Audra picked up a lavender crepe that had a sheer floral overlay. Lovely. "Have you ever made any of these full size? For a real wedding?"

"I thought about it, but I wasn't sure how to go about doing it—getting the business, I mean."

Audra swept a hand over the bed. "Oh, that's easy. You have the samples right here. All you have to do is bring the brides in, let them choose a dress from these doll-size models, and you sew them up, custom-made for the bridesmaids."

Heddy's eyes grew wide. "Oh. Oh my. My heart has started beating a million miles an hour."

Audra's mind swam with the vision. "You could have photos of the dresses in a catalog and do a mass mailing."

"My designs? In a catalog?"

"Sure. You have a real talent here, Heddy."

They took a moment and looked over the dresses. Finally, Heddy spoke. "I . . . I can't do all this myself."

Audra made an instant decision. "I'll help." Upon hearing her own words, she backtracked. "Oh my . . . this is happening so fast. Too fast maybe. We'll have to be smart about this, but . . ."

"But what?" Heddy asked.

Lord, guide us . . . Audra took a deep breath. "But I could sew the basic parts of the dress, and I could help with the catalog and the orders, handle the business part of it." Audra suddenly felt Evelyn's hand grip her arm. "What?"

"Don't you see? We were just trying to decide what you should do with yourself, to use your business degree. This is it! You and Heddy could start a wedding business."

Summer adjusted the doll's veil. "It can be Catherine's Wedding Creations."

The three women looked at each other and laughed.

It was perfect.

And God-sent?

•   •   •

Audra heard Russell's key in the door. She called to Summer, "He's here! Stay in your room until I talk to him."

She heard Summer's door click shut. Audra fluffed her hair and placed herself in front of the door. Russell did a double take at her presence and quickly hid some flowers behind his back. She pretended not to notice. Flowers? He was too good for her.

He shut the door with his foot, looking a bit apprehensive. "Hi, luv." He pulled the flowers front and center. It was a bouquet of yellow roses. "These are for you. I'm so sorry about this afternoon, and all that I did with your raise, causing prob—"

In one quick movement, she set the roses on the top of the couch and drew him into a deep kiss. He responded immediately.

When they separated, he was slow to open his eyes. "Wow."

"Why thank you, Mr. Peerbaugh."

He took a deep breath. "No, thank *you*." He pointed to the flowers. "I expected you to still be upset."

She bounced twice on her toes. "Nope."

His face displayed the epitome of male confusion. "I don't get it. What changed between you quitting this afternoon and you grinning at me this evening?"

This was fun. "Everything."

His eyebrows raised.

She pulled him around the couch. He sat at one end, and she close by, facing him. "Actually, I have Heddy to thank."

"The elusive tenant whom Mom rarely sees?"

Audra laughed. "If everything works out, we'll be seeing her plenty now."

"Uh-oh. Am I going to like this?"

She turned serious and took his hand. "I hope so, dear one. I hope so."

She told him everything, searching his face for support or dissent. He was wary at first, but little by little she saw his suspicion change to acceptance—and even excitement.

She leaned back, not realizing she'd been sitting so far forward she was practically in his lap. "There. What do you think?"

During her recitation, he'd turned to face her too, so now he also sat back, increasing the space between them from one foot to three. He studied his wife. "Do you actually think brides would buy dresses from little samples?"

"I'm sure we *would* need to make full-size samples in the different sizes, but the doll-size versions are a novelty. Fun. Interesting. Every girl grew up playing with a doll. It brings back good memories. And more importantly, I think a lot of brides are frustrated by the lack of choice in the stores. Heddy's creations are unique, feminine, and cover every style preference."

"What about cost? Surely custom-made dresses cost more than store-bought."

"Sometimes. That's where I come in. I'll set up a direct connection with a fabric supplier, and we'll have swatches to choose from for each dress. Getting the fabric at wholesale will help us keep the costs reasonable."

"You're going to sew too?"

Audra frowned. "You doubt my abilities?"

"I've never seen you sew anything."

"That's because I haven't had the space. But when Summer and I were living with my parents, I made Summer clothes all the time, and even made my mom some valances for the kitchen. I know the basics and Heddy can teach me the rest."

He looked around the apartment. "Heddy lives in one room. We live in a two-bedroom apartment. Would you work from here?"

She leaned toward him again. "Which leads me to another idea."

"To which I offer another uh-oh."

"No, no. This is *your* idea. Your talk about getting us a home of our own? A house? One big enough to entertain your clients . . ."

He got the connection. "And yours?"

"Well, yeah."

"And you want it big enough for a workroom, right?"

"We'd need an area where clients could come and see the samples, and a small office area."

"It sounds like you need an office downtown."

"No, Russell. The whole point in all this is to let me be home for Summer—for all of us. If we do this, it has to be from our home. We're partners, remember? Helping each other be all we can be."

"Sounds like a jingle."

"I can sing it if you want."

He played with his lower lip just as she'd seen his mother do. She was silent, letting him think.

"You'll need start-up costs."

"I'll put together an estimate." She traced a finger along his leg. "And I just so happen to know a banker who might help us get a loan."

He watched her finger. "What would you use for collateral?"

She smiled. "I'll think of something."

She heard Summer's bedroom door open. "Can I come out now? I'm hungry."

Audra felt bad. She'd forgotten all about telling Summer to stay in her room. What a good girl. "Come out, baby."

Summer ran to the couch. She looked at her mom, then at Russell. "So?"

Audra tugged at her shirt. "Catherine's Wedding Creations is now in business."

"Yeah!" Summer climbed into the space between them. "My favorite dress is the purple one because it has this see-through stuff on top that has flowers—"

"Uh-uh," Audra said. "I like the green one with the long sleeves."

Summer turned toward her mom. "That one's too plain."

"It's classic."

"I like ones that poof out when you twirl."

"You don't twirl walking down the aisle, baby."

"But you could . . ."

Russell raised his hands in surrender and slipped off the couch.

It took a wise man to know when to retreat.

•　　•　　•

In bed that night, Audra snuggled close to her husband. "Thanks for being so supportive, dear one."

"You're welcome. I just hope this is the right thing."

"Oh, it is. I know it is."

"How do you know?"

"Because Evelyn and I prayed about it."

"Oh."

She disengaged herself from his arms and sat up, the covers falling off her shoulders. "Don't discount prayer like that, Russell."

"I don't."

"Your bland 'oh' just did. Before we even got the idea, your mom and I prayed for direction. And moments after the idea came to me, I prayed for God's guidance. Things are falling into place. It feels right. God's answered those prayers. It's a fact you can't dispute."

"Sure I can."

"Russell!"

He fluffed the pillow under his head. "I know your faith is strong, and my mom's is growing. I'm just a rookie in the faith department compared to you two, but I don't think you should give God credit for everything that happens."

"Then who *should* get credit?"

"You and Heddy. You're the ones who came up with the idea. God wasn't involved."

She couldn't believe he'd said such a thing. "So you think Heddy and I are more powerful than God?"

"I didn't say that."

"But you're implying that we're smarter, more business savvy, more in control, than God."

"I'm just saying that God gave people brains to use. You and Heddy used yours."

"Through His inspiration. Through His direction."

His shrug angered her.

"He answered our prayers directly, Russell. He arranged for me to quit, for me to go to Evelyn's, for Heddy to come home just when we needed her to distract Summer. He gave Heddy the idea

123

to show Summer the bride doll and the clothes. And He gave me the idea about the bridal business—*plus* the abilities and gifts to carry it out. Heddy and I were paired up by Him, not by us. What if Heddy hadn't moved into Peerbaugh Place? Even that was arranged by Him while we were on our honeymoon." She thought of something. "He even guided you during our lunch to plant the seed about me not working at the bank."

"And I suppose He made Susan and Kendra gossip."

She thought a moment. "He hates gossip. But He also can use a bad thing for good. The gossip got me to quit and the rest fell into place."

Russell shook his head. "You're making it sound as if God's got His hand in everything."

She clapped her own hands together once. "Exactly!"

"Audra . . ."

She sighed, trying to think of some way to get through to him. "Do you believe God created the world—the universe—and everything in it?"

"Sure."

"Have you ever wondered why He created thousands of species of trees and plants and fish and animals?"

"Not really."

She got on her knees and faced him. "Why not just create one kind of tree, or maybe one deciduous and one coniferous and call it done? Why not create one fish . . . say, a bass."

"Make it salmon."

She shook her head. "Nope. One fish."

"At least you didn't say carp."

"Consider yourself lucky."

He sat up to face her, adjusting his pillow against the headboard. "Go on. I'm dying to know how you're going to tie fish into your wedding business."

Me too. Lord, help me here. An image came to mind. "Have you ever seen mist rise up on a lake in the early morning and wondered why?"

"It's because the cold air drops toward the water at night and—"

Audra swatted his arm. "No! It's because it's beautiful. It's because it's lovely and amazing and awesome to watch." She took his hand. "Stop thinking like a logical banker for just one minute and think of the world like a child. Find that awe again."

"That's a tough one."

"Try."

Russell closed his eyes and made an exaggerated face. "Okay. I'm ready."

This was hopeless. "Oh, pooh."

He opened one eye. Then both. "Go on, luv."

"Not when you're making fun."

He squeezed her hand. "I'm sorry. Go on. Make your point."

What is *my point?* She was afraid she'd lost it, but then suddenly, it came back to her. "The point is that God is a God of details. He does some things just because they are lovely and wondrous to behold. He even creates fish and plant life that are so deep in the ocean no man ever sees them."

"I know. I *have* wondered about that."

"Though I don't know His mind, I imagine God does it because He loves to create. He loves variety. He loves beauty. And if He cares about such details in nature, then surely He cares about such details in the lives of men and women. For we're the crowning glory of God's creation." She thought of the hundredth Psalm, which she'd memorized years ago: "'Acknowledge that the Lord is God! He made us, and we are His. We are His people, the sheep of His pasture.'"

Russell smiled. "So we're sheep."

"We're *His*. And we're unique. We each have special talents." She thought of another verse, but she couldn't remember it word for word so she flipped on the lamp and grabbed the Bible off the bedside table.

"Uh-oh. You're breaking out the big guns now."

She flipped to Romans, knowing it was there somewhere. "*The* big gun. The answer to everything." Her eyes pegged it. "Here. Listen to this."

"Do I have a choice?"

"None." She cleared her throat, ready to read, then decided a preamble was required. "This will prove that God gave Heddy and me different talents, but that we're supposed to meld them, use them together. And you have gifts to give to the project too."

He crossed his arms. "This I gotta hear."

She read: "'We are all parts of His one body, and each of us has different work to do. And since we are all one body in Christ, we belong to each other, and each of us needs all the others.'"

He reached for the Bible. "It doesn't say that."

"It most certainly does." She turned it around for him to see.

He read it for himself, then looked up. "Wow."

"That seems to be your word today."

"It's appropriate."

She scooted close. "Do you understand now? Do you accept that God had something—if not everything—to do with Heddy and me coming up with this idea?"

"Let's just say I'm considering it."

Audra began to say more, but Russell pulled her close and she knew it was time to be quiet.

"You're quite the advocate for the Almighty, aren't you?"

"I do my best." *And He does the rest.*

I cry out to God Most High,
to God who will fulfill His purpose for me.

PSALM 57:2

*S*he's not coming today.

Those words slapped Evelyn upon waking. They kept her in bed and caused her to hug a pillow to her chest.

It wasn't fair. Summer was her new granddaughter. She'd babysat for her all last semester, and they'd had it all arranged for her to babysit for her after Russell and Audra were married. Now, for Audra to disrupt the entire arrangement by quitting her job and staying home . . . plus finding an exciting new business to start with Heddy.

Evelyn turned to her other side, dragging the pillow with her.

No, ma'am, it wasn't fair at all.

It seemed as if everyone was deserting her. First Mae, then Tessa, then Audra, now Summer. Their Sister Circle was getting frighteningly small. And no way would Heddy and Gail fill the vacancies.

You have Piper.

Yes, she did. Sort of. Piper had moved in, but she wasn't going to be around that much. Between work and spending time with her parents . . .

"Oh, Aaron . . ."

She hadn't meant to call out for her late husband. And in truth, Evelyn was getting her grief under control quite nicely. But every once in a while, her need for him pounced, demanding attention, nudging her, prodding her, just like *he* used to do, pestering her until she paid him his due.

And though she hadn't been particularly happy in the last few years of their marriage, she did miss Aaron's companionship. The sound of his familiar voice, the Old Spice smell of him, and the comfort of his constant presence, always there, no matter what. At the time, she'd considered that more of an annoyance than a blessing—until he wasn't there at all. Now, annoying would be a welcome change from the isolation she suffered.

She rolled to her back and stared at the ceiling, her eyes skimming the faint swirls of the texturing. Even though her life was inhabited by others, she was isolated. She was the only widow. She was the only grandmother. She was the only one who had no clue as to why she was alive. Why she was here.

This last idea overwhelmed her. How had her thoughts progressed from Summer to Aaron to leading a purposeless life?

Heddy's and Audra's talk about their new business was to blame. Their fire and excitement. The perfect way it had all come together—especially since Audra and Evelyn had just prayed for God's direction in Audra's life.

Pray for your direction, Evelyn.

She sat up in bed, pulling the pillow to her lap. Why had she not thought of this? Why had she never thought about asking God point-blank to show her His plan for her life? Everybody else was off on her own road, tooling along as if everything was so clear, yet Evelyn was stuck on the shoulder, sitting there waiting. For what?

She remembered Aaron's tendency to never ask directions. Up until now she'd been exactly like Aaron. But no more. No more!

She tossed the pillow aside and got out of bed, falling to her knees beside it. She clasped her hands and drew them to her forehead. "Lord? Piper and Audra and even Mae have said that everyone has a unique purpose. I hope that's true. And if it's true, then I want to know what my purpose is. Why did You make me? Why am I here, now, in this place and time? What do You want me to do with the rest of my life? Show me. Please."

She waited a few moments in silence, hoping—but not expecting—God to make some brilliant idea pop into her mind. Nothing happened.

And yet . . . as Evelyn stood to get dressed, she did feel different. Hopeful. Exhilarated. As if something fantastic was promised, even if the details weren't known. And she found that flame of anticipation very, very warm, a fire that could fuel her through the hours and days that were her life.

●   ●   ●

After doing her normal chores, Evelyn found she had to get out of the house. Besides her disappointment over not having Summer after school, the threat present in Anabelle's letter continued to eat at her. Although she'd acted strong in Piper's presence that first day, the lurking pall of dread lingered. The letter had said Evelyn had fourteen days to respond. Seven of those days had already passed. Although she didn't have money for a lawyer, she did need advice.

And in Aaron's absence, Russell was the best advisor she had.

As soon as she entered the bank's lobby, she was greeted by the receptionist. "May I help you, Mrs. Peerbaugh?"

"Yes . . . I mean maybe." Evelyn looked toward Russell's office. He was not alone, but had a couple seated in the chairs across from his desk. Although he'd always said she was welcome anytime, maybe she should have made an appointment.

But then he looked up, saw her through the glass of his wall, smiled, and waved. *Whew.* It was all right. She was welcome.

The receptionist had obviously witnessed the wave because she said, "I'm glad he's seen you. I'm sure he won't be much longer. Would you like to take a seat?"

She sat in a royal blue chair and flipped through a copy of *Inc.*

A few minutes later, she spotted the couple passing by. She looked up. Russell was coming toward her. He gave her a kiss on the cheek. "Mom. To what do I owe this pleasure?"

He was such a nice boy. She patted her purse containing the letter. "I need your advice."

Russell's face turned serious. "Let's go in my office."

She took a seat across from him. The chair was still warm.

"So. Tell me. What's wrong?"

She handed him the letter. He unfolded it and read through it. His strong chin combined with the Peerbaugh nose reminded her of a younger Aaron. An odd thought flashed: *He's really grown up.*

"Hmm," he said. "I thought I'd scared her off the other day. Obviously not."

"Obviously not."

"Hmm." As he studied the letter some more, she suddenly feared this was much more serious than she'd first imagined.

"Does she have a case?" she asked. "Can she really make trouble for me?"

Russell sat back. "I don't know. But I know someone who might. I'll call the bank's lawyer and let him take a look at this."

Evelyn let herself relax. "So he'll take care of it for me?"

"I didn't say that. He'll look at it. We'll go from there."

Her dread returned. "I didn't discriminate, Russell. I didn't."

"I believe you." He stood.

She'd taken up enough of his time, but her hope for a quick resolution died.

• • •

"Have a good day in school, baby."

Summer looked up at her mother and squinted one eye. "This is going to be weird. Me coming here after school, instead of going to Grandma's."

"I know. But it will be nice too. I'll have a special snack waiting. What would you like?"

"What do we have?"

Audra thought about the meager pickings in the pantry. What with being gone on the honeymoon and working full time . . . she suddenly felt a twinge of jealousy that Evelyn provided something she hadn't. "I'll make something. Your choice."

Summer concentrated as she zipped her coat. Audra knew better than to offer help. When Summer was done she said, "Chocolate-chip cookies? With cinnamon in them?"

"Cinnamon?"

"It's how Grandma makes them."

Strike one.

"Sure, baby. I'll call her and get the recipe. Just for you."

Summer opened the door to leave, then thought of something else. "Can you get some chocolate milk? Grandma has chocolate milk."

Strike two.

"We have chocolate powder in the—"

"No. Real chocolate milk. From a carton. It's richer."

Strike three. And she's out. "Anything else?"

Summer cocked her head, actually thinking. "No, I guess that's it."

And good thing too. Audra was losing patience. She gave Summer a kiss good-bye and shut the door. So much for her first free day at home. She had to call Evelyn for the recipe, take a trip to the store for ingredients—and real chocolate milk—and then spend a chunk of time baking cookies. Summer had always been satisfied with Oreos and powdered chocolate milk before. . . .

Too bad Grandma Evelyn had raised the bar on snack time.

•   •   •

Considering the mood she'd been in when she left the house on Summer's snack excursion, Audra was surprised to find an amazing amount of exhilaration in the simple act of going to the grocery store. It was one of her least favorite errands. And yet today she actually found herself humming. Joyfully humming.

What gives?

Freedom and time. That's what was at work here. Of course she'd hated grocery shopping before. It had always been something that cut into her precious free time. But now, with no nine-to-five job, shopping could be part of her job as wife and mother, leaving her free time available for other things.

She laughed at the thought. Life was good.

•   •   •

Mae was hungry, and if the world knew what was good for it, it would make way so she could get fed. When Mae's stomach growled, she growled.

She looked at her watch. It was one o'clock. No wonder. She was used to eating with the girls at Ruby's at noon. But today she'd had to take a trip to Jackson to deliver a commissioned necklace, bracelet, and earrings set that a customer had ordered for his wife for their twenty-fifth anniversary. Though customers at Silver-Wear usually came to her, since this was one of the biggest commissions she'd ever taken, she'd promised to do the delivering herself. It was the least she could do.

She spotted Burger Madness up ahead on her right. Perfect.

And considering the amount of the check burning a hole in her pocket, she might even splurge and monster-size it.

She pulled into the drive-through and looked at the menu. At the last minute, knowing there were enough calories in a regular-size meal to cover her allotment for the entire day, she restrained herself and nixed the monster-size idea. She drove around to pay.

But when she handed her money to the employee she did a double take. For behind the cashier she spotted Gail. Gail from Peerbaugh Place, handing an order to an inside customer.

The cashier handed her change. "Fifty-three cents."

"Is that Gail Saunders working over there?" Mae asked.

The boy turned around. "Yeah. Gail. That's her. You want to talk to her?"

"No, no," Mae said. "I was just curious." She drove into traffic and headed back to Carson Creek.

My, my. Gail working at a Burger Madness. What did it mean?

•   •   •

Collier Ames fingered the handle on his mug of tea. "Now, now, Mae. Don't go jumping to any delusions."

Mae paced in front of the kitchen sink. "It's *conclusions*, and I'm not jumping. It's standing smack-dab in front of me waving a hand in front of my face. Gracious gophers, Collie, she was standing in front of me, plain as day."

"Lots of people have a second job."

"Maybe. But why has she never said anything? From what I've seen and heard, Gail makes a big deal about being some executive at Lanigan Marketing. She's even put down Heddy's job as the hostess at Ruby's."

Collier took a sip of tea. "Maybe she likes the food at Burger Madness? They do have a super pork tenderloin."

"Oh, puh-leeze. Next you'll be saying she took the job so she could wear the spiffy uniform."

He shrugged.

Men. Mae stopped pacing and tapped her lips. "I've got to go tell Evelyn."

"Oh no you don't."

She grabbed her coat. "Oh yes I do. It's my duty as her friend."

Collier got up and took Mae's coat from her. He hung it up on the hook by the back door. "Since you don't know the facts behind Gail's job, I suggest you remain quiet. There's got to be a reasonable explanation."

"Not necessarily."

"Yes, necessarily. Gail's not working at a burger place in a town thirty minutes away for the fun of it."

"Then I have to know why."

"You don't have to know why. It's none of your business, Mae."

"But Evelyn's my friend and she's being conned."

He made a face. "How so?"

"She's rented to a con artist. Gail's pretended to be something she's not."

Collier nodded and riddled his fingers on the table. "Let me ask you this: As far as you know, has Gail paid her rent—in full?"

"As far as I know."

"Has she brandished any firearms, carried out any drug deals, or been seen entertaining any shady characters on the porch of Peerbaugh Place?"

Mae dug her fists into her hips. "Collie."

"I rest my case. Leave it alone, Mae. If Gail is lying, she must have good reason. The truth will come out eventually. It always does."

Mae felt a pout coming on. He was right, but Mae never found any fun in that. Or in waiting.

• • •

Mae held the phone book open with one hand while she dialed with the other. Her finger marked the listing for Lanigan Marketing.

The connection was made. "Lanigan Marketing. How may I help you?"

"Gail Saunders, please."

A moment's hesitation. "I'm sorry, Ms. Saunders no longer works here."

The phone book fell off her lap. "For how long? I mean, how long has she been gone?"

"About a month. Can someone else help you?"

Nope. Mae had all the information she needed. She hung up the phone, her mind racing. She moved to the living room window and saw her husband getting the mail. Her first thought was to go outside and tell him what she'd found out. But then he'd know that she hadn't dropped the subject, and she didn't feel up to going there right now.

Her second thought was to march across the street to Evelyn's and tell her everything. Quickly, before Gail got home. But Evelyn's car wasn't there.

Mae let the curtain fall. Fiddle-dee. More waiting.

• • •

After talking to Russell at the bank, Evelyn stopped at home and put together a plate of cookies for Wanda and Wayne Wellington. Even if Wanda didn't feel up to eating them, Wayne would polish them off.

It was strange knocking on the door to Piper's apartment, knowing someone else would answer the door. Having prepared herself for that, she was surprised when Piper answered.

"Piper! Why aren't you at work?"

Piper took the tray of cookies. "Work's done for the day, Evelyn."

Evelyn looked at her watch. Where had the time gone? Without Summer's schedule to dictate her day, the hours had flown by unannounced.

"Come on in."

Evelyn went inside, not knowing what to expect. She'd thought Wanda would be in the bedroom asleep and was surprised to see her propped up on the living room couch. She was pale, but her smile was her own.

"Hiya, Evelyn. Nice to see you."

Wayne moved some newspapers off a chair. "Have a seat. We were just watching the end of *Rear Window*."

Evelyn hurried to her seat. "I love that movie. Grace Kelly's clothes are magnificent."

"I know," Wanda said. "Those filmy huge skirts, her tiny waist."

Piper put her hands around her own waist. "I have never had a waist that tiny."

"And then when she pulls that negligee out of the little suitcase . . ." Wanda said. "I wish the movie was in color so we could see the clothes better."

Wayne rolled his eyes. "How can you ladies take an Alfred Hitchcock thriller—one of the most suspenseful movies ever made—and turn it into a fashion review?"

"You can't ignore the clothes, Dad."

"Wanna bet? You don't hear me commenting on what Jimmy Stewart is wearing." He raised the pitch of his voice, "Oh, that pajama top when he's fighting with the killer is just too-too."

They laughed, but when Wanda laughed, she pulled a pillow to her midsection.

Wayne was at once attentive. "Sorry, honey."

Wanda smiled sheepishly at Evelyn. "It's a sad day when one's husband has to apologize for making his wife laugh, but it hurts a bit. And coughing? A pillow helps."

"How are you feeling otherwise?" Evelyn asked.

Wanda shrugged. "Pretty good. They make me walk a bit more every day. Exercise that old heart of mine."

"Did the procedure work?"

"I'm going in soon to be checked. We pray for the best. I take comfort in knowing God won't give me more than I can handle." She sighed deeply. "So what's going on with you, Evelyn?"

Evelyn's answer was interrupted by the ring of the phone on the coffee table. Piper picked it up and took a few steps away. Evelyn didn't know whether to talk or wait. When she heard Piper say "Dr. Baladino," she remained quiet.

Piper was answering questions. "Yes . . . yes . . . sometimes . . . that would be nice." She covered the receiver and whispered, "He's going to stop by to check on you."

"That *is* nice," Wanda said.

Then Piper's face changed, and her eyebrows rose. She turned so her back was to them, and she lowered her voice into the receiver. Evelyn, Wanda, and Wayne exchanged curious glances.

"I don't know, Doctor. That sounds very nice, and no, I've never heard that group play."

"What group?" Wanda whispered.

"Can you hold on a moment, please?" Piper covered the receiver a second time. "Dr. Baladino has invited me to go hear the Bryson String Quartet next Tuesday night when they play for the Winter Festival."

Wanda's face lit up. "That's wonderful."

Piper shook her head, whispering. "But I can't. He's your doctor."

"So?" Wanda pointed a finger at her. "You go, young lady. He's a nice man and it sounds wonderful."

"You do need to get out more," Wayne said.

Evelyn nodded wholeheartedly. Piper's social life was only slightly more exciting than her own—the difference being that Piper was only thirty-four and should be spending a lot of time with friends. And boyfriends.

Piper wagged a finger at all of them. "This is a conspiracy."

Her mother wagged a finger back. "I don't care what you call it. You go!"

Piper unclamped the receiver. "Doctor Baladino? . . . Yes, it appears I'd love to go."

While Piper got the details, the other three applauded softly. And Wanda—making sure Piper wasn't watching—mouthed, "A doctor!"

Evelyn agreed completely.

• • •

"What's got into you today, Heddy? You're practically glowing."

This kind of comment had been repeated throughout her workday at Ruby's. And she knew it was true. She was glowing from the inside out. Glowing with anticipation about Catherine's Wedding Creations.

But she couldn't tell them that. Not yet. She'd see the customers to their tables, refill their coffee, and take their money, all the while nodding, saying little, and smiling some more. That's all she could do. She and Audra had a lot of planning to do, and she couldn't risk losing this job before it was time to move on. She needed the money.

Money. If only a person didn't have to think about money.

She felt a bit guilty for not telling Audra the truth about her money situation, or her past—failed—attempt at starting a business. She didn't have anything to invest. Audra was the wife of a banker. She had plenty of money at her disposal.

But every time Heddy felt her glow dampened by such thoughts, she found herself offering a simple prayer: *Help us.* Those two words allowed her to shove the doubts away. It would work out. Somehow. She felt it.

•   •   •

Audra retrieved a fallen rose petal and adjusted the bouquet in the vase at the center of the table. She stepped back to look. The china and crystal they'd received for their wedding glistened.

"It's pretty, Mommy," Summer said. "Can I put the napkins in the ringy things?"

"Sure, baby."

Summer got to work, her little forehead wrinkling in concentration. Audra went back in the kitchen and checked the fontina chicken. The aroma was enticing. She'd seen the recipe on the cooking channel just that afternoon, which had given her the idea for a home-cooked feast—which also meant another trip to the grocery store. She was sure every day wouldn't be this chaotic. She'd get organized eventually.

The point was, for the first time in her life she actually cooked. And enjoyed doing it. When she and Summer had been living with her parents and even at Peerbaugh Place, she'd taken her turn, but it had always been simple stuff like putting a roast in the Crock-Pot or browning some hamburger for tacos. Never real cooking with a recipe and ingredients that needed chopping and dicing.

She checked the apple pie in the oven, its aroma overpowering the smell of the chicken. It was golden brown and lovely. She almost didn't want to cut into it. Sure, she'd cheated a bit in getting those sheets of frozen pie dough because she hadn't wanted to risk making her own from scratch, but she bet—if truth were told—that a lot of good cooks took shortcuts where it really didn't matter. Maybe that's what made a good cook good?

She heard the key in the door and her stomach tensed. She moved out of the kitchen to stand beside the beautiful table, pulling Summer under her arm.

Russell came in and stopped in his tracks. "Wow."

Just the reaction she'd hoped for. "Do you like it?"

He touched the edge of a place mat. "It's beautiful. Is this our new stuff?"

"Uh-huh. Fresh from the wedding boxes."

"I like it."

"I told you you would."

"I helped," Summer said.

He kissed the top of her head. "I bet you did." He took off his suit coat. "Do I smell pie?"

Audra knew she was beaming but couldn't help herself. "Apple pie, fontina chicken, garlic cheese bread, and a fresh salad."

He gave her a kiss. "I didn't know you could cook."

"Me either."

He headed toward the bedroom to change, but backtracked, pulling a small magazine from his pocket. "I got this for you." It was a realty brochure featuring all the houses for sale in the area. "I'm taking what you told me to heart. You need a house with office facilities. If you'll do the preliminary looking, I'll come see whatever you find."

She fanned through the pages. Good thing she didn't work outside the home anymore. This domestic life was becoming all-consuming.

●　　●　　●

Gail took a basket of her laundry down to the basement of Peerbaugh Place. She was mad at the world. It wasn't fair that a bunch of whining, giggling teenagers from Burger Madness bragged all day about their plans for Friday night, while she didn't have a thing to do. No, no, she, Gail Saunders, was forced to spend her "date night" doing laundry. She might as well wash her hair and make the image complete.

As she divided the darks from the lights, she remembered doing laundry for Jacob and Terry. She hated the chore and was notorious for forgetting it in the washer.

Jacob. She wondered what he was doing tonight. Did he have a football game? Was he even playing football this year? Or was it soccer?

The fact that she didn't know was pitiful. But she couldn't insert herself into their lives again. She just couldn't.

She stuffed her dirty uniform in the washer with an extra shove. Yes, yes, when it came down to it, she was the one at fault, the one with too many faults. She could not expect her family to tolerate such imperfection. She would not.

But wanting to change and actually changing were two different things. Maybe she was doomed to be who she was.

If people didn't like it, they could leave her alone.

Which is exactly what she was.

Alone.

*   *   *

Mae loved going out to dinner Friday nights with Collier. They always had a great time eating through many courses, talking for hours, sharing a dessert and coffee.

But tonight Mae regretted getting home so late. As they turned into their own driveway, she noticed that Gail's car was in the driveway of Peerbaugh Place. There was no way she could tell Evelyn tonight.

Oh, well. One more day of deception couldn't be helped.

Tomorrow was Saturday. Tomorrow Mae would blow the whistle on Gail Saunders.

Do not despise these small beginnings,
for the Lord rejoices to see the work begin.

ZECHARIAH 4:10

*I*t was the first time in a long time that Heddy Wainsworth got up early—voluntarily. Today was the day she and Audra were going to discuss the new business.

Before getting dressed, she lingered over the doll clothes spread over every available surface in her room. She remembered designing each one, pooling her allowance to buy a bit of lace or trim to make them match the image that was in her head.

Always a bridesmaid dressmaker, never a bride.

One of these days . . .

•   •   •

Summer appeared in front of Audra and Russell as they drank their morning coffee at the kitchen table. She had on a coat and a Powerpuff Girls backpack. "I'm ready."

Russell looked at the clock. "The museum's not open for another hour, chickie pie."

Summer's shoulders sagged.

Audra helped her out of her backpack and coat. She weighed the pack in her hands. "What's in here?"

Summer set the pack on the table and unzipped it. "Here's my monkey 'cuz I thought he should see the other monkeys; here's two books on animals; here's a water bottle, a hat, two granola bars, and . . ." She squeezed open a rubber coin holder and removed a folded bill. "Here's five dollars."

"That's a lot of money," Russell said. "You going to use it to buy a hot dog and candy?"

She shook her head as if his suggestion was preposterous. "It's to buy Mommy a present 'cuz she doesn't get to come."

Audra pulled her close. "How did I ever get lucky enough to have a daughter like you?"

"My Sunday school teacher says there's no such thing as luck. Good things aren't luck; they're God's blessings."

"I think your teacher's right," Audra said. She looked at Russell. "Don't you, Russell?"

He shrugged. "If you're asking me to take the phrase *good luck* out of my vocabulary, I'd tell you good luck."

Audra helped Summer pour a bowl of cereal. "But don't you think Summer's teacher is right? that Summer's right? that she's not here by good luck but because of the blessings of God?"

Russell's mug stopped halfway to his mouth. He looked at Audra, then at Summer. "Is this a trick question?"

"It's a simple one."

He took a sip of coffee, then stood. "I'll leave the theology to you ladies. I'd better get dressed. We don't want to keep the monkeys waiting."

Summer dunked her cereal into the milk with the back of her spoon. "He doesn't believe in God, does he?"

Audra dropped her piece of toast—jam side down. "Of course he does!"

"He doesn't pray with us."

"He comes to church with us."

Summer shrugged, and Audra knew her shrug spoke volumes. Naturally, before they got too serious in their dating, Audra had made sure Russell shared her faith in Christ. But she had to admit that while Russell came to church with them, he never showed any signs of being moved by the sermon, the music, or the worship. She wondered if he only went because she asked him to. And now that they were married and the shine of courtship had waned, would he start finding excuses to stay home?

Summer wiped a dribble of milk from her chin. "How will God find Russell if he isn't looking?"

Good question.

"Hurry up and finish, baby. You don't want to keep him waiting."

Or *Him* waiting.

•　•　•

Evelyn took the basket of laundry down the stairs to the unfinished basement. Sometimes she envied those who had new houses with light and airy laundry rooms on the first floor. Being in a dank basement lit by bare bulbs made a dismal job even more depressing. She set the basket on the washer and took a moment to look around.

The concrete-block walls were unpainted, and the two small windows, full of cobwebs. Metal shelves full of paint cans and boxes of Christmas ornaments lined the walls. In the corner was a conglomeration of larger items she and Aaron had kept for reasons she'd long forgotten. Between this basement and the attic there was a lot of wasted space—and a lot of unneeded junk. There was no reason why most of it couldn't be cleared out. And maybe she could paint the walls a sunny yellow and have some real light fixtures put in. It would be a good start.

She smiled at her thoughts. The old Evelyn had gone on year

after year, never letting herself see the possibilities in her home—or in herself. But in the past eleven months it was like the pages of her life had been turned to a new chapter. A chapter *she* was free to write.

She got back to the task at hand, realizing there was a smile on her face. Funny how even laundry was endurable when the mind was brewing with the excitement of a new project.

She opened the washer lid and found it full of damp clothes. By the dark colors she guessed they were Gail's. Oh, well. She'd just move them to the dryer and even fold them when they were done. It would be her good deed of the day since Gail was working another Saturday.

But when she started to transfer the clothes to the dryer, one of the items caught her eye. It was a red, white, and blue polyester top. It looked familiar. Evelyn held it up and within moments recognized it. It was the uniform of Burger Madness. What was it doing in Gail's laundry?

She continued the chore, her thoughts reeling with impossible answers. When she got to the bottom of the washer, she found a dime—and something else.

A name tag: *Gail*.

Evelyn felt a surge of rage heat her insides. She left the laundry as it was and headed upstairs. She was going to drive to Jackson and confront Gail, right there in front of everyone.

She stopped halfway up the stairs. No. The better idea was to clear out her room and have everything on the porch when Gail came home.

A memory flashed. Gail coming home and leaving for work wearing professional suits. What did she do? Dress in the rest room at Burger Madness? The premeditation of this act smacked of such deep deception that Evelyn felt used. Compromised. Violated.

Had Gail ever worked at Lanigan Marketing? Why the farce?

And yet, as long as Gail could pay the rent and had an honest job, Evelyn didn't care where she worked.

But what she did care about was the lying. That was unacceptable.

She continued upstairs, flipping off the light behind her.

* * *

Mae had fretted that Collier would never get out of the house to go on his hardware-store errands. It wasn't that she couldn't go across the street to visit Evelyn. She did that all the time—with his blessing. But this morning, when Mae had real news to share with her neighbor, news Collier had told her *not* to share, she preferred to have the coast clear.

Finally it was, and Mae was across the street before Collier's car completed the first turn at the end of the street.

She knocked and went inside in one motion. "Knock, knock. It's me." She stopped to listen for an answer, but got none. "Evelyn? Your car's here. Are you? Evelyn?"

She caught the hint of movement in the parlor and took another step. Evelyn was sitting in the wing chair, her hands gripping the armrests.

"Evelyn. What's wrong?"

Her chest heaved and it seemed to take effort for her to grab a breath. "She lied to me. Gail lied to me."

Mae sank onto the couch, deflated. "You know."

Evelyn's eyes flashed. "*You* know?"

"I was in Jackson yesterday. I went through the Burger Madness drive-through. I saw her there. How did you find out?"

"I was doing laundry. I found her uniform." Evelyn looked up, her chin set. "I can't believe how angry I am. I don't get angry."

"Maybe you should. In this case you have every right to rant and roar. She deceived you."

Evelyn nodded and fingered the armrests. "I was heading out to Jackson to confront her. Either that, or I was going to empty her room onto the porch."

Mae laughed. "Zounds, Evie. I didn't know you had it in you."

"Me either. And I didn't realize honesty was so important to me."

"My question is why did she lie? It's not like you wouldn't have rented her the room if she'd said she worked at Burger Madness. And why live thirty miles from work? Why not live in Jackson?"

Evelyn shook her head. "And why develop this elaborate lie about working as some executive at Lanigan if she doesn't even—"

"She *did* work there."

"How do you know?"

"I called and asked for her. They said she hasn't worked there for a month." Mae sat back on the couch. "I bet she got fired."

"She could have quit."

"If it was her choice, she could have said so. You know Gail. She'd make sure the world knew that Lanigan is some awful company that she wants nothing to do with. If she quit she'd pass herself off as better than they are. But she's presenting them as a great company. Which means she was fired."

"I wonder why."

"How about lying? She seems good at that."

Evelyn let go of the armrests. "Did you know she has a little boy she never sees?"

Mae was tempted to jump on that one but didn't. Until she'd contacted her own two children—Ringo and Starr—last Mother's Day, it had been over a year since she'd seen them. Of course, they were grown and Gail's boy was young . . . Mae softened her tone to encompass her own faults. "Did she say why she doesn't see him?"

Evelyn shook her head. "The husband has custody."

"Boy, that's rare."

"I know. Which pretty much means she didn't want him.
Or she did something so awful to him . . ."

"I can't imagine. How old is he?"

"Nine."

Mae let out a puff of air. "An age when every darling needs
their mom."

"And dad."

Mae shrugged. "Oh, to live in a perfect world."

Evelyn put a hand to her mouth. "Oops. Sorry, Mae. I forgot
you brought up your children alone."

"In my case, alone was better than *with* Danny." Silence
settled between them. Finally Mae stood. "So, Evie. What are you
going to do? I take it you've calmed down enough not to trek to
Jackson or dump all her worldly goods on the porch."

"What should I do?"

Mae smiled. "Now this is the mild, meek, forgiving Evelyn
I know."

"The pushover Evelyn, the gullible Evelyn."

"The kind, open, trusting Evelyn."

"You can rest assured I won't trust anymore."

"Don't say that."

"But by blindly trusting, I allowed her to take advantage—"

"This is Gail's fault, not yours. There was no way you could
have known what she was up to. And in truth, there's got to be a
good reason for it. Keeping up the pretense can't have been easy."

Evelyn shook her head. "How should I confront her?"

"You sit her down and tell her what you found out. Then you
listen."

"Should I tell her to move out?"

"That's up to you. But I think it would depend on the whys
of it—her excuse."

"It will have to be some excuse."

"Want me to hang around?"

Evelyn's relief was palpable. "Would you?"

"Sure. Unlike you, Mae Fitzpatrick Ames never runs from a fight. She may skitter around it, and high-jump over it, but run? Never. It's not in my Irish blood." She pointed to the kitchen. "You got some hot water brewing? I'd like a cup of tea while we wait."

●　　●　　●

Heddy hesitated before knocking on the door to Audra's apartment. She put a hand to her midsection and took a deep breath. Her stomach was dancing the tango. The last time she'd felt this nervous had been when she'd had to confront Carlos. But this was a good kind of nervousness—nerves caused by pure excitement and anticipation.

She knocked. Audra answered, ushering her inside. It was a nice apartment, though a bit stark.

She felt Audra's eyes on her. "I know, I know. It needs some warming up. It was Russell's place before we were married."

Heddy touched the back of a black leather sofa. "It does look a bit masculine."

Audra turned to the kitchen. "Would you like some tea?"

"Love some."

Audra talked while she poured. "We're just starting to look for a house. I was a bit reluctant at first, not wanting to appear as if I was taking advantage of Russell's finances. No one is going to call me a gold digger."

"I'm sure they wouldn't."

She handed Heddy a teacup and saucer. "I'm sure *some* would. Let's sit at the table." They sat and Audra added a plate of poppy-seed muffins. "People can be brutal."

Heddy knew that to be true—which is why she'd kept the

Carlos fiasco a secret. But she could tell there was experience behind Audra's words. "*Have* they been brutal?"

Audra shrugged. "I was working as a teller at Russell's bank until this last week when I overheard some mean comments. That's when I quit."

"Lucky for me."

Audra cocked her head. "More and more I realize it was the right thing to do. Actually, I think God's been nudging me in this direction for a long time. It just took those nasty comments to make me take the step."

Nudging. It was an interesting term. Especially used in conjunction with God. "Does He . . . I mean, do you get these nudges often?"

Audra cut a muffin in two and slathered on some margarine. "Actually, yes. More and more. Or rather, I notice it more and more. I'm sure God's been trying to get my attention for years but I ignored Him."

Heddy's thoughts sliced through the moment. In the span of a few seconds the faces of all the men she'd dated flashed before her. All the men who had been wrong for her, who had taken advantage of her, whom *she* had taken advantage of, in her desperate attempt to find a mate.

"Heddy?"

She left the images behind. "Sorry."

"You left me for a moment. Where were you?"

Oh, how she wanted to share with Audra, share with anyone. But they barely knew each other. Maybe someday . . . "I was just wondering if God's been nudging me."

Audra laughed. "If that's what He's been doing, I suggest you start taking note, because you know He won't let up."

"He won't?"

"Nope. And good thing too, because He's always right, though I say that begrudgingly. Just one of these times *I'd* like to be right."

Heddy smiled. She liked how Audra thought about things. It seemed so clear, so simple, so . . . full of hope that things *could* be the way they were supposed to be.

Audra licked her fingers. "Speaking of God, would it be all right if I prayed for us before our meeting? I'd like Him to be involved in this new venture of ours."

"Sure. That would be wonderful."

As Audra prayed aloud, Heddy felt her nervous knots calm. She knew it wasn't because of anything she'd done. The God Audra spoke of so openly seemed present, and because of that, everything seemed right. Positive. This new business was going to work. She knew it.

And she found herself thanking God for it.

●   ●   ●

"Can you hold my backpack so I can get my monkey out?" Summer asked.

Russell obliged as Summer held her stuffed monkey next to the glass that separated them from the jungle scene. She talked softly to the toys, pointing out the details of the display.

He took a few steps back to watch and wait, reminding himself that he didn't really like natural history museums much. But Summer certainly did and so that made it tolera—

Suddenly, out of nowhere, it was as if Russell were observing Summer from afar, seeing the scene both analytically—like a stranger—yet also poignantly and piercingly, like a father watching a daughter with love in his heart.

And with the image, his heart began to ache, expanding and contracting as if adapting to something new. The feeling took him by surprise and his banker's mind rebelled, demanding an explanation for this emotional mutiny.

At that moment, Summer turned her head and smiled at him.

She pointed to the stuffed monkeys in the display. "Do you see that monkey way up high, Daddy?"

Daddy. His throat tightened, and he realized its ache was caused from a staggering desire to sob.

Sob? Bankers didn't sob. And what was there to sob about? He was in a public place, at the museum with his wife's daughter. It was an ordinary moment experienced by hundreds of people a day. Nothing amazing or extraordinary.

Wanna bet?

He saw Summer's face lose its smile, her eyebrows dipping. "What's wrong?" she asked.

Russell shook his head and attempted to clear his throat, but it felt like there was a rock in it. He tried to say something, but nothing came out. He motioned to a bench behind them and fled to it, hoping in the few seconds his face was hidden from her view he could regain his composure.

He failed. When the backs of his legs felt the edge of the bench, they buckled and he collapsed onto it.

Summer ran to his side. "Daddy?"

He glanced around the museum, feeling like a fool. Luckily, at this particular time, there were few people nearby. But it wouldn't have mattered if there had been a crowd of thousands. He would not have been able to control the emotions that were assaulting him.

Summer put a hand on his arm. "What's wrong?"

He managed to eke out, "Nothing" and was amazed to find it was the truth. Nothing was wrong. Something was right. He was now the father-protector of a beautiful little girl. Although that fact had certainly been a part of his consciousness as he'd fallen in love with Audra, up until now it had been set in the wings, as if he'd only been playing a part, doing what was expected of him. Sure, he'd cared about Summer—who wouldn't care about her? But until a few minutes ago when he'd seen her—really *seen* her—

he had not realized he loved her for herself, not because she was the daughter of the woman he loved. He cared for her. Wanted to protect her, teach her, hold her close.

She was looking up at him, her innocent face pulled with concern. He surprised himself by finding a smile to offer. Her features loosened and she smiled back. "Are you okay?"

Was he? He took a deep breath and let it out. The ache had subsided, and the rock had left his throat free to swallow and talk again. He felt purified, as if his insides had been scraped clean. Yet they were not empty but filled with an airy fullness that made it easier to breathe in and out, easier to think and feel.

He had to say it out loud. He took Summer's hand. "I love you, Summer."

She beamed and reached her arms out to him. He leaned close and she wrapped them tight around his neck. "I love you too, Daddy."

He pulled her onto his lap and they rocked and swayed, a daddy-and-daughter moment he would never forget.

And then Russell knew what he had to do.

•   •   •

Audra was organizing the notes she'd taken during her meeting with Heddy when Russell and Summer came home.

Summer burst through the door, waving a sack. "Here's your present!"

"Oh, baby, I told you not to buy me anything."

Russell hung up his coat. "She was adamant. We spent a half hour picking it out."

"Open it! Open it!"

Audra pulled out a small bundle of tissue and unwrapped it.

Summer bounced on her toes. "With tax it was $5.12, so I didn't have enough, but Daddy paid the twelve cents."

Daddy? She looked to Russell for an explanation, but he seemed oblivious.

"Twelve cents was the least I could do," he said.

Audra finally got to the end of the tissue paper. A ceramic monkey fell into her hand. Its hands and feet were oddly placed, as if it was climbing something.

Summer picked it up. "It goes on your teacup or your cereal bowl. See?" She hooked the monkey's hands on Audra's cup.

"It's very cute," Audra said.

Russell helped Summer off with her coat. "I told her it might make drinking a little awkward, but assured her you'd find a place for it to hang permanently."

Audra looked around the apartment and immediately spotted her pencil holder next to the phone. She hooked the monkey on its rim. "There. A perfect place for him."

"His name is Percy."

"Where did you get that name?"

"I dunno. He looked like a Percy."

Audra couldn't argue with her and gave her a thank-you hug and kiss.

"Can I go see if Morgan can play?" Summer asked.

Morgan lived down the hall. "Sure, baby. But come right back if she can't."

Summer was out the door in seconds. Russell stood at the table, fingering the back of a chair. The fact that he didn't sit made her take notice. "Sit down. I bet you're exhausted."

He shrugged. "I prefer to remain standing."

Mental alarm bells rang. "What's going on?"

He stopped his fidgeting and gripped the back of the chair. "I had what *you* might call a revelation at the museum."

What an oddly worded sentence. "I might call it a revelation? What do *you* call it?"

He hesitated. "A revelation, I guess. It's just that I'm not used to this sort of thing."

"What sort of thing?"

"Having a revelation sort of thing."

"And I am?"

"You are."

He was driving her crazy. It wasn't like Russell to be so cryptic. "What exactly are we talking about here?"

Russell changed his weight to the other foot. "I . . . this is going to sound really odd, but at the museum, I realized I love Summer."

"I'm glad. But I always thought you loved her."

She was relieved when he pulled a chair out and sat. "I did. But not like this. It's as if I've loved her out of obligation to you, because she's your daughter. But today I realized I love her like a dad loves a daughter." He ran a hand through his hair. "Frankly, that realization blew me away."

Audra could tell how moved he was. She felt a little stupid for assuming his love was deeper than it was. And yet, if she was honest about the situation, she had to acknowledge that just because he fell in love with her didn't mean he automatically fell in love with her child.

She reached across the table and put her hand on his. "I heard her call you Daddy."

He glanced up, then down. "I know. And maybe that was part of it. Whatever caused the moment, it happened. One second she was a cute little girl who was the daughter of my new wife, and the next she was *my* daughter."

"Oh, Russell, that's wonder—"

She stopped talking when he looked up, his face serious. "I want to make her my daughter. Legally. I want to adopt her."

Audra expelled a puff of air that turned into tears. She'd

always hoped . . . "Oh, dear one, that's great. That's fantastic."
Then a thought. "Have you told her?"

"No. I wanted to talk to you first."

"Do you want to tell her now?"

He glanced toward the door. "No. She's at Morgan's. Besides,
I'm not sure she'll be pleased."

Audra left her seat and wrapped her arms around him. "Of
course she'll be pleased. She loves you."

"Too bad I was slow loving her back."

She kissed Russell's cheek and nuzzled herself onto his lap.
"But you do now. You do now."

"Actually, I was thinking it might be nice to ask her over a
fancy dinner at a restaurant Summer's never been to. We could
get all dressed up and—"

"We could go to Chez Garsaud, where we went for our first
date. It would be perfect."

"Consider it done."

What had she ever done to deserve such blessings?

Nothing. Yet God blessed her anyway. Amazing.

•   •   •

It didn't hit Gail until she was on the way home from work. She'd
left a load of laundry in the washer! And the load contained her
other Burger Madness uniform. If anyone had gone downstairs to
do their laundry . . .

She drove faster.

•   •   •

Mae drummed her fingers on the kitchen table. "I feel like a lion,
lurking in the shadows of my cave, waiting for a gazelle to happen by."

Evelyn refreshed their tea. "We're not going to pounce on Gail. We're not." When Mae didn't answer, Evelyn persisted. "Mae? Is that agreed?"

Mae dipped a butter cookie in her tea and took a bite. "Like it or not, Evie, I think pouncing will be involved. We can't pretend nothing has happened and then slip in, 'By the way, Gail, we know your secret; the jig's up.'"

"Maybe not, but I'm afraid you're leaning toward telling her to put her hands above her head while you read her her rights."

Mae made a face. "I could, you know. I've watched enough cop shows to Mirandize anybody."

"Ah. Another hidden talent."

"I got a million of 'em."

"Then why don't you draw on your talent of tact for this particular situation?"

Mae shook her head. "That's your talent, not mine."

"In my case it's not tact; it's cowardice."

Mae took another cookie and pointed it at Evelyn. "Now stop that. I think your greatest fault is not appreciating your strengths. You put yourself down too much, Evie. You're stronger than you think."

Evelyn shrugged, though she knew Mae was right. Just yesterday she'd acknowledged a new strength stirring within her—a new sense of impending purpose.

"If you beef yourself up and I tone myself down, then maybe—"

They heard the front door open. Evelyn was not comforted when Mae fumbled her cookie onto the table. *Maybe Gail will go directly upstairs and we can put off—*

Gail rushed into the kitchen and pulled up short at the sight of Evelyn and Mae. "Oh. Hi."

"Hi, yourself," Mae said.

Evelyn immediately noticed Gail was wearing a pair of jeans

and a sweater. For her to have to constantly change clothes . . . the ever-present black bag was on her shoulder, its purpose suddenly clear.

Gail headed to the basement door. "I forgot and left some things in the washer. Sorry about that. I'll go down right now and—"

Mae made the sound of a game-show buzzer. "*Awwwk!* Too late."

"What?"

Mae extended a hand in Evelyn's direction. "Evie already moved your clothes to the dryer."

Gail froze in place.

"So. What do you say to that?" Mae asked.

Evelyn stifled a sigh. Mae was zooming toward a head-on collision. Evelyn made sure her voice was nonthreatening. "I saw your uniform, Gail."

Gail's chest heaved and her eyes darted between this patch of air and that patch of air.

"What do you have to say for yourself?" Mae asked.

"Mae!"

"It's a logical question."

"But your tone . . ."

"Fine—" Mae crossed her arms in a pout—"do it your way."

"Thank you." Evelyn wished Gail would talk, offer an explanation on her own. She didn't want to pull it out of her.

But Gail remained mute.

"Please know that it doesn't matter to us where you work, Gail," Evelyn said. "But it does matter that you—"

Gail took a step forward. "But it matters to me! And it matters to me that you snooped—"

"I did not snoop," Evelyn said. "I was merely doing my own laundry and had to move yours from the washer to the dryer."

Mae nodded. "If you'd finished your own—"

"That's not the point," Evelyn said. "I don't mind moving a load of laundry. The point is, your secret is out. The point is, it didn't have to be a secret at all."

Gail ran the back of a hand across her mouth. "That's your opinion."

Evelyn had never witnessed someone with such a big chip on her shoulder. Gail took everything as a challenge, an affront, an attack.

Gail moved toward the basement door. "I'll collect my things and be gone by this evening."

Evelyn sucked in a breath. "Gone?"

"Move out. I assume you don't want me here anymore."

"Of course I want you here." Though as she said the words, Evelyn wasn't so sure.

Gail stopped with her hand on the doorknob. She looked to the floor. Evelyn waited—and was relieved Mae didn't break the moment. Finally Gail spoke. "You wouldn't understand about the job thing."

"Wanna bet?" Mae said. "You think you're the only one who's ever been fired?"

Gail spun around, her eyes blazing. "How do you know?"

"I called Lanigan Marketing."

"They told you I'd been fired?"

"They said you no longer worked there." Mae shrugged. "Considering your cover-up, I figured you didn't leave of your own accord. So what happened? You get caught playing computer games during working hours? Or caught with your hand in the till? Or maybe your lips on the boss?"

"Mae! That's enough!" Obviously tact *wasn't* one of Mae's strengths.

Gail took a step toward the table, pointing a finger at Mae. "You don't know anything, and you have no right to judge me or make such awful accusations."

Evelyn was glad to see Mae's face turn red. She needed to be embarrassed for her outburst.

"Sorry, Gail," Mae said. "That *was* over the line." She ran her hands over her face. "Arggh. Sometimes my mouth runs away from my brain so fast I need a lariat to lasso it in."

"And tie it up."

"With double knots," Mae agreed.

Evelyn pointed to a chair. "Sit down, Gail. Let's talk about this. Maybe we can help."

Gail's head lowered and swung like a pendulum. "No one can help. I don't need anyone's help. I have to handle this myself."

"Handle what?"

She looked up. "Failure."

Mae let out a laugh, then clapped a hand over her mouth.

"Your rope job isn't working," Gail said.

Mae took a deep breath and slowly removed her hand. Evelyn almost expected something visible to escape from her mouth, like the words in a balloon extending from the mouth of a comic-book character.

They all waited. Finally, Mae said, "I wasn't laughing at you. Not exactly. I was laughing at the idea that you were a failure because you lost one job. Maybe Lanigan was a failure, not utilizing you to the extent of your abilities. Maybe it just wasn't where you are supposed to be."

"And Burger Madness is?"

"Burger Madness pays the rent until you find something you like better," Mae said. "Did you like working at Lanigan's?"

Gail shrugged and crossed the room to the table. Evelyn was hopeful she'd sit, but Gail just stood there. "It could have been better. They were a very unorganized company."

Mae smiled and nodded. "And you told them so, didn't you?"

Gail blinked. "They needed to be told."

"Ah. The fog lifts."

"You don't believe me?"

"Oh, I believe you," Mae said, turning sideways and draping an arm over the back of her chair. "But I also believe you and I are sisters in one main regard."

"And what's that?"

"Neither one of us has mastered the art of being tactful."

Gail didn't respond—at first. Then she started to laugh. "Perhaps I *was* a bit too direct in my suggestions to them."

"Perhaps," Mae said.

Gail looked behind her to the counter. "I could use some tea . . ."

Evelyn popped up to get a cup.

As Gail took a seat, Mae leaned forward. "So what exactly did you say to them?"

Evelyn poured the tea, the sound of Mae's and Gail's calm voices adding to her relief.

Phew. That wasn't so bad.

●　　●　　●

"I'll get it." Wayne Wellington answered the doorbell of Piper's apartment.

Piper was just helping her mother get comfortable on the couch after taking her for a stroll to the mailbox and back. She looked up when she heard Dr. Baladino's voice.

Her father backed into the apartment, making room. "Come in, come in, Doctor. It's very nice of you to stop by."

Piper felt her mother's tug on her shirttail and caught her wink. "Yes, it is, Doctor. Certainly you don't do this for all your patients?"

Dr. Baladino came to her side with his bag. "I try to. I'd like to." He glanced at Piper. "And how are you this afternoon, Ms. Wellington?"

"Call her Piper," Wanda said.

"Mom!" They were as obvious as an *Ozzie and Harriet* episode. Next, they'd be finding something to do in the next room, leaving her and the doctor alone.

"And you can call me Gregory." He pulled a chair closer to his patient. "Piper's an unusual name. Is there a story behind it?"

Wayne took a seat in the wing chair nearby. "Wanda and I used to love to watch the old Piper Laurie movies."

"*Son of Ali Baba* is our favorite. Rock Hudson," Wanda added.

"No, Tony Curtis," Wayne said.

Dr. Baladino opened his bag and took out a stethoscope. "I'm afraid I missed that one."

"You need to rent it," Wanda said. "Piper loves movies. She'll watch it with you."

Piper felt herself blush. "Mom . . ."

Dr. Baladino winked at her. "Maybe we'll have to do that."

Piper was relieved when her mother remained silent as the doctor checked her over. He took the stethoscope out of his ears. "Sounding good. Are you getting some exercise?"

Wayne answered for her. "We walked to the corner yesterday."

The doctor closed his bag and stood. "That's good. Try to go a bit farther every day."

"Will do."

He headed to the door. But Wanda wasn't through with him yet. "Can I go to church in the morning, Doctor?"

"Certainly."

"Would you like to come with us?"

Piper wanted to vaporize and disappear under a couch.

The doctor smiled. "Actually, I don't go to church, Mrs. Wellington. I'm Jewish."

Wanda's face deflated.

The doctor said his good-byes and left. "See you Tuesday night, then," he told Piper.

Yes, yes, see you then.

She had barely closed the door when her mother reacted. "Jewish? How can he be Jewish with an Italian name like Baladino?"

"*Shh*, Mom. He's probably still in the hall."

Wanda crossed her arms. "And I thought he was so perfect for you."

Piper sank onto the couch, putting her mother's feet in her lap. "It's just one concert. I'm not going to marry him."

"Hmm."

"Now you're acting like you don't want me to go out with him."

"Oh, I suppose you can go."

"Thank you, I will."

Wayne spoke up. "Don't mind your mother; she enjoys acting like a yenta."

Piper saw the irony and laughed. "Yes, sirree, Mom is acting like a *Jewish* matchmaker." She began the song from *Fiddler on the Roof*, "'Matchmaker, matchmaker, make me a match. . . .'"

Her father joined in, hugging a couch pillow to his chest in adolescent longing. Piper rose from the couch and stood by her father. They moved together, swaying with the music. When they were finished, they bowed, and waited for Wanda's applause.

She glared at them. "You make fun, but somebody has to find you a man."

Piper returned to the couch. "There you're wrong, Mom." Piper hated when this topic came up. Yes, she wanted to be married. Yes, she wanted a family. She'd prayed about it for years. But obviously God had other plans. She had to trust Him.

"You must admit that even you were hopeful when our good doctor invited you out," her mother said.

"I was hoping to enjoy some good music and good conversation."

"You were hoping for more than that."

"No, I wasn't," Piper said, hoping she wasn't lying. "I don't even know him, so how could I have thoughts of having any kind of serious relationship?"

"It's easy," her mom said. "I used to do it all the time."

Wayne perked up. "You did?"

"Sure. I had lots of boyfriends whom I considered marrying at one time or another."

"Name one."

She raised her hand, ready to count them off. "There was David and Bobby, Carl, Tim, Tom . . ."

Lots of names but no Gregory. Not for her mom, and not for her.

C'est la vie.

* * *

Gail turned off the light to go to sleep. She had not been so full in a long time. Nor so satisfied.

After the confrontation about her job, she and Evelyn had decided to order a pizza. They'd eaten the entire thing and talked. Evelyn was a nice lady who seemed to really care about people—care about Gail.

Imagine that.

But I know! I, the Lord,
search all hearts and examine secret motives.
I give all people their due rewards,
according to what their actions deserve.

JEREMIAH 17:10

*H*eddy seated the two women by the window and handed them menus. "The special this morning is blueberry pancakes and sausage links."

"That's why we're here," the older woman said.

"Your waitress will be here in a moment." She went back to the front counter, where two more customers were waiting. Blueberry Pancake Day always filled Ruby's to capacity.

She was glad they were busy. Today was the big day. Today she and Audra were going to Russell's bank to ask for a loan to start up Catherine's Wedding Creations. It had been Audra's idea to get a loan. Heddy was oblivious to such things as business plans, spreadsheets, and projected costs. And in truth, the idea of a loan was frightening. Heddy had never owed money to anyone. She'd always lived in an apartment and had paid cash when she'd bought her car from a friend. And yet, Audra acted as if this was a logical step. A necessary step.

It's not like they needed tens of thousands of dollars. But there were start-up costs with printing brochures and buying some sewing equipment. Heddy had sold her sewing machine after the Carlos incident; it had been a simple model anyway. There were so many new ones out that could better handle the intricacies of sewing with slippery fabrics such as satin, chiffon, and voile. And if there was enough money, Heddy would really like a serger.

The steady influx of customers made it impossible to dwell too long on her nervous stomach. The waitresses on duty—Connie and Agnes—were struggling to keep up, so Heddy grabbed the coffeepot and made the rounds. As she walked by the two women she'd just seated, the elder pointed to her coffee cup. "Can you fill 'er up until Agnes gets to us?"

"Sure."

The younger woman moved her cup close. "Me too."

The older woman shook her head. "You're not old enough to drink coffee, honey."

"I'm getting married, Mother. If I'm old enough to get married, I should be old enough to drink coffee."

Faced with that logic, the mother sat back in her chair. She looked to Heddy. "My daughter got herself engaged this weekend. This is a mother-daughter breakfast to start planning the wedding."

"Congratulations," Heddy said. She turned to leave, then remembered *she* was in the wedding business. She turned back. "You'll be needing bridesmaid dresses?"

"Five of them," the daughter said.

"Five?" the mother said.

The girl listed them. "There's Donna, Mary, Jennifer, Amanda, and Suzanne."

The mother's eyebrows lifted. "Suzanne?"

"Yes, Mother. Suzanne's a good friend."

"You didn't list Erin. She's your cousin and she had you in her—"

"Mom . . . we don't need to get into this now." She nodded to

Heddy. "To answer your question, yes, I'll be needing bridesmaid dresses. Why do you ask?"

Their first potential customer. Heddy could hardly wait to tell Audra.

•   •   •

Heddy had never been past the teller area of a bank. She'd led a simple life—at least financially—and so had never had reason to venture into the inner sanctum. Russell's office was lovely, with burgundy leather chairs and a large cherry desk.

"Ms. Wainsworth, Ms. Peerbaugh, come in and sit down," Russell said.

Audra took the seat near the window. "Ms. Peerbaugh? What happened to honey, sweetie, sugar pie?" Audra asked.

"That comes after I see your financial statement."

"You're no fun."

Heddy ignored their banter, her mind stuck on one term: *financial statement*. She didn't have a financial statement. She didn't have any finances to state. *This is never going to work. I need to leave right—*

"So, Heddy," Russell said, "you have created quite a flurry around our home."

Is that bad?

"I've never seen Audra so excited about anything."

Phew.

"Except you, dear one," Audra said.

Russell blushed. "Exception noted." He organized some papers on his desk. "Audra's given me the projected costs and the business plan. I think you two have a wonderful idea. But for the bank's records, we need to know what assets you bring into the business."

Uh-oh. "Assets?"

"Things you own. Collateral. Real estate, cars, savings accounts, CDs, stocks . . . that sort of thing."

Heddy thought of her 1987 Oldsmobile Cutlass Supreme. She'd bought it for two thousand dollars two years ago. What was it worth today? She hadn't a clue.

There was silence.

"Do you own a car?"

Heddy told him the details and he wrote it down.

"Real estate?"

"No."

"CDs?"

She managed a smile. "Not the kind you're talking about."

"Stocks?"

"None." Heddy knew her voice was getting quieter and quieter with each negative answer. She wanted to leave. Forget the whole thing.

Russell sat back and sighed. "That leaves a savings account."

Heddy drew in a breath to answer with her final, "None."

His eyebrows raised. Audra sat forward. "You don't have a savings account?"

"I have some money in my checking account."

"How do you live?" Audra asked. "I mean, most people have *something* in savings."

Heddy thought of the nice nest egg she'd had before Carlos wiped her out. "I had one at one time," Heddy said. She chose her next words carefully. "But there were . . . circumstances that arose that took that money and—"

"Was there a bankruptcy?" Russell asked.

"No, no. I don't owe anybody anything."

"That's good."

Heddy fidgeted in her chair. She was glad something was good.

Audra spoke. "Russell, when it comes down to it, I don't have any collateral either. My car is about it."

"But you have savings."

Audra shrugged. "Yes. Some. But not a lot, if you count only what I brought into the marriage. *You* have plenty. I'm just getting started."

He cleared his throat, "Yes, well . . ."

Heddy suddenly thought of something. She removed a ruby ring from her finger and set it on his desk. "I have this ring. It was my grandmother's. It's a real ruby and those are real diamonds."

Russell picked it up. "It's very pretty."

"I'm sure it's worth something."

After a moment's hesitation he handed it back to her. "I'm sure it is." With the intake of a new breath, he seemed to change gears. He wrote something at the bottom of a page and turned it around to face them. "Sign here and we'll call this a done deal."

"We got the loan?" Audra asked.

"You got the loan."

Audra ran around his desk and kissed him. He glanced nervously toward the lobby and she backed off.

Heddy looked at the legal paper in front of her. The idea of signing such a thing was daunting, especially when she knew they were *not* getting the loan based on her background or financial status. She felt like a barnacle attaching itself to a fresh new boat.

"Sign it, Heddy," Audra said. "Then it's my turn."

Heddy signed her name and handed it over. It was a done deal. Heaven help them.

●   ●   ●

"My, my," Russell said, getting up from his desk. "What a day. To have both my wife and my mother visit my office."

Evelyn accepted his hug and took a seat. "Audra was here?"

"She was getting a business loan with Heddy."

"I love their idea."

"I do too. And I think it will go." He rocked in his chair. "But that Heddy . . . has she told you much about her past?"

The way he said it sounded ominous. "Not really. Should I be concerned about something?"

"She seems like a nice lady. It's just the banker in me talking, and as a banker who now has Heddy as a customer, I'd better stop this conversation right here." He picked up a file and opened it. He handed his mother a piece of paper. "Here's the letter from our lawyer to Anabelle Griese regarding her discrimination complaint."

Evelyn scanned the page, which was on a heavy linen letterhead. There were a lot of *therefore*s and words such as *complainant* and *client*.

Russell summarized it. "It basically tells her to back off. There is no basis for her complaint. She knows it, and we know it."

Evelyn reread some of the paragraphs, feeling a bit sick to her stomach. What kind of woman was Anabelle that she would try to sue? If only they could work it out without the legalese.

"Mom? It's all right, isn't it? Joe Graham wrote it as a favor to me. He won't charge you anything for it."

She set the letter on the edge of the desk, feeling better when it was out of her hands. "I'm sure it's fine. And it's quite . . . legal sounding."

"Exactly. I'm sure once Ms. Griese gets the letter you'll never hear from her again." He paused. "That *is* what you want, isn't it?"

"Uh . . . yes. That's what I want."

"Good." He stood. "Because she'll be getting the letter today. We sent it certified yesterday morning."

Oh dear.

●   ●   ●

On the way home from the bank, Evelyn stopped at the hardware store. As soon as she entered she was assailed with pleasant memories of Aaron. Not that he'd been any whiz fix-it man. Just the opposite. Most of his fix-it projects fizzed more than whizzed. But when Aaron had decided to paint the fence or put in a new faucet in the kitchen, Evelyn had gone with him to Handy Hardware.

There was something thought provoking about a hardware store. Evelyn loved to stroll up and down the aisles. She'd discover all sorts of gadgets invented to make life easier, and she was always inspired to attempt some other project.

But today she had a project in mind. She was going to paint the basement. She headed to the display of paint colors, feeling like a kid in a candy store.

"Kind of boggles the mind, doesn't it?" said the clerk.

She glanced around to see Herb Evans. "Hi, Herb. Yes, it does. They're all so pretty."

"What are you painting?"

"The basement." She told him about her plans to clean things out and lighten things up. "I was thinking about a yellow."

He laughed and pulled out a card. "That narrows it down to about twenty-five. You can choose from Daisy to Daffodil to Cheerful. I don't know who comes up with these names."

Herb helped her choose a lemony shade called Optimistic Yellow and collected the tools she'd need. He started checking her out, but paused between ringing up the paint and the roller. "I know what you really need for this project."

"What's that?"

"Help." He grinned. "I'm available if you need me."

Evelyn felt herself redden. She still was not used to being single. "Thanks, Herb. I'll remember that."

●　　●　　●

Evelyn pushed the screen door open with her hip, balancing yet another load of giveaway items from the basement. She set the box on the porch and straightened her back with a groan. She imagined the reward of a long, steamy bath when she was through. But that was then. This was—

"Mrs. Peerbaugh."

Evelyn turned toward the voice—the voice that had presented her name as a stern statement, not a question. Anabelle Griese strode up the front walk.

Evelyn eyed the door, wanting to escape inside, throw the bolt, and cower in the corner until she went away. But no such luck. Anabelle continued up the porch steps, placing herself in the escape route.

"I got this today," Anabelle said, waving a paper.

The lawyer's letter. Evelyn edged around to the far side of the giveaway box. Not as good as a door, but better than nothing.

"Aren't you going to say something?"

Evelyn had no idea what *to* say. *"I'm sorry"*? Or *"Take that, you meanie"*? She took a deep breath and fell back into repeating the obvious. "You got the letter."

"You bet I got it. From a lawyer, no less."

"But your letter was from a lawyer."

"A lawyer, yes. Me. It was from me."

The absurdity of the semantics game gave Evelyn courage—and also gave her a moment to send up a quick prayer for divine help. "But you're a lawyer. You threatened to sue me."

"You bet I did. You didn't rent to me because I'm fat."

"I didn't rent to you because your references weren't good."

Anabelle's forehead became a washboard. "I'll deal with them later."

It was a ridiculous statement. And in spite of Anabelle's ready-to-pounce stance, Evelyn realized she was uncharacteristically calm. Gone was Evelyn's need to flee. *How did that happen?* Then she remembered her quick prayer and said another one—of thanks. She stepped out from behind the box and motioned to the front door. "Would you like to come in and sit down?"

Anabelle seemed taken aback. Evelyn didn't wait for her to respond—nor for herself to question what she was doing—but headed inside. She entered the parlor, extended a hand toward the couch, and sat on the rocker.

"Would you like some tea? coffee?"

"No, I'm fine."

As Evelyn looked across the quiet of Peerbaugh Place, Peppers strolled into the room and made a beeline for her calf. As soon as fur met skin, the cat started purring. "Ah, the peaceful purr of a cat . . ." Evelyn was taken aback by her own words. *Why did I mention peace to this, the most unpeaceful woman I've ever met?*

Anabelle sighed, letting a single word escape. "Peaceful . . ." She allowed the lawyer's letter to fall into its folds. She creased it shut. "That's one of the reasons I wanted to live here. The setting is so nice. Calm."

"Yes, it is." Evelyn agreed. "I'm . . . I'm sorry things didn't work out."

Anabelle looked to the floor and nodded. "My ex-landlord said I was difficult?"

It was disconcerting to have the roaring lion replaced with a mewling lamb. "A bit."

Anabelle nodded again, then drew in a breath that seemed to affect her entire body. "I am difficult. I know it." She set the letter beside her and patted it.

Evelyn couldn't believe the change. Without the attitude, Anabelle's entire presence was transformed. Her voice was quite melodic, and her face pretty. She had fabulous skin. "Did you find a place to live?"

Anabelle nodded. "Actually, it's bigger than the rooms you had to offer, but the yard isn't as nice. It will do."

"I'm glad."

She stood, taking the letter with her. "I'm sorry I wrote the letter, Mrs. Peerbaugh. Don't worry. I'm not going to pursue anything."

"Because there's nothing to pursue?" Evelyn asked.

Anabelle smiled. "Because there's nothing to pursue." She headed for the door.

"Feel free to stop by for some tea," Evelyn said.

"Thanks. I may do that."

Evelyn let her out and remained at the opened door until Anabelle's car disappeared from sight. Then she bounced twice on her toes, did an about-face, and headed to the basement, scooping up Peppers on the way.

Thank You, God! Would wonders never cease?

*   *   *

"Mademoiselle?"

Summer looked a bit confused as the maître d' held out the chair for her.

"Sit, baby," Audra said. "He's being polite, treating you like a lady."

Russell gave Summer a wink. "The lady you are."

Summer settled into her chair and handled it well when the maître d' gracefully laid a napkin in her lap. In fact, she beamed. It was apparent Audra's little girl could get used to this.

So could Audra. Chez Garsaud had the potential to make a person feel incredibly special or incredibly stupid. For amid the elegance and personal service, there were unspoken words of etiquette that one did not often have to incorporate into day-to-day life. Like the pulling-out-the-chair thing, using more than one fork, and setting your utensils neatly across the plate to indicate you were finished. Yet Audra kind of liked being challenged to achieve a higher level of manners. Life was often *too* casual, a variety of manners *too* acceptable.

The oversize menu extended from Summer's lap to a good eight inches above the top of her head. She leaned toward her mother and whispered, "I can't read most of these words."

Audra whispered back, "That's because a lot of it is written in French."

"Oooh." Summer's eyes grew wide and sought out the foreign words as if they were a display in a museum.

"I'm sorry they don't have a children's menu," Russell said.

"That's okay," Summer said. "I'll eat big-people food. I want to eat big-people food. Tonight."

Audra and Russell exchanged a smile. They hadn't told Summer why they were going out to a fancy dinner, only that it was a special occasion—a surprise special occasion. She had accepted eagerly, taking great care in getting dressed in her favorite kelly green corduroy dress with the big white collar and her patent leather shoes. She looked the epitome of "little girl."

Russell closed his own menu and pulled Summer's close so they could look at it together. He pointed to *Tournedos Rossini.* "This is steak with *foie gras*, truffles, and Madeira sauce."

"What's a truffle?"

He made a face. "A fungus that grows underground that dogs and pigs sniff out."

"Eeww."

"And *foie gras* is goose-liver paste."

"Yuck. What else is there?"

He looked for something more child friendly, but decided this was an occasion that could benefit from a little more shock value. "How about *Timbales de Foies de Volaille*: unmolded chicken liver custards?"

Audra gave him a look. "Russell . . ."

"Okay, okay," he said. "I bet you'd like this one. *Poulet en*

Cocotte Bonne Femme. That's casserole-roasted chicken with bacon, onions, and potatoes."

Summer nodded vehemently. "That. I'll take that."

He closed the menu. "A good choice." He looked at Audra. "And what is your pleasure, madame?" He grinned. "By the way, how do you like being called *madame* instead of *mademoiselle*?"

She took his hand and pulled him close enough to kiss. "I like it a lot."

"Me too. It means we're a family," Summer said.

Was that a perfect lead-in or what? Russell set the menus aside. "Actually, that's why we're here."

Summer wiggled in her seat. "The surprise?"

"Yes, the—"

They were interrupted by the waiter introducing himself and taking their order.

"Where were we?" Russell asked.

"The surprise!"

"Oh, yes. That." Though his attention was on Summer, he extended his hand to Audra. She took it, offering support. "Since your mother and I are married . . ." He took a deep breath. Audra couldn't remember ever seeing him so flustered or unsure of himself.

"Right," Summer said. "We're a family."

"Yes, we are," he said. "But I would like to apply some stickum to the family."

Summer looked confused. "We already had a wedding."

"Which was the stickum for your mom and me. But I want there to be stickum between *you* and me."

"Do we need a wedding too?"

He laughed. "Not a wedding—an adoption."

Summer's eyes flitted past them, as if she was thinking hard. "James Crinney is adopted."

"Lots of people are. Piper is. Some are adopted because they have no parents, and some are adopted when they have one parent, but that parent marries someone new, and . . ." Russell sighed. Then he took Summer's hand and made eye contact with both the women in his life. "The point is, I love you, Summer. As a father loves a daughter. And I want you to truly be my daughter, in real life *and* on paper, for all the world to know. If you'll have me."

Summer carefully took her napkin from her lap and stood. She placed it on the chair. Then she stepped over to Russell's side and put her arm on his shoulder, peering at him eye to eye. "I would love to be your daughter, Daddy. I love you too."

If hugs and kisses were not proper etiquette for Chez Garsaud, no one said a word.

●　●　●

Piper looked in the mirror. She adjusted the hair around her ears. Then she pulled it free. Then she hooked it behind her ears again. She turned to Evelyn, who stood in the doorway to their shared bathroom. "Which is better?"

"I like it behind your ears best."

Piper took another look in the mirror. "I agree."

"You don't need blush—you're blushing naturally."

Piper caught her grin. "It's warm in here."

"It is not warm in here."

"Don't make more of this than there is, Evelyn."

"Oh, I won't. I don't have to. It's a date, plain and simple. Piper's dating a handsome doctor. 'Nuf said."

Piper didn't want to put a damper on Evelyn's enthusiasm, yet also didn't want her getting her hopes up. They returned to her bedroom where Piper put on pearl earrings. "Actually, there *is* more to say. He's Jewish."

Evelyn's shoulders slumped. Then she recovered. "Well . . . so?"

"Hello? I'm a Christian. An up-front Christian."

Evelyn leaned against the dresser. "You both believe in the same God, don't you?"

"Yes."

"That's important."

"Yes, it is. But . . ."

"But he doesn't celebrate Christmas."

Piper smiled. "That's one way to put it. Though actually, from what I've seen, a lot of Jewish people celebrate the secular part of our Christmas and just leave out the Jesus part."

"Actually, a lot of so-called Christians do that too."

"Point taken."

Evelyn handed Piper's cologne to her with a smile. "What's the harm in one date? You yourself said it was no big deal."

After spraying the cologne on her neck, Piper picked up her purse, ready to go. "Then why did I just spend ninety minutes primping?"

Evelyn touched her arm. "You look lovely. Don't worry so much. Go out and have a nice evening. Maybe you can win him over to our side."

Winning a soul for Jesus. Now there was a unique incentive for a date.

●　　●　　●

Dr. Gregory Baladino looked amazing in his khaki trousers, pine green V-necked sweater, and brown suede jacket. The jacket matched his eyes.

Back off, Piper!

The Bryson String Quartet did not play until eight, so Piper and Gregory strolled through the Winter Festival in Jackson's town meeting hall, looking at the booths of watercolor paintings, handmade pottery, and wood carvings. At a carving booth, Piper was drawn to an intricate cross.

"Ooh," she said, reaching out to touch it. Then she glanced toward Gregory and withdrew her hand.

He stood with his hands behind his back, as if assessing a piece of art. "That's nicely done. It must have taken hours."

Piper chastised herself for being overly sensitive. There was nothing wrong with her pointing out a pretty cross, any more than there would be anything wrong with Gregory pointing out a Star of David.

"Would you like to have it?" he asked.

She would. But she found herself unable to say the words for a myriad of reasons.

She didn't have to say it. Gregory took it down and pulled out his wallet. Within a minute, it was hers.

She cradled the package. "You didn't have to do that."

"I wanted to. It will be your souvenir of the evening." With a gentle hand at her back, he led her into the stream of people. "Do you want something to eat? Are you hungry?"

"Starved."

He laughed. "I love an honest woman. The three words I detest are *I don't care.*"

"You're a decisive man."

"Yes, I am."

"And you like decisive women—people, I mean."

He smiled. "Yes, I do."

She found herself filing the information away. He liked honesty and decisiveness. She shook her head. *Stop it! This is not a real date. It can't be. There are too many obstacles.*

"What was the shake of the head for?" he asked.

She felt herself redden. "You don't miss much, do you?"

He pointed to a corn-dog stand. "I bet you're a corn-dog woman."

She wasn't sure what he meant by that but had to admit, "I love 'em."

"We'll take two, please."

•   •   •

Piper closed her eyes and let the lilting melody of Schubert inundate every cell. How could a man on the other side of the world have created music that could touch so many, hundreds of years after the fact?

She laughed to herself, thinking of the Bible. Its influence began even further back and had even more far-reaching effects on people's lives.

She felt a nudge against her shoulder, then heard a whisper. "You find Schubert funny?"

Gregory *didn't* miss a thing. But she couldn't go into it now during the concert. And she wasn't sure if she could go into it at another time either. She hated to admit it, but she'd never had a lengthy conversation with a Jew. Or a Muslim. Or a Buddhist. There was something wrong in that. If Christ's great commission was for believers to spread the good news of His coming—His coming for *all* people— then shouldn't she venture beyond telling a few safe acquaintances who merely needed a little nudge in the right direction?

The quartet ended. The concert ended. The thought ended.

For now.

•   •   •

Piper pushed her plate away with a groan.

Gregory pointed at what she'd left. "You have cheesecake left."

"This chocolate, chocolate-chip cheesecake is almost too much—even for me."

"You've reached your limit?"

It seemed a loaded question. "On this, anyway." But not on him. Not on him at all. He was a wonderful conversationalist, and if ordering another piece of cheesecake would make the evening last longer, she'd consider it.

He took a bite of his carrot cake. They'd been talking about her mother's illness. "She's a strong woman, your mother."

"Strong spiritually anyway."

He nodded twice. "From my observation, that seems to help the physical part too. There have even been studies . . ."

He'd opened a door. "Faith *does* help in the healing process. I know it."

His grin was crooked. "You're a doctor now?"

"I'm a believer in the power of faith—the power of God."

He took a sip of coffee. "I figured that."

"How?"

"Your mom's invitation to join you at church. The cross . . ."

"Jesus. Yes, Jesus," she said. She suddenly felt inept. Christ was the person who stood between them, yet He was also the One who could—and should—bind them.

"My dad was a Christian," Gregory said.

Piper felt a gawk coming on, but stopped it. "But you said you were Jewish."

"My mother was Jewish."

The implications were boggling. "That must have been confusing."

He shrugged. "Not really. My parents couldn't agree so we didn't go to any church or synagogue."

"You got no religious upbringing?"

"Bits and pieces. They considered Christianity and being a Jew more of a cultural tag, like being an Italian or a Republican. We celebrated a few of the holidays, but only went through the motions."

"How sad. Empty."

"It wasn't so bad."

Piper shifted in her chair. "But when you grew up, when you could choose on your own, which did you choose?"

"Neither."

"Neither?"

He raised a finger to the waitress, signaling for the check. "Never saw much point."

Piper's insides screamed. *Not much point? Not much point!*

"You're upset."

She tossed her napkin on the table and tried to get control of her emotions. She failed. "I'm shocked. Flabbergasted."

"Belief in God is not a requirement for living, Piper."

The arrogance of that statement turned her stomach. "You'll accept being alive because of the Creator, but you won't acknowledge Him or worship Him?"

"I'm a doctor. A scientist."

"Don't give me that. I know plenty of scientists and doctors who have strong faith. They have faith *because* they are people of science and realize that the intricacies of the universe and the human body could not have happened by chance."

Gregory got out his wallet and tossed some bills on the table. "Fine. I acquiesce. I do believe there is a God."

She forced herself to breathe. "Good."

"But that doesn't mean I have to bother Him with a few gimme prayers or by going to a special building once a week."

"Prayer is much more than asking for things. And going to church is an act of worship and—"

"I'm getting along fine as things are. As I am. Why should I change?"

She moved her chair back an inch. "So you consider yourself perfect?"

"Of course not. I see my flaws as well as the next—"

"Good."

He reached across the table and touched her hand. "We've had a wonderful evening, Piper. I like you. A lot. You're one of the few women I've ever gone out with who doesn't put my doctor status on a pedestal. Let's not ruin things by bringing religion into the picture."

She pulled her hand away. "I'm not talking religion. I'm talking relationship. Heavenly Father–child. Savior-sinner. God-man."

He smiled. "How about man-woman?"

She stood. "I don't think so."

He looked up at her, his face incredulous. "You're willing to give up whatever we might have—*might* have developed—because of God?"

"Absolutely."

●　　●　　●

The drive to Peerbaugh Place was silent. And tense. A thousand thoughts ricocheted in Piper's mind. Was she doing a good thing or a bad thing by breaking it off with Gregory before it could even begin? Did God really need her defending Him? She knew God loved Gregory more than she ever could, and He wanted him to draw close and love Him back. God also had the power to zap Gregory into submission—if He wanted to.

But He didn't want to. God rarely worked that way. He was big on free will and giving people a choice and a chance to willingly come to Him. God was not about force but about love.

Piper's methods were less altruistic. *How dare you not admit you need God! You are wrong and I am right! So there!* So much for loving her neighbor as herself or winning a soul to Christ through love.

She glanced at Gregory. He gripped the wheel, staring straight ahead. He had many good qualities. She'd felt a connection to him, and he fit so many of the criteria she'd always wanted in a man. Maybe there was a way to work things through. Maybe she could still be a shining example of Jesus' love, so much so that he'd want what she had for himself.

No way. She hadn't shown Gregory God's love but only Piper Wellington's stubborn, know-it-all defensiveness. "I'm sorry, Gregory. I didn't mean to—"

He pulled into the driveway. "I'm sorry too. Maybe I'll see you next week when your mother comes in for her checkup."

To his credit he came around and opened the door for her and took her up to the front door of Peerbaugh Place. He was a gentleman.

But was she a lady?

•　　•　　•

Evelyn got up from the couch when Piper entered. "How was—?" She stopped short, along with her words. "What happened?"

Piper headed upstairs.

Evelyn ran after her. "Piper? Tell me."

Piper opened the door to her room, but did not invite Evelyn in. "You want to know what happened? I had one of the most delightful evenings of my life, with one of the most fascinating, kind, generous gentlemen I've ever met. But I blew it."

"What did you do?"

What exactly *had* she done? She thought about it a moment. "I threw God in his face, but Gregory couldn't catch Him because he was too busy holding up his hands, fending off my assault."

"You what?"

Piper could only shake her head. "I'm tired, Evelyn. I just want to go to bed. Good night."

She closed the door.

•　　•　　•

Piper couldn't sleep. The could-have-saids, and should-have-saids assaulted her like arrows finding their mark. As a believer she was supposed to be winning souls for Christ, not turning people off so they would never want anything to do with Him.

She sat up in bed and stared at the beautiful, moonlit cross

Gregory had bought for her. The symbol of her faith. The symbol of Christ's ultimate sacrifice, taking the rap for *her* sins, even though He Himself was without sin. The epitome of unfair, yet also the epitome of hope. For because He died—and rose again, cleansed, up to heaven—Piper could be assured of a similar heavenly future.

How miserably she'd failed God. He'd put in her path a man who needed Him, and yet she'd been disrespectful and arrogant and—

She thought of the verse she'd remembered earlier. She flipped on a bedside lamp, grabbed the Bible from the table, and looked up *neighbor* in the concordance in the back. She chose a verse in Paul's letter to the Galatians because Paul was always good at cutting to the chase, getting to the point. She read: *"For you have been called to live in freedom—not freedom to satisfy your sinful nature, but freedom to serve one another in love. For the whole law can be summed up in this one command: 'Love your neighbor as yourself.' But if instead of showing love among yourselves you are always biting and devouring one another, watch out! Beware of destroying one another."*

Piper covered her face with her hands and sobbed.

What had she done?

11

What is important is faith expressing itself in love.

GALATIANS 5:6

$\mathcal{I}$t was one of those days when Piper could not have told anyone whether she'd put eye makeup on both eyes or whether
her shoes matched. As she headed downstairs to grab a cup
of coffee she assumed so, but honestly didn't care one way or
the other. The God-Gregory disaster sat on her shoulders like a
yoke, heavy with two full buckets. With every movement regret
splashed from one bucket or the other and sopped her shoes.
What a mess.

She'd asked God for forgiveness—and had received it, but
that didn't make the regret and shame disappear. At three in
the morning, she'd even tried to tolerate her feelings by accepting them as normal and inevitable. If she *didn't* feel regret and
shame, *that* would be cause for worry. And so she had to endure
what she had to endure. Take her licks like a man. Woman.
Whatever.

She'd asked for God's forgiveness, but still needed to ask for
Gregory's. That was number one on her agenda this morning.
As soon as it was a decent hour, she'd call him and verbally fall
prostrate before him, hopefully receive a full pardon, and move

on—to what, she wasn't sure. She wasn't even sure what she *wanted* to have happen to the relationship except that she didn't want to leave it as it was.

Evelyn was at the table, drinking tea. It smelled minty. "Morning." She eyed Piper, her face full of questions. "There's muffins if you—"

Piper poured coffee into a travel mug. "No thanks; coffee will do."

The phone rang and Evelyn answered it. "Oh, hi, Wanda."

Piper waved her arms violently, shaking her head. The last person she wanted to talk to this morning was her mother.

Evelyn hedged. "Uh, just a minute." She covered the receiver. "She wants to talk to you."

"Does she sound as if she's hurting?"

"She sounds normal," Evelyn said.

Her duties as a daughter to a sick mother took over. "Ask if she's okay, and if she is, tell her I've already left."

"I won't lie, Piper."

"Fine." She edged to the kitchen door. "Ask the question."

Evelyn did as she was told. "Is everything all right, Wanda? Are you all right?" As she received the answer, she nodded.

Piper waved good-bye and headed for the door. She heard Evelyn continue, "Sorry, I think she just left."

Bad daughter. Bad.

* * *

Piper sat at her desk in the high school counselor's office. She looked up Gregory's phone number and had it pegged with a finger when Joey Kensington appeared at her door.

"Yes, Joey?"

"My math teacher says I'm supposed to talk with you."

Yes, yes, many of Joey's teachers pawned him off on Piper

when they reached the end of their bag of tricks to get him to buckle down. "Can you give me just a minute, Joey?"

He shrugged, shoved his hands in the pockets of his jeans, and took a step away from the door. She wanted to get up and close the door but realized that would look odd. She was proud of her open-door policy. And would it really hurt if a student heard her apologizing? Wouldn't that be a good life lesson? For him to know that adults had to apologize too?

She dialed Gregory's number. After the third ring, it was picked up by his service. She nearly said, "No message" but changed her mind and left her name and number. At least he would know she called.

•   •   •

Evelyn carried her painting tools downstairs, eager to get started on the basement after spending hours cleaning it out. She heard a faint knock on the door, then heard it open and the sound of Summer's feet, running toward the kitchen.

"Grandma!"

"Down here."

A moment later, Summer and Audra joined her. "Wow. It's so clean. This explains the pile of stuff on the porch."

"I'm redecorating the laundry area." *Redecorating* was too strong a word. "I'm fixing it up."

Summer ran the dry brush over her hand. "What color are you painting it?"

"Optimistic Yellow."

"I like yellow."

Evelyn pulled her head close. "Me too." She looked at her watch. "Don't you have to get to school?"

"She had to come over to tell you the good—"

"I'm going to be 'dopted!"

191

"A-dopted, baby," Audra said. "Russell wants to adopt her. Make it legal."

Evelyn's heart swelled. She lifted Summer into her arms. "That's the most wonderful thing I've ever heard."

"We'll be a legal family now," Summer said.

Evelyn looked to Audra. The "legal" term was obviously Russell's. "When did he decide this?"

"The other day, believe it or not, at the museum. We went out to dinner last night and he asked Summer if she agreed."

"And I said yes!" Summer said.

"I should hope so." Evelyn let Summer down. "So what happens next?"

Audra's sigh was deep. "First I have to track down Luke and get him to relinquish custody."

"I thought he did that when she was born."

"Nope. He wouldn't." She eyed Summer, who was taking the roller up and down the walls, pretending to paint. She lowered her voice. "Not that he ever showed much interest in . . . things. He refused, just to be contrary, because I wanted him to sign."

"Do you know where he is?"

"Jackson, I think."

"What if you can't find him?"

"Then we have to run an ad. I hope it doesn't come to that." Audra held her hand out. "Come on, baby. We need to get you to school."

Summer put the roller away and gave her grandma a kiss. "I'm going to be a Peerbaugh too," she said.

Hopefully.

•   •   •

Evelyn didn't get to her painting for another forty-five minutes, because when they went upstairs, Heddy corralled Audra, wanting to show her the logo she'd created for Catherine's Wedding Creations. They needed to talk, so Evelyn took Summer to school.

"How do you like being home with your mom after school?" Evelyn asked in the car. *Was that a pitiful plea for attention or what?*

"It's okay. But you make better cookies than Mommy. I like the chocolate drop ones the best."

"I'll give her the recipe."

"And I miss you, Grandma. I miss seeing you."

The pity plea is fulfilled! "I miss you too, sweetie. But remember, you can come over anytime you want."

"Can I help you paint?"

Oh dear. They turned into the school driveway.

•　　•　　•

"I gave him the messages, Ms. Wellington," said Gregory's answering service. "Would you like me to tell him you called again?"

What good would it do for him to know she'd called six times, not five? "No, thank you. I'm done bothering you."

"It's no bother."

"Thanks for your help." She hung up. Gregory didn't want to talk to her. Period. End of story. End of relationship.

She hated consequences. Even if they were deserved.

•　　•　　•

Evelyn was just pouring the yellow paint into the roller pan when she heard another *knock-knock*, another opened door, and another voice: "Evie? It's me."

"Down in the basement."

Mae came downstairs, her olive green clogs *ka-chunk*ing on each step. Evelyn had never analyzed it before, but at the sight of Mae's shoes, she realized she'd rarely seen her friend with her entire foot covered. It was either flip-flops, sandals, mules, or clogs—open-toed in warm weather, and these close-toed versions in the winter. Psychologists would probably find some deep-seated reason for that, but Evelyn let it go as just another of Mae's eccentricities that continued to entertain and delight.

Mae shielded her eyes with one hand while pointing at the paint tray with the other. "Gracious goldenrod, Evie. That's bright."

"It's not goldenrod; it's called Optimistic Yellow. And yes, it's bright in order to lighten up this dingy basement."

"Hey, I'm all for color—you know that." With an amazingly deft move, Mae hopped onto the dryer, using it as a chair. "But I didn't know you were talented in regard to decorating." She put a hand to her mouth. "Oops. I think that came out wrong. Peerbaugh Place is lovely and—"

Evelyn stopped her friend's backpedaling. "No need for apologies. Ever since Piper helped me redecorate my bedroom I've been seeing things a bit differently, realizing things don't have to stay the same."

"Bravo. Change can be good."

"Especially if it's Optimistic Yellow." Evelyn dipped the brush and applied the first paint to the wall, edging around the window. She stepped back. "I like it."

"Me too."

Evelyn kept working, liking that she was able to do so in Mae's presence. "You come for a reason or just visiting?"

"Actually, I need the recipe for your hash-brown casserole. Collie says we're supposed to bring a covered dish to the church dinner tonight, and he had the audacity to choose your hash browns over my brown rice."

"That's because my recipe is more tasty—being chock-full of fat and calories."

"That man. If only he'd give tofu a chance."

Evelyn laughed. "Face it, Mae, Collier Ames is not a tofu–bean sprout kind of guy."

Mae swung her legs, banging them against the dryer. "But he is cute."

"That, he is. The recipe's in the blue recipe book on the shelf. Help yourself."

Mae jumped down and headed upstairs. Then Evelyn remembered and called her back. "Mae!"

Mae put a hand to her chest. "Don't do that! I nearly fell off the steps."

"Russell's going to adopt Summer."

"Yee-ha to that!" Mae came back down to hear all the details. "Who would have thought our single mom Audra would settle down and marry a banker? Actually, who would have thought hippie me would be married—to a man who likes meat loaf and wears Hush Puppies?"

"True on both accounts."

"You're next, Evelyn."

She thought of Herb Evans. "I don't think so."

"Don't give me that. It's been nearly a year since Aaron died. "There are loads of nice older men out there, just aching for a wife."

"I don't know about that . . ."

"Well, maybe not loads, but surely a gaggle or two."

Evelyn shrugged. Dating was the last thing on her mind.

Mae readied herself to ascend the stairs a second time. "Any other news before I disappear into the world of tasty fat and calories?"

Evelyn thought a moment, then remembered. "Anabelle! She came over and we made up. I got her to drop the lawsuit."

"You got her to—?"

Evelyn shuffled her shoulders. "I should tell you not to act so surprised, because I'm the most surprised of anybody. But I handled it, Mae. She came over, all huffy, and I was calm and asked her to sit down, and . . . and I handled it. We're not going to be best friends, but we're not enemies either."

"And that's a good thing."

"You bet."

There were footsteps moving about in the kitchen. They both looked up. *Gail.*

Mae whispered, "How's she doing since being found out?"

"I haven't seen much of her, but I think she's okay."

Mae nodded. "Is she working today?"

"I don't know."

"Think she'd want to come over sometime?"

Evelyn raised an eyebrow. "You *want* her to come over?"

"Hey, why not? You know I can be friends with a chair if I set my mind to it. And I think Gail needs a friend."

Evelyn laughed. "Then I say go for it, or as Gail says, 'knock yourself out.'"

"Don't mind if I do."

•   •   •

Mae lingered on the top step of the basement long enough to take a deep breath and send off a prayer: *For once in my life, Lord, help me not say too much.*

She entered the kitchen. Gail was eating a bowl of Cinnamon Life, reading the back of the box. She was *not* wearing her Burger Madness uniform. Gail looked up. "What are you doing here?"

"Bugging Evelyn."

"Hmm."

"When I heard footsteps overhead, I decided to come up and inflict my bugging on someone else."

"Don't knock yourself out on my account."

Mae smiled and took a seat across from her. "Hey, no problem. It's what I live for."

"Bugging people?"

She shrugged. "It's a gift."

Gail shoved her chair back and took her bowl to the sink even though there was cereal left.

Mae wanted to call a time-out. Why wasn't Gail responding to her charm? It was the one sure thing in her life—other than Collie and Jesus. Gail's unresponsiveness was totally unacceptable.

She slapped her hands on the table. "Well, Gail. I must say you are a tough nut to crack."

"Excuse me?"

"If you'd ever get that girder off your shoulder, you might find that the rest of us aren't so bad after all."

"I do not have a chip on my—"

"Girder. I said girder. Reinforced steel."

The corner of Gail's mouth quivered, but she managed to get the smile under control. "You think you have the power to knock it off?"

Mae stood. "Knock it off? Probably not. But I'll be glad to chip in for a crane to do some heavy lifting. You can always put it back later."

Gail leaned back against the counter, crossing her ankles and her arms. "And why would you want to do that?"

"Because we're neighbors, silly. Because we're two potential sisters just waiting to happen."

"I don't have any sisters."

"Not yet, you don't. Sisters are *not* allowed to wear girders. It gets in the way of the hugs."

"Is this a rule?"

"Number 438." Mae got out the blue recipe book Evelyn had mentioned and looked up the hash-brown casserole recipe. "Besides, you and I have a lot in common."

"Ah, yes. I remember. We both share a lack of tact."

It took Mae a moment to remember their conversation from the other day. "Yes, that. But something else too."

"Gumption beyond all measure?"

Mae laughed. "See? We are sisters. Actually, I was referring to our children."

Gail's face clouded. "What do you know about my son?"

"I know he doesn't live with you. I know you don't see him much. And I understand that. Because up until last spring, I'd been out of contact with my two darlings: Ringo and Starr."

Gail's jaw dropped. "Ringo and Starr? You've got to be kidding."

"You've got your Burger Madness . . . chalk their names up to hippie madness." She motioned toward the door. "Want to come over and help me make something delicious but fattening for a potluck Hubby and I are going to tonight?"

Gail shrugged. "Sure. Why not?"

Mae wanted to pump a fist into the air, but managed to restrain herself.

•   •   •

Gail had a half hour before her visit to Mae's. She finished getting dressed, and Mae made a quick trip to the grocery store for the necessary ingredients. The extra time gave her a chance to regret her quick decision. Mae was the last person she wanted to be chummy with. She was like hot fudge on Rocky Road ice cream. Too much of a good thing.

As Gail tied her shoes, she tried to think of a good excuse not to go, but nothing credible came to mind. And so she was stuck, cooking with a crazed hippie who named her children Ringo and Starr.

What a hoot.

• • •

The sour cream fell from its carton into the large metal mixing bowl with a loud *schlup*. Mae made a face. "You got that can of soup opened?"

Gail made the final turn of the can opener. "Ready."

Mae moved the bowl closer. "Add away." The cream of chicken soup exited the can, retaining its shape. She added the frozen hash browns. "This *can't* be healthy. Potatoes are not supposed to be bought frozen."

Gail laughed and added the grated cheddar cheese. "You're too much of a purist. This is home cooking for the twenty-first century."

Mae held the recipe card at arm's length, squinting. Then she held it toward Gail. "Tell me this does *not* say to put crushed corn flakes on top."

Gail read the card. "Corn flakes mixed with melted butter. Yum. Sounds great."

Mae poured some corn flakes into a plastic bag and crushed them with extra fervor. "What I do for Collie."

"Collie is your dog?"

Mae burst out laughing. "Oh dear me, no. Though he can produce the most amazing puppy eyes. No, Collier is my husband. I just call him Collie." She held the nine-by-thirteen pan so Gail could transfer the mixture. "I'm afraid I have a habit of adapting everybody's name. Collier becomes Collie, Evelyn becomes Evie, Tessa becomes Tessie." She looked at Gail. "Hmm. Can't do much with *Gail*."

"Sorry to disappoint you."

"No matter. If I can't desecrate your name I'll think of some other way to bug you."

"Right. It's what you live for."

"Now you're catching on." Mae stirred the cornflakes into the melted butter, then handed the bowl to Gail. "You sprinkle these on top. I can't bring myself to do it."

"Cornflake snob."

"Now if they were bran flakes . . ." Mae put the pan into the oven, setting the timer. She wiped her hands on a towel that was slung over her shoulder. "There. All done."

Good. Now I can go—

"Now we have time for some real sister talk."

"I thought you said I wasn't your sister."

Mae waved a finger at Gail's shoulders. "I think it's time. I see the girder is gone."

Gail actually glanced at her own shoulders, feeling immediately ridiculous.

Mae laughed. "See? It *is* gone. It feels better without it, doesn't it?"

Actually, it did.

Mae took a seat in the breakfast nook, which was actually two booth seats with a table in between. She patted the far side of the table. "Sit, Gail. Sit and tell me about your son."

Gail tensed.

"What's his name?"

The direct question could not be ignored. "Jacob."

"He's ten?"

"Nine."

"Boy, I remember when Ringo was nine. That boy could trip over air yet walked like he weighed three hundred pounds. His bedroom was right above the kitchen. I was constantly yelling up at him to quit being an elephant."

Gail had to smile. She slid into the booth. "Jacob is all legs. We can't keep him in jeans—he outgrows them so fast."

"Typical boy. So different from girls. Starr wouldn't outgrow things physically as much as she would outgrow the style."

"Girls are more faddish than boys."

"You got that right. What grade is Jacob in?"

"Fourth."

"What's his favorite subject?"

Gail had to think, and that fact disturbed her—and reinforced her decision to leave her family behind.

"Gail? His favorite subject?"

Gail set her jaw. "I don't know, okay?"

Mae's eyes widened for the shortest of seconds. "I see."

Those two words flipped an inner switch in Gail. "No, you don't see."

"Then enlighten me."

Gail studied Mae's face. It was an open face, full of compassion. There was no judgment there. Mae clasped her hands on top of the table, waiting. Gail imagined she'd be willing to wait a very long time.

"I'm not a good mother."

"Join the club."

Gail felt her eyebrows rise.

"You think you're the only one who has doubts about her abilities? You think you're the only one who questions why she doesn't feel maternal more of the time?"

"You felt that way too?"

"More often than I felt I was getting it right."

That's fine but . . . "I couldn't take it anymore."

Mae's eyebrows dipped. "Take what?"

"Being a mediocre mom."

"So . . . ?"

"I left."

"Gracious Gobstoppers, Gail. Because you weren't a perfect mom?"

Gail snickered. "Far from perfect."

"Give me an example of this horrible imperfection."

Gail didn't have to think long. "I hated going to my son's baseball games. I had to make myself go."

A laugh escaped and Mae squelched it with a hand. "You didn't like sitting in the blazing sun for hours and hours on a Saturday afternoon when your to-do list at home remained undone?"

"Uh . . . right."

"Did you ever do a poll of the other parents in the stands?"

"A poll?"

"To see how many really loved being there—above and beyond their love for their babies?"

"No."

"Well, you should have. Both my darlings used to play sports, and both played in the orchestra too—which had *long* concerts with music that was barely discernible as melodic."

Gail nodded. "Jacob plays clarinet."

"*Squeak, squeak, squawk, squawk.*"

"Pretty close."

Mae reached across the table and touched Gail's arm. "The good mothering doesn't come in liking to do those things for our children, but in *doing* those things for them in spite of the fact we'd rather be doing most anything else. It's about being there. Supporting them."

It made sense, but Gail didn't like that it made sense, because if it made sense, then her moving out . . .

"Are you and your husband divorced?"

"I'm going to file soon."

"Why?"

"Because I'm not a good wife either."

"Because you don't like to do his laundry or watch the fishing channel with him?"

Mae was alarmingly close. "If I love my family, shouldn't I like doing those things?" Gail asked.

"Ideally. And it *is* something to strive for. Loving well is the hardest thing we're asked to do."

The question popped out even though Gail knew how Mae would answer. "By whom?"

"By Jesus."

"Oh."

Mae slapped the table. "Uh-uh. Don't say 'oh' like I just said a bad word. *Jesus* is a good word, a great word, *the* Word."

"I'm not a religious person."

"Neither am I."

"Huh?"

"I'm not religious, as in getting high on ceremonies and reciting rote prayers and such. But I am a believing person—thanks to Collie—and I do get high on living with Him by my side every minute of the day."

Him or him?

Mae answered the unspoken question. "Him, as in capital *H*." She laughed. "And him, lowercase *h* too. Collie is a gem."

Gail felt a surge of something fill her up from the center out. Could it be hope?

"Just a minute." Mae got up and returned with her Bible. "I was just reading a cool verse the other day and—"

Gail smiled. "You call a Bible verse 'cool'?"

"Absolutely. Old JC is the coolest." She made the hippie peace sign. "Peace, flower power, love, baby." She found the verse. "How's this for love?" She read: "'God is love, and all who live in love live in God, and God lives in them. And as we live in God, our love grows more perfect.'" She closed the Bible. "Perfect love. That's what we're supposed to strive for."

Gail shook her head. "I'm so far from perfect . . ."

"And you'll stay far from perfect as long as you keep plugging at it alone. You need help."

"You *have* been a help, Mae."

"Oh no, not me—though I do thank you for the compliment. I'm talking divine help. Jesus Christ help."

Gail looked down. "Don't push me, Mae."

Mae patted her hand twice. "'Nuf said. Let's just call it a little nudge. The when, where and how of your making that kind of life-changing decision is not up to me anyway. It's between you and God. Just know that He's doing the calling, and He's doing the waiting, and He's ready whenever you are." She took a deep breath through her nose. "Zounds, though I hate to admit it, that potato concoction is beginning to smell mighty tasty."

"Smells perfect to me," Gail said.

They laughed.

●　　●　　●

Evelyn washed out her brush, paint roller, and pan. The laundry sink ran with yellow water in a swirl of marbleized color. Peppers sat on the dryer watching.

"What do you think, Peps?" Evelyn looked over the room. It was lovely. Happy. Sunny. Not like a basement at all. Maybe if she bought a bit of flowered fabric, she could get Audra or Heddy to sew a little curtain for the window. And Summer could paint some pretty pictures Evelyn could frame for the walls. What was homier than kid paintings from her granddaughter?

Granddaughter. She smiled at the thought that Russell was going to make it legal by adopting her.

Like someone adopted your baby girl.

Evelyn sucked in a breath. The memory continued to assail her at odd moments. She didn't regret giving up her baby. It had happened before Aaron had come into her life. She'd been a single mother, and the baby's father had died in the Vietnam War, never seeing his daughter. Times were different then. She would never have been able to bring up her baby girl like Audra had brought up Summer.

Maybe that's why Evelyn had bonded with Summer so readily. Summer reminded her of the daughter she'd given up for adoption.

Evelyn found joy in knowing that the adoption of her daughter had been a blessing in some couple's life. Just as now, Summer's adoption was a blessing in hers.

Summer Peerbaugh. It was a wonderful name for a wonderful little girl.

Everything had worked out for the best.

Hadn't it?

● ● ●

Piper carried the Chinese takeout up the stairs to her apartment as if she were traveling her last mile, getting ready to eat her last meal. The last thing she felt like doing was being upbeat and chirpy with her parents. How could she possibly endure her mother's hopeful face? Or worse, her questions? *How was your date, dear? Was it wonderful? Are you going to marry the doctor? Are you? Huh? Huh?*

Yes, the date was wonderful, but no, marrying him was out of the question. For a myriad of reasons.

Piper used her key and went in. Her parents were watching TV. Piper heard the voice of Hawkeye Pierce from an old *M*A*S*H* rerun.

Her father got up. "Hey. Food. Good. I'm starved. Come dear."

Piper shook her head. "No, stay put. I'll bring it to you, Mom."

Her mother got off the couch to join them. "No, I'll come. Though little good it will do."

Piper unpacked the sack. "What do you mean by that?"

She looked at both of them as if they were dense. "Sodium? I'm supposed to watch my sodium. And fried foods. What has more sodium than Chinese? And the rice and sweet-and-sour pork are fried."

Piper put a hand to her forehead. "I'm so sorry. I didn't think . . . but I did get some steamed rice."

Her mother slid onto a breakfast stool. "Goody." She made a face.

"You could put sweet-and-sour sauce on it," Wayne said. "Just stay away from the soy-sauce dishes."

"Whatever. It will have to do." She sighed deeply . "I suppose a lot of things will have 'to do' from now on."

Piper longed for chirpy and upbeat. She looked to her father for more explanation.

"Dr. Baladino called today . . ."

He called you, but he didn't call me?

Her father took her mother's hand. "The angioplasty was only partially successful. The right ventricle still has blockage. He might want to go in and fix it."

"Then do it," Piper said.

Her mother shook her head. "My blood pressure's high. They've got me on medicine for it. They want to get that under control before doing more surgery to put in another stent."

Her father added, "But for now, all we can do is make some lifestyle changes."

"Like what?" Piper asked.

Her mother poked a fork in the rice, but didn't eat any. "Normal stuff I've heard a thousand times, but ignored. Eat healthy, exercise."

"That doesn't sound so hard." She looked at her mother's petite frame. "And it's not like you're overweight or eat junk food all the time."

Her mother shrugged, then looked up. From the look on her face, Piper could tell that whatever was coming next was the real issue. "Dr. Baladino wants me to stick around Carson Creek. We can't go back to RVing."

"For now," her father said. "Once we get you squared away, we'll be off and running."

Piper's mom toppled a pile of rice. "I'm ruining our retirement."

"Now stop that," her father said. "Without your health, we have no retirement."

"Enough of this," Wanda said. She set her fork down, seemed to shuck off her depression, and managed a smile. "Tell us all about your date with the doctor."

Piper had predetermined how much she would say and how she would word things. "I had a wonderful time, but he's not the man for me. Our home base is too different."

"Him being Jewish?" her father asked.

"Him not really believing in God."

"Oh my."

"How can anyone not believe in God?" Wanda asked. "Especially a doctor who has studied the minute details of the human body. That kind of miraculous order didn't happen by accident."

"I know. I mentioned that very point," Piper said. She didn't want to discuss it further. "Anyway, that's that. He's a nice man, a good doctor, but I won't be seeing him again."

"Whatever you think is best, Piper-girl," her father said.

Her mother didn't answer, and the cleft between her eyebrows told of deep thoughts. Piper didn't want to ask, but she had to. "Out with it, Mom."

Her mother took a bite of rice and chewed. Only after she swallowed did she answer. "Maybe you're the one. His one."

"I'm not the woman of his dreams, if that's what you're—"

"No, no. Maybe you're not his romantic one, but his spiritual one. The one person who could have a profound effect on his faith. On his life—both now and forever."

Piper thought of her mishandling of their God discussion. "You give me too much credit."

"You give yourself too little. What if you're supposed to be an influence in Dr. Baladino's life? What if, by your very presence and example of faith, he ends up turning to Jesus and gaining eternal life?"

"Mom, we went on one date."

"It's a start."

Piper paced behind the counter. "No, it's not a start. The subject of God *did* come up, and let me tell you, I was not a shining example of Christianity or faith of any kind. I was rude, sharp, and—"

"Not you," her father said.

Sometimes she hated that they were her most steadfast fans. "Yes, me, Dad. I'm sure the sum total of heaven was cringing about how I handled the God issue. I feel awful about it and have called Gregory all day, trying to apologize, but he hasn't returned my calls."

"He called us," her mother said.

"Exactly. Which proves he could have called me but chose not to do so. He and I are done. *Fini.* Over."

"But, honey . . ."

Piper shook her head. "Even if he accepts my apology, I'm sure any chance of me having a positive effect on Dr. Gregory Baladino's life is gone."

"But—"

Piper raised her hand as a stop sign. "No. That's the end of it. Let's move on to another topic. Something happier."

But between her aborted relationship with Gregory and her mother's heart disease, no happy topics came to mind. They ate in silence.

•   •   •

Piper's dad took a load of dirty clothes down to the apartment laundry room, leaving Piper alone with her mother. Piper was alarmed to find her stomach knotted, as if she was nervous. How odd. She and her mom had always had a great relationship. Yet when she thought about it, ever since her mom had taken sick, Piper had gone out of her way to make sure the two of them were never alone.

Why was that?

And yet, Piper's reaction was unmistakable. Instead of lolling on a couch, chatting or watching a TV program with her mother, Piper found herself making busywork in the kitchen as if activity could encircle her in a protective shield.

A protective shield from what?

Wanda took a seat on the stool at the breakfast bar. She pointed to the pitcher Piper was washing. "You already washed that."

Piper froze and saw the pitcher for the first time. She rinsed it and set it upside down to drain. She picked up a sponge and wiped the clean counters.

"Piper . . ."

Piper didn't turn around. "Hmm?"

Her mother's voice became more adamant. "Piper."

She had no choice but to face her. Why did she have trouble looking at her mother's eyes? She waited. For something. Anything.

"What's wrong with you?" her mother finally asked.

"Nothing."

The lowered chin showed her mother's unbelief. "I'm sorry for being so negative earlier. I didn't mean to upset you. It was nice of you to bring home Chinese. I was rude."

Her mother's ridiculous apology broke through Piper's

unease. She was way off the mark. Her previous comment about the Chinese food was incidental and inconsequential, mundane and meaningless. "Mom, that's not . . . it has nothing to do with . . ." Why couldn't she put her feelings into words? Expressing herself was usually her strong suit.

Her mother smiled the slightest bit, and her eyes revealed that she knew food was not the issue, but in normal mom fashion she had wanted Piper to realize it herself. "I'm not going to die, Piper. Not yet, that is."

Piper tried to back away from the words, but found the sink blocking her way.

"Don't be afraid for me, honey."

The truth burst to the surface like a volcano erupting hot lava. "But don't you get it? I'm not afraid for *you*. I'm afraid for me! You're the one going through the pain, the operations, and the uncertainty, and I'm only worried about how your illness affects me!" She covered her face with her hands. "I'm the most selfish daughter."

Before Piper could elaborate, her mother's arms were around her, pulling her close as they had done for thirty-four years. "*Shh, shh.* You're a wonderful daughter, and far from selfish . . . you gave up your apartment for us. That was not the act of a selfish daughter."

Piper stood more erect and sniffed. "But still . . ."

"Uh-uh. None of that. Your reactions are normal. You think your father hasn't had thoughts about how all this affects him? That doesn't mean he's selfish or that he doesn't love me. It means he's human." She pushed Piper's hair behind her ears. "And when I was so negative earlier, that was me being selfishly human."

"But you have a right to be."

She shrugged. "I think that's the danger of any serious illness. The patient can become so absorbed in me, myself, and I that the entire focus of their life is veered onto a side road that sooner or later leads them far away from the *right* road. Their *life* road."

"You're fighting for that life."

"Yes, I am. And I will be the first to admit to moments of wishing it were happening to someone else."

Piper let out a puff of air. "Yay."

"Yay?"

"Don't be too perfect, Mom. It makes it hard on the rest of us."

Her mother looked toward the comfort of the living room. "Can we sit?" They took a place on opposite ends of the couch. "There. That's better," she said.

"I wish this were happening to someone else too, Mom."

"Understood. But this is my struggle. And in spite of the fact that I don't want it or understand it, I know God has given it to *me* for a reason."

"What reason?"

She laughed. "I haven't a clue. But I'm sure someday, in hindsight, you'll all see it clear."

Piper didn't like the *you* reference. "*We'll* see it clear. We, including you."

Wanda agreed. "You're right. We'll all see God's plan. And He does have one. He 'saw me before I was born.'" She closed her eyes and looked utterly peaceful as she continued to quote the verse in Psalms: "'Every day of my life was recorded in Your book. Every moment was laid out before a single day had passed.'" She opened her eyes. "It's a plan, Piper. It's not haphazard."

How many times had Piper referred to God's plan in talking with someone else? How many times had she flipped the phrase as a catchall for whatever issue was being discussed? Not that it wasn't the truth, but now, said in such a life-and-death context as her mother's illness, it suddenly sounded trite, almost as bad as someone saying, "It's God's will."

"You don't like the notion that this sickness is God's plan for my life? It is, you know."

Piper squirmed on the cushion and took a pillow into her lap. "Oh yes, I know it's His plan, but no, I don't like it."

"Me neither. But fortunately, God doesn't ask our opinions on such things. He's smart that way."

"How so?"

"Because if He asked us, we'd always shy away from the struggles, the trials, and the heartache. We'd always choose the sunshine and the easy path."

Piper shrugged.

"Don't shrug at me. You know I'm right, and you know it's an important concept. We gain our greatest education through struggles. We learn more in the darkness than in the light because we are forced to trust without evidence. Trust that He knows best."

"I'd like to argue with Him in this particular case."

Wanda flipped a hand. "Then do it. Argue. You think God can't handle our debate? Do you think He's going to abandon us because we doubt, disagree, or even get mad?"

"But don't doubt and debate show our lack of faith?"

"If they pull us away from Him, sure. But if we feel those very human things and take them *to* Him, they show the very essence of our faith." She pulled one leg under the other. "And wouldn't you rather have some dark, struggling times and learn God's principles than live in the light without them?"

Piper knew the correct answer, but still found it hard to say.

"Come on, honey. Don't fail me now."

"Yes, yes. I agree with you."

"Because I'm right."

"As usual."

Her mother leaned back with a satisfied look just as her father came back with a load of warm clothes from the dryer.

"Okay, ladies, who wants to help fold?"

•   •   •

Audra pulled her sleep shirt over her head and folded back the covers on her side of the bed. "Heddy and I are going to Jackson on Saturday to visit the fabric distributor and choose some preliminary fabrics." She crawled into bed and pulled the covers up. "I thought I'd ask your mother to go along."

"Why?" Russell asked. "She's not involved in the new business, is she?"

"No. But I think she feels left out since I took Summer away from her."

"You didn't take Summer away; *you're* home for Summer after school. That's a good thing."

She snuggled under his arm. "I know. But I don't want her to feel lonely."

He kissed the top of her head. "You're a good woman, Audra Peerbaugh."

She smiled at the sound of her name. And now Summer would share that name.

Russell seemed to sense her thoughts. "I want to get going on this adoption thing. But we need to find Luke, have him sign the papers. Do you know where he is?"

The smile left her. The last thing she wanted to do was talk to Luke. "Not really."

"So how are you going to go about finding him? Should we place an ad or—?"

"I suppose I can talk to his mother."

He jerked back. "You know how to reach her?"

She nodded against his chest.

"Then do it," he said. "Talk to his mother."

Goody.

Teach me Your ways, O Lord,
that I may live according to Your truth!
Grant me purity of heart, that I may honor You.

PSALM 86:11

When Audra woke up Saturday morning, she realized it had been forty-eight hours since she'd called Luke's mother. She'd left multiple messages, but in truth, had been relieved that Dorthea had never called back. Putting an ad in the paper to get in contact with Luke might take a little longer but seemed far less stressful than dealing with the Ottingtons in person. If Dorthea didn't call by Monday, Audra would contact the adoption lawyer Russell had found and place the ad. Time would take care of the rest.

She slipped out of bed, letting Russell sleep. She passed Summer watching cartoons quietly in the living room. They waved to each other as Audra shuffled toward the kitchen to put the coffee on. Her notes for the wedding business lay strewn over the kitchen table. Today was going to be an exciting, fun day, choosing fabric for each design and setting up an account with the fabric distributor Audra had found in Jackson. Things were progressing nicely. Everything was looking up. Life was—

The phone rang and Audra lunged for it, not wanting it to wake Russell.

"Audra? This is Dorthea. You called?"

The sound of Dorthea's voice brought back memories of the first time they'd met. It had been in the parlor of the Ottington home where Audra and Luke had gone to explain their pregnant situation. Dorthea had evidenced no moral concern for their condition, just a fear that Audra would be a burden on her son's future, be after her son's money, or besmirch the Ottington name with this illegitimate birth.

The irony was that her precious son wasn't so precious. After Summer was born, Audra discovered that Luke had gotten two other girls pregnant—one before Audra, one after. His baby-in-every-port history added to her own self-condemnation. To think she'd been impressed with his charm, good looks, and social status. What *had* she been thinking?

"Thank you for calling back, Mrs. Ottington." Audra decided the best way to get Luke's mother to cooperate was to follow the social amenities. "How have you been?"

While Dorthea droned on about bridge clubs, trips, and committees, Audra glanced toward the bedroom where Russell lay sleeping. Russell was just as charming, good-looking, and high on the social ladder as Luke had been. Interesting. Subconsciously, did she need a successful man, a man who had money and style?

She wedged the phone in the crook of her neck and poured herself a cup of coffee. No. She had not been drawn to Russell because he was vice president of the bank. His status and success were a perk of their relationship, not a requirement. Truth be, money was not that important to Audra. If it was, she would have taken the money Dorthea had offered as payment to get lost.

Dorthea droned on, "And Mr. Ottington and I decided that it was in the best interest . . ."

Mr. Ottington. Audra had always found it odd that Dorthea spoke of her husband in this manner. It was so . . . . distant.

In his defense, Luke *had* wanted to marry her—or at least he'd offered. She would never forget his face during his halfhearted proposal while his parents were out of the room. He said all the right words—Luke Ottington always said all the right words—but there was something in his eyes that revealed his hope that she'd say no, his assumption she'd say no. And when she'd seen that look, a part of her considered saying yes, just to prove those eyes wrong.

But she'd known that marrying out of spite wouldn't be a marriage at all. She'd heard it said: "Don't marry a man you can live with; marry a man you can't live without." Luke was *not* that man. And so she'd graduated from high school seven months pregnant, lived at home with her parents while she went to college, ever determined to bring up Summer alone.

Until now. Until Russell.

Dorthea was describing some villa in Italy . . .

Audra heard Summer's soft giggle and peeked into the living room. Her daughter was draped over the ottoman, her head resting on a stuffed monkey. Her legs were in constant motion, rising off the floor, dropping down, pushing the ottoman this way and that, like a dance being done to the music of the cartoons.

If it weren't for Luke, she wouldn't have Summer. Summer was a consequence turned into God's greatest blessing. And now their two had become three as Russell's presence completed the family.

When Dorthea finished the Ottington family update, Audra felt as if she'd just heard a quarterly report. "So," Dorthea said, "why did you call?"

"I need to talk to Luke."

"What about?"

"I've married."

"Oh, really."

Audra was not surprised she didn't receive a congratulation. "Can I have Luke's phone number, please?"

"*May* you."

"Fine. May I?"

"Why do you want to contact him?"

It wasn't Dorthea's business, and yet the question was not unexpected. "I don't want anything from him, Mrs. Ottington—no money, nothing like that. I just want a few moments of his time."

"Did you marry well?"

I married a banker. How's that? "I adore him."

"Oh."

"Summer adores him."

There was a pause, and Audra had the feeling Dorthea was trying to remember who Summer was. *You remember her, don't you? Your granddaughter?* But to receive satisfaction in saying the words aloud would also be to acknowledge a relationship Audra did *not* want to encourage. It was best Dorthea continued with the mind-set of "Summer who?"

"Luke is doing very well for himself. He lives in Jackson now."

Although Audra would have loved to ask if Luke was married or what "doing well" entailed, she left the questions unspoken.

"Perhaps it would be better if I let him contact you."

As long as he *did*. "I suppose you could give him this phone number."

"Fine. I'll have him call."

Audra wanted to add, "It's important" but knew those two words would ignite more questions. "Thank you. I appreciate it." She hung up, drained, and joined Summer in the living room, lying down on the couch. Within seconds, Summer left her ottoman and snuggled beside her. Her child's scent expelled all bad thoughts, and her warm body made the world all right.

It was just what Audra needed.

●　　●　　●

"Two umbrellas! I get to go again!" Summer snatched the two umbrella cards and continued picking matches from the over-turned cards.

Russell was amazed at her recall. She always won when they played Memory—and it wasn't because he *let* her win. However, it *did* have a lot to do with the fact that she concentrated on the game and he let his mind wander. At least that's what he told himself.

She turned over a turtle and an ostrich. "Ahh. Your turn, Daddy."

Russell remembered seeing an ostrich card somewhere . . . he turned over a donkey. He'd never seen another donkey. He was cooked.

The telephone saved him from further humiliation. He groaned as he got to his feet, getting it on the third ring. "Peerbaughs'."

"Who?"

"Peerbaughs'. May I help you?"

"I don't know. I was looking for Audra Taylor?"

Russell felt a swell of possessiveness. "You mean Audra Peerbaugh?"

A laugh. "That's her last name now?"

"Who is this?" Russell asked.

"This is Luke Ottington, her old boyfriend. My mother said she'd called?"

Russell regretted his previous short tone. Now was not the time to antagonize Summer's birth father. "Audra's not here right now. Can I get a number and have her call you back?"

"What's this about?"

"I'd rather she talk to you."

"You her husband?"

"Yes."

"Where's the girl?"

Didn't he know her name? "I'm not sure what you mean, 'where's the girl?'"

"Is she living with you? Or is she living with Audra's parents?" He sighed. "Where's the girl?"

"She's with us." *Right here. Six feet away.*

"She okay?"

"She's fine."

"Can I talk with her?"

You don't even remember her name but you want to talk to her?
"She's at a friend's house right now." *A friend. Me. She's at my
house.*

"Oh."

Russell wanted this conversation ended. "Can I have your
number so Audra can call you?" He wrote it down and hung up.

"Who was that?" Summer asked.

"Nobody important." *Just the person who fathered you.* He sank
back to the floor. "Whose turn is it?"

●　　●　　●

"Oooh." Heddy was drawn to a bolt of mint green satin. Her hand
sought the cool smoothness. "I like this one."

Audra and Evelyn came close and also seemed compelled
to touch the fabric. "This weight would be perfect for the sheath
dress, wouldn't it?"

Heddy turned to the fabric rep. "We need a sample card for
this one too."

The man jotted down a note. "No problem."

They continued through the display room, touching and draping the bridal fabrics. Heddy felt more alive than she had in years.

Evelyn whispered to her, "You're in your element, aren't
you?"

Heddy pulled fabric from a bolt and draped it around her
shoulders. "I could die now and call it heaven."

She heard Audra ask the other fabric rep about credit terms.
She was so lucky to have Audra as a partner. Heddy didn't want
to deal with money or shipping or credit. She wanted to create

and share her excitement for the beautiful dresses with the brides and bridesmaids.

Evelyn fingered a navy moiré. "Are you going to make up full-size samples of each of your designs?"

"We decided we have to," Heddy said. "We have to give the women something to try on. Of course once they choose, we'll custom fit each design so it looks wonderful on them."

"That's a lot of work," Evelyn said. "Work you have to do before you open your doors for business."

"I'll love every minute of it."

Evelyn ran her hand along a row of pastel sheers. "Hmm."

Heddy couldn't tell whether it was a good *hmm* or a bad *hmm.*

Audra finished her financial discussion and joined them. "We're all set. John will put the sample cards and swatches in my car."

"Are we getting the yardage for the sized sample dresses now?"

Audra looked toward the salesmen, who were talking between themselves. "You want all that fabric now? We could get a little at a time. I don't want to overwhelm you with the work. Or overwhelm us with the expense."

Heddy was glad Audra was the practical one, but didn't like being confronted with that practicality. "We have the money from the loan, don't we?"

"Sure."

"And you're going to help with the sewing."

"Of course, but that doesn't mean I don't feel the pressure of it. But I defer to you. You're the designer; I'm just a seamstress." Audra turned to Evelyn. "Would you like to help, Evelyn?"

"I don't sew. Not like that anyway."

"You could work on the pamphlet or the flyers or—"

Evelyn shook her head. "This is your business, Audra. I'm

glad you invited me along for the day—it was fun seeing all these lovely fabrics—but this isn't my thing. It's your thing."

Audra's face sagged. She'd confided in Heddy about wanting to have her mother-in-law involved in the new business. She was worried that Evelyn didn't have enough to do since she didn't take care of Summer every day. Obviously, Evelyn had other plans.

Heddy wondered what they were.

•   •   •

Audra was too quiet and Evelyn didn't like it. Ever since they'd left the fabric warehouse, she'd lost her perkiness and was pensive. Was it because Evelyn had declined to be a part of the wedding business?

What Evelyn hadn't told Audra and Heddy was that she *wanted* to be a part of it. Or rather, she wanted to want to be a part of it. That's why she'd accepted Audra's invitation to go with them today. But as Heddy swooned over the fabrics and Audra was in her element handling the business end, Evelyn realized she had no passion for the project. Sure, she thought it was a great idea, and sure, she could help—and would help if they needed her. But then she realized she didn't want to get involved in something just to be involved. She wanted to find something that made her glow like Catherine's Wedding Creations made Audra and Heddy glow.

She wanted to find her purpose. It was a prayer that snuck into her day with more and more frequency. *Lord, why am I here? What do You want me to do with my life?* Peerbaugh Place was part of it—Evelyn was sure of that—but it was as if the boardinghouse was a cake missing the frosting. And until Evelyn found out the flavor of that missing frosting, her life would only be partially full and fulfilling.

As they turned onto the highway leading to Carson Creek, she reached from the backseat and touched Audra on the shoulder. "I'm sorry if you're disappointed I don't want to be involved."

Audra shrugged. "That's your choice. I was just trying to be nice."

Evelyn fell back against the seat. Audra's tone made her insides boil. How could the word *nice* make her so mad? "I'm not a charity case, Audra. I don't need people finding me busywork."

Audra kept her eyes on the road. Heddy glanced back, then forward again. "No offense, Evelyn," Audra said. "I merely thought since Summer isn't with you during the day, and since you have so much time on your hands . . ."

"I'm not bored."

"Good."

"I have things to do."

A pause. "Good."

Evelyn hated feeling defensive. She was basically content in her life at Peerbaugh Place. True, the maintenance of the house didn't take more than an hour a day. True, she'd quit most of her committee work after Aaron died, wanting to start her life fresh. And true, she was searching for something meaningful. But Catherine's Wedding Creations wasn't it.

Then what was?

• • •

Piper was suspicious the moment Evelyn answered the phone. The smile that took over Evelyn's face was full of mischief. "Just a minute, please." She covered the receiver and whispered, "It's for you. It's Dr. Baladino."

Piper hated the pull in her stomach—a pull of anticipation. "Piper . . . take it."

She took the receiver along with a fresh breath. "Hi, Gregory." "Piper."

The way he stroked her name . . . but she didn't know what to say next. She'd been the one to call him—multiple times—days ago. The ball was in his court.

He volleyed. "Sorry to take so long getting back to you."

"Four days."

"I know."

"I'm sorry. That's the reason I left so many messages. I wanted to tell you that I'm sorry."

"I know."

His short answers were exasperating. "So? Do you forgive me?"

"Actually . . . that's the problem."

"What?"

"Forgiveness. You asking me for forgiveness. I've never . . . that's not something I've experienced before."

"No one's ever said they're sorry to you?"

"Sure. But no one's ever mentioned the forgiveness part."

"Maybe because that's the God part."

"I wouldn't know."

Oops . . . here we go again. But even as she regretted the challenge of their exchange, Piper thought of her mother's notion that maybe she was *the* one who could have an impact on Gregory's faith. *Lord, guide me here.* "Would you like to go out to dinner again? My treat?"

"Will you promise not to bring up any controversial issues?"

Piper hesitated, but only a moment. "No."

He laughed. "Then you're on. When?"

"How's tonight?"

"Eager, are we?"

Piper was glad he couldn't see her blush through the phone. "Hungry."

They made arrangements to meet at Adolpho's. When Piper hung up, she was greeted by Evelyn's grin. Might as well give in. "Yes, we're going out again."

"Tonight?"

"Tonight."

"Hmm."

Hmm indeed.

•   •   •

Gail hated to shop. And as a woman, that made her as odd as a man who hated sports. To her, shopping was a necessity, not entertainment. When she needed something, she went in, bought it, and left. One, two, three strikes and she was out of there.

But today she had a mission. She had to buy Jacob a birthday present, but she had no idea what to get him. Would it have been different if she was still at home? Was she trying to think of an extraordinary gift that compensated for her absence? Could *any* gift compensate for her absence?

She wandered to the foyer of Peerbaugh Place, coffee mug clutched beneath her chin, its rising steam matching the fog of her thoughts. She saw Mae across the street pinching off wilted mum heads. Only Mae would be working on her flowers in the dead of winter. She was wearing a royal blue sweater with snowflakes embroidered all over it. Quite conventional. Something Gail could imagine most women wearing. But on Mae, coupled with bright orange pants, it became a bold statement, a pronouncement of rebellion against winter, like those seasonal flags that could be seen flying from many houses. Gail had to smile. Only Mae could take the ordinary and make it extraordinary.

You need an extraordinary gift for your son . . .

Gail set down her mug, wrapped her long cardigan closed, went outside, and perched on the top step. "Hey, Mae."

Mae straightened from her mum-pinching position. "Hey, yourself." She headed across the street, carrying her bucket of blooms.

Gail met her halfway up the front walk.

Mae held up the bucket. "There has *got* to be some use for dead flower blooms. We've got a zillion of them over there."

Gail looked across the street. The entire front of the Ames home was lined with huge mum bushes. Brown, crisp mum bushes.

Mae shook the bucket. "I was wondering if they'd make good tea. If I crushed them and—"

"You'd drink them?"

She shrugged. "It's a thought." She lowered the bucket. "So what's up with you this fine day?"

"I need to go shopping."

"Don't sound so thrilled."

"I hate shopping."

Mae felt Gail's forehead. "You don't feel feverish."

"I know, I know. I should like to shop."

Mae nodded. "It's in the female handbook."

"But I don't."

"Then give *me* your shopping list. After years of practice, my sale radar is finely honed."

"I don't even care if things are on sale."

Mae feigned a heart attack. "Now I know you're sick. No self-respecting shopper pays full price."

Gail ran a toe along the edge of the front walk, making the edge of a snow pile fall. "Would you go with me? I need a birthday present for my son."

Mae did a one-eighty and ran back across the street. "Give me five minutes."

Gail hoped she wouldn't regret this.

* * *

Mae was perplexed. Gail had informed her she was a quick in-and-out shopper, yet she had proved to be anything but. They had tried the stores in Carson Creek, found nothing, and had driven all the way to Jackson to go to the mall. An hour later they were still looking for the perfect gift. As Gail meticulously read the package on some science-lab kit—which Mae was certain she would also reject—Mae found a chair along the wall. It was the tagalong chair, reserved for those innocents who were dragged along on a shopping spree, only to hit their weary wall eons before the shopper was satisfied.

Gail glanced over. "Uh-oh. Have I worn you out?"

Mae was tempted to pop up from the chair to defend her top-gun shopper status. But she was too tired. "Yes, you have."

Gail put the science lab back on the shelf. "I'm sorry. I can't find anything that feels completely right."

Mae rubbed her cramped right calf, then stopped as an idea formed. "Maybe any*thing* is the problem. Maybe you don't need to buy him anything. Any *thing*."

"You lost me."

Mae stood, needing space to illustrate. She swept an arm to encompass the store. "Answer this: Would Jacob's life be enriched through the ownership of any of these toys?"

"Enriched? Probably not. But he'd like them. Some of them. I just wish I could figure out which one."

Mae started to pace. "Forgive me for the food analogy I'm about to offer—seems I always go back to food; go figure—but I want you to consider something." She waited while a toddler and his mother walked between them. "Tell me about the most enjoyable, memorable dinner you've ever had."

"Mae, I don't think—"

"Exactly. Don't think, just remember. What dinner comes to mind?"

Gail looked to the ceiling. "I suppose a good one was a dinner Terry and I had on our honeymoon. It was in Cancún. We called room service, and they set a table on our balcony overlooking the

Gulf." Her face softened and she sighed. "We watched the sunset. It was glorious."

Mae was thrilled at her answer. The analogy was going to work perfectly. "So you liked the meal."

"I loved it."

"It was delicious?"

The question seemed to pull Gail out of a daze. "Hmm?"

"Was the food good?"

"Yes . . . I think so. Yes, I know it was."

"But that food memory is hazier than the sunset, than the balcony, than the ambiance and the company?"

"Sure. In a way the food was inconsequential."

Mae clapped her hands, sending a four-year-old running toward her mother. "Gracious game-o-rama, Gail, you've got it."

"Got what?"

Mae set a hand on a Tonka truck. "These toys are the food at your dinner. They appease the appetite and are wonderful, but they do not make the moment."

"What moment?"

"The moment that makes the memory. The memory moment you want to create for Jacob on his birthday."

"Memory moment."

"Exactly. I bet if you ask Jacob what birthday present he'd like best, he'd say he'd like to spend time with his mom."

Gail shook her head. "I doubt it."

"Doubt nothing. If you had a chance to recapture the memory moment of your sunset dinner with Terry on that balcony, would you?"

"I suppose."

Mae tossed her hands in the air. "Come on, woman! Give a little here. Admit I'm right."

Gail smiled. "If I do, will you stop making a scene?"

Mae looked around the store. Other customers stared back.

She'd obviously been heard. And seen. "If they can't take a little passionate concern from one sister to another, then they can go tangle a Slinky." Eyes looked away and Mae turned her attention back to Gail. "They heard me, but did you?"

"Yes, I heard you."

"Did you understand me? Did you get where I'm coming from, Sister Gail?"

"You want me to spend time with Jacob for his birthday. Do something special, just the two of us."

"Create a memory moment. You got it."

"Where would I go? What would we do?"

"You'll think of something." Mae wrapped an arm around Gail's shoulder and led her out of the store.

Phew.

●　　●　　●

Audra shoved her half-eaten plate of meat loaf aside in order to show Russell one of the sample books of fabric. "And these are the samples we'll show the customers."

"Oooh." Summer shimmied off her chair and took up residence between them. She touched the crepe de chine. "Soft."

"Which color do you like best?" Audra asked.

Summer thought a moment then pointed. "This one."

What was it with little girls and purple?

Russell flipped the pages quickly, obviously not compelled to ooh and aah. "How long will it take to get the fabric once the bride has chosen?"

"Just a few days. They have these in stock in Jackson."

"They extended you credit?" Russell asked.

"Yes—" The doorbell rang. Summer ran to answer it while Audra finished her sentence. "Yes, everything's set. We don't have a huge credit limit, but enough to get us start—"

"Hi, kid."

The buzz of Audra's nerves turned into a shiver. She bolted toward the door, yanking Summer behind her.

"Mommy!"

Audra looked to Russell. "Take her. Please."

Russell eyed Luke, then Audra. "Come on, chickie pie. Let's go in your room. I want to see what you did in school yesterday."

As they walked away, Luke draped himself against the door-jamb. He grinned wickedly and eyed Audra from head to toe—and back again. "So, Aud. Look at you."

Look at him. Luke was a pose in *GQ*. Suave, slick. And he still had the ability to command whatever space he occupied. She forced herself to concentrate. "How did you find me?"

"Hey, you called me. Or called my mother. I phoned here and talked with your hubby." He snickered. "Peerbaugh? What kind of last name is that?"

Audra took a breath, reminding herself not to get drawn into Luke's web of conversation where she would certainly be the loser. "It's *because* of my marriage that I contacted you."

"Sounds intriguing." He stopped leaning. "You going to ask me in?"

It was the last thing she wanted to do. But she had no choice, not if she wanted him to cooperate. She took a step back and he sauntered in, his eyes scanning the place. "Not much bigger than a bread box in here, Aud. I'd have thought you would have chosen someone who could provide for you better than this."

Audra's heart pounded. "We're getting a house soon." As soon as she said it, she hated herself for it. Why did Luke always put her on the defensive? *I've married just fine, thank you. Russell is the vice president of a bank and I'm starting my own business and—*

Luke moved to the table and helped himself to a piece of bread. He sat at Russell's place and flipped a page of the sample book. "What's this?"

Audra snatched it away. "Can we get to the point here?"

He sat back. "Whatever you say. You *are* in charge."

Yeah, right. She remained standing and took hold of the back of Summer's chair. "My husband wants to adopt Summer."

"He's not her dad."

"Sure he is."

Luke shook his head. "I'm her dad." He grinned and tried to reach for her hand. She pulled it away. "If it's money you're after, my mom's offer is void."

Why did he always think it was about money? "I don't want your money, Luke. And if I did, shouldn't it come from you, not your mother? You're supposed to be paying child support, you know."

He shrugged. "I'm without employment at the moment."

And Dorthea had said he was doing fine. . . . It was her turn to smile. "Did you get fired again?"

"It's not my—"

She laughed. "Oh, that's right. It's never your fault. Do you ever wonder about that, Luke? How the entire business community can be in a conspiracy against one laborer?"

He checked his manicure. "I have never been, and will never be, a *laborer*." He made it sound akin to being a criminal. "I've had some bad breaks."

She was already weary of it. "Whatever. Your not having a job is not the only reason I don't expect any money from you."

"Oh, good. More insults?"

Her mind dipped into one thought, then another, finding it hard to land. "If pointing out the existence of your other children is an insult, then yes."

"How—?"

Even as she pursued this tack, Audra wondered how she'd got there. "Where are your other children, Luke? And are there more than two—other than Summer?"

"Who's been blabbing?"

"Where are they?"

"They're around."

"Where, Luke? The girl must be seven now. How old is the boy?"

He bolted from the chair and headed to the door.

A wave of panic propelled her after him. Now was not the time for revenge. "Luke. Don't go. I'm sorry. I shouldn't have brought that up."

He stopped with a hand on the doorknob. "No, you shouldn't have."

Although she hated to do it, she touched his shoulder, hoping it would soften the moment. It did. He turned around. She was stunned to see actual hurt in his eyes and hurried to dispel it. "I want what's best for you, Luke. I want you to be happy." It was a stretch beyond her true feelings. "But more than that, I want Summer to be happy. And she *is* happy now. With us. We're a family."

He glance toward the bedroom. "I think about her sometimes."

She held in a rude response. "That's good. I'm glad."

He stood straighter. "I'm her father."

Audra took a breath. "You *fathered* her, Luke. Any man can be a biological father, but it takes someone special to be a real daddy. Someone who's around. Someone who loves her day in and day out. Someone like Russell. He loves her and she loves him. We would like you to relinquish your parental rights so he can adopt her. Legally."

His hands found his pockets. He bit his lower lip.

"You've never taken any interest in her," she added.

He sucked in a breath and his words were adamant. "I could."

Audra's insides welled with panic. Why had she said that last comment? It had only given him ideas. She went to the desk and retrieved the legal paper he needed to sign. She got a pen from her purse and held both toward him.

He looked at the paper, but did not take it. He opened the door.

"Luke . . . I need you to sign."

He went out to the hallway. "I'll think about it."

"But—"

"I'll think about it."

He walked away, leaving her standing in the hall looking after him. She went back inside, closed the door, and found she needed to lean against it.

Russell peeked his head out the door of Summer's room. Three feet lower, Summer's head appeared. "You all right, luv?" he asked.

She meant to say yes, nod yes, imply yes in some way. But the tears spoke the larger truth. She sank to the floor, and moments later found two sets of arms surrounding her, making it all better.

Family. There was nothing like it.

●　　　●　　　●

Audra tucked Summer into bed and kissed her. "There. All cozy?"

Summer nodded. "Daddy said that other man was my dad."

So simply said. So horribly complicated. Audra had no clue how much a five-year-old could—or should—understand. She smoothed the top of the sheet as it fell over the side of the bed. "It takes a man and a woman to create a child. He was the man."

"The dad."

"The man." Audra sighed and tried to put herself into the mind-set of her daughter. What exactly did Summer want to know? want to hear? "A child is supposed to be born out of the love between two people—a man and a woman. After they've committed themselves to each other in marriage."

"Like you and Daddy."

"Yes, like me and Daddy." Next came the hard part. "But

sometimes people get it wrong. They do the creating part before they set up the commitment part. Before the love has had time to be real and deep and—"

"Before it's had time to stick?"

Audra flicked the end of Summer's nose. "Well said, baby. The stickum wasn't there between Luke and me. And without the stickum a relationship doesn't work."

"That's why it's been just you and me."

"Right."

"Until Daddy came along and joined us."

Russell stepped in from the hall. "And I am the most stickiest person around." He made monster hands and crept toward the bed with a roar, causing Audra and Summer to cower in mock horror. "Here I am! Full of stickum! Watch out!"

Giggling was a glorious by-product of stickum.

•　　•　　•

Since Piper was going out with Gregory, Evelyn decided to spend the evening with Wayne and Wanda. Piper had said her mom was kind of down about the prognosis for her heart troubles, especially having to give up the RVing for a while. As nice as Piper's old apartment was, it was not home. They had no home. Not really.

Evelyn called first and Wayne said to come on over. She decided to make one of the recipes from the time they'd taken a cooking class together. A spinach dip with some crackers. Healthy fare.

When she got there she found Wayne setting up a Monopoly game on the kitchen table. "Welcome, Evelyn. We found ourselves in the mood for a friendly game of—"

Wanda came out from the kitchen. "Friendly nothing. I only agreed to play if you and I can conspire to keep him from getting Boardwalk and Park Place. Is it a deal?"

"Absolutely." Evelyn handed over the covered tray of dip and crackers. "Maybe we can lull him into making a mistake by feeding him."

"I do not lull. Ever."

Wanda took off the lid. "Yummy. And Wayne's right. As far as games go, he is tightly wound."

"I'll remember that."

"And he'll insist on being banker."

"Fine with me," Evelyn said.

They gathered food and drink and settled around the table. Wayne shook the dice next to his ear. "Let's see who goes first."

And it began. Three hours of Monopoly. Hotels, passing GO, and Last Chance cards. And Wayne did *not* gain control of Park Place and Boardwalk—Evelyn buying up one and letting Wanda buy the other. Evelyn found it interesting how she and Wanda played with compassion, mercy, and cooperation while Wayne played as if world finance was on the line. Was it a man-woman thing?

At twenty minutes after ten, Evelyn looked at her watch. No way was it that late. She stood, nearly toppling her money. "Oh, I'm so sorry. It's late. You need your rest and—"

Wanda looked at her own watch. "My, my, I haven't stayed up this late since the surgery."

Evelyn started putting her money back in the bank's coffers. "I'm so sorry to keep you up."

"No, it's wonderful," Wanda said. "You made me forget. You made me laugh. I needed that."

"Indeed you did," Wayne said. "Never mind the board. I'll clear that up later." He took the snack tray into the kitchen and put the lid on it. "Thanks so much for coming over, Evelyn."

She hurriedly got her coat and gave Wanda a hug good-bye.

"I'll see you to your car," Wayne said. He carried the tray for her and opened her car door.

She got behind the wheel. "I had a wonderful time, Wayne. Thanks—"

"No, Evelyn. Thank *you*." His face was serious. "I don't think you understand what a blessing you were to us tonight. We've had other friends stop by, and Piper is usually around, but they all seem to focus on Wanda's illness. You helped her forget it."

Evelyn realized she hadn't even thought about mentioning Wanda's condition. She figured if Wanda wanted to bring it up, she would. And since Wanda hadn't, Evelyn had taken her cue and spoken of other things. "It's no big deal, Wayne."

"It's a huge deal. You're good at this, at being around people in need. You seem to sense what they need and give it to them."

"Do I?"

He smiled. "You do. It's quite a gift, Evelyn." He moved to shut the door. "Have a safe trip home."

Evelyn didn't drive home. She flew. She had a gift.

She had a gift!

•   •   •

Piper loved the way Gregory spun his spaghetti on his fork and found the realization ridiculous. She was not sixteen, drooling over Mr. Big-Man-on-Campus. She was a mature, thirty-four-year-old. But still . . .

So far the dinner had gone smoothly. Gregory had accepted her apology and offered one of his own for being so blunt. Then they'd talked about college basketball, the kids Piper counseled at the high school, and the conflicts all the doctors had with the administration of the hospital. Normal conversation that delved into the problems and conflicts of life and yet didn't touch upon the one common solution to all those problems and conflicts.

During the salads, Piper had remained silent, reminding herself to be good and not sabotage the evening. But by the time they were halfway through their entrées, she was ready to burst with the strain of not mentioning faith.

She sighed and put down her fork.

"Uh-oh," he said. "Piper is frustrated."

"Well, actually . . ."

"I saw it starting when we were eating our salads."

He was amazing. "What gave me away?"

He touched the space between her eyebrows. "This dipped and the wrinkle deepened."

She pulled back an inch. "I don't appreciate you mentioning my wrinkles."

"Worry lines, then."

It did not sound any better. Piper hated that she was getting wrinkles. Her mother had always kidded that hers were caused by bringing up Piper. So it followed that Piper—who was husbandless and childless—should have a face free of those life lines.

Piper rubbed the space between her eyes, attempting to iron the offenders away. "I was trying to be good."

He laughed. "Being good is not supposed to be so stressful."

She tried to clarify. "I was trying to be good for you."

He set his fork down. "I want to make a deal with you. Do you agree?"

"I have to hear it first."

"I want you to quit putting on a front. Just be yourself and I'll be myself."

She eyed him suspiciously. "But it was my *self* that got me in trouble last week."

He returned her look. "I'd prefer dealing with the real Piper head-on rather than this contained, frustrated, ready-to-burst Piper who's skirting around every issue she's passionate about."

"But just because I'm passionate about things, doesn't mean you are."

"So be it."

"We may not agree."

"So be it."

"I may offend—"

He took her hand. "Piper, I would rather spend time with a real, honest, sincere, intelligent person who makes me think than a sickly sweet, yes-man who makes my mind turn to mush."

She smiled at him. "I hate mush."

"Me too."

"So we agree on something after all."

"What do you know."

She pushed her lasagna aside. Might as well get it over with. "So, are you ready?"

He raised an eyebrow. "Ready for what?"

"For a proclamation of who I am and what I'm passionate about?"

He pushed his plate aside and placed his hands, palms down on the table, bracing himself. He took a deep breath. "Okay. I'm ready."

"It's not *that* bad."

"I want to be prepared."

"Are you always so exasperating?"

"Hey, exasperating is part of the real me. Take it or leave it."

I'll take it. She pulled in a breath and began. "I am Piper Marie Wellington. I'm thirty-four years old, the only adopted child of Wanda and Wayne Wellington. I am a counselor at Carson Creek High School, a job which I alternately love and hate. I stay on because I love children and continue to hope I'll reach the ones who need to be reached—that I'll make a difference. I have never been married and would love to be married and have a passel of children. I don't understand why this hasn't happened, but am slowly coming to terms with the fact that it might not be God's will for my life."

"Not in the cards?"

She shook her head. "Not God's will. Which brings me to the passion of my life. His name is Jesus and I love Him so much it sometimes hurts physically. I continue to be in awe of the fact that He is God, that He came to earth as a man—feeling every emotion I've ever felt—and then took the rap for my sins on the cross. He died for my sins so I won't have to. And because I believe in Him, I know I'll spend eternity in heaven. It's a fact. A certainty in my life—because He said so."

She risked a glance at Gregory's face. He was smiling slightly, but otherwise showed no emotion. "Because He did all this for me, I have dedicated my life to Him one hundred percent—lock, stock, and garlic bread. My biggest prayer is that He gives me the ability to obey Him in every aspect of my life. More than anything I want Him to be proud of me, and the greatest moment of my life will be when I die, go to heaven, meet Him face-to-face, and hear Him say, 'Well done, My good and faithful servant.'" She let out the rest of her breath. "That's about it. My life is His. Everything I do and everything that happens to me has to be weighed against what He wants."

"What would Jesus do? That saying?"

"It's not a saying; it's a lifestyle, a scale upon which everything else is weighed."

"Sounds too simple."

She thought a moment. "It is, yet it isn't. With the Bible God's given us the guidebook for life. As with everything else, if you read the manual, things have a better chance of running smoothly and to their greatest capacity." She cocked her head. "It's like the word-processing program on my computer. It does a ton more than I ever tap into, and all that wealth of ability and knowledge is there if only I'd take the time to read the directions, try things out. Same with the Bible. Even though I've read it completely through many times, I continue to find new things it can do for me."

Gregory sat back, his arms crossed. "Many times, you say?"

"Five to be exact."

"Five sparkle stars for Piper."

"Thank you."

"Do you get extra points for that?"

"No. But I have gained a zillion extra points for living life better and to the fullest." She let her spine relax against the chair. "There, I'm done. And I'm glad to *not* see you sprinting for the door."

"I would, but I want to order dessert later."

"I see." She matched his cross-armed stance. "Your turn."

He reached for his plate, took his fork, and spun another bite of spaghetti around it, but never picked it up. "I don't think I'm going to be as good at this as you are."

"No grades, no scores from the judges. I promise." She reached over and touched the edge of his plate. "Just say it, Gregory. Tell me who you are."

He took a sip of water and cleared his throat. "I'm not nearly as complex as you. I've told you a bit about my childhood, so I won't go into that. I got an undergraduate degree at Northwestern, went to medical school at the University of Ohio, and have been working in Carson Creek for two years."

"Why here?"

"Why not here? I wanted to settle into a small-town setting where I could really get to know people one-on-one. There are plenty of doctors who want the big hospitals in the big cities. It's the small towns that need us." He shrugged. "So I came."

"My mother is glad you did."

He nodded, then fingered the stem of his water goblet. "I am thirty-three years old, I would also like to be married and have children. I am passionate about people and helping them, healing them."

Piper wanted to add that God did the ultimate healing, only using Gregory as a vehicle, but kept quiet. He was a good doctor—that was a fact.

"Until our little discussion the other night, I hadn't thought much about God and certainly never thought about Jesus. As far as I knew, He was a good man who died tragically."

"Triumphantly."

"So you say. Anyway, I think it's wonderful we did this. I find your views challenging and interesting. I'm not planning on being won over to your way of thinking, but I don't mind the exposure either." He grinned. "Not when it comes from a woman such as you."

Such as me? Her stomach did a silly flip. "You flatter me."

"I don't do so lightly. You, Piper Wellington, are unlike any woman I've met. You're strong yet naive, dedicated to your beliefs, pure—"

Piper laughed. "Pure?"

"Although we haven't talked about it, you give the impression you don't have a history with men."

"I beg your pardon?"

"I mean that in the best sense. So many women today—people today—address physical affection flippantly, as if it has no meaning. You don't. If you hadn't noticed, I haven't even tried to hold your hand."

She'd wondered about that. "Are my nonverbal cues that strong?"

He smiled. "Perhaps that, combined with the whole of you. It's hard to define. But I didn't want to breach something that was held sacred."

She was very impressed. "So you're a gentleman."

"Occasionally. With you."

Cryptic. Did that mean he *did* have a history with women?

"You're blushing."

She took a bite of her fettuccine. "Eat your spaghetti, Doctor. Eat your spaghetti."

Progress had been made. Was God proud?

Piper hoped so.

Search for the Lord and for His strength,
and keep on searching.

1 CHRONICLES 16:11

$\mathcal{E}$velyn paused at the kitchen door. "Are you sure you don't want to come to church with us, Gail? We're picking up Accosta— that friend of mine from the hospital—but there's still plenty of room."

Gail dunked her Cheerios with the back of a spoon. "No thanks. I've got things to do."

Before leaving, Evelyn and Piper exchanged a look that made Gail feel the appropriate amount of guilt. But she didn't let it bother her too much. She was used to it. Back when she was home with her family, Terry had pressured her to go to church with him and Jacob every single week.

Okay, so maybe *pressured* was too harsh a word. He'd asked, invited, cajoled, begged. In truth, it had gotten to the point where she might have said yes, but saying no had become such a habit that to agree to go was a matter of principle. To go would be to give in, to surrender. To lose. It would be a sign of weakness.

Besides, God didn't miss her. He was not interested in imperfect people like Gail. Maybe someday, when she was a better mom, a better worker, a better person, then she could go to Him and feel worthy. Until then, she would work hard to improve herself.

Trouble was, she hadn't made much progress in that regard. She was still stuck working at Burger Madness, still stuck in a boardinghouse, and still stuck feeling so . . . mediocre.

She shut off her brain and ate her cereal.

• • •

Gail arranged the last of the Sunday paper neatly on the kitchen table. She checked her watch. Terry and Jacob should be home from church by now. And if Gail didn't call them soon, Piper and Evelyn would also be home from church, and they would be all ears as Gail talked with her son. It was none of their business.

Yet it was business that needed to be attended to. Tuesday was Jacob's birthday, and Gail was intent on following Mae's advice to create a memory moment for him. But in order to do so, she had to call home, and with that call, she would risk having to talk with Terry.

But the reason for her reluctance was not what most people expected. She didn't hate talking to Terry because they argued— as so many separated couples argued—but because he was so *nice*. It was nearly impossible for Gail to hate him. And she wanted to hate him. How else could she justify her abandonment?

She headed to the phone, disgusted that her heart was beating like Morse code. She took the receiver along with a breath. *Please . . .*

Please what? Please who? Had she just prayed? Certainly not. She dialed. If only Jacob would answer—

"Hello?"

It was Terry. Why couldn't things ever play out easily? "Is Jacob there?"

"Gail. How are you?"

"Fine, fine. Is Jacob there?"

"Sure. We just got back from church."

Predictable, totally predictable.

"He's changing clothes. I'll get him for you in a minute. In the meantime, tell me how work's going. Did Lanigan get that big contract you were working on?"

"I really don't feel like talking about work, Terry. I told you I'm fine. That should be answer enough."

"An answer for a stranger. I'm your husband. I care about you. I love—"

"Don't."

His voice hardened. "Don't say *I love you?* Don't say that I—we—miss you? Those are words most people ache to hear. Why can't you hear them, Gail? Why can't you accept that they're true?"

"We've been through this."

"*You've* been through it!" She heard his sigh. When he spoke again, his voice was back to normal. "I will not give up on you, nor on us. You are loveable, Gail—when you let yourself be. And even if you soften up or ease up on yourself, Jacob and I will continue to love you. You can't do anything to make us *not* love you. Don't you understand that?"

No, she didn't. Love was a reward for good behavior. A reward for being perfect. It was not something given away for free. "I—"

"Here's Jacob."

"Hi, Mom!"

His voice was an elixir that warmed her entire being. "Hey, bud. Did you have fun in church?"

"We're doing a skit and I get to be Joseph."

Even I know that one. "Jesus' dad."

"No, the other Joseph."

"There was more than one?"

"Sure. I'm going to be the one who was the son of Jacob—the guy who has my name. Joseph was thrown into a well by his brothers and was a slave, but then he got to be the most powerful man in Egypt, right under the pharaoh, and then his brothers came back and didn't recognize him and—"

It sounded like a soap opera. "It's your birthday Tuesday."

"Are you coming to my party?"

Her stomach clenched. "Your dad is giving you a party?"

"Uh . . . actually, it's just for some boys at school. I wanted to invite Amanda Lewis, but Dad said she might feel dumb being the only girl, so it's just guys." He hesitated. "But you can come, Mom. You can be the only girl."

A wave of hurt broke over the top of her. She hesitated until it passed. "Actually, I was wondering if you'd like to come here some day next week and spend the evening with me. I could pick you up after school and we could go to dinner and—"

"Yes! When?"

"How about Wednesday?"

"I have choir. But how about tomorrow?"

Gail thought of her work schedule. She was supposed to work but she'd get someone to fill in. She had to. "Tomorrow it is."

"Let me ask Dad."

Oh, yes, do ask the king of the hill . . .

Jacob came back on the line. "Dad says it's fine. Pick me up at three, okay, Mom?"

"I'll be there."

"This is going to be so fun. I can't wait."

Gail hoped he wasn't just pretending to sound sincere.

•　　•　　•

Piper always paid attention during the sermon—Pastor Wilkins was a dynamic, inspiring speaker—but this morning she wished she were one who could daydream during church or sleep. Not because it was boring or inapplicable to her life, but because it was as if he (along with the really big *He*) was speaking directly to her.

It all started with prayer. After the service started, during their time for silent prayer, Piper prayed for Gregory. She found herself wishing he were by her side, sharing the passion of her life: Jesus. Then they had the Scripture reading from 2 Corinthians 6:14-15. The words clanged like an alarm in Piper's brain: *"Don't team up with those who are unbelievers. . . . How can a believer be a partner with an unbeliever?"*

A personal question surfaced: *How can you be a partner with Gregory? God says no.*

She almost tuned out the sermon, not wanting to hear what Pastor Wilkins had to say. But the truth seeker in her tuned in, needing to hear it—whatever it was. For what good would it do to ignore God's direction? If she went off on her own volition she'd just mess things up. It was a fact she'd proven many times.

Maybe it wouldn't be as bad as she feared. She knew the danger in teaming up with a nonbeliever—in marriage or business—was that such associations might cause her to compromise her faith. That wasn't a problem. If Gregory didn't know who she was and who she stood for after last night, then he was as dense as a slab of concrete.

And wasn't it like her mom had said? Jesus *wanted* believers to share their faith. They weren't supposed to shut themselves off in their safe little world and talk shop. They were supposed to carpet the world with the Good News. The trick was not to let the world soil the carpet. And Piper wouldn't allow that to happen. She wouldn't.

And yet all her rationalizing couldn't change the clear and concise statements of God: *"Don't team up with those who are unbelievers. . . . How can a believer be a partner with an unbeliever?"*

The Word of God entered Piper's psyche like an impenetrable phalanx of Greek soldiers, marching forward, shoulder to shoulder, shield butting against shield. Piper's desires and Piper's wants shot their sputtering arrows, but the army of God's Word did not waver, but calmly raised its shields, deflecting the attack as if it were as threatening as a pinprick.

Piper shook her head. The disappointment at not getting her own way made her want to pout and cry and demand and—

Evelyn leaned over. "What's wrong?"

Piper shook her head and let a tear fall onto her lap.

Nothing was wrong. Nothing and everything.

•　　•　　•

"Talk to me, Piper!"

Piper looked at Evelyn in the seat beside her and realized she hadn't said a word since church had let out. She'd made her way through the maze of the narthex, nodding her greetings, but not really seeing or acknowledging anyone. She'd been aware of Evelyn and Accosta hurrying after her as they made their way to the car.

Her friends deserved an explanation. "I'm breaking it off with Gregory."

"But you're just getting started. I thought you liked him."

Piper snickered. "Oh, I do like him; that's for sure. I haven't felt a chemistry like this since—" she tried to think—"since never. We have a connection that's very special."

"Then why would you break it off?" Accosta asked.

"Because God told me to."

She glanced at Evelyn in time to see a raised eyebrow. "And when did He tell you this?"

"During the sermon, during the Scripture reading: Don't team up with unbelievers. Don't partner with them." She sighed. "Don't date them with the intent of getting serious with them."

"I never heard that last part," Evelyn said.

"That's a Piper paraphrase."

"Perhaps you could help him find God. You helped me."

"That's the hard part. I could and I should. Just like I could and should with everyone I meet. But that doesn't mean I should bond with him, make a commitment to him. God draws the line there."

"Why?" Accosta asked.

"It could be dangerous to *my* faith, to *my* convictions."

"But no one has stronger faith and convictions than you do."

Piper pulled over to the side of the road, put the car in park, and faced her friends. "Don't say that."

"It's true. What's the word? You're a *bulwark* of the faith."

Piper shivered. "Talk like that will get me thinking too much of myself and then Satan can jump in and cause all sorts of havoc."

"Satan? How did he get into this conversation?"

Piper wasn't sure, but the uneasy feeling continued. And as she recognized it—and hated it—she realized how dangerous such a situation could really be. "No one is above temptation. I may seem strong to you now, but that's because my faith has never really been tested. I grew up with two godly parents; I have a career I love; I have awesome friends, sisters in Christ, who buoy me up and fill my soul. The one vulnerable aspect of my life is my singleness. It's my weakness, the soft underbelly that the armor of my faith doesn't quite cover." She gripped the steering wheel, knowing she was on the right track. "Satan knows that. And he'll attack me there. *I* know it. And God knows it too."

Piper suddenly ran her hands through her hair, yanking at handfuls, needing the tug and pull to solidify the moment. She looked at the ladies. They were pensive, concerned. "What is a common need in every human?"

It only took Evelyn a moment to answer. "To be loved?"

"Exactly. Ingrained in us is the desire to join, to bond, to couple. That's why God told us to be careful in this kind of situation. Because the desire for two to become one is *so* strong and deeply rooted, it can take over. We've all seen it a hundred times in person, in books, in movies. People falling head over heels in love, giddy with love, all logic leaving them, so consumed with being together that they will do anything, risk everything to be together. It's Romeo and Juliet played over and over, in a myriad of ways."

"You and Gregory aren't going to die for each other."

"Not now. But if we truly fell in love, we'd feel that way. We'd be willing to sacrifice anything for each other. Even our own lives. That goes with the territory of deep loving and of marriage."

"What's wrong with that?" Accosta asked.

Piper looked out the windshield. "That kind of intensity scares me as it excites me. If two people are on the same wavelength in *all* important areas of their lives, it can be an awesome, soul-lifting experience. But if they aren't . . . if I believe in God and have dedicated my life to Him and Gregory doesn't and hasn't, then at some point, there's going to be a waterloo. A battle for supremacy. And if God isn't first in both our lives, then He might lose. Even though I think my faith is strong, I might give *in* to Gregory—out of love for him. And I might give *up* Jesus, putting in His place a flesh-and-blood man who means well, but who's led me astray."

"Gregory wouldn't do that."

"He might. That's the danger. That's the unknown. That's why God—like a loving, caring, concerned Father—says, 'Don't do it, children. Don't go on that road. It's too dangerous.'"

Evelyn fingered the strap of her purse. "Aaron and I didn't share a faith and we were together over thirty years."

"But that's okay—I mean, that's sad, but that's not what God's talking about here. You were the same. You were equal in your non-faith."

"But I found faith recently. Does that mean if Aaron were still alive, I'd have to leave him like you're leaving Gregory?"

"No, no." Piper tried to remember the Bible passage from one of Paul's letters in the New Testament. "I remember reading that a believing spouse is supposed to stay with the unbelieving spouse, to be a shining example so that maybe they too can be won over to Christ. Marriage is sacred. That vow is not to be broken—or taken lightly. Or unequally, in my case. I am to be equally yoked or not yoked at all."

Evelyn let out a breath. "Wow."

"Yeah."

"When are you going to tell him?"

"Soon. Actually, I *will* give him a chance. We'll talk about it all. For more than anything I want him to turn to God—with or without me in his life. But until he does, our relationship can't go any further. I can't let it. I could fall in love with him and *that* would really hurt."

"You're so brave," Accosta said.

Piper laughed and put the car into drive. "If I were brave I'd do what I wanted to do, no matter what God wanted. *That* would be the essence of bravery."

"Or stupidity."

"God is slow to anger and He loves us, but we're also told not to test Him. I think I'll do things His way. In the long run it's easier."

"I don't know about that," Evelyn said. "But it's probably best."

Piper was counting on it.

• • •

"Hello, ladies," Heddy said. "Table for three?"

Piper pointed toward the window. "A table with a view, if you please."

Heddy laughed. A view of the street was better than a view of the kitchen, but hardly made for inspirational dining. She led them to the table and handed them menus. "The Sunday special is fried chicken, mashed potatoes, corn bread, and green beans with almonds."

Piper glanced at Evelyn and handed the menus back. "Yes. Two, please."

Heddy nodded to Accosta, remembering that Evelyn had said the older woman had to watch her diet. "Don't let them influence you, Mrs. Rand. There *are* a few healthy things on the menu."

"I'm sure I'll find something yummy *and* healthy," Accosta said.

Heddy saw another couple come in the door. "If you'll excuse me, I'll send Connie over. I'll try to come chat later." She left them and put on her best hostess smile for the new customers who—

She stopped, bumping into the edge of a table. *Carlos!*

When he saw her, his eyes flitted wildly and his feet shuffled as if he wanted to run.

You'd better run, mister. But leave the money you bilked from me behind.

The woman accompanying Carlos tugged at his arm. "What's wrong with you?"

"Uh . . . maybe we should go someplace else."

The woman straightened her shoulders, her gray suit falling crisply over her frame. The gold around her neck and at her ears had to be real. And the rings . . . she tugged at one of the earrings. "There is no place else. The man fixing our tire said so. And if you even dare suggest that we *grab* a hot dog and *zap* it in the microwave at his service station, then you don't know me at all." She seemed to notice Heddy for the first time and offered a condescending smile—and a final whisper in Carlos's direction. "This is fine dining compared to that."

She nudged Carlos and he spurted out, "Two, please." He looked at Heddy then to the floor.

So that's how he was going to play it. How dare he pretend they didn't know each other. After all they'd . . . shared.

The woman interrupted Heddy's thoughts. "Nonsmoking," she added.

Heddy became aware of the diner. She was not alone and this was not the place for a confrontation. She found her voice. "Right this way, please."

"Come, Carlos."

Those two words, said with the air of a mistress calling a dog to heel, told Heddy the story. Carlos had found himself another sugar mama.

As she told them the special, Heddy took the opportunity to study the woman. She was probably in her fifties, though good grooming and good skin made her look ten years younger. She oozed money and social status. And the way she was careful not to touch the top of the table with her carefully manicured hands earned her the title of snob.

"Your waitress will be right with you," she finally said and turned away. She felt Carlos's eyes on her, but did not look back. Although she couldn't risk a careful study of him, from what she'd seen their breakup had *not* aversely affected his good looks and *had* affected the cut and quality of his suit. She wondered what had brought them to Carson Creek, all dressed up . . .

"Excuse me, ma'am?"

A family had come in and she hadn't even noticed. She sat them at the last table in the corner. She busied herself, taking customers' payments, and pouring water and coffee to help out the waitresses. She refilled Piper's coffee.

"Who's that over there?" Piper asked. She pointed to Carlos and his mark.

Heddy glanced but looked back quickly. She felt heat in her cheeks.

"You know them?" Evelyn whispered.

Heddy shrugged. "I need to make the coffee rounds."

She knew they knew she was lying. She wasn't good at it. No, indeed, heart-on-her-sleeve Heddy was an open emotional book. But she had a secret. Having it and being confronted with it now made her feel like a balloon about to pop.

If only she could quit wanting to look at him . . .

They'd been engaged and would have been married if she hadn't caught him pocketing the money she'd given him to start the new business—their new business. When she'd confronted him, he'd had a slick explanation for everything. In fact, his excuses had been so smooth and so good—at least to her naive ears—that she'd come to the conclusion her only option was to cut her losses and move on.

She'd gone to the police, but since she'd written the checks to Carlos, since they'd been engaged, since he was so good at what he did, there was nothing they could do to avenge her own stupidity.

But here he was, probably doing it again.

When Carlos reached across the table and took the woman's hand, when he gave her the smile that Heddy had once called her own, she was assaulted with an idea. A mission.

She had to stop him.

"Ma'am, you gave me too much change here."

Heddy thanked the customer for his honesty and recounted the change. As soon as the task was done, her mind ran to meet its goal. How should she do it?

Get her alone. Tell her the truth about him.

But how? The diner was full and even if it had been empty, there was no private place to have such a talk. And what about Carlos? There was no reason for him to leave the woman's side. Except maybe to go to the rest—

To her surprise, Carlos stood, excused himself, and disappeared down the short hall to the rest rooms.

There was no time to think or consider any longer. And even

as Heddy's feet found themselves walking toward the woman, her mind was screaming, *What are you doing? This is none of your business!*

But it *was* her business. One victim to another potential victim. *Help me, God*, she prayed as she neared the table.

The woman looked up. "Yes?"

"May I join you a moment?" Heddy didn't wait for an answer but sat quickly in Carlos's chair.

"Well. This is highly unusual," the woman said.

"I'm afraid it's only going to get more unusual." Heddy took a breath. "Carlos is a con man after your money."

The woman sat back. "Excuse me?"

Heddy glanced over her shoulder toward the rest room. She only had moments. "I was engaged to him. We were going to start a business. He stole all my savings. I don't want him to do the same thing to you."

The woman's expression was very undignified. "I . . . he . . . we were going to start—"

The woman looked up as Carlos appeared. "Get out of my seat."

Heddy was glad to comply. She skittered toward the front counter.

But the woman wasn't so willing to let her go. She called after her, "Are you telling me the truth? Is he really a con man?"

All conversation died. Heddy turned around slowly, hating all the eyes upon her. The woman must have had some suspicions of her own or she would have consulted Carlos first. "Yes, it's true."

Carlos glared at Heddy. "It is not!" He turned to the woman. "Whatever she told you . . . she's a liar."

"Did you get engaged to her and then rob her of her savings?"

Two dozen eyebrows rose.

Carlos slid into his seat, lowering his voice for the woman's ears alone. He tried to touch her hand.

She yanked it away and stood. "I should have known. You said all the right words, did all the right things. My lawyer will be contacting you." She tossed her napkin on the table and strode out.

Carlos ran after her, stopping only a moment to point a finger in Heddy's face. "You had no right."

Heddy found an untapped store of strength and looked him in the eyes. "No, *you* had no right. You have no right to prey on women who are looking for love and companionship. You're a crook, Carlos. I didn't have the power or clout behind me, but apparently your newest ladylove does. I say you deserve whatever she can dish out."

He did a quick scan of the diner, and obviously not finding any support, he left the building, running after the woman.

The diner erupted in applause. Ruby came out of the kitchen and wrapped an arm around Heddy's shoulders. "Way to go, little lady. I didn't think you had it in you."

People swarmed around Heddy, and she was overcome with relief. They were on *her* side? They didn't think badly of her for being stupid enough to fall for someone like Carlos?

She began to cry and found Ruby's shoulder.

Ruby laughed. "Sake-a-day, honey. You think we haven't all been conned in the game of love once or twice?"

There were nods all around.

"Get back to eating, folks. And I'll get back to cooking. Carson Creek has had its excitement for the day."

Evelyn and Piper joined Heddy at the front counter. Piper handed her a tissue. She blew her nose.

"That was quite a display," Piper said.

"You were very brave," Evelyn said. "To tell that woman the truth. To save her from experiencing the same thing." She shook her head. "I'm proud of you."

"Me too," Piper said.

Would wonders never cease?

•   •   •

"Hell-o-o." After finishing lunch at Ruby's and dropping Evelyn and Accosta off, Piper unlocked the door to her apartment. She found her mother putting a lid on a coffee cake.

She took it off. "Want a piece?"

Piper eyed it appreciatively. Her Aunt Betty's coffee cake. "Love to, but better not. Evelyn and I had lunch at Ruby's." Her mother didn't know Heddy so she decided not to mention Heddy's ruckus. She took a seat on the stool. "Where's Dad?"

"He had to go back to church for some building-committee meeting."

"I didn't know he was on the building committee."

"He wasn't. Couldn't be, since we were on the road. But now that we're stuck here . . ."

"Mom . . ."

Her mother's face lit up. "Actually, we *are* heading out. Tomorrow."

"What?"

"Now don't get your feathers flocked. We're just going for a short spin. A few days. We're not going far." She ran a hand along the lid of the pan. "We need to go."

"But should you go?" Piper asked. "What does Gregory say about all this?"

"He says it's fine. As long as I'm smart this time and pay attention to what my body is trying to tell me." She set the pan aside. "Speaking of Gregory . . . how did your dinner go?"

For once, Piper appreciated her mother's segue. "I wanted to talk to you about that."

"Really?"

Piper nodded and cocked her head toward the living room. "Let's get comfortable."

"Uh-oh. Another serious conversation in the living room. I initiated the last one, and now it's your turn."

"Do you mind?"

Her mother reached across the counter and chucked her under the chin. "Of course not. I'm just giving you a hard time. Let's sit."

They got comfortable at opposite ends of the couch.

"Okay. Fess up," her mother said. "What's the problem between you and Gregory?"

"I could fall in love with him."

"Is that a bad thing?"

"That's what I'm asking you." Piper hugged a couch pillow. "Last night I declared myself to him."

"Declared?"

"I told him who I was, that I was committed to Jesus. All of it."

Her mother looked relieved, then leaned closer. "How did he react?"

"He said he appreciated me sharing with him, but made sure I knew he wasn't planning on being won over to my way of thinking."

She sat back. "Oh."

Piper sighed. "It wasn't that I was expecting him to ask me more about Jesus—I was hoping, maybe, but not expecting—but it doesn't sound promising. He's pretty set in his ways. Content with his life."

"Contentment makes it hard."

"Exactly. We both know most people come to Jesus when they're searching for something better in their lives."

"Yet you said you could love him."

"Which is the problem. He's charming, handsome, and we can talk about anything. He's a good man. An honest man. I'm glad he isn't pretending to be won over to my faith. I wouldn't want that."

Her mother smiled. "But sometimes a little less honesty makes us feel better?"

"That's the trouble with genuine people, they are so . . . sincere it's hard not to like them."

"Love them."

Piper shrugged. "I was reading the Bible and Paul says a believer shouldn't partner with an unbeliever."

Her mother nodded. "You shouldn't become unequally yoked."

"Right."

"First Corinthians seven."

Piper shook her head. "Second Corinthians six."

"There too. Here, we'll look it up." Her mother got up to retrieve a Bible and took a seat close to Piper. She flipped the pages. "Here. First Corinthians seven, starting with verse six." She held the Bible so Piper could read with her. "'This is only my suggestion. It's not meant to be an absolute rule. I wish everyone could get along without marrying, just as I do. But we are not all the same. God gives some the gift of marriage, and to others He gives the gift of singleness.'"

"I wish it *felt* more like a gift," Piper said.

"Let's keep reading. I know there's a passage that mentions single women specifically." They read in silence a few moments; then her mother said, "This is it: 'In everything you do, I want you to be free from the concerns of this life. . . . A woman who is no longer married or has never been married can be more devoted to the Lord in body and in spirit, while the married woman must be concerned about her earthly responsibilities and how to please her husband. I am saying this for your benefit, not to place restrictions on you. I want you to do whatever will help you serve the Lord best, with as few distractions as possible. . . . So the person who marries does well, and the person who doesn't marry does even better.'" She closed the Bible. "See?"

Piper did see. And she didn't like what she saw. For to follow the Word of God would mean sacrifice. And hadn't she *been* sacrificing? She was thirty-four years old. Most of her friends were married with children. Yet she was alone. Oh, yes, she was free to serve the Lord without distractions. But love and companionship weren't distractions. Were they? And what kind of serving was she doing that was so great anyway? It wasn't as if she was—

She felt her mom's hand on her knee. "You're disappointed."

A snicker escaped. "Uh, yes."

"You want a loophole."

"A big one."

Her mother nodded and they shared a moment of silence. "Maybe you could just be friends with him?"

It was a nice thought—and Piper gave it a moment's consideration before saying, "I can't. It would be like standing two feet from the waves of the ocean and not being allowed to wade in, experience the feel of the water on my feet."

"Feel the pull of the undertow?"

Her voice broke. "Maybe. But isn't that part of love?"

"It most certainly is. Which is exactly why God's instructions are for our own good. He *knows* the danger—and excitement— that can come with a relationship. He's trying to protect us."

"Sure. So He can have our full attention." Piper put a hand to her mouth. "Oh . . . that sounded terrible. As if I begrudge God my commitment." She let her head fall into her hands and bent over, wanting to fold in on herself, make her awful nature disappear. "Why would He want me to serve Him anyway? My attitude is wrong, all wrong." She felt the old desire raise its hand, demanding attention. She sat up and faced her mother. "I want to be married! I want children. I want a life like everyone else has. What's so wrong with that?"

She fell into her mother's arms. Her mother. *A* mother. Something she would never be.

•   •   •

When Piper came into Peerbaugh Place, she found Evelyn dusting the dining room.

"How's your mom?" Evelyn asked.

Piper hung up her coat and headed upstairs. "Fine."

"Gregory called."

She froze on the second step. *No, I can't talk to him* warred with *Get it over with*. She turned to Evelyn. "When did he call?"

"Just a few minutes ago. He said something about going ice skating out at Miller's Pond and getting hot chocolate."

It sounded wonderful. A perfect winter afternoon.

She'd fix that quick enough.

•   •   •

Piper looked out the window as the patchwork of snow-covered hills slid by. *This is the last time I'll ever be with him. This is the last time I'll ever hear his voice, or be in his car, or smell the scent of his aftershave, or—*

"You're quiet."

Piper burst into tears, surprising both of them. Gregory quickly pulled off the highway onto a gravel side road, easing the car to a stop. He shut off the engine and angled toward her. "Out with it," he said.

She hid her face behind her hands and shook her head.

He gently pulled a hand free, peeking at her. "Piper. What's got you so upset?"

She battled the impulse to fling open the car door and run away, stumble through a field until she tripped into the cold snow, where she could continue her dramatic cry. It would make a great scene in a movie, but what purpose would it serve?

With a final swipe to her tears, she forced her hands into her lap. She took a deep breath. "Sorry about this."

"I don't want your apology. I want your explanation."

How should she word it? "The good news is also the bad news."

"Sounds intriguing."

"I think I'm falling in love with you."

His smile was genuine, then faded. "How is that bad?"

"My faith says I can't do that."

"Can't do what?"

"Can't fall in love with you."

"Because . . . ?"

"You're an unbeliever. You don't believe in God, much less Jesus."

"So what? I'm sure there are a lot of things we don't agree on."

"But this is *the* thing. It's a nonnegotiable thing."

He moved back an inch. "So I have no say in this? You're just giving me an ultimatum?"

"I didn't give you an ultimatum."

He crossed his arms. "Sure you did. Either I believe in God and Jesus like you do, or you're out of my life."

He'd hit it square on. But it sounded so cold, so . . . dumb.

His head shook back and forth. "You'd give up us—and the possibility of us. If this is the kind of direction your God gives, I'd rather stay far away from Him."

Piper's soul screamed at the same time her voice did. "No!" *Lord! This can't be what You want. By my action I'm pushing him farther away from You!* "You can't do that. He wants you to be as close to Him as I am."

"But until I make that decision, He's going to take away a person I've come to love."

You love me?

"You know what, Piper? I have an ultimatum for you. Until

you can be a person who can take off her blinders and be a part of this world and see it clearly, I want nothing to do with you."

He turned on the car and did a three-point turn, heading back to town. A cloud of gravel dust marked their journey back to where they started.

Separate and alone.

• • •

Evelyn heard the door open and caught a glimpse of Piper as she ran up the stairs. "Piper? Back so soon?"

Piper's door slammed.

Evelyn and Heddy exchanged a look.

"Are you going to see what's wrong?"

Evelyn looked up the stairs. The closed door spoke of Piper's preference. "I think I'll let her be alone a little bit."

Chicken.

• • •

Piper buried her face in the pillow, only easing up when she needed air. Then she punched the pillow. Hard.

It's not fair, Lord! It's not fair!

She tossed the pillow on the floor and glared at it. She had just thrown away a relationship with a wonderful man—maybe her last chance to ever be married and have a family. Her biological clock was ticking so loudly the whole world could hear. And now God had forced her to give it all up. Throw it away.

I didn't force you. You chose.

"Some choice I had," she said aloud.

You chose. And I will honor your choice.

Her laugh was thick with sarcasm. Honor. What honor could measure up to the companionship and love of a good man? What honor could relieve the ache of empty arms that had so much love to give a child?

Piper got on her knees and raised her fists to the ceiling. "I'm giving up everything for You!"

But as her words ricocheted off the ceiling and hit her in the face, her fists released and her body crumbled onto the bed. She pulled her legs beneath her and touched her forehead to the bedspread, her hands flat on its surface. She bowed before the King, totally humbled. Totally appalled at her words. Totally supplicant before Him.

She dared not look up, but spoke into the bed. "I'm so sorry, so sorry. This is nothing compared to what You gave up on the cross. You sacrificed Your Son."

Just as I'm asking you to sacrifice the son you might have had someday.

She was stunned to silence. God understood her sacrifice. He was not asking her to do anything He hadn't done Himself. Felt Himself.

Piper remembered some words of King David: *"I cannot present burnt offerings to the Lord my God that have cost me nothing."* Anything of worth had a cost. A big cost. And if the cost for Piper further dedicating her life to the Lord was this big, then it must mean . . .

She sat upright. "I have worth. I have worth in the eyes of the Lord."

She dried her tears and took a moment to weigh her words, let them sink in.

Yes.

It *was* enough.

It was more than enough.

●　　●　　●

Audra had always dreamed of her own home and now . . .

She, Russell, and Summer had spent the afternoon going through open houses. They'd found a few prospects, but nothing that was perfect for them as a family and for Catherine's Wedding Creations.

Until this one. It was a newer two-story that had a den in the front that could be turned into the business office. It boasted a backyard with trees, empty flower urns by the door, red shutters, and a huge pin oak crowning the front. Inside, lots of closet space and a walk-in pantry.

The real-estate agent had been discreet after the initial showing, letting them walk through the house a second time on their own, letting them dream and talk. Summer had already claimed the bedroom that was painted yellow and had a window seat. They made their way back to the living room.

"What do you think?" Russell asked.

Audra let her eyes graze the fireplace. Her mind's eye placed two wing chairs in front of it, one for her and one for Russell. She smelled fresh popcorn and imagined Summer lying on her tummy between them, reading a book by firelight. Perfection.

She fingered the lace curtains, pulling one aside to look—

Luke was outside! Sitting in his car, staring at the house!

"Russell!"

He came running.

"Look!"

"What's he doing out there?"

"He followed us." She looked toward Summer, who was chatting with the Realtor in the kitchen, twirling on a bar stool. "I don't like this."

"He wouldn't snatch her, would he?" Russell asked.

She'd never thought of that, but she quickly discounted it. Luke was a jerk, but he wasn't violent. She shook her head. "He didn't want anything to do with her until last night when he wouldn't sign the papers. I can't imagine—"

"He only wants her now because I want her."

She glanced at the door. "I need him to sign, Russell. I can't have him following us around, stalking us. I can't live in fear of him inserting himself into Summer's life."

Russell edged the curtain aside, taking another look. He let the lace fall. "What do you want me to do? Go out there and confront him?"

"Actually, I'd like a knight in shining armor."

"I accept the role, but in the end, I'm not sure that will help us accomplish our goal."

But it sure would make me feel better. "So you're a reluctant knight?"

"A prudent one."

Audra sighed. Why did Luke have to show up now and ruin the excitement and thrill of finding the perfect house? She couldn't let him ruin this day for them. She opened the front door.

"Where are you going?" Russell asked.

She was already halfway down the walk.

Luke got out of his car. He smiled.

She did not smile back. She stopped, leaving the car between them. "Why are you following us?"

"I wasn't—"

She shook her head. "You were. You did not just happen by. This was intentional."

Caught in the lie, his face hardened. "I want to see my kid."

"She doesn't want to see you."

"That's a lie."

Audra was caught off guard. Was it a lie? Did Summer want to see Luke? She realized she'd never asked, never made it an option. She forced herself to change mental gears. "Luke, face it. The only reason you're showing interest now is because I contacted you and reminded you of your daughter. This newfound attention does not stem from any deep-seated need to be a part of her life, but is a novelty, something new to capture your interest."

"You make me sound as shallow as a pan."

Though he was serious, she had to smile. "You're not shallow; you just have other things going in your life right now that do not include the time, money, and emotional fortitude needed to be a father."

Luke nodded toward Russell, who stood in the open doorway of the house. "But he does."

"He does." Audra wished she had the papers with her. Maybe she should carry them around with her at all times. . . .

Suddenly Summer appeared in the doorway. She launched herself toward Russell and grabbed his waist, yelling, "Daddy!"

Oh, baby, why did you show up now?

Luke's face lit up at the sight of the little girl, and Audra knew that all the progress she'd just made had been negated. She didn't know what to do. What to say.

So she hurried back up the front steps and herded her family inside, away from the man who might shadow their future.

The Lord is good and does what is right;
He shows the proper path to those who go astray.
He leads the humble in what is right,
teaching them His way.

PSALM 25:8-9

*P*iper couldn't sleep. She tiptoed downstairs in the dark, avoiding the creak in the center of the third step from the top. She winced at the brightness when she flipped the kitchen light and stumbled to fill the teapot with water.

She took a seat at the table to wait for the water to heat. She straightened the salt and pepper shakers, then gave the lazy Susan a spin. *Round and round it goes and where it stops, nobody knows.*

It wasn't that she was changing her mind about breaking up with Gregory. No sir, the time she'd spent communing with the Lord in her room had been profound, and the decision she made there, intact. She would not renege on her dedication to the Lord's will.

But that didn't make it easy, and God never implied that it would be. People often had the misconception that once you gave your life to Him, the road would run smoothly, with no jigs, jogs, or ruts. Not so. Piper knew each jig, jog, and rut was there for a reason, to make the upcoming road even smoother. Faith was a lifelong process, not just a onetime decision.

She heard the water rattle the teapot, getting hot and stirred up within its confined space. She knew the feeling and knew she'd better prepare herself for all the heat she'd get about her decision. People wouldn't understand. They'd try to stir her up—even with the best of intentions. She had to be strong, remain firm. Be vigilant.

The image of a sheepdog standing guard over a flock came to mind. She had to be like that dog, staying focused on her goal, doing what she'd been told to do, being obedient to the Master. How does it look to the other dogs when the vigilant one is sitting so long, doing its duty? Does it look like fun? Does it look like a waste of time? Do they make fun of the dog because all it gets to do is guard the dumb sheep who don't know enough to keep themselves out of a ditch?

But what about that dog as seen through the eyes of the Master? It is being obedient to the command it has received. It may not understand why it has to stay and watch and wait, but the trust involved makes the Master proud. And that is worth more than the approval of any mortal.

The bottom line was, did Piper believe there was a more worthy calling, a better plan outside the will of the Master?

The answer was no.

And so she would stay and be still and watch and wait. None of them particularly fun aspects of life, but all worthwhile in the long—

The kitchen door opened and Heddy appeared. "Piper. I saw the light and thought someone had left it on."

Heddy was dressed for work at Ruby's. Piper glanced at the clock: 5:30. "You heading to work?"

"Um-hmm. Is that hot water?"

"I'll get the mugs."

They made their tea and took seats at the table. "How are you doing after the Carlos incident?" Piper asked.

"Fine, I guess. It was such a shock seeing him again."

"He conned you out of all your money?"

"That's why I'm here at a boardinghouse. I have nothing left. What money he didn't take I used to pay the bills we'd incurred to start our business. After paying those, there wasn't enough for rent on my apartment so I had to move."

Piper thought of the small furnished room that was now Heddy's. "What happened to your things?"

Heddy attempted to sip her tea but it was still too hot. "Had a garage sale with most of it. Put a few things in storage. It's amazing what you don't need when you set your mind to it."

Piper understood. She still was amazed that she didn't miss the things back at her apartment.

Heddy continued. "It gave me a chance to start fresh. And that's what I'm doing."

"So you're content here?"

Heddy shrugged. "For now. I'd still like to be married and have a family."

Piper snickered. "Join the club."

Heddy peered at Piper over her mug. "How's the love of your life?"

The image of the vigilant sheepdog reappeared. *Stand firm, Piper.* "I broke up with him yesterday."

"Why?"

How to put it in twenty-five words or less . . . "Gregory doesn't share my faith and the Bible instructs us not to become 'unequally yoked.'" She let her shrug say the rest.

"So you gave up Gregory for Jesus?"

Piper smiled. "Yes, I guess I did."

"I'm impressed."

Piper raised her eyebrows.

271

"Shouldn't I be?"

"Maybe. But I was expecting some comment about how dumb I am. Some argument against it."

"I am not one to offer advice about men."

Piper laughed. "No, I guess you're not."

"And I do admire your dedication to Him—to God. I'd like . . ."

The unspoken words set off Piper's radar. "You'd like to what?"

Heddy turned her mug in a circle. "I'd like to have what you have. God-wise. I'd like to be so in tune with Him that I do the right thing, no matter what."

"We all would. And you can have what I have. Anyone can."

"How?"

Piper was once again amazed at how God slipped these sharing opportunities into her life unannounced. She leaned closer. "You admit you need a Savior. You admit you need Jesus to be that Savior. You tell Him so. He's ready and waiting for you to do just that."

"Do I have to say something specific?"

"Not at all. It's the attitude and the ache for Him that God responds to, not any exact words."

Heddy fingered the handle of the mug. "I do need Him. I've done so many things wrong in my life, and I need Him to forgive me for all that."

"He'll do it. He's already paid the price on the cross. He died for our sins—past, present, and future."

"That's nice to know."

"You bet it is."

Heddy let go of her mug and rubbed her hands on her thighs. "So I just say it? Now?"

"Now is always good."

And so Heddy Wainsworth and Piper Wellington became true sisters in Christ that morning over a cup of tea. And the heavens celebrated.

• • •

Heddy drove to work, but she wished she had the day off. She felt like running through a park, swinging on a swing, lying in the snow to look at the heavens.

The heavens where her Savior lived.

And yet Piper had told her that Jesus lived within her now. Through the Holy Spirit. He was her ever-present counselor, anytime she needed Him. The comfort in that knowledge went beyond words.

Heddy pulled into the alley behind Ruby's and parked. Yes, indeed, she would love to have the day off, but it was also imperative she show up at work to reinforce her presence after yesterday's Carlos outburst. Ruby and the other employees had been very supportive, so Heddy felt a responsibility to be worthy of that support.

She went inside and hung up her coat. Mel Hibbs, one of the daily regulars, was coming in the front door.

"Morning, Mel. You're too early. You know we don't open for another fifteen minutes."

Mel's eyes scanned the diner. Ruby and the cooks were in the back, and the two waitresses were chatting in the far corner. He angled his back to them and shoved his hands in his pockets. His voice slithered across the space between them. "Don't give me a hard time, Heddy. I came in early to see you."

Heddy had the feeling a beetle was climbing up her spine. "Me?"

His smile was crooked. "I was in here yesterday when that classy lady was in here with your ex—her new gigolo."

Heddy slid behind the counter. "He wasn't her gigolo."

"But he was yours, right?"

She swallowed. "He was no such thing. We dated. We were close."

Mel traced the edge of the counter, his finger coming perilously close to Heddy's midsection. She took a step back.

Ruby came out of the kitchen. "Mel? 'Lantic Ocean, can't you wait? We're getting your biscuits done as fast as we can."

He waved a hand. "No hurry, Rube."

Before Ruby disappeared into the kitchen, she locked eyes with Heddy. Heddy tried to send an SOS, but it must not have been received, because Ruby withdrew.

If only I could get to the door. But Mel stood between her and escape. And maybe she was overreacting. Maybe Mel was just making conversation. Maybe—

Mel touched her arm. "Let's you and me go out, Heddy. I may not be as slick as your young stud, but I have my moments and—"

Heddy pushed past him toward the door. She had it open when Ruby's voice called out, "Hold it right there."

She froze. Mel froze. Ruby sauntered out of the kitchen, wiping her hands on her fresh apron. She pointed at Heddy. "You, over there. Go help Mary and Becca fill saltshakers."

Ruby waited until Heddy was in the safe care of the waitresses in the corner. Then she strolled toward Mel as if she were a confident sheriff confronting an outlaw. Her index finger rose and zeroed in on his chest, where it poked. Hard.

"And you, Mr. Hibbs, this is what I say to you: back off, bucko."

Mel's eyes grew wide.

Ruby continued. "Our Heddy is a good woman, a woman of virtue. She did a courageous thing yesterday, exposing that man for what he was before he could add another victim to his trophy case. If she's guilty of anything, it's trusting too much. Which is one thing she is *not* going to do with you."

"I didn't do nothing."

"But you tried. And that's just as bad." She put her hand on his shoulder, whipped him around, and pushed him toward the door. "Go eat your biscuits and gravy somewhere else today, Mel."

"You're throwing me out?"

"For today. If I were a stronger woman, I'd throw you out for good, but for some reason my forgiving nature won't do that."

He opened the door and gave Heddy one last look. Ruby grabbed his arm. "But know this, Mel Hibbs. If you ever proposition one of my employees again or speak suggestively to them in any way, I will raise the hood of your truck and pour a day's worth of gravy on the engine. Put that through your carburetor and chug it awhile."

He made a face and left. Heddy hurried toward her. "Ruby! Thank you. I didn't know what to—"

It was her turn to be on the receiving end of Ruby's finger. "I'll tell you what to do, Ms. Wainsworth. You learn from your mistakes and wait for the right man to come along. Me and my Bobby were married forty-eight years before he passed, and though he wasn't the fanciest talker or the prettiest looker, he was the man meant for me. Wait for that man and don't settle for less." The finger skimmed her nose. "You hear me?"

"I hear you."

"Good. Now get back to work."

Heddy marveled at the fact that she'd experienced two saviors that morning.

•   •   •

Audra's assignment for the day was twofold: forget about Luke and go back to the pin-oak house for one last look. She and Russell had talked that morning, and Russell had agreed they could make an offer on it if she gave it her final approval.

She had just gotten Summer off to school and was putting on

her shoes, when there was a knock on the door. Never would she have guessed who was on the other side.

Dorthea Ottington. Luke's mother.

She pulled back from the peephole as Dorthea offered a second set of knocks. Audra opened the door.

"I knew you were in there."

Nice to see you too, Dorthea. "How did you know?"

"Are you going to ask me in?"

Audra stepped aside. She did not close the door. "Actually, I'm on my way out."

Dorthea took three steps inside, did a quick scan of the apartment, and apparently deemed it too mundane for comment. "This won't take long. I just wanted you to know that I am on the way to meet Luke at the bank, to take care of this thing once and for all."

"This *thing*?"

"I do *not* approve of my son's notion to be a part of your daughter's life."

"His daughter too." *Why did I say that?*

"Yes, yes. Whatever. Anyway, I wanted to tell you that I am your ally in this. Nothing would please me more than to have my son move on and forget—" She stopped herself.

"Forget he ever had a daughter? Forget he ever met me?"

Dorthea walked out of the apartment into the hallway. "Don't act as if you don't wish the very same thing."

Audra planted her feet. "My daughter is the joy of my life, and I do not regret having her or meeting your son. I have learned from my immature choices and built on them. But honestly, I would never wish them canceled out. They helped me be me."

Dorthea clapped softly. "Well, well. Little Audra Taylor has gained some gumption in her mature years, hasn't she?"

It was the perfect cue. Audra took hold of the door. "Yes, I believe I have. Good-bye, Mrs. Ottington."

"But—"

She closed the door on her. *But nothing.* Audra had Dorthea as an ally. It was yet to be determined if that was a good thing or a bad thing. But the stitch in her stomach spoke of the latter.

She suddenly remembered some of Dorthea's words: *"I am on the way to meet Luke at the bank, to take care of this thing once and for all."*

The bank? Russell's bank?

A dozen questions demanded attention and none of them had the chance to be answered. What was Dorthea planning to do?

Audra grabbed the phone.

●   ●   ●

Russell hung up the phone after talking with Audra. It didn't make sense. Why would Luke and his mother be meeting at a bank—maybe *his* bank?

Russell typed in Dorthea Ottington's name on his computer. Nothing. He put in Luke's name. There was one account with three hundred dollars in it. It had been opened the day before. Was that timing significant?

He made a call to Lynda, who handled new accounts. "When did Luke Ottington come in and—"

"Oh, *he* didn't come in, Mr. Peerbaugh. She did. The mother."

"Mrs. Ottington opened the account for her son?"

"Is there something wrong?"

"No, no. Thank you, Lynda."

Russell turned his chair so he could see out the front of the bank. He needed time to think.

He didn't get it. For there in the parking lot was Luke, talking with an older woman. His mother?

It was evident the mother had arrived first and caught Luke

before he could completely exit his car. He stood behind the opened car door, and Russell couldn't help but think it was a shield between them.

The mother was arguing, making sweeping gestures with one hand, while in the other she held an envelope. This seemed to be the object of contention. She pressed it toward Luke. He shook his head and pushed it away. She persisted and got in his face, pointing a finger.

Luke looked away, but otherwise made no move. Obviously, he'd been put in such a situation before and had found the avoidance of eye contact with his mother to be his best defense.

When Mrs. Ottington slapped the top of Luke's black Camaro, he looked at her. And even from a distance, Russell could see the contempt and hatred in his eyes.

Only then did Luke take the envelope. That accomplished, the mother got in her car and drove away.

Luke just stood there, staring at the envelope. His shoulders sagged. His head seemed too heavy for his neck.

Russell tensed, as he would if he were witnessing someone in trouble. He had rarely seen such despair, such utter collapse of will. It was horrid. *God, please help him!*

Finally Luke stirred, but his movements were those of a zombie. He closed his door and walked toward the entrance of the bank, the envelope hanging from his hand like a weight.

Russell scrambled to the door of his office. The sight of Luke was mesmerizing, like watching a convict walk the green mile to his death. Luke ignored the chirpy "Good morning" from the receptionist and slogged his way to one of the tellers.

"I have a deposit."

Russell's suspicions were confirmed. On impulse, he hurried to Luke's side. "Morning, Luke."

Luke turned; it took his eyes a moment to register. It was like he was drugged, not with anything medicinal but with the drug of despair, defeat, and surrender.

"Hi." His voice had no life.

Russell put a hand to his back. "Why don't you come with me a moment, Luke." He nodded to the teller. "I'll take care of Mr. Ottington, Susan."

Luke let himself be led into Russell's office. He sank into the guest chair like a being without a spine.

Now, confronted with the man who could thwart Russell's wish to become Summer's legal father, Russell didn't know what to do and wasn't sure why he had instigated the actions that had led from there to here.

Sure he did. He may not be a religious man, but he was a compassionate man. And no man with any honor could let Luke continue. Until the bribe was deposited, it could still be given back. Russell suddenly realized he could use a little help. And so he found himself praying, *God, help me help this man. Help me do the right thing.*

In the inaction and silence of the room, Luke seemed to wake up from his daze. He looked around. He stood. "I gotta go."

"No, stay. Please."

Luke sat back down.

Where to begin? "I saw you and your mother . . ."

Luke looked past him to the front window, then down to the envelope in his hand.

"Is she paying you off? bribing you?"

Luke shrugged. "She's being my mother."

"She's done this before?"

"Money talks."

"You don't have to take it."

His laugh was bitter.

"You could stand up to her. Make your own choices for your life."

"Oh, yeah, as if I have such a good track record with choices."

Russell leaned forward. "So you agree with your mother's choices?"

Another shrug. "What difference does it make? At least it keeps me in spending money."

They both looked at the envelope. "Can I ask . . . how much is she paying you?"

"Ten thousand."

"Ten thousand to . . . ?"

"Forget about Summer. Let you adopt her."

Russell was forced back in his chair by his own expulsion of breath. Audra had mentioned that Dorthea had called herself their ally, but this . . . "Don't take it."

Luke blinked. "What?"

Even as Russell was thinking, *What am I doing?* he found himself saying, "Don't take the money. Stand up to her."

"But you want to adopt Summer."

Russell looked squarely at Luke. "Yes, I do." He ran his hands over his face, trying to force logic into his pores.

"By giving me that advice you're hurting—"

"I know. But I think there's a larger issue here." He pointed to the window. "Seeing your mother run over you like that . . . seeing you give in. You've got to take control, Luke. Make decisions based on values, logic, and what's right. You can't let money make decisions for you."

"But you work in a bank. You make money decisions all the time."

"But they are logical, hopefully wise decisions. They are not decisions that stem from blackmail or bribes."

"So you think I shouldn't sign away my parental rights to Summer?"

Ah. The big question. "Actually, I think you should. From every standpoint I can think of, I believe you should let Summer go."

"So you can adopt her."

Russell opened his mouth to give one answer, but decided on another. "So I can adopt her. And love her."

"I love—I could love her."

"Maybe."

"Maybe I need someone to love. Maybe loving her would get my life in shape. Get me to pull things together."

Russell shook his head adamantly. "A child is not a guinea pig. She should not be used as a self-help tool. You can't go into a parental relationship thinking about what *you* will get out of it."

"So you have no selfish thoughts about becoming an instant daddy?"

"Sure I do. Being around Summer, being a parent to Summer, makes me feel better about myself. She makes me happy. But the point is, to be a good parent I always have to be thinking of her happiness and well-being first. I'm willing to do that."

"Are you?"

"I am. The question is, are you?"

Luke held the envelope in both hands. "I need the money."

The blatancy of Luke's statement made Russell's altruism fade. He'd had enough. He pointed toward the tellers. "Then deposit your mother's money and be on your way."

"But I also like the idea of standing up to her."

Russell was drained. He picked up a pen. "Do what you want, Luke. Lecture over."

Luke left his office. And though Russell pretended not to look, he watched as Luke headed toward the teller. Then he saw Luke change his mind and walk away, envelope in hand.

Way to go, Luke!

Then it hit him.

What have I done?

• • •

A half hour later, Russell received a phone call from Dorthea Ottington. Had Luke confronted his mother so soon? He braced himself for a tirade.

"Mr. Peerbaugh, I wanted you to know that my son was just in your bank and deposited a rather large sum of money in an account that *I* opened for him."

"Is that so?"

"It most certainly is. It's important that you know I chose *your* bank on purpose, as evidence of my goodwill in this child situation. I want to work with you and Audra to resolve this issue so my son's life can get back to normal."

"I see." What else could he say?

"'I see'? That's it? That's all the reaction I get?"

"Thank you?"

"That's better."

"Is there anything else I can do for you, Mrs. Ottington?"

A hesitation. "No, nothing. I believe I have everything under control."

Wanna bet?

• • •

Gail hated the nervous knots in her stomach. Why was she nervous about picking her own son up at school?

She pulled into the drive-up lane, scoping out the kids gathered outside. It had been a long time since she'd last done this. Back when things were normal, when she still lived at home. *Normal. Home.* Nice words. Unobtainable words.

Jacob saw her, waved, and ran to the car. He climbed in with a flurry of movement and fresh air. A heaving of the backpack. A slammed door. His smile. "Hi, Mom."

"Hey, bud."

"Where we going to eat?"

"You hungry so soon?"

"I'm always hungry."

She'd forgotten. "I was thinking maybe we'd have your birthday dinner at that Italian place in Jackson, over near the—"

"Can we go to Burger Madness?"

Her heart stopped and she nearly slammed on the brake. No way. This couldn't be happening. "Why?"

"Dad won't go there because he says the food's not healthy."

Which is one reason I felt safe getting a job there . . . "Why do you think I'll feed you junk food?"

His grin was contagious. "Won't you? For my birthday? They have a special on their Triple Madness Burger."

"Since when can you eat a triple burger?"

"Since I'm ten."

"You're not ten until tomorrow."

"Ah, come on, Mom. I won't waste any food. Not one single fry."

"But I'd planned on a fancier—"

"I don't want fancy. I want good food. Besides, eating fast will give us more time to do fun stuff. What stuff are we going to do?"

She was glad she'd planned ahead. "I thought we'd go to the planetarium. They have a new laser show."

He nodded, his bangs bouncing against his forehead. "Cool. Let's go eat."

"But—"

"Mom . . ."

She was doomed.

●　　●　　●

Gail considered going through the drive-through, but knew eating in the car wouldn't be appropriate for a birthday dinner. They *had* to go in. The jig was up—in two directions. Jacob didn't know she worked at Burger Madness, and Burger Madness didn't know she had a son. Joy.

As Jacob burst through the entry door, Gail steeled herself. She only had seconds.

"Hey, Gail," said Tom, as he wiped off tables. "I thought you couldn't work tonight."

Jacob looked at Tom, then at Gail. She put a hand on the back of his neck. "I couldn't. Can't. Tom, this is my son, Jacob. It's his birthday. Jacob, this is Tom. I work with him."

"Hey, hey, birthday boy," Tom said. "You too old for balloons?"

Jacob didn't answer.

Gail steered them away. "See you later, Tom."

Jacob sidled out of her grasp and stepped to the side to face her. "You work here?"

There wasn't enough breath in her lungs for more than, "I do."

"Since when?"

"A few weeks." She didn't want to go into the firing. She didn't *need* to go into the firing, did she?

Jacob looked around the restaurant as if seeing it for the first time. Then he nodded. "Can I see where they make the fries?"

He could have anything he wanted.

•　　•　　•

"Ha! Got it!" With an extravagant motion, Mae put the corner piece of the sky in the puzzle. "I'm good. I'm so good."

Collier pointed to a hole in the picture of a barnyard. "If you're so good, find *this* piece that has a tiny bit of red in one corner."

"What shape?"

"Soup bowl."

"Gotcha."

Mae loved how they'd given puzzle pieces distinguishing names: There were two-handled soup bowls, gingerbread men, sniffing dog-left and sniffing dog-right, and the beloved edge pieces.

She *was* good. She found the piece and placed it in the hole.

Collier sat back. "No fair. You're supposed to give it to me and I get to put it in."

"Uh-uh," Mae said. "Them that find it, get to place it."

"Who says?"

"It's a common rule. Ask anyone."

"You make up your own rules."

"Absolutely. If I don't, somebody else—"

There was a knock on the door. Mae got up and peeked through the window. "It's Gail." She opened the door. Gail sailed inside, glowing. "My, my. What's got your beacon beaming?"

Gail nodded to Collier. "I just had a memory moment with my son. Thanks to you."

Mae patted a chair. "Sit. Tell me all about it."

As Gail talked, Mae thanked God that things had worked out. She loved to give advice, but sometimes it was hard to rein in the Mae advice, and purify it into good God advice. This time, she'd been successful.

Collier got up. "That calls for a celebration. How about a piece of carrot cake? I just—"

"No, no thank you," Gail said, also getting up. "Jacob and I had a Triple Madness Burger–eating contest, so I doubt I'll eat for a week." She moved toward the door. "I need to be going but I just had to tell you how things went." She hesitated a moment, then gave Mae an awkward hug. "Thank you, Mae."

"No problem."

Mae shut the door after her and bounced her way back to the puzzle table.

"Warning! Warning!" Collier said. "If your head gets any bigger, I'll have to move into the guest room."

"Gracious goose," Mae said, taking her seat, "let me enjoy my victory."

Collier reset his reading glasses on his nose and looked for the next piece. "Oh, I will. But I also want you to consider the phrase 'physician, heal thyself.'"

"What's that supposed to mean?"

"Think about it."

Mae didn't want to think about it. "Just tell me."

He took off his glasses. "Your advice helped Gail connect with her son; that 'memory moment' term you gave her."

"It's good advice. It worked."

"Then I advise you to use it on yourself. Create a few memory moments between you and your kids."

"It's not the same. My kids aren't kids anymore. My darlings are grown."

"It's exactly the same. You haven't seen them since our wedding."

She let her fingers walk up his arm. "I've been busy."

"Not that busy."

She withdrew her hand with a pout. "Ringo and Starr are independent people. They don't need—or want—a mom interfering in their lives."

"I'm not talking about interfering. I'm talking about a visit now and then. Have them come down for Easter."

"That's almost three months away."

"So?"

"I don't plan my life that far ahead."

"Maybe you should."

"I'm sure they have other plans."

"Oh, I get it. You're *hoping* they have other plans."

She swatted his arm. "You act like I don't want to see my own children."

"No, *you* act like you don't want to see your own children."

He had a point. "I'll think about it."

He put his glasses back on. "Do more than think, dear wife. Act."

●　　●　　●

Mae finished applying the oatmeal-sandalwood mud mask to her face, washed her hands, grabbed an afghan, and lay down on the bed—upside down, her feet elevated on the pillow for improved circulation. She cozied in and closed her eyes. But they would not remain closed. Though her body was in the relax mode, her mind was jumping about, working up quite a sweat.

"You act like you don't want to see your own children."

Collier's words were true. That *is* how she'd acted the last few years. But was it the truth? If she wanted to see her dear darlings, wouldn't she go out of her way to arrange it? make it happen?

What was wrong with her?

She looked at the flickering jasmine candle on the bed stand. Its flame helped her eyes and thoughts to focus. She'd never been a touchy-feely mom. No "koochy-koo" or "Do *we* need to go potty?" for Mae. She'd spoken to her children like she spoke to everyone else. Direct and to the point. She always figured if you treated them with respect, as if they had a working brain in their heads, then they'd be more likely to use that brain.

And it had worked. Both her children were independent and successful. Ringo had been a roadie with a rock band for three years, handling the intricacies of the sound system, and Starr was working for a publishing house in New York. Neither was married, though Starr was engaged to and living with a broker named Ted. After a few years with very little contact, last

Mother's Day, at Evelyn's urging, Mae had called Starr. They'd kept in sporadic contact since then, and both Mae's children had come to their wedding. They seemed to like Collier, and he, them. Maybe Collier wanted them for Easter because he'd never had children.

She sat upright, her shoulders leaving the warmth of the afghan. That's it. Collier wanted them to be a closer family for his own benefit. He'd shared his regret at putting his career above marriage. He'd traveled worldwide with his company, fixing pipelines in places from Saudi Arabia to Panama. A wife and family hadn't fit into that mix.

Maybe she needed to ask the children home for him.

Maybe you need to ask the children home for you. For them.

She sank back onto the bed, soaking in the truth. And then another truth hit her: She was good at giving advice to other people but not so good at applying it to her own life.

Physician, heal thyself indeed. She was a hypocrite.

She covered her eyes, feeling the tears come. She proceeded to have a memory moment.

With God.

•   •   •

Sketchpads, fabric swatches, and dolls littered Heddy's bed. She set the pencil down, leaned against the headboard, and rubbed her eyes. She'd worked all evening on the sketches of the dresses, and only had one ready for the catalog. But things were progressing nicely. By the end of the week they'd be ready to go to the printer. The rest of the fabric was being delivered Friday, and they'd get busy making the sample dresses. So much work, but so rewarding too.

Pretty soon she'd be able to quit her job at Ruby's.

The memory of Mel Hibbs returned. Heddy had made so

many mistakes in her life, mostly involving her relationships with men. Any thought of the future brought with it the fear she'd make another mistake. And another. It was easy to say she'd be smarter next time, but when the man-woman chemistry got going, things happened. If only she could have some assurance she wouldn't blow it again.

You do. Because I'm here.

The words were an inner whisper, yet they startled her. *Could it be . . . ?*

Needing to hold on to something of substance, she reached for the Bible she'd just bought. The weight of it in her hands was both comforting and daunting. So many pages. So many words. Where to start?

But with each breath a calm settled in. An assurance. It was His book, so certainly He'd do the leading.

She stroked the cover and took a deep breath. *If a willing heart means anything, God . . . I'm ready.*

Heddy Wainsworth and God had a nice conversation.

There are three things that will endure—
faith, hope, and love—and the greatest of these is love.

1 CORINTHIANS 13:13

$\mathcal{M}$ae was at the phone first thing. That alone was an accomplishment, because Mae was not a morning person and *first thing* usually involved nothing more taxing than getting a cup of tea or reading the paper. But after her talk with God amid the facial mask the night before, she knew she had to follow through as soon as she woke.

Besides, if she got up early enough and made the phone call before Collier got up, she might not have to endure his I-told-you-so smirk. He may be a dear man, but his smirk could make her teeth grind glass.

So she tiptoed downstairs, put a coat over her muumuu, slipped her feet into her clogs, grabbed a quilt from the couch, and took the phone out on the porch, away from the prying ears of her too-wise husband. She settled onto the swing and pulled a slip of paper with her children's phone numbers out of her pocket. She realized how pitiful that was—that she didn't have their numbers memorized. But she had never been one to clutter her mind with numbers. At least that was her excuse.

She dialed Starr's number and got the swing moving. Starr answered and Mae's stomach flipped.

"Hey, Starr baby."

"Mother?"

"Does someone else call you Starr baby?"

"No, it's just . . . what's wrong?"

Mae deserved that. "Not a thing. I was calling to see how you were doing, plus I wanted to ask you down for Easter."

Starr laughed. "You? Make a holiday dinner?"

"Are you disparaging my cooking abilities?"

"Let's just say that Swanson and Smack Ramen were familiar names around the Fitzpatrick household."

Mae decided it was safer to concede the point than to argue that her cooking abilities had improved—and gotten healthier. "Collier is an excellent cook."

"Glad to hear it."

"So, will you come?"

"Are you calling Ringo?"

"Of course."

"Do you have his new cell number? He's in Indianapolis today, on the last city of the tour. You need to call him." There was an urgency in Starr's voice.

"I planned on it, but what's up?"

"Just call him. I know he'll come."

"You *know*?"

"Just ask him, Mother. I'll call him too. In fact, why wait until Easter? How about this weekend?"

"This week—?"

"Why not? Ringo's finishing up his tour tonight. He's available. I'm sure he is. I'll call him and make sure. Is that all right?"

"Sure, I guess so." This was all very odd.

"Super. Gotta get to work. Thanks for the call, Mother. Ted and I will be there, probably late Saturday. Don't worry about dinner."

Mae hung up, confused. Easter was less than three months away. Since when was that not soon enough? She called Ringo's cell, but as soon as it started ringing, she realized people in the concert business were not early risers. She was about to hang up when he answered.

"Yeah?"

"Ringo, I'm so sorry to wake you. I forgot; I didn't think—"

"Mom?"

She told him why she was calling.

"This weekend? I'll be there."

This was *way* too easy. What was going on? "You okay, Son?"

He cleared his throat. "Yeah, I'm fine. Real good even. We'll see you Saturday."

"We?"

"Uh . . . me and Starr."

Hmm.

●　　●　　●

Russell tossed a pen across his desk. If the president of the bank came in and asked him to prove that two plus two equaled four, Russell would have greeted him with a blank stare.

Ever since Luke had left the bank yesterday, Russell had expected a phone call informing him that Luke had stood up to his mother and would indeed be a part of Summer's life. And by the way, thanks for the good advice.

Or—even worse—Russell expected a call from Audra, furious and confused. *"Whatever were you thinking, Russell? Whose side are you on?"*

He was on the side of "right." He'd done an unselfish thing, helped another human being to try and better his life, to become stronger. No matter that the consequences of that advice might inconvenience his own family.

Inconvenience? How about destroy?

His nerves threatened to burst through his skin. He stood, grabbing his coat. He had to get out of there. Walk, move, run—

The intercom buzzed. "Mr. Peerbaugh?"

He paused with one arm in the sleeve. "Yes?"

"Call on line three. It's a Mr. Loughgrin from A-1 Realty."

The house.

Russell returned to his chair. "Russell Peerbaugh here."

"Good news, Mr. Peerbaugh. The owners took your offer. The house is yours."

Russell extracted his arm from the coat and tossed it aside. "We got it?"

"They agreed to all the conditions and you can have immediate possession. Just name a day."

They finished discussing the details and Russell hung up. He leaned back in his chair, relieved. At least he had *some* good news to tell Audra. A little padding for the bad news to come?

He grabbed his coat for the second time. Yes, indeed, he had to get out of there. He had some padding to do.

●   ●   ●

Russell found Audra at the computer, putting the finishing touches on the wedding-catalog layout.

"What are you doing home in the middle of the morning?" she asked.

He pulled a package from behind his back. He knew he earned extra points for gifts. He was glad he'd thought of it.

"What's this for?"

"You'll see."

She ripped off the paper and opened the box. A "Home Sweet Home" plaque greeted her. She looked up at Russell.

He nodded. "We got it."

She shot out of the chair and into his arms.

Russell deemed the padding successful.

●　　●　　●

Audra stood alone in the entryway of their apartment. Russell had just left to go back to work, leaving Audra to start planning their move. He'd handle the money part of the house purchase, but it would be up to her to organize and pack and plan.

Audra spread her arms wide. "We're getting a house!"

Before her words could sink into the carpet, her practical side took over and began making lists. In a way it was good that she'd been so busy planning Catherine's Wedding Creations that she hadn't had time to completely unpack all the boxes she and Summer had brought with them when they'd moved into Russell's apartment. She had a head start.

She grabbed her shoes. The first order of business was to go see their new house, take some notes, and really look at it with the new eyes of an owner. *An owner!* What furniture went where, what would be stored in what cupboard. Lists, organizing, and planning. Audra was in her element.

She had just detoured to the phone to call the Realtor when there was a knock on the door. Russell must have forgotten something.

It wasn't Russell.

"Luke."

"Hi, Audra."

Her first thought was one of relief—at least Summer was at school. "What do you want? I was just on my way out."

"Can I come in?"

She pulled the door a few more inches toward closed. "I don't think that would be appropriate."

He nodded once, then stuffed his hands in his pockets. He

shifted his weight from right to left, then back again. What was going on? This was not the usual smug, confident Luke.

"I would rather say this in a more appropriate setting, but I guess this will have to do."

Audra's jaw clenched. "Say what?"

He looked to the floor. "I want to be a part of Summer's life."

Speechless, she held the door for support.

"I realize I haven't done right by her. And I want to change all that and be there for her."

Audra finally snapped out of her shock. "But we don't want you *there*. She and I have been perfectly happy with you out of our lives. We even managed without the child support you should have been paying."

"I'll pay—"

She shook her head so hard, her hair flapped against the door. "The only reason I contacted you at all was to get you to sign away the parental rights you so obviously didn't care about anyway, so that Summer's true daddy could make it legal. Russell cares for Summer from his heart. All this sudden attention from you is just a whim. It will pass and then where will Summer's heart be? Broken? Because her birth father pretended he wanted to know her but really didn't?"

"I wouldn't do that."

"You would. I know you."

His hands came out of his pockets and a finger pointed at her. "You don't know me. I've changed."

She snickered. "No you haven't. You're still the immature pawn of your mother and—" Suddenly, something didn't fit. "You can't be a part of Summer's life. Your mother is totally against it."

He straightened his shoulders. "She still is."

It took Audra a moment to grasp the implications. "You stood up to your mother?"

"I did. Thanks to your husband."

It took Audra a few more moments to truly hear what he'd said. But the words made no sense. "Thanks to Russell?"

"He was the one who urged me to stand up to my mom."

"No, no. You must be mistaken."

"No mistake about it," Luke said. "I was at his bank, ready to deposit a ten-thousand-dollar bribe from my mother when your husband stopped me."

Audra put her hands to her ears. It couldn't be true. Russell wouldn't work against her. Against them.

"He's a good guy, your husband. I know by helping me he might have hurt himself but he—"

Audra waved Luke's words away. She couldn't hear any more. His words floated like oil on the pool of everything she knew and believed. If he kept talking, his words ran the risk of being stirred in, mixed with what she knew was true.

"Get out of here." She began shutting the door, forcing him to step back into the hall.

"But, Audra—"

"Go!"

She slammed the door, locked it, and leaned against it. She stared at the ceiling. This couldn't be happening. White was black, and black was white.

And Russell had betrayed her.

She grabbed her coat and keys.

•   •   •

Russell happened to see Audra's car drive into the bank parking lot and he knew—he *knew*—this was not a social visit. The way she slammed the door and marched toward the bank's entrance made him want to run and hide in the men's room.

But he held fast. He took a moment to close his eyes and take a few good breaths. He clasped his hands across his midsection, wishing the hand-to-hand contact would calm his inner shaking. Their first real argument was about to begin. An inevitable milestone. How would it play out? Who would win?

Would anyone win?

Audra did not do her usual stop at the door to his office nor offer him her usual *tap-tap*, "Hi. Are you busy?" She stormed in, shut his door, and sat across from him. He had never seen Audra seethe. Until now.

"You don't deny it?"

It was an odd way for the conversation to begin. No preamble. No explanation. But maybe none was needed.

"I do not."

"But to help him is to hurt us."

"I knew that."

"And you chose to do it anyway?"

Russell knew that what he wanted to say next would sound too convenient, almost as if he was saying it because he knew the words would placate her. But as the truth, it had to be said. He kept his hands clasped, but moved them to the desk and leaned toward her. "I prayed about it, luv. I actually prayed."

The aura that had shrouded Audra since she'd walked in evaporated before his eyes. Their eyes met and held. She bit her lower lip. "You prayed?"

His hands unclasped and raked through his hair. "I didn't plan on it. I didn't plan on any of it. But you should have seen him, Audra." He pointed to the window overlooking the parking lot. "I watched the way his mother badgered him and offered him an envelope—a bribe to do things her way. She was scary enough, but what scared me more was the way he stood out there after she'd driven away. He was a broken man. A man without hope. He was a lifeless shell that could walk and talk but had nothing inside that gave him any substance or meaning."

Russell was appalled when he felt tears form. He hesitated,

willing them away. "When Luke came into the bank and headed for a teller to deposit that money, I knew that to let him follow through with it would make me an accomplice to him selling his soul."

A tear escaped. Russell flicked it away and tried to get control.

"Is that when you prayed?" Audra's voice was soft.

All he could do was nod. He looked through the glass wall of his office and wished it were solid so the whole bank couldn't witness his weakness. Audra must have seen the direction of his gaze because she got out of her chair and positioned herself at his side, blocking all view of him from the outside world.

With her so close, there was nothing he wanted to do more than pull her into his arms and accept her comfort, her anger, her presence.

But that was not possible, and so instead, he put a hand on his desk within inches of her. She skimmed her fingers along the edge of the desk until her fingertips touched his. He looked up at her, aching for her forgiveness and understanding.

She returned his gaze. Finally, she spoke. "We'll work it out."

He nodded. "I love you, Audra. And I love Summer."

She nodded. "You're a good man, Russell Peerbaugh."

At that moment, no words meant more to him.

●　　●　　●

With newfound confidence because of her decorating success in the basement, Evelyn decided to tackle the sunroom. The dark paneling some earlier Peerbaugh had installed was horrible. Hardly sunny. She'd been watching do-it-yourself channels on TV and had seen paneling painted successfully. So she headed to the hardware store again. Although Optimistic Yellow would certainly have been appropriate for a sunroom, she was thinking about green or maybe even a blue. A cool color to compensate for the sun that sometimes made the room *too* warm.

She'd planned to handle the decision alone, but when she drove by Mae's Silver-Wear, she decided another opinion wouldn't hurt. And Mae could always be counted on for an opinion. She pulled up front and went inside.

Mae was sitting behind the counter, her feet up, a sketchpad in her lap. "Hidy-ho, Evie. What are you up to?"

Evelyn told her. "Care to come along and give me some advice?"

Mae's feet hit the floor with a *plop-plop*. "That's the nice thing about having one's own business." She retrieved a "Back in a jiff" sign from behind the counter, hung it in the door, locked up, and they were off.

If there had been twenty-five shades of yellow, there were even more shades of green and blue. Oh dear. And then Mae got sidetracked looking at oranges.

"I'm not an orange person, Mae," Evelyn finally said. "That's your color."

"Actually chartreuse and fuchsia are my colors." She stuck the orange paint samples aside with a sigh. "Fine. Green and blue. I'll acquiesce."

Herb Evans had been eyeing them from the brush rack. He moved closer. "Green and blue suit you, Evelyn—if you don't mind my saying so."

"Hi, Herb."

"Howdy, Herb."

Evelyn was curious. "I appreciate you agreeing with me, but why do you say they suit me?"

When he shrugged, his shirt collar bent against his neck. "They're calm colors, fresh, relaxing yet invigorating."

Evelyn felt herself blush.

Mae nudged her in the side. "You take an eloquent pill this morning, Herb?"

Evelyn was pleased to see that he blushed too. "Just making an observation. About Evelyn." He looked away. "About paint."

"Uh-huh." Mae grinned like a talk-show host.

Evelyn needed to change the subject. She fanned a handful of paint samples. "This is for our sunroom, Herb. I'm going to paint the dark paneling."

"That's quite a job."

"I handled painting the basement all right."

"Oh, I'm sure you did. But paneling . . ." He shook his head. "You'd have to prime it first so the color doesn't bleed through. Do a light sanding. Then you could paint the color. I'm sure it would take at least two coats."

"Sand it?" This *did* sound like more than Evelyn could handle.

Another nudge from Mae. "I bet Herb would help you, wouldn't you, Herb?"

"Mae!"

"Of course I'd help. I'd be happy to help."

"But I don't have money to hire—"

"Oh, you wouldn't need to pay me, Evelyn. I'd do it for free. As a . . . friend."

There was more twinkle in his eye than that of a friend.

Mae clapped her hands. "I bet Evelyn would be more than willing to swap you a home-cooked meal for a little elbow grease. Wouldn't you, Evie?"

Mae! "I—"

"I sure would like that," Herb said. "Since my wife died, my eating habits have been pretty pitiful, though I have mastered hamburgers and frozen potpies."

"Evelyn can do better than that," Mae said. "She's even taken cooking classes and can whip up all sorts of fancy things."

Herb smiled. "Sounds wonderful."

Evelyn was properly cornered. "I'd appreciate your help, Herb, and I'd be happy to cook you a dinner as payment."

"Wonderful," he said. "Now, let's get that color picked out."

• • •

As soon as they got in the car, Evelyn let Mae have it. "How could you?"

"Gracious goose bumps, Evie. He's a nice man—nice *single* man—who was born in a suitable decade, still has most of his hair, keeps his shirt tucked in, and has a smile that could cook a pot roast."

"A what?"

"A warm smile." Mae put on her seat belt. "Zounds, Evie. I thought you'd known me long enough to decipher my words, know what I'm trying to say, even though what I *actually* say is often twenty eons from where I started."

Evelyn started the car. "I will never completely understand what you say."

"Then understand what I mean."

"I do understand. I do."

"Then explain it back to me."

Mae could be so . . . difficult.

She crossed her arms. "I'm waiting."

Evelyn groaned, but followed through. "You're saying that Herb is a respectable, fairly attractive, available man, and it's time I start dating—or at least think about dating. I'm only fifty-seven. I have years and years left in my life, and I don't have to live them alone." She pointed at Mae. "Though I could, mind you; I think I could if that's the way things played out. I'm doing pretty well, if I do say so myself. I'm fixing up the place, handling the money just fine, and even handled the Anabelle Griese incident—or rather, Russell got a lawyer to handle it for me, which is totally acceptable. Knowing when and where to ask for help when it's needed is part of being a successful, independent woman, don't you think?"

Mae applauded. "Bravo! Encore! Encore!"

Evelyn suddenly realized she'd presented a monologue. "Sorry. I got carried away."

"Oh, no, no," Mae said. "It was wonderful and was evidence of the new Evelyn Peerbaugh, woman of the new century!"

"Just keep in mind it's not a date. Herb's coming over to help me paint."

Mae tapped her fingernails on the armrest. "Whatever you say, sister. Whatever you want to believe."

•   •   •

The lunch rush was just subsiding when the manager of Burger Madness called Gail aside.

Gail's mind ran through everything she'd done that day. Had she made some mistake? Had she breached some point of Burger Madness etiquette? She couldn't think of anything, though she had gotten a bit annoyed at the high school kid who'd tried to use an expired coupon. But hadn't she smiled when she'd dealt with him? The little creep.

Mr. Stanborg led her to the small office in back. He offered her a seat. He closed the door.

A bad sign.

He took a seat behind the desk, moaning in relief. "A busy lunch today."

"Uh-huh," Gail said. *Brilliant, Gail. Profound. You could at least use real words.* "Yes."

"You work well under pressure."

"I do?"

"And other people work well with you. You're a leader."

"I am?"

He laughed. "You don't have much self-confidence, do you?"

"Haven't seen much reason for it lately."

"You have reason for it now. Because I am about to offer you the position of assistant manager."

"You're kidding."

He laughed again. "No, I'm not kidding. There will be a few more hours involved, but there is also a raise. Would you take the position?"

Dumb question.

•   •   •

After dropping Mae off at Silver-Wear and doing some more errands, Evelyn came home to a house that smelled of nutmeg and cloves. She headed toward it and found Gail in the kitchen, checking on something in the oven.

"Is that pumpkin pie I smell?" Evelyn asked.

"I had a craving."

"Glad to hear it." Evelyn set her packages on the counter.

"I also had a reason to make pies."

"And what's that?"

"A reason to celebrate. I got a promotion. I am now the assistant manager at Burger Madness."

Evelyn hesitated, but only for a second. "That's wonderful."

Gail put the mixing bowl in the sink and ran water in it. "I know it's a far cry from the job I pretended to have at Lanigan's or the one I thought I deserved, but I'm happy about it." She glanced at Evelyn. "I hate to admit it, but I like working there."

"Good for you."

"It's not a very glamorous job."

"But if you like it . . ."

Gail pointed to the hardware-store sack. "What are you up to?"

"I'm going to paint the sunroom." She got out the sample of Celery Green. Herb would be bringing the actual paint when he came to help Saturday. "Of course we'll have to prime the paneling and sand it first, but Herb Evans from the store is going to help me."

"That's nice of him."

"In exchange for a home-cooked dinner."

Gail grinned. "Is this Herb single?"

"Actually . . ."

"Good for you, Evelyn. It's nice you're finding someone to do things with."

"He's just a friend."

"A male friend."

Evelyn had to concede that point. Then she thought about Gail's situation and felt bad. "Have you ever considered dating again? After all, you're single."

Silence. "Actually, I'm not."

"What?"

"I'm not divorced. I'm still married."

"Why did you tell us you were divorced?"

"Because it seemed more decisive. Being separated like we are . . . that's wishy-washy. That reveals a weakness. Divorce reveals a stronger decision."

"No it doesn't."

"Sure it does. If I had the guts to get divorced, it would show that I'm in control, that I know what I want and have the fortitude to set out to get it. But just being separated . . ."

Evelyn's head shook adamantly. "Staying married shows fortitude. Staying married is the hardest thing in the world. Divorce is easy. Too easy. People don't work at their marriages anymore. At the first sign of trouble, they cut and run."

Gail threw the empty pumpkin cans into the recycling bin. "I ran. I ran here."

"But you're not divorced yet. You're trying to work it out." Evelyn hesitated. "Aren't you?"

Gail put the spices back in the rack. "My husband is. He never wanted me to leave."

"Why did you leave?"

"Because I felt out of control and totally unworthy of him and my son. They are both so good and the joy of my life, while I am this flawed, horrible person who can't even appreciate what she has. They deserve better." She put a hand to her midsection. "A few months ago, this feeling of discontent grabbed me from the inside out. It gnawed at me, made me doubt, made me feel depressed and full of despair, and—"

Evelyn raised a hand, stopping her words. Her mind searched for the reason why Gail's words raised a red flag: *discontent, doubt, depression, despair*. Then she remembered something she'd learned in church a few months previous. "Those are the *D*-words."

"What are the *D*-words?"

"You mentioned your feelings: *discontent, doubt, depression, despair*. The *D*-words that Satan uses to bring us down, to keep us away from God."

"How did Satan get into this?"

Evelyn realized how all this must sound to Gail, who wasn't close to God. Evelyn had felt the same way. "We don't like to talk about Satan, but that doesn't mean he doesn't exist. In fact, that's the key to his greatest power over us, another *D*-word: *deception*. He's subtle and gets us thinking and acting negatively so we withdraw and become consumed with those feelings. They take over."

Gail's nod was a good sign.

"The key is, when things seem so totally bad, we have to wake up, recognize what's happening, and say, 'I'm not going to do this! I'm not going to be drawn into this quicksand.' And then you tell Satan to go away and leave you alone."

Gail smirked. "I tell him. *I* tell him?"

Oh dear. Evelyn knew that every believer had the power to

order Satan away—through the power of Jesus' name. But what about an unbeliever? or a borderline believer like Gail?

A thought loomed: *First things first.*

And somehow Evelyn understood. She felt an almost physical ache for the right words to come, and when she opened her mouth, she knew they'd be there. "Gail. You want out of this mess you're in? You want some answers? You want some relief and peace in your life?"

"Sure. You got some extra peace lying around?"

Evelyn smiled at the perfect segue. "Actually, I do. Or God does. Or more specifically, Jesus does."

Gail raised a hand. "Uh-uh. Don't go there. Terry's told me this a hundred times."

"Then isn't it about time you paid attention?"

"I don't think you have any right—"

"What does God have to do to get you to stop procrastinating and make the choice? *The* choice."

Gail closed her mouth with a click. For a full minute the only sounds in the kitchen were the whir of the refrigerator, the ticking of the clock on the wall, and the breathing of the two women. Evelyn became conscious of the pounding of her own heart in her ears. What had made her so gutsy? Yet she knew the answer to that was the answer to everything. *Please, Lord, she's come this far.*

"Fine," Gail finally said. "What do I have to do to get everything on the right track?"

Evelyn's heart did a back flip. This was it. This was actually happening. Someone was looking to her, Evelyn Peerbaugh, for help about their faith. And she, in turn, needed help. . . .

Help me do this right, God. Thus fortified, Evelyn began. "First, you let Jesus into your life. Then, with His power behind you, you order Satan and evil out."

"And that will do it? All my troubles will disappear?"

"Absolutely not. We do have to be careful not to attribute

every negative thing to evil. But with God on your side, you won't be handling things alone anymore. You'll have the full power of Jesus behind you, helping you, guiding you, comforting you. That's where the peace is. In Him. Through Him." She put a hand on Gail's shoulder. "He changed my life, Gail. He can change yours too. I promise."

Their eyes met and Evelyn could see that a decision had been made even before Gail spoke. "Let's do it."

●　　●　　●

Gail went up to her room, and Evelyn went into the sunroom and shut the doors. Her pounding heart had been replaced with a fullness so complete she thought she would burst. She had to let it out. And so she jumped into the air and pumped a fist. "Yes!"

The movement was awkward and she nearly stumbled, but Evelyn had the feeling that in God's eyes, her jump for joy held the grace of an angel's dance.

Alleluia!

●　　●　　●

Gail sat on her window seat and pulled her knees to her chest. A flurry of snow sailed by, floating so gently. So unconcerned. Suddenly Gail realized that these attributes were also present in her own heart. She felt gentle and unconcerned. Calm.

Peaceful.

Her throat tightened and she put a hand to her chest. Was this *Him*? Was this God? So soon? So completely?

She bowed her head. Finding no words of her own, she relied on God to hear the gratitude and sense the awe that flowed through her veins.

And somehow she knew He did just fine. Just fine. Message received.

·   ·   ·

It had been a busy day for Piper. She'd stayed long after school to counsel two girls, then had attended a staff meeting. By the time she got home, it was nearly nine. She unlocked her darkened apartment and went inside. She flipped on the lights, but the room did not come to life as she'd expected. True, her parents were gone on their short RV trip, meaning Piper was free to return home, make herself at home. Settle back in. Then why wasn't there any life here? Here, in this home.

She ran a hand along the back of the couch, hoping the tactile experience would spur the right feelings. It was as though she were experiencing the apartment for the first time, reclaiming it as her own. It wasn't as if she hadn't been there since her parents moved in. She had. Daily. But with them in residence, the whole atmosphere changed. Every piece of furniture, dish in the cupboard, and knickknack on the shelves had seemed different. Removed. Altered.

But now that she was back and they were not there, everything should be the same as it was. She should be able to mentally restore the scene to her old image of home.

Yet she couldn't.

Maybe she needed a little help . . .

She kicked off her shoes, turned on an Andrea Bocelli CD, and curled up on the couch, pulling the afghan over her shoulders. It was a familiar, cozy position in a cozy apartment. This would work. She would enjoy a quiet, soothing time, with the strains of a handsome, Italian tenor filling every corner.

Handsome, Italian . . .

Gregory Baladino.

She began to cry.

Dear friends, let us continue to love one another,
for love comes from God.
Anyone who loves is born of God and knows God.
But anyone who does not love does not know God—
for God is love.

1 JOHN 4:7-8

$\mathcal{P}$iper woke up on the couch. The lights were on. All was quiet. Bocelli had stopped singing. She looked at the clock: 2:15.

She stumbled into her bedroom to get into her pajamas, wash her face, and brush her teeth. She hoped the movements wouldn't wake her up too much. She wanted to get back to sleep. In her own bed. In her own apartment. What a concept.

She did her duties and pulled back the covers. She was just about to turn off the lamp when she saw the corner of a piece of paper sticking out from the bedside table. She pulled at it, then opened the drawer to aid its exit. It was a piece of stationery lined with birdhouses. She recognized her mother's handwriting. It was a letter. But the date was over a week ago. Had her mother forgotten to mail—

My dearest Piper,

Piper? The letter was for her? She sat on the bed and began to read.

My dearest Piper,

You have just left here after we had a discussion about my dying. You said you were selfish for wondering how my death would affect you. I hope I convinced you it's okay to think of yourself. I don't want you to feel any guilt. You are too good a woman for that.

But I have to admit something to you that I have not admitted to anyone. Not because I want to burden you with my feelings but because I need to share them, get them down, so that someday when you read this, you will understand all that I went through and maybe grow from it. Find strength for your own road.

This heart of mine is going to give out. I am going to die.

Piper's stomach grated against itself. Her first reaction was one of anger. Had Gregory lied to her? Had her mother and father lied to her, not telling her the total truth, putting on a front when things were much more serious? How dare they? She looked at the phone, feeling the urge to call Gregory and demand the truth. But there was more letter to read . . .

Dr. Baladino says with treatment and careful living I'll be fine. Your father says I'll be fine. The tests and medical science say my condition is treatable and my life livable. So it's not because of anything they've said that I feel this way. It's a gut feeling: I'm going to die. And in the not-too-distant future.

Please believe me when I say I've done everything in my power to rid myself of this notion. Begging God to remove the thought has come into play. But the feeling does not go away. And so I've come to accept it as a blessing rather than a curse. How much better for me to realize my time is short so I can wrap things up right, say the words that need to be said, appreciate the moments that are a gift.

Please know I'm not giving up. After all, Hezekiah asked God for fifteen more years and God granted his request. But in truth, that turned out to be a huge mistake. During that fifteen years Hezekiah sired the worst and most evil king Israel had ever had. So maybe he should have gone when God called him. . . .

Hmm. Let's just say I'm accepting my death as a possibility but leaving my options open. If God decides to remove this notion from my mind, then I'll be the first to say, "Whew! Glad that's gone!" and be totally happy living another thirty years.

But if He doesn't . . .

I just need to tell someone. I need someone to know that I sense time is short. And I also want someone to know that I am okay with it, that I've come to consider the knowledge a gift not a burden. That's the one advantage of a death by illness rather than by accident. The person is given time to say good-bye.

I'm not ready to do that yet. Not in this letter. But I want you to know how special you are and how special our relationship is, and that you are the one person in the world I felt I could share this with. For you are my greatest gift, dear daughter. And I hope these letters will be of comfort to you when I'm gone.

All my love,
Mom

Letters? Plural?

Piper opened the drawer wide. Stacked neatly were a dozen letters, all to her, dating back to the day they called Piper and told her they were coming home.

Piper started to read another one, then pulled it to her chest. Should she be doing this? It was clear her mother was writing these for Piper's viewing after she was gone. Would it be wrong to read the rest? Now.

Probably. But she did it anyway. She needed to know what was in her mother's mind. She needed to hear her words. Now, not later.

She settled onto the bed, drawing the pile of letters onto her lap. She read them in order. From her mother's first realization that the pains she'd been feeling were not "nothing," through her disbelief, her anger, her pleading to God. It was better than a diary, for her mother spoke directly to Piper in the letters, not to an anonymous "Dear Diary."

While she read, Piper ignored her own tears, accepting them as part of the deal. As she finished, she took a breath, and realized it was the first full one she'd taken since she'd started.

There were two facts that were irrefutable: Her mother had sensed the seriousness of her illness from the very beginning—why else would she start writing to Piper before she'd even seen a doctor? And second: Her mother's faith was seeing her through. Sure, Piper's dad was helping and so was Piper, but their attempts to understand and offer comfort and encouragement were clumsy compared to the presence of God—the Father, Son, and Holy Spirit. These letters were her mother's testimony. They were her legacy. They were an inspiration.

Piper set them aside and got on her knees, her entire body aching with the need to have God hear her prayers. She rested her clasped hands on the bed, bowing her head upon them. "Lord God! Heal my mother! You cannot take her away from me. I need her here. Though these letters are wonderful, they are not enough. Shouldn't such a woman of faith live? She can do great things for You, Lord! Great things, alive. You've healed before. Heal now!"

Her voice was shaking and she felt a wave of shame. "How many desperate pleas for healing are You getting today, Father? this hour? this minute? How do You choose which ones to answer and which ones to ignore?" She caught herself and shook her head. "No. That's wrong. You don't ignore any prayer. I know that. You hear them all, but You can't say yes to them all."

Piper sat on her heels, burying her face in the side of the bed. "Oh, give me strength, Jesus! Help me be a good daughter to my mother. Show me how to help her." She felt a wave of surrender envelop her and gave in to it. "All this has come from my heart, but I know what else I have to pray." With difficulty she grabbed a fresh breath. "I have to pray Your will be done." She began to cry. "Whatever it is, I realize You know best. And truly, that's what I want. So do what You must, Lord Jesus. But if it fits into Your plan that my mother be healed, then please grant my request. In Jesus' name, amen."

The silence of her apartment pressed down on her. She hadn't really noticed that she'd been speaking aloud. But now that her voice was silent . . . Piper was drained.

She set the letters back in the bedside table with the reverence of handling sacred writ. Then she climbed into bed and tried to sleep.

●　　●　　●

Heddy recognized the woman and her daughter as soon as they came into Ruby's. They'd been in before when she and Audra had just come up with the idea to start Catherine's Wedding Creations.

"How are the wedding plans going?" she asked.

The daughter looked at the mother. "Actually, that's the real reason we're here. We'd like to talk to you about the bridesmaid dresses."

"Do you have an office somewhere? A showroom?" the mother asked.

Soon. Soon. Heddy thought fast. "Our official showroom is in progress. Would you like to meet at Peerbaugh Place? There's a lovely parlor there where we could talk."

"That Victorian boardinghouse?"

"That's the one."

"I've always wanted to see the inside," the mother said. "Do you have time later today?"

"Absolutely."

As soon as they left—with two cinnamon rolls and coffees to go—Heddy called Audra. "Guess what?"

This was going to be great.

* * *

Mae really liked the new insulated gloves Collier had bought for her. Wanting to try them out, she went outside to sweep the newest flurry off the porch.

She looked across the street and saw Summer come outside to play. Audra stood in the doorway, gave Summer instructions, waved a hand at Mae, then disappeared inside. Summer jumped down the porch steps carrying a doll, then back up again, then down. Where did little girls get their energy? Especially when weighed down by boots, scarf, and hat.

Mae arched her back. "Hey, there, doll face. Whatcha doing?"

"I'm supposed to play good because Mommy and Heddy are going to have a wedding meeting with a bridesmaid lady."

"They have a customer?"

"Their first one." She held her doll front and center. "I'm going to hide Sally in the snow and then try to find her."

Okay . . . "If you get bored you can come over here and help me sweep the porch."

Summer nodded, heading to a pile of snow. Within seconds the doll had disappeared and Summer was back on the steps calling for her as if she was lost. What an imagination.

A few minutes later, Mae noticed a Camaro drive by. Slowly. Then it turned around at the corner and returned. A lone man sat inside, looking toward Peerbaugh Place. Mae's nerve endings stood at attention. When he stopped out front, she was about to ask him his business, when he got out and approached Summer.

Mae's muscles tensed and she left the porch, heading toward

the street to make sure he knew she saw him. "Afternoon," she called from the curb.

He gave her a backward glance and nodded but kept walking up the front walk of Peerbaugh Place.

He stopped a few feet from Summer. "Hi," he said.

Summer got up from the step and took a position at the top of the porch. "I've seen you before."

"Yes, you have. Do you know who I am?"

"You're the man."

"I'm your dad."

She stared at him and then shook her head. "I have a daddy."

"Yes, you do. Me."

Mae had heard enough. She hurried across the street. "Luke?"

He turned toward her. "How do you know my name?"

"Audra, Summer, and I are sisters—of the heart, if not by blood—so I've heard *all* about you."

"I wouldn't believe everything Audra says."

"You'd rather I believe you? You who has fathered—" She looked at Summer and decided not to complete the sentence. She strode past him, up the porch steps, and took Summer's hand, heading inside.

"I wasn't hurting anything."

"You weren't helping either." She nudged Summer through the door. "Go inside, doll face. I'll be in in a minute." She closed the door and went down the stairs toward Luke. She gestured for him to follow her to his car. She was amazed when he followed.

Looking back at the house, she saw Audra's, Evelyn's, and Heddy's faces at the window. She raised a hand to them. She had it under control.

Luke saw the exchange. "What is this? A conspiracy?"

"No, it's a family. As I told you, we're sisters, and as sisters we will not let anything hurt any of us."

"I'm not going to hurt Summer."

She leaned close, jabbing a finger into his chest. "You ever see a mother bird protecting her brood? Flapping her wings, cawing, dive-bombing the offender?"

He didn't answer.

"Answer me, Luke."

"Yes, I've seen that."

"Well, let me tell you right now that is *nothing* compared to the defensive measures we will take to protect that precious child from anything that can hurt her: physically, mentally, emotionally, or spiritually."

She saw his shoulders fall. "I don't mean any harm. I just want—"

On impulse, Mae took another tack. "You just want to do the right thing, don't you? The noble thing. The magnanimous thing. Something that rises above yourself and achieves something nearly divine."

"All I want is to have her—"

"But that's the point. You can't have her. Summer is not yours. I don't know why you've suddenly decided to take this road, but let me assure you, it's the wrong one. Summer has a father, a *daddy* in the truest sense of the word. He loves her and is ready to sacrifice everything for her, even if it would mean a hardship on himself. Are you ready to do that?"

"I'd like to be."

She patted him on the back. "I'm sure you would, Luke. But Summer can't wait five to ten years while you attempt to become the man she needs. She's been without a father the first five years of her life so she needs that man now. *Now.* And Russell Peerbaugh is that man."

Luke jerked away from her touch, got into his car, and pulled away. Mae looked after him, feeling a wave of empathy for the man. *Help him, Lord. Help him do the right thing.*

Upon his departure, the other women poured out of

Peerbaugh Place, Audra taking the lead. "Mae! Thank you for saving Summer!"

Mae walked toward them, needing to leave the spot where she and Luke had had their exchange. "I didn't save her from anyone, Audra. Luke didn't mean any harm."

Audra pulled up short. "How can you say that?"

Mae rubbed her forehead. Relationships were a constant testing ground for character. "He's not a bad man. He's a searching man."

Audra took Summer under her arm. "Well he can do his searching somewhere else. We want nothing to do with him."

Mae shrugged. What could she say, especially in front of the girl?

"You had a long discussion with him, Mae," Evelyn said. "What did you tell him?"

"I encouraged him to do the right thing."

Audra's eyes blazed. "But did you tell him what the right thing was?"

Mae longed for the nonjudgmental atmosphere of her porch. "Yes, Audra. I told him."

"What did he say?"

"He didn't." Mae turned and walked back home.

•   •   •

"Are you all right?" Evelyn asked.

Audra's insides seethed. How dare Luke show up like that and talk to her daughter? She shivered at the memory. What would have happened if Mae hadn't been there?

She spun around. Where was Summer?

The little girl was at the dining room table where they had set up their presentation for the bride and her mother. Heddy had brought down her doll wearing one of the bridesmaid creations, and Summer was fingering the lace on the bodice. Totally unconcerned. Totally normal.

Audra felt she was about to blow, but couldn't do it in the presence of her daughter. She fled to the kitchen. Evelyn came after her, standing silent. Waiting.

Audra got a drink of water then turned around. "I hate him, Evelyn. I hate him so much it's like a fire burning me up from the inside out. I want him gone. Out of our lives forever. If that means he's dead, then—"

"Audra!"

Audra covered her mouth, appalled she'd said the words aloud. "I despise how I feel. I know it's wrong. But he can*not* be in our lives. He can't! Summer and I are just getting to a place that's good and stable and full of love. Why did he have to come back now and mess things up?"

"*You* contacted *him*."

Audra let out a breath. "I had to. But why couldn't he just sign the papers and fade away again? His mother wants him to do that. I want him to do that. If only Russell hadn't spurred him into taking a stand against his mother . . . I mean, of all times. Let Luke stand up to her about something else, but not about this. Not about this."

Evelyn shifted her weight. "What Russell did . . . even though it seems bad . . . I think was good. Actually, I'm rather proud of him."

Audra let the pride of a mother toward a son break through her hatred of another mother's son. "Did I tell you he prayed about it first?"

Evelyn's eyes lit up. "He did?"

Audra nodded, then began to pace. "I should be celebrating that fact, instead of zoning in on the negative. My husband prayed."

"Then he did the right thing. *Because* he prayed. Which means God wanted Luke to confront his mother. Stand up to her."

Audra stopped pacing as a statement flashed in her mind. "God cares about Luke. He wants what's best for Luke."

"God loves Luke."

Audra covered her ears. "Why don't I want to hear that?"

Evelyn came close and rubbed the back of Audra's shoulders. "Russell did the right thing. Luke did the right thing. Now, it's up to you to do the right thing."

"Which is?"

Evelyn shrugged. "Don't ask me. Ask God."

The doorbell rang. "They're here."

Evelyn held Audra by the shoulders. "Your first customers. Go get 'em."

But Audra couldn't go. Not yet. "Will you go for me—for just a few minutes? I have to do something first."

Evelyn looked into her eyes, then nodded. "Good girl."

•   •   •

Audra grabbed her jacket and slipped out the back door. She shoved her hands in her pockets, took a deep breath of cold air, and looked up. The trees were barren, their branches stark and empty. They'd been that way for months, yet it was as if she was seeing them for the first time. Somehow in the busyness of planning the wedding last fall, she hadn't noticed the transition between resplendent and radiant to bleak and barren.

Just a few weeks ago she'd come back from their honeymoon, resplendent and radiant. The new bride starting a new life. But now this ordeal with Luke left her feeling cold and naked, like a tree without leaves.

But it wasn't a permanent condition. Come spring, the trees would get a new beginning and fresh leaves would bud and grow and make them full. It was all part of the plan, the process, God's design.

Was it also His design that she go through such horrid times of barrenness? It had to be, for Audra believed there was a reason for everything. Nothing—no emotion, no act, no thought—was wasted in God's kingdom. All could be turned for bad or good. It was a matter of attitude and perspective.

Audra had a choice. She could let her hatred for Luke fester and become vile. Or she could surrender it to the only One who could turn it around and banish it from her heart.

She sat on a lawn chair, the bite of the cold metal quickly filtering through the fabric of her pants. She leaned her elbows on her thighs, her head in her hands. "Lord, make it right. Take this hate away from me. Replace it with Your love. I can't do it without You."

She sat still a moment, waiting for an overwhelming feeling of love to pour over her. It did not. And yet the hate *had* lessened, just a touch.

She got up. It was a beginning.

Those who know Your name trust in You,
for You, O Lord, have never abandoned anyone
who searches for You.

PSALM 9:10

$\mathcal{P}$iper was a lazy bum. As a proponent of the "early to rise" axiom, "lazy bum" was a title she gave herself for sleeping until nine thirty on Saturday morning. But considering how little sleep she'd gotten the past three nights since reading her mother's letters, she forgave herself.

Yet she awoke with a dilemma. Her parents would be home before lunch. Should she tell her mother she'd read the letters or remain silent? She lay in bed awhile, considering the pros and cons. Unable to come to a decision, she got out of bed. Maybe coffee would help.

• • •

Piper was just starting to make chipped beef on toast when her parents came in.

"We're back!" There was a pleasant flush to her mother's cheeks. Maybe the trip had been a good idea after all.

Her father brought in the suitcase. "Hey, Piper-girl. How were things while we were gone?"

She wiped her hands and hugged them both, trying not to look at her mother differently. "Not much new here. How did your trip go?"

Her father's voice was too loud, his few words stressed oddly. "Fine. It was *fine*."

The face of Piper's mother revealed no details.

"I was just starting lunch. Are you hungry?"

Her father took a step toward the door. "Can it wait a half hour? I need to get the RV out of the parking lot and back to the storage lot."

"Do you need me to go with you to bring you back?"

"I've got a bit of cleaning out to do. I'll call you when I'm ready." He returned to give his wife a kiss. "You okay?"

"I'm fine. Now go."

He left. Something had happened on the trip. Something not good. Piper wanted to give her mother a chance to come clean. "So how was the trip, *really*?"

"It was fine. Just—"

"You can stop pretending, Mom. I found the letters."

Piper expected a horrified look. A "how could you?" She didn't get it.

"I was hoping you would."

Piper could only blink and stare.

"That's why I pulled the one up a bit so it stuck out of the drawer. I wanted you to see it."

"Why didn't you just give them to me?"

Wanda fingered the edge of the breakfast counter. "I don't know. When I was writing them, I truly intended for you not to see them until I was gone. But when I was writing the last one, I got the notion to let you in on my little secret."

"Little secret? Thinking you're going to die soon is a flashing billboard!"

Her mother closed her eyes and recited: "'Lord, remind me

how brief my time on earth will be. Remind me that my days are numbered, and that my life is fleeing away. My life is no longer than the width of my hand. An entire lifetime is just a moment to You; human existence is but a breath.'" She opened her eyes and sighed. "The Psalms hold such comfort for me."

Piper's head was shaking in short bursts. "I didn't get much comfort from those verses. They're about death."

"They're about the brevity of life and how we can't waste it. Not one moment." She placed both hands palms down on the counter. "Which mirrors my new philosophy. I'm not going to waste another moment."

"Sounds like you have a plan."

"I do. I plan to be here with you and your father. Stay in Carson Creek among my friends. No more RVing."

"How does Dad feel about this?"

"He's in denial. Partly because I haven't shared with him all that I've shared with you through the letters. But I think he knows, deep down. I think he senses things are worse than they seem."

Piper's throat tightened. "How *are* you feeling?"

"Just as I should at this point in my life."

Piper groaned. "I'm not sure if I should ask you to speak more plainly or less plainly. You're vacillating all over the place."

Her mother reached across the counter and took Piper's hand. "I'm not giving up, honey. I'm being honest with myself. At this point, my biggest goal is to ban worry from my life. It is not allowed. Not by me, by your father, nor by you. You have to promise me that."

Piper pulled her hand away. "Are you kidding? I can't promise not to worry."

"Of course you can. If you trust God. 'Don't worry about tomorrow, for tomorrow will bring its own worries. Today's trouble is enough for today.'"

"Easy enough said . . ."

"And totally possible to do. Consider it my prefinal request."

"Mom . . ."

"Piper. Do it for me. Do it for you. Do it for your own faith. You'll come out better for it. I promise."

Everything her mother said rang true. But how could she not worry? How was that possible? "I'll try," she finally said. "That's all I can promise you."

· · ·

Piper's father called from the RV-storage lot, ready for a ride back. Piper went to get him, glad for some time alone with him.

As she pulled onto the street, he took a noisy breath. "There. That's done."

It was time to hear his version. "How *was* your trip?"

He looked out his window. "Just fine."

Piper hated that word. "Are you planning to go out again?"

He whipped his head toward her. "Of course we are. Why wouldn't we?"

Piper pursed her lips together. Her mother had said he was in denial.

"You've been talking to your mother," he said.

"She wants to stick close to home, Dad."

"She wants to give in and give up."

"No she doesn't. She wants to enjoy what—" Piper stopped herself from finishing the sentence with "time she has left." Her father had not read the letters. He didn't know the extent of his wife's foresight.

"She's not going to die. Not yet. Not if I can help it."

So he *did* know. She reached for his hand. "Everyone wants her to live. But she wants some stability during this uncertain time. I think it would be a good idea if the RV sat for a while."

He shrugged. Then he said, "If only we hadn't sold the house."

An idea formed and was out of her mouth before Piper could raise a mental hand and ask any questions. "You can have my apartment. Permanently."

"What? No, no. We couldn't do that."

"Sure you could. I'm fine at Peerbaugh Place. I think moving in there, being away from my things, made me realize how little I miss them. And I like being around the other tenants and Evelyn."

He was quiet. "Have you told your mother this idea?"

"I'll leave that to you. Do it, Dad. It's the best thing."

She hoped she was right about that. When she'd awakened that morning she'd never expected to give up her home.

•   •   •

As soon as Piper got in the door, her mother popped off the couch. "Gregory called!"

Piper felt as if her emotions were on a spinning wheel in a game show. The wheel passed Elation, edged by Pleasure, closed in on Fear, and finally stopped on Apprehension.

"Well?" her mother said. "Aren't you going to call him back?"

Piper hung up her coat. "*I* broke up with *him*, Mom. I don't want him to call."

"He said you'd say that."

"He did?"

"He said, 'I'm sure Piper doesn't want to talk to me, but tell her to please call. She won't regret it.'" Her mother sank onto the couch, drawing her feet beneath her like an excited little girl. "You think he's found Jesus? You think he's made the choice that can keep you together?"

The emotion wheel nudged into the next category: Anticipation. But then it edged back to Apprehension. *If* Gregory had dedicated his life to the Lord in less than a week—after her ultimatum—then how sincere could he be? It was too convenient. She didn't want him to turn to God in order to *get* something he wanted, namely their continued relationship. She wanted him to do it because he *had* to. Because his soul cried out to do it. Calling Jesus Lord was a means to an end—in regard to salvation—but not in regard to one's love life.

Her father shut the closet door. "You should call him back, Piper-girl. Do you want us to leave for a bit?"

She shook her head. "I'll use the phone in the bedroom. You talk to Mom about my proposal."

"What proposal?" her mother asked.

Piper went into the bedroom, sat on the bed, and pulled the phone into her lap. *Lord, please, please . . .* she hoped God could finish her prayer and put in the details of "please what?" because she wasn't sure her motives were pure. She wanted Gregory in her life. And she wanted him bad.

He answered on the second ring.

"Hi, Gregory. My mother said you called?"

I've found Jesus! We can be together now!

"I *did* call because I need to tell you something."

"Oh?"

"I've been doing a lot of thinking this week—and a lot of missing you."

A fire sparked inside. "I've missed you too."

"And though it's been hard, and though I've gone through anger and hate as well as longing to be with you so much my legs ache, I've come to a conclusion."

Piper put a hand to her chest. This was it. He'd accepted Christ! "Go on . . ."

"I've concluded that you are the most amazing woman—

person—I've ever met. I have never known anyone who believed in their convictions so completely, so sincerely, that they were willing to sacrifice their own happiness for those convictions. You are an extraordinary woman, Piper Wellington."

"Thank you."

"And though I can't agree to your terms, I can—and do—admire you for . . ."

Piper's ears grabbed on to "I can't agree to your terms," missing the rest of his sentence. This was not an I-found-Jesus call. There was not going to be a happy ending.

". . . maybe someday I'll make the decision you think I need to make, but I know you wouldn't want me to make it just to get something I want so desperately, even if it is you."

Wanna bet? Her throat was so tight she couldn't speak.

He went on. "But I wanted you to know that you have affected my life profoundly. You are an inspiration. You are the kind of person I want to be. And maybe someday I'll come to the point of needing this God of yours so much that I will sacrifice for Him, like you have sacrificed for Him. But until that time, I am honored to call you friend."

Friend? Piper wanted to scream the word. All that came out was an odd gargling.

"Piper?"

She swallowed hard. "I . . . I'm glad you think so much of me."

"I do. I just wanted you to know that."

Piper nodded to the phone but could not talk.

"Well . . . I'd better go. Please keep in touch."

"Sure." Her voice broke and she tried again. "Sure."

He hung up.

She hung up.

It was over.

A tap on the door. "Piper? Honey?"

Piper did not wipe away her tears, but accepted her mother's comfort. After all, she was an amazing, inspirational woman.

Big deal.

Piper was still alone.

It was out of her hands.

●　　●　　●

"Can I go over to Morgan's?" Summer asked.

"No!"

Audra hated the look on Summer's face. She set aside the T-shirt she'd been folding, pulled Summer's head close, and kissed the top of it. "Sorry, baby. I just don't want you to go out of the house today."

"Why not? It's Saturday. I always play with Morgan on Saturday."

Russell looked up from the computer desk in the living room. "I'd like to hear this too."

Audra folded the shirt, then pulled another one from the laundry basket. "Russell . . . you know why."

"He's not dangerous, Audra."

"How do you know?"

Russell didn't answer. He had no answer.

"I rest my case," she said.

Russell left the computer. "Then tell me this: How long are you going to keep our daughter prisoner?"

Summer looked up at him. "Am I a prisoner?"

"Of course not, baby."

"Fine," Russell said. "Then let her go to Morgan's."

Audra shook a towel with a snap.

"It's just down the hall, Audra. Twenty-five feet, max."

He was right. She pulled the towel to her chest, hugging it. What had gotten into her? Luke was not an evil man. Three days ago she'd prayed that her hate would lessen. And it had. But in its place were fear and anxiety which seemed just as bad.

Russell came close. "It'll work out, luv. It will."

Tears surprised her. "How? How will it work out?"

She felt Summer hug her waist. "Pray about it, Mommy. That's what you always tell me. Pray about it."

She didn't deserve this child, this man. Audra fell to her knees, to Summer's level. She took her hand and held the other one out toward Russell. He took it and dropped to his knees too. Were they actually going to pray together? As a family? Just like that? Out of the blue?

"You start, Daddy," Summer said.

Audra's stomach knotted. Would Russell—?

He cleared his throat, then began. "God, we need You. We love each other and want desperately to be a family in every way we can. To do that we need Luke to sign the papers. He won't do that and frankly, he's making us nervous and afraid."

"And we don't like that feeling," Audra added.

"Make it all work out," Summer said. "Please."

What else could Audra add? "Amen," she said.

Russell and Summer added their own amens.

It was out of their hands.

•   •   •

Evelyn looked at the shirts tossed across her bed. How could it be so difficult choosing a shirt to paint in? One made her look fat because it was too small. Another made her look fat because it was too big. She finally settled on an old pink plaid.

She buttoned the top button and looked in the mirror. Why did her hair have to be flat today of all days?

Today of all days?

Evelyn looked herself in the eyes. "Don't be ridiculous." Then she sprayed herself with Tuscany cologne and went downstairs to work on the dinner.

The dinner for Herb Evans.

Ridiculous.

•   •   •

Evelyn couldn't remember laughing so much since Mae had done her John Wayne imitation. It wasn't that Herb told jokes or did imitations of celebrities. He was just a funny man. Witty. Good with words.

He was a hard worker too. They'd moved the furniture to the center of the sunroom and applied a coat of primer in less than an hour. While they waited for it to dry, Evelyn put ingredients into her bread machine. *The way to a man's heart is through his—*

Ridiculous.

Herb came out of the washroom. "Put me to work."

"Nonsense. This meal is payment for your work in the sunroom. You're not supposed to help."

"Nonsense back at ya. Now tell me what to do."

Evelyn got a green pepper and an onion out of the fridge and pointed him toward the cutting board. "Diced small, please."

"You got it."

She watched him work. He was pretty good at it. "Have you always been good in the kitchen?" she asked.

"Not at all. But since Samantha died, I've had to make do or starve." He sighed. "I sure miss her. How about your husband? Did Aaron help in the kitchen?"

Are you kidding?

They spent the next hour talking about their late spouses, drawing into the conversation their good and bad traits—and some of their own. They talked about grief and being alone. About life.

Maybe their spending time together wasn't so ridiculous after all.

It was out of her hands.

●   ●   ●

Heddy straightened the menus in their holder. The bell on the front door of Ruby's opened. She looked up, her hostess smile already in place. It was Steve Mannersmith, the English teacher at the high school.

He smiled at her, then at the floor, then back at her. "Afternoon, Ms. Wainsworth."

"Afternoon, Steve. And you know it's Heddy. Please call me Heddy." She took a menu. "Dining alone today?"

His eyes skimmed over the other diners while his hands found the pockets of his fleece-lined jacket. "Actually, no."

"How many will be joining you?"

He blushed. "Actually, no one. Actually, I didn't come in to eat. I was wanting . . . would you . . . I mean, I was wanting to ask if *you* wanted to go out with *me* to dinner. Tonight. Dinner and a play."

She felt her eyebrows rise.

"I know it's late notice, but . . ." He shrugged and laughed. "You'd think I'd be better at this. I witness my students asking each other out every day. But I'm a bit out of practice."

When Steve had been in the diner before, Ruby had told her all about his divorce. A horrible experience all around. As trite as it sounded, his wife had run off with her personal trainer from the health club. They didn't have any children.

Heddy noticed Ruby peering out of the kitchen. She received a wink. Was Ruby behind this?

When she turned back to Steve, she saw that he'd witnessed the wink too. He hurried to say, "I've been meaning to ask you for a long time."

Did it matter if Ruby had nudged him a bit? Not really.

She smiled at him. "A play, you say?"

"Nothing professional. But our church is putting one on and there's a dinner too."

A churchgoing man.

"I'd be happy to go," she said.

She'd never been out with a churchgoing man.

It was out of her hands.

•　　•　　•

Audra wanted to like college football—for Russell's sake. And so she agreed to watch a game with him Saturday afternoon while Summer was at Morgan's—safely at Morgan's—playing.

She made it through the first quarter before she fell asleep. Every once in a while, she attempted to open an eye and pretend she was awake, but the fact that she suddenly found herself covered with an afghan meant she wasn't fooling her husband. She'd try watching the second half. She would.

She didn't have to worry about it because there was a knock on the door. Groggy, she sat up and let Russell get it. It was probably just the girls, wanting to play here for a while.

But then she heard Russell's strident whisper. "Audra! It's Luke."

She was wide-awake now. She scrambled off the couch. Russell had not opened the door yet, but had seen him through the peephole. "Don't open it!" she whispered back.

Luke knocked again. "Aud? Come on. Open up. I come in peace."

Russell looked at Audra with a question in his eyes. She sighed. Earlier they'd prayed together, relinquishing control. If God *was* in control, then maybe Luke's presence here this afternoon . . .

"Let him in," Audra said.

"You sure?"

She nodded but took a step back.

Russell opened the door.

"You're here," Luke said.

"What do you want, Luke?" he asked.

He looked past Russell to Audra. "Hey, Aud."

"What do you want, Luke?" she asked.

"Can I come in?"

Russell stepped aside. Luke came in, but he was not his usual cocky self. Something was up. "Is Summer here?" he asked.

"No, she's not." Audra's voice was mean.

Luke nodded. "Good."

Good?

"Maybe you need to get to the point," Russell said.

Luke shoved his hands into the pockets of his leather jacket. "I've changed my mind. About the girl."

Audra's heart stopped beating, then started up again with a vengeance. "How? What exactly do you mean?"

"I'll sign over my rights." He nodded toward Russell. "She can be your daughter."

Audra and Russell exchanged a look. Russell was the first to ask the question. "Why the change?"

Luke shrugged. "I don't know. A combination of things . . ." He looked at the floor, scuffed a toe on the carpet, then looked up again. "I do realize she needs a family, and my family is just me and my parents and they're . . . well, you know."

Audra was well aware of the limits of the Ottington family.

Luke shifted his weight and continued. "I wish I were a different kind of man, but I'm not." He took a deep breath and wiped his palms on his pants. "The right thing is to let her go. Let her be happy, with you."

Audra's first thought was *Quick! Get the papers!* But to act so desperate after Luke's honest admission would be rude. She was glad when he was the one who brought it up.

"Do you have the papers handy? And a pen?"

He gave his signature. It was done.

"I guess that's it," he said, opening the door. "I hope you're all very happy. I mean it."

"You too," Audra said. He looked so pathetic, standing alone in the hall. On impulse, Audra gave him a hug. "Take care of yourself, Luke."

He nodded and left.

Russell and Audra closed the door and stared at each other. "What just happened?" Russell asked.

Audra couldn't hold it in any longer. She hurled herself at her husband, encasing him in a hug. "God just answered our prayers, that's what!"

•   •   •

Gail smelled the food when she walked in the door after work. The aroma drew her into the kitchen, where she found Evelyn, Piper, and a pudgy man wearing a oxford shirt spattered with green paint.

Evelyn was laughing. She let her laughter wind down when she saw Gail. "Gail! Just in time. We're nearly ready to eat. We're having quite a feast."

Gail hung her Burger Madness visor on a hook by the back door. "What's the occasion?"

The man answered. "It's a case of bribery, pure and simple. I was bribed into helping paint the sunroom by the promise of this wonderful meal."

"Come see," Evelyn said, heading for the doorway. "We still need another coat, but Herb's coming over tomorrow to finish it up."

"Is there another meal involved?" Gail asked, taking a look at the sunroom. It was a nice color.

The man looked at Evelyn, a twinkle in his eye. "I don't know. Is there?"

Evelyn actually blushed. "I'm sure we could work something out."

Well, I'll be.

The doorbell rang. "I'll get it," Gail said. "I'm headed that direction to change anyway."

She was removing her name tag as she opened the door. At the sight of the ringers, she pricked herself. "Terry. Jacob. What are you doing here?"

"We've come to see if you want to go to church with us tonight, Mom. They have a special gospel choir coming in and it should be really cool."

"Uh . . . we were just sitting down to dinner." For the first time she noticed the dining room table was set.

Terry looked past her. "It's not until seven. We'll come back and get you."

The timing was too coincidental. Gail had experienced a God breakthrough, and a few days later Terry appeared, asking her to go to church with them again?

"Who put you up to this?" she asked.

Terry looked confused. "What?"

"Did Evelyn call you and tell you I was ripe for the whole church thing?" *Or did God send you?*

"Ripe? Gail, ease up, okay? We were talking about the gospel group this afternoon and Jacob thought of you. He was the one who wanted to stop by."

Jacob tugged at her sleeve. "Mom . . . we want you to go."

His eyes were sincere. She was acting paranoid.

At that moment Piper came out of the kitchen. "Hello. Who have we here?"

Gail was forced to make introductions.

"We asked Mom to come with us to a gospel concert tonight."

"At Christ Covenant?"

"That's the one."

"Ooh," Piper said, "I heard about that. Sounds wonderful." She looked at Gail. "You're going, aren't you?"

"Well . . . we were just going to have dinner," Gail said.

"Indeed we are," Piper said. "And there's always room for more, isn't there? Will you two stay?"

Jacob sniffed the air. "It smells really good."

Terry laughed. "I think that's a yes. That is, if it's all right with Gail."

Actually, Gail was too confused to say a thing. It was as if things were out of her hands.

●　　●　　●

Evelyn's painting spree had been the inspiration for Mae to repaint the kitchen at the Ames residence. Collier was none too pleased to have this chore added to his honey-do list today, but as usual he was amicable. Basically, Mae knew that her wish was his command. What a guy.

Mae despised the prep work that went with painting. Taping off the cabinets, the counter, the baseboard. Yuck. Putting down drop cloths. Double yuck! If Mae had her way, the paint would be on the wall within minutes of getting the notion. So she got a little paint where it didn't belong. It added character to the room.

Their kitchen was saved from a drippy dotted fate because Collier had come through and taken over the prep jobs yesterday—though she had to promise him a back rub for doing it.

She stirred the orange paint. It was the color she'd picked out for Evelyn to use in her sunroom. Evelyn might not have had the courage to paint a room Tangier Ocher, but Mae certainly did. The name alone made the choice inevitable. How could Mae *not* choose an orange named Tangier Ocher? The name was exotic, exciting, and mysterious—though Mae had no idea what an ocher was.

Mae's plan was to be done with the work by the time Ringo, Starr, and Ted showed up. "Late" had been Starr's only hint as to when they'd get there. Whatever.

When the oldies station on the radio began playing "It's My Party," Mae ran to the radio and cranked it up, using the paint brush as a microphone as she sang along. Collier shook his head. But he was smiling. And that's all that mattered.

As Mae started to do the frug (or was it the pony?) she spun around and was pulled up short by the sight of Ringo and Starr in the kitchen doorway.

"Kids!"

"We knocked," Starr said, "but no one heard us. Then we heard you singing." She grinned. "We can all be thankful it wasn't 'Barbara Ann.'"

Mae pinched her daughter's cheek and kissed her nose, giving Ted a salute. "Oh, pooh. That's one of my best songs." She looked to Ringo, who was behind them. "Come here, son of mine. Give your mother a—"

As Ringo stepped forward, she saw a young woman behind him. A tiny thing of Asian background. "Mom, I'd like you to meet Soon-ja. My fiancée."

It was rare that Mae was shocked beyond words, but this was one of those times. She'd thought Ringo was the consummate bachelor.

Collier stepped forward. "Hi, Soon-ja. I'm Collier, Mae's better half. Why don't we get away from these fumes and go sit in the living room so you can tell us all about it."

• • •

Mae didn't object to Soon-ja. Not a bit. She was charming and held her own in the discussion, a trait Mae held dear. No, indeed, she was thrilled Ringo was finally getting married. Both children engaged. How exciting.

"Are you going to have a big wedding?" she asked, trying not to pounce.

Soon-ja and Ringo held hands and looked at each other. "I don't think so," the girl said. "My parents died when I was little. I was brought up by grandparents. And they don't have the money to—"

Mae tried not to jump off the couch. "Then we'll do it! We'll give you the wedding of the century!" She turned to Collier, praying he wouldn't burst her bubble. "Won't we, Mr. Husband?"

Collier just shook his head. "As if anyone else has a choice?"

Mae ignored him. She turned to Starr. "Would you want it to be a double wedding? Twice the fun . . ."

Starr laughed. "I see Mother is still the shy, retiring sort."

Mae flipped away the distraction. "Would you let me—us— do that for you? Would you?"

Ringo looked skeptical, but the glow Mae saw on Soon-ja's face gave her the answer she wanted. "I'd love it," the girl said.

"Starr?"

Starr exchanged a look with Ted. "We'll think about it."

It was as good as a yes. Mae jumped up, nearly toppling the puzzle table next to the couch. "Yee-ha, children. I know just the people to make your bridesmaid dresses." She looked out the window and pointed across the street where she saw Audra, Summer, and Russell pull up. "In fact, there she is right now. Come on!" She hurried to the front door and stepped out on the porch. The others followed. "Audra!"

Audra looked over and waved. "Who you got there, Mae?"

"My darlin' darlings and their spouses-to-be. Ringo just announced he's engaged."

"That's wonderful." She and Russell exchanged a few words Mae couldn't hear. "We have some good news of our own. Come on over. All of you. We were just about to tell Evelyn."

Mae gathered her brood. "Come on, family. I never want to miss good news."

•   •   •

Summer ran into Evelyn's arms. "Daddy's my daddy! Daddy's my daddy!"

Evelyn looked up to see Audra and Russell come into the kitchen. "What's this?" she asked.

They both were beaming. "It's true. Luke came over and signed the papers."

Russell kissed his mother's cheek. "I'm going to be a daddy. A real daddy."

Mae, Collier, and a passel of other people came into the kitchen. Evelyn recognized Ringo, Starr, and Ted, but who was the other young woman?

"So what's the good news?" Mae asked.

Audra told her.

Mae put an arm around her son. "We have some good news too. Ringo is engaged." She beckoned the young woman forward. "Soon-ja, meet my extended family."

Hands were shaken all around. A moment later, Heddy came in the back door.

"Join the party, Heddy," Piper said.

"My, my, Peerbaugh Place is cooking tonight."

Mae took a deep whiff. "Literally, I'd say. What's that wonderful smell?"

"Smothered steaks with mushrooms." Evelyn looked toward

the oven, did the math, and offered the invitation. "There's plenty for all who can stay."

"I'm in," Collier said.

Ringo tilted the lid on the pan of creamed corn. "Yum. Us too."

"I can't," Heddy said. "I have a date."

A chorus of *ooooh*s followed.

"Who is it?" Audra asked.

"You probably don't know him. Steve Mannersmith, the English teacher—"

"At the high school," Piper said. "Of course I know him. He's a nice man."

"Doesn't he go to your church, Mae?"

"Sure he does," Collier said. "He played the ukulele at May Madness last year."

"He did?" Mae asked. "I must have blocked him out of my mind."

"He wasn't that bad."

"It appears you have the approval of the house, Heddy," Gail said.

She blushed, then excused herself to go change.

"I saw the dining room all dolled up. Want me to add some place settings?" Mae asked.

Evelyn nodded. "I used the good china. It's in the—"

"Buffet. Gracious goblets, Evie, I used to live here. Come on, Starr, help me rearrange the table."

The kitchen had too many cooks. Evelyn shooed them into the parlor. "Go on now. Piper can stay and help me. The rest of you go get acquainted."

"There'll be a quiz later," Mae said. "This way, people."

The kitchen emptied. Piper and Evelyn looked at each other, then started laughing. "Nothing like instant chaos," Piper said.

"I love it," Evelyn said. And she meant it. She paused before tackling the food, letting herself listen to the sounds of the house. "Isn't the laughter wonderful, Piper? It's like old times."

"Though a few of the players have changed."

"Actually, all of the players have changed—inside. But the fun of being together never changes."

Piper gave Evelyn's shoulders a squeeze. "You getting sentimental on me, Evelyn?"

"I believe I am."

"Nothing wrong with that."

Evelyn opened the oven door, trying to figure out how to make the main dish feed nine extra mouths. "The funny thing is, I'm getting used to the changes. It seems like every day holds something new around the corner."

"Life certainly does keep us guessing."

"Indeed, it does. Now let's get this meal on the table. Peerbaugh Place is full."

"And hungry," Piper said. "Always hungry."

Evelyn wouldn't have it any other way.

How wonderful it is, how pleasant,
when brothers live together in harmony!

PSALM 133:1

A Note from the Authors

$\mathcal{D}$ear sisters,

Welcome back to the sisterhood!

It is such a joy writing the Sister Circle books. Returning to Peerbaugh Place is like going home. Yet things have changed; things have happened since we've been gone. There are surprises to share. Surprises even to us.

But you created these characters. Certainly you know what's going on.

We wish!

This might sound strange, but it's a common phenomenon in the novel-writing world. Regarding the actions of the characters, we are often just as surprised as you are. We expect them to do something, think something, say something, but then they surprise us. We can fight it—or give them their freedom. We choose the latter. God chooses to give us free will, and so we do the same for our characters.

It's for the best. Keeping the peace is essential for a smoothly run novel. And besides, would you want to argue with Tessa or Mae?

In this second of the Sister Circle books, we always planned on having Evelyn and Piper stick around. But the rest would either be away, living the rest of their lives off-page, or would have a minor role. Having won a three-month world cruise, Tessa agreed to this idea, and so did Gillie with her new job opportunity, but . . .

Tell that to Mae. To quote Dylan Thomas, Mae would "not go gentle into that good night." She hung around and insisted on putting her two cents' worth into everything. (The question is, do we get our money's worth?)

That left Audra and Summer. No way did they want to be left out—and Evelyn took a stand and cast her vote to have them stay close (yay, Evelyn!). And so they were drawn back into the fold.

What were we supposed to do? Tell them to get out? move on?

No indeed. That would have been against the code of sisterhood. We welcomed them back, made them a cup of tea, and settled in to listen to their latest news. And while we were chatting, we welcomed some newcomers too—though to be honest, it was not always easy. We do like things to stay the same, don't we? It's comfortable. It's known. And letting strangers enter our lives takes an act of love. Sometimes a very deliberate act. Romans 9:25 says, "Those who were not My people, I will now call My people. And I will love those whom I did not love before."

So that's what we offer you with this book, and the next, and the next. . . . It's our offering of love to our sisters—old and new. May the blessings of God be with you 'round every corner.

Nancy and Vonette

P.S. If you've had some wonderful Sister Circle experiences, we'd love to hear about them. Post them to the Sister Circle Web site (www.sistercircles.com) or write to us in care of Tyndale House Author Relations, 351 Executive Drive, Carol Stream, IL 60188. Or if you have comments about the books, feel free to e-mail a note to nancy@nancymoser.com.

P.P.S. We used a wonderful sheepdog analogy in chapter 14 and would like to give credit for its inspiration to Phillip Keller's *Lessons from a Sheep Dog*. Thank you, Mr. Keller.

About the Authors

NANCY MOSER is the best-selling author of seventeen novels including *The Good Nearby*, *Mozart's Sister*, and the Christy Award–winning *Time Lottery*. She also coauthored the Sister Circle series with Campus Crusade cofounder Vonette Bright. Nancy is a motivational speaker, and information about her Said So Sister Seminar can be found at www.nancymoser.com and www.sistercircles.com. Nancy and her husband, Mark, have three children and live in the Midwest.

VONETTE BRIGHT is cofounder of Campus Crusade for Christ along with her late husband, Dr. William R. Bright. She earned a degree in home economics from Texas Women's University and did graduate work in the field of education at the University of Southern California. Vonette taught in Los Angeles City Schools before joining Bill full-time in Campus Crusade. Bill and Vonette have two married sons and four grandchildren.

Vonette's commitment is to help others develop a heart for God. She founded the Great Commission Prayer Crusade and the National Prayer Committee, which helped to establish a National Day of Prayer in the U.S. with a permanent date on the first Thursday in May. She presently serves as chairwoman for the Bright Media Foundation and maintains an amazing schedule from her home in Orlando. Vonette's desire is to see women of faith connecting, serving, and supporting each other with such genuine love that women who do not know Christ will be drawn to them and will want to meet Him.

Scripture Verses in *'Round the Corner*

CHAPTER	TOPIC	VERSE
Chapter 1	Needs	Isaiah 65:24
Chapter 2	Trouble	Psalm 25:17-18
	Worry	Luke 12:25
	Worry	Matthew 6:34
Chapter 3	Companionship	2 Timothy 2:22
Chapter 4	Hope	Psalm 31:24
Chapter 5	Confusion	Ephesians 4:17
Chapter 6	Deception	Isaiah 28:17
Chapter 7	Purpose	Psalm 138:8
	Being	Psalm 100:3
	Purpose	Romans 12:5
Chapter 8	Purpose	Psalm 57:2
Chapter 9	Beginnings	Zechariah 4:10
Chapter 10	Motives	Jeremiah 17:10
	Love	Galatians 5:13-15
Chapter 11	Love	Galatians 5:6
	Love	1 John 4:16-17
	Plan	Psalm 139:16
Chapter 12	Truth	Psalm 86:11
	Praise	Matthew 25:21

Discussion Questions

CHAPTER 1

1. People come into our lives, affect us, then leave. It's inevitable. Which special "sister" from your past moved out of your life? Do you still keep in touch? If you haven't before, can you make the effort to contact her now?

2. Women often fall back on intuition. Evelyn lets Heddy move in based on feelings. Then she has second thoughts. When has your intuition been right about someone? When has it been wrong?

3. Anabelle Griese has a chip on her shoulder. And yet, do you think Evelyn *was* prejudiced against her because she was overweight? Have you ever been the victim of prejudice? or the one who has shown prejudice? What happened?

Faith Issue

Evelyn is impatient with God. He filled Peerbaugh Place so quickly the first time (and so well). This time . . . How are you impatient with God? When has God's timing ever been wrong?

CHAPTER 2

1. Evelyn almost goes into Heddy's room to snoop. Have you ever snooped? What were the consequences? What were your feelings, even if you weren't caught?

2. Even though it's Piper's mom who's sick, Piper gets comfort from *her*. Are you usually a comforter or the one needing comforting? Who among your group of sisters is the greatest comforter?

3. Evelyn wants things in Peerbaugh Place to be like they were

before and hopes that by cooking something she'll help it happen. How have you tried to recapture a past time, shape things into an established mold? What happened?

Faith Issue

When Evelyn successfully conquers her desire to snoop, she felt a surge of satisfaction. "She'd done the right thing. This time." Name a time when you did the right thing, this time.

CHAPTER 3

1. Neither of Evelyn's new tenants is exactly as she'd hoped. Yet often people whom we don't expect to be a positive influence in our lives turn out to be one after all. Without knowing how the story turns out, what positive influence might Heddy, Gail, Evelyn, and Piper have on each other?
2. Heddy is caught kissing a man she barely knows. What do you think about that? Does Evelyn have a right to say no-go to such behavior?
3. Heddy is desperate to be married. What do you think are the pressures to be married? or single?

Faith Issue

The Bible speaks clearly against sex outside of marriage. How would you handle a potentially immoral situation with guests in your home?

CHAPTER 4

1. Piper is understandably worried about her mother's surgery. How do you handle worry? Are your methods successful? How could your sisters help?
2. A "coincidence" leads Evelyn into volunteering at the hospital. Many people don't believe in coincidence, feeling it's God's plan set in motion. What do you believe?
3. "One of the good things that had happened since Aaron's death

was that Evelyn had developed a backbone. It wasn't straight and strong yet, but it was getting there. And when she had occasion to stand up tall and take a stand, it felt good." What crisis situation has given you some backbone?

Faith Issue
It's a scientific fact that prayer affects health. How have you seen the power of prayer affect health issues?

CHAPTER 5
1. Heddy has a list of goals, what she wants out of life. Do you have such a list? If not, would it be advantageous? What would be on your list?
2. Anabelle and Evelyn have it out at the bank. How would you handle such a public situation—fight or flight?
3. Accosta Rand ignites Evelyn's desire to help. Have you ever met anyone who had this effect on you? Was it a short-term or long-term relationship?

Faith Issue
Heddy thinks "that people could mess up His plan and choose wrong. Free will and all that." What are your feelings about free will?

CHAPTER 6
1. Gail finds that keeping up the pretense regarding her fast-food job exhausting. Have you ever put yourself in such a situation? Were you found out? What were the consequences?
2. Mae "reads" Heddy by watching her, studying her. Are you good at reading people? Are you usually wrong or right? What do you think your sisters "read" about you?
3. First Audra and Russell, and then Gail and Heddy, have discussions about being a stay-at-home mom, living out the traditional woman's role. What do you think about this role?

Do you think problems are caused—or solved—when women test the role?

Faith Issue

As with the Anabelle Griese lawsuit situation, everyone gets treated unfairly at times. Why do you think God allows such situations to happen?

CHAPTER 7

1. Although she didn't mean to, Audra eavesdropped on two coworkers. What she heard made her angry and affected her life. Have you ever overheard something that drastically changed a situation? Have you been on the giving end of gossip that someone else overheard? What happened?
2. Audra had a horrible day, one thing after another. Is it possible for us to perpetuate such days, making them worse? How does attitude play into this?
3. Heddy has a hidden talent with her clothing design and sewing abilities, one that's been dormant for years. Do you have such a talent? What could you do to use it now?

Faith Issue

Audra lives out the adage "When God closes a door, He opens a window." If she hadn't quit her job, Heddy wouldn't have shown Summer her dolls, and Catherine's Wedding Creations would not have come to be. When has this closed door/opened window scenario happened to you?

CHAPTER 8

1. It's said that if you don't ask a question, the answer is already no. Evelyn realizes she's never asked God point-blank for specific direction in her life. What question have you *not* asked? What's held you back? Can you ask it now?
2. Mae knows a secret about Gail. Have you ever known

someone's secret and felt it bursting to get out? Did you tell someone? When is it okay to share such information?

3. Piper's mom and Evelyn conspire to hook her up with Dr. Baladino. Was there a time matchmaking worked in your life—or one when it didn't?

Faith Issue

Gail has a self-image problem—one that is so strong it's taken her away from her family. We're often harder on ourselves than God is. How can we replace these feelings with the knowledge that He loves us? How can we help others know of His love?

CHAPTER 9

1. When she finds Gail's uniform and knows she's been lied to, Evelyn says, "I can't believe how angry I am. I don't get angry." What pushes your button and makes you really angry? Do *too many* things push your button?

2. Evelyn and Mae confront Gail about the uniform. They have different styles in doing so. Which best matches your style? Is one style of confrontation better than another?

Faith Issues

1. Summer says, "My Sunday school teacher says there's no such thing as luck. Good things aren't luck; they're God's blessings." What do you think?

2. Audra and Heddy discuss God's "nudges" in their lives and how people can ignore them. How has God nudged you? Tell about a time you followed a nudge—or a time you didn't.

CHAPTER 10

1. Heddy's and Audra's wedding business is a good idea but also a big undertaking. Do you think they're handling it correctly? What advice would you give them?

2. Evelyn makes peace with Anabelle, an enemy. When have you

made peace with someone you used to dislike? How did you handle it if it was someone you had every reason to dislike?

Faith Issues

1. Piper dating Gregory . . . what do you think of evangelistic dating?
2. When Anabelle Griese shows up on Evelyn's porch, Evelyn sends up a quick prayer for help and gets an immediate response. When has God answered a prayer nearly as fast as you've prayed it?

CHAPTER 11

1. Piper deals with guilt for saying something she shouldn't have. We've all done that. Do you find it hard to apologize? Is there someone you should apologize to right now?
2. Evelyn wants Summer and Audra to need her; she wants her daily presence to be missed. This is natural. Who needs you? Whom do you need? How can you let them know?
3. Evelyn is attracted to Herb. It's been eleven months since Aaron's death. Do you think there is a prescribed length of mourning? When is it okay for a widow or widower to start dating?

Faith Issue

Mae is a strong influence in Gail's faith life. Do you think Piper will be an influence in Gregory's? How? Whose life can you change?

CHAPTER 12

1. Audra would rather put an ad in the paper to find Luke than make a simple phone call to his mother. Why do we avoid the direct solution? direct contact? Tell about a time you've avoided someone like this.
2. Audra thinks the perfect plan would be to have Evelyn involved in the wedding business. Have you ever pushed to

get someone involved in one of your projects? What were the results?

3. What "memory moment" have you had with a loved one or fellow sister? What new one can you create today?

Faith Issue
Audra has a hard time forgiving Luke and feels compelled to verbally assault him. Whom do you need to forgive? What effect will it have on the person? on you?

CHAPTER 13
1. Gail's husband repeatedly asked her to go to church to the point that she said no on principle. When have you refused to do something a loved one asked because to give in would be to lose the battle?
2. In order to prevent someone else from getting hurt like she did, Heddy has to reveal her secret in public—a courageous, selfless act. Have you ever had to show such courage? What were the results?

Faith Issues
1. While reading the Bible Piper comes across a hard truth, a hard piece of direction. What do you think about God's direction to not be "unequally yoked"? Name a hard truth the Bible's taught you.
2. Piper ends the relationship—for God. It's the hardest thing she's ever done. When have you followed God's direction above your own? Or is there some act of obedience you should be doing now?

CHAPTER 14
1. Dorthea Ottington is used to getting her own way, even if it means manipulating her own son. Have you ever manipulated (or been manipulated) in this way? What were the consequences?

2. Luke almost capitulates to his mother's wishes. He's obviously done this before. There's a balance to be found between honoring a parent's wishes and becoming your own person. When have you had to take such a stand?

3. Russell is spurred to help Luke be a better man—at his own expense. How have you urged someone to aim higher, at a cost to yourself?

Faith Issue

Mae is good with the advice, but slow to apply it to herself. She finds herself to be a hypocrite. What does God think of hypocrites? What does He teach us about walking the talk?

CHAPTER 15

1. Mae wants Evelyn to paint the sunroom orange, but Evelyn rejects the idea: "I'm not an orange person, Mae." That may sound like an odd statement, but it's true. What's your color? Or what's not your color?

2. Gail felt that working at a fast-food place was beneath her and didn't fit her self-image. Do you think we put too much stock in position and job titles? If you had your pick, what job or position would you have? Why?

Faith Issues

1. *Discontent, doubt, depression, despair* are the *D*-words Satan can use to keep us from God. What is your experience with these *D*-words?

2. Evelyn—a new believer herself—is put in a position to lead Gail toward Christ. Do you think God can use every believer no matter what their faith maturity?

CHAPTER 16

1. Piper finds her mother's letters. Is there a letter to a loved one

you'd like to write? and send? What would it say? What's holding you back from writing it?

2. Mae looks out for Summer, protecting her from Luke's influence. That's what neighbors—and sisters—are for. When have you come to someone else's defense? or been defended by a sister?

3. Audra hates Luke and it's eating her up. Whom do you hate? How can you let the hate go?

Faith Issue
Wanda Wellington has a marvelous faith that is carrying her through her illness. When have you witnessed such a faith? What are the elements of faith you'd need to carry you through a crisis?

CHAPTER 17

1. Wanda vows not to waste another moment. Why does it often take a life-or-death crisis before we live this way? How can you live this way starting today?

2. Do you believe there's "someone for everyone"? One special person meant for each of us? Or are there many "someones" and we're allowed to choose?

3. Evelyn comes to realize that the new ladies of Peerbaugh Place can be her sisters—different than before, but sisters nonetheless, marking a new phase in her life. What "phases" of sisters have you had in your life?

Faith Issue
If Gregory had called and said he'd become a Christian, how would Piper know it was sincere? What would be the signs? How should she have reacted?

an undivided heart

$\mathcal{S}$omething was up.

Evelyn knew it from the moment Herb Evans knocked on the door to pick her up for their date. He usually rang the doorbell, but this time he announced his presence with a snappy rhythm.

Herb was nice . . . but snappy?

She opened the door and found him grinning at her, holding a bouquet of yellow mums. "Hiya, Evelyn."

She drew in a breath. "Hi, Herb."

He shoved the flowers toward her. "These are for you."

"What's the occasion?"

"Oh, nothing."

Just the way he said it told her it was something. And her first inclination was to push the mums back into his arms, keep pushing him out the door, shut it, and flip the lock.

How odd.

Herb bounced twice on his toes. "Ready to go?"

I have a headache, a backache. I have to clean the oven. . . .

For the first time, Herb's face clouded. "Evelyn? Is something wrong?"

Evelyn was saved from having to answer by the sound of footsteps coming down the stairs. "Hi, Herb. Where you two heading?"

365

"Hi, Piper." He put a hand on Evelyn's shoulder. "It's a surprise."

She was doomed.

Piper gave her a questioning look, letting Evelyn know she wasn't hiding a thing. If only she didn't have such a transparent face.

"Can I steal her away from you a moment, Herb?" Piper slipped a hand through Evelyn's arm.

"Sure . . . I guess."

"Have a seat in the parlor. I'll get her back to you in just a minute." Piper led her away. Evelyn had rarely felt such relief and would have been content if the "minute" would be extended tenfold. Or a hundredfold.

They entered the kitchen. Piper made sure the door was shut before she spoke. "Okay. Spill it. Why the look of total panic?"

It would sound dumb because it was. It didn't make any sense at all.

"Evelyn . . . you're acting like you don't want to go out with him. You've been dating Herb for eight months."

"Has it been that long?"

Piper let out a sigh. "Evelyn! What's happening?"

She moved to a chair and sat. Piper joined her. "He brought me flowers."

"How dare he."

"He's smiling . . ."

"A sure sign of a scheming man."

Evelyn's left hand found her right one. "He's not a scheming man. He's a nice man."

"I figured as much, or else you wouldn't have dated him so long."

"He's . . . he's serious about me."

"Of course he is. You're both in your late fifties, Evelyn. People your age generally don't date around. They're done playing the games of youth."

Evelyn felt herself being studied. She didn't like it.

"Have you been toying with his affection, Evelyn?"

"No!"

Piper's right eyebrow raised.

"I didn't mean to."

Piper sat back, looking at the kitchen door. "Do you think he's going to propose? Is that what you're afraid of?"

That *was* it. "I don't *know*, but when he showed up today, my entire body started vibrating—and it wasn't from anticipation." She leaned toward Piper, whispering, "I wanted to run."

Piper shook her head. "Oh, Evelyn . . ."

"I know! What should I do? I don't want to hurt him."

"I'm afraid there's no way not to."

"Oh dear."

"Surely this isn't a total surprise. Surely the idea of marriage crossed your mind at some point these last eight months."

Evelyn rubbed the space between her eyes, wishing all her thoughts and feelings would become clear. "I suppose it did. But I never let it get past the idea stage."

"Do you love him?"

She opened her mouth to speak, then closed it. "I like him a lot. I like being with him. I like . . . I like having a man tell me I'm pretty. Aaron never did that."

"Herb fills a need."

It sounded so callous. "Well, sure. I guess. But I think I fill a need in him too."

"Obviously. But now he wants more."

So simply said. *He wants more.*

They shared a moment of silence. "He's waiting," Piper said finally.

"I know."

"What are you going to do?"

Evelyn sat up straight. "Maybe he won't ask me tonight. Maybe I've read the situation wrong."

"But maybe you haven't."

Evelyn had a thought that contradicted the rest and yet was so strong. "But maybe I shouldn't fight it."

"What are you saying?"

What *was* she saying? "What would be wrong with marrying Herb?"

Piper made a time-out T with her hands. "What just happened here? One minute you're scared he will propose, and now you're thinking about saying yes?"

"It would be nice to be married again."

Piper sprang from her chair and began to pace. "If you love someone, Evelyn. If you love him."

Love. What was love? "But like you said, Herb and I are in our late fifties. Maybe the type of love we're supposed to experience in order to get married has changed. Maybe there isn't supposed to be that . . . that passion anymore."

Piper stopped pacing and gawked at her. "Don't you dare say that."

"Companionship is good. It's nice."

"Then be his friend. But you don't marry someone as an antidote to eating alone."

"But maybe you do."

Piper shoved her hands on her hips. "Fine. Go marry him. Go *settle*."

Settle. It was an awful word.

The kitchen door swung open a few inches. It was Herb. "Evelyn? Is everything all right?"

Piper also waited for her answer. Two against one.

Evelyn stood. "Everything's fine, Herb. Let's go."

She felt Piper's eyes on her back even after the kitchen door swung shut.

Discover
THE SISTER CIRCLE HANDBOOK!

A companion to
the four Sister Circle
novels by
Nancy Moser and
Vonette Bright.

THE SISTER CIRCLE HANDBOOK:
DISCOVER THE JOY OF FRIENDSHIP

The Sister Circle Handbook is a celebration of women's unique capacity to bond. It contains 12 studies of real-life issues and offers biblical, sister-to-sister solutions. The tone of the studies is not preachy-teachy but a mixture of fun, female wit and substance.

Includes:

- • 12 lessons, each lesson approximately 90 minutes
- • Scripture references and text
- • Discussion questions
- • Illustration excerpts from *The Sister Circle* novels
- • Also, *To-do Ideas* "For Me" and "For Others"

ISBN 978-0-7644-3571-3